# The Crossroads of Space and Time

# The Crossroads
# of Space and Time

CHARLES & IRENE NICKERSON

Rev. date: 02/11/2015

**To order additional copies of this book, contact:**
Xlibris
1-888-795-4274
www.Xlibris.com
Orders@Xlibris.com
551935

# CONTENTS

# INTRODUCTION

THANK YOU FOR reading Crossroads of Space and Time, the first in the Tiberius Maxumus series. This book takes place after **Andreas Prime: The Legend of Home,** The second book in the Beary Maxumus series.

I hope you enjoy it.

I wish to thank my 19 year old daughter who is my Co-author in all these books. Without her encouragement and swinging that *cat-of-nine-tails* these stories would have never been told. I also want to thank her for adding the feminine touch and romance to the stories.

One other point, I talk about the race that originally lived in the Aldrin System as using Gates that created artificial wormholes. This idea has long been used in Science fiction. From Babylon 5, to Star Gate SG1. A round gate that allowed you to past through time was even introduced in the original Star Trek Series created by Gean Roddenberry. While I do not claim the idea of artificial wormholes or gates that can create them as my own, it is a widely used device in Science Fiction. I also sometimes mention races that were created by Mr. Roddenberry for Star Trek. It is a large galaxy we live in and part of me hopes those races exist. They are not central to my story, but it is my way to pay homage to a man, who dreamed of a larger Universe.

Most of all I want to thank the Creator of the Universe and His Word Jesus Christ without whom creative endeavor could not exist.

I also want to thank Harley McCoy who helped me edit this work.

Lastly I want to thank, my wife Linda who allows me the time to feed this addiction.

Charles L Nickerson.

I would like to dedicate this book to the unseen warriors that risk their lives for this country. Often all they leave behind is a gold star on a wall.

God Bless

# PROLOGUE

THE *ALDRIN SYSTEM* is at the edge of the *Bearilian Federation* influence. It was not actually part of the Federation but an acquired territory. It lies at one end of a stable wormhole that Bearilians were quick to exploit once they started interstellar space travel.

This particular wormhole is called *Kalaallit's Passage* named for the Captain of the *BAF Wander*, a small Frigate like research vessel the Bearilians at that time used and preferred. It had a six bear crew.

Thirty-six hundred years ago Captain Nuuk Kalaallit, a Polarian and his five bear crew discovered the wormhole and the *Aldrin System*. Several things struck the young Polarian Captain as they emerged into this planetary system. First the inner four planets seemed to be in a constant state of geological upheaval. Second, that there were ancient ruins on the fifth, sixth, and seventh planets but no other signs of intelligent activity. Third, that there was an enormous amount of space traffic through the area.

The young Captain hailed a passing Sirius cargo ship and asked about the System. Other than it had once had a thriving and advanced culture that had long since vanished no one knew. The Captain believed that the civilization that had lived there had established the current trade routes. Also no one entered the haunted planets of *V, VI*, and *VII*.

Captain Kalaallit decided to solve the mysteries of this system. He launched several probes towards the inner planets and what he thought was the sun. Much to his surprise he found that the system had not one but two yellow suns. Identical twins locked in a gravitational struggle with each other and orbiting each other at a high rate of speed of one revolution every two hundred cycles. (A cycle equals the time it takes light to travel $1.079 \times 10^9$ KSMU) The Solar Tidal, forces emitted by the two stars was constantly tearing at the four inner planets. Yet for the middle three it provided the ideal situation. Plant and animal life seemed to flourish on all three planets especially the sixth planet.

The probes he had launch toward these planets showed what his life form scanners showed, rich plant life, and wild life. They also showed long abandoned cities. At one location high in the mountains on the North Central Continent of the *VI* planet they spotted a large pyramid complex. On the *V* they located a similar complex in a central desert region. Again on a large Island on the *VII* planet a pyramid complex with the same lay out on the Equator.

Kalaallit decide to investigate each complex. They landed in the late afternoon at the desert complex the pyramid was huge. It was also obvious that it was a building not a hive ship or similar structure. A painting on the floor showed two demons in a struggle to destroy one another and the planets revolving around them. The words *Αλδριν τηε Δεστροψερσ, Aldrin the Destroyers*) was written.

On the sixth planet the next day they landed at the mountain complex. Here they found a different picture. In these painting two lovers held each other in a loving embrace as the planets revolved around them. Here the words *Αλδριν τηε λоωερσ* (*Aldrin the Lovers*) was engraved on the floor around the painting.

On the seventh planet, a planet of water and islands the pyramid complex was on the equator. Here on a beautiful lush island the crew found yet a third depiction of the stars. This time two young creatures were holding on to each other for dear life, as they were being turned around by a large whirlpool. Here the words *Αλδριν τηε Τωινσ* (*Aldrin the Twins*) was chiseled into the rock.

After several weeks of mapping and surveying the system Captain Kalaallit was left with more questions than answers. It was obvious that the people of the *Aldrin System* had been an advance race. Very different from Bearilians, they were more humanoid. Yet they were not human. They were not the sons of Adam or daughters of Eve. The three planets seem to share a culture. But they differ in their interruption of the relationship between their two stars. The biggest question was where had the creatures that had built the temples and the cities gone. There were no signs of war just natural decay.

Captain Kalaallit returned to *Bearilia Prime* submitted his report. He suggested colonizing the system. He pointed out that no one else seemed to want it and if the Aldrinans returned they could offer to leave.

Since that time only the *Colony on Aldrin VI* has really flourished. It has turned into a major trading center and supply stop for many different groups. A meeting place for emissaries and spies. It is a place of beauty, culture, entertainment, intrigue, and death.

Tiberius and Babs have left *Ashland* and have arrived at *Saint Elaina's* this is where our story begins at *Grace Castle* the day of the departure from *Andreas Prime*.

# CHAPTER 1

# Departure

TIBERIUS AND BABS arrived at *Grace Castle* and were met by Justinian.

Justinian greeted them. "Well, we have your bags all packed. Here, are your traveling, credits." He opened up a small metal case with three point two million *Darius Dinars* in it. "That is a lot of credits Ti."

Ti opened a small lock box. He took out identification cards, a wallet with debit cards, corporate cards, and a wedding ring. He watched as Babs stepped out of another room transformed into Mrs. Allis Tornbow.

Ti gulped. "Allis dear, here are your papers, purse, and wedding ring."

Babs cooed, "Thank you, Brinton dear. Do I meet with your approval?" She asked in a sultry voice.

Justinian shook his head. "If not my dear, I will need to call a medic. The cub wouldn't have a pulse."

Ti replied. "Keep the com unit handy. She tends to take my breath away."

Babs dropped her head and blushed. She smiled and her eyes danced.

"Cousin, we're going to slip some of Babs' gems in with the Governments stuff. I figure we can sell some of it along the way. It is all good quality gems. Can you get me two more display cases?" Ti asked.

"They are here Sir Ti." Jonae said. "Lady Babs called yesterday."

"Also Babs, I talked to Pompey's father. He likes your idea but would like to haggle on the split." Justinian said.

Babs rolled her eyes. "Tell Sire Pompey, that I am the junior partner. He will have to bargain with Lady Maxumus."

Justinian smirked. "He was afraid you would say that. He said that when it came to business his daughter was a shrew. That she wouldn't budge from a position. Of course he taught her."

Babs replied. "We are putting up over 75% of the capital investment to start with. Cousin you are building the ships. He will be supplying the linens and other goods. You each put up 12.5% and make 100% profit before Pompey or I make so much as a copper. I think the terms are fair."

Justinian shrugged. "I agree my dear. I am a pirate, but not a greedy one. The best point is the jobs it will create and hopefully the tourism."

Ti and Babs climbed into the limousine transport and headed for the spaceport. Two large luxury space transports were there *The Dream of Days* and *The Dream in the Night*. The later was to be the ship to take them to the *Aldrin system* and *Aldrin VI*.

The Captain, an older Ursa Americanus by the name of Hamilton Thorn, and his First Officer, Eric Taylor, were waiting as the young couple got out. They looked nervous, then surprised. "Mr. Tornbow? We were expecting…"

Ti waved off the comment. "Yes, I know my father. He has retired. I have taken over at least part of his duties gentlebears. May I introduce my bride, Mrs. Allis Tornbow? I suspect you have everything arranged as we requested?"

The captain stuttered. "Sir I…, yes, of course the purser will show you to the vault room. Also there is a safe in your stateroom as you requested. Sir you realize it will take six months to get to the *Aldrin system*. You could have taken a faster transport."

"Captain, I looked at your itinerary. You are traveling to *Candaris Prime, Pandarus VI*, and *Helios IV* before taking the *Kalaallit Passage* to the *Aldrin system*. All three are resort planets. We will be there three days each. They all have high end jewelry shops. I can move a great deal of merchandise between here and the *Aldrin system*. Plus this is our honeymoon." Ti pointed out.

The Captain thought, *alright he is the old skinflint's son. Who else would think about business when they had that next to them?* "I see you are your father's son. If you need anything just let me know."

In their stateroom Babs carefully swept the room. "It's clear. How did he know father so well and how did you?"

"He helped raise me; this is one of his favor ships when he travels as Mr. Thaddeus Tornbow. You realized he never left the game completely didn't you." Ti asked.

"But, he has… other responsibilities." Babs said.

Ti shrugged. "Don't underestimate him. He is a dangerous bear. The only one more dangerous, when she is mad is herself."

She looked at him, "You're serious."

Ti smiled. "It wasn't his father that taught him to be a fifth degree Master of Banche. It was herself and I don't think Beary or I to this day could take her. Of course being a neurosurgeon does give her some advantages."

Ti finished putting things away in the two wall safes. As Babs assembled their weapons and stored them.

Babs whispered, "Now what, my husband?"

Ti shook his head and kissed her. "If I were the answer would be different. I think we go to the Casino and check it out. Maybe, we should hit some of the shops. Remember, I am supposed to be a high roller and you my trophy wife." He looked at her. "Where..?"

Babs laughed lightly "A girl has to have some secrets."

Before they left the stateroom, Ti hacked into the ships manifest. There were five hundred ninety passengers. Only five had joined the ship at *Andreas Prime*. An older Bear, who was traveling to *Candaris Prime*, and two others, that also had tickets through to the *Aldrin system*. It said that they were transfer passengers from *The Dream of Days*. Something about these two bothered Ti.

Babs looked at him. "Got something?"

Ti shrugged. "It is just a feeling. Why would you travel from *Darius V* to *Andreas Prime* to go to the *Aldrin System?*"

Babs looked at him. "You wouldn't. It's a three week trip to the passage from the *Darius system*. It's even faster, if you take a fast transport. But then if we were in a hurry we could make the trip in a month and a half."

Ti looked at their pictures, two young Bearilians. They were supposedly from the *Darius System*. Perhaps, they were after one last fling, before seeking their fortune on the wild frontier of space. According to their travel documents they were brothers in their early twenties. They had been raised in a State ran orphanage till they were sixteen. When they had ran away, turned up, three years later, working on a mining moon of *Darius VIII.* Now they are here. "Ok, we keep our eyes on these two. However, we better keep an eye out for the ones that don't make since." Ti said.

Babs draped his coat over his shoulders. "Come on show a girl a good time. We left spaceport five STUs ago."

Ti, shrugged, "Right, where to first?"

Babs smiled. "Where else, the casino, we are supposed to be high rollers. Remember?"

The casino was already packed. Babs looked around, as she took his arm. "What's your pleasure?"

Ti replied. "To let you work the room and let me watch."

Babs looked around. "Triads table, in the corner."

Babs walked over to the table. "Gentlebears, is this seat taken?"

The dealer looked at her and the gentlebear with her. "This is a gentlebears game!"

Babs daintily sat down and leaned over the table. She looked into each of the older bears' eyes. "Surly these gentlebears wouldn't mind playing cards with little old me. Would you?" She said in a voice so sweet honey almost dripped from it.

Ti watched in amassment, as each older bears mouth dropped, and their head shook no.

One straightened. "My lady, I am Mr. Brownstone. Who might you be?"

"Oh, how silly of me, I am, Mrs. Allis Tornbow. This is my husband Brinton." Babs said.

"Mr. Tornbow, I know your father Thaddeus. How is the old scoundrel?" Mr. Brownstone asked.

"He is semi-retired for health reasons. My mother threatened to break his arms and legs if didn't turn over this part of the business to us." Ti said.

There was general laughter. Then the pit boss arrived. "Mr. Tornbow is there a problem?"

Ti smiled. "The dealer seems to think there is a problem, with my wife playing cards, with these gentlebears, at this table."

The pit boss turned white. "Not at all, Mr. Tornbow, all VIB guest are welcome at these tables."

Ti nodded. "Very good, bring my wife five hundred thousand credits worth of chips. Do you wish for me to pay for them now or charge them to my cabin?"

"We will put them on your cabin, Sir." The pit boss said, as he gave a quick look at the dealer.

A chair for Ti was brought over, along with Babs' chips.

Triad is a card game of luck and skill. The players are each dealt six cards. Each card has a numerical value from one to ten and three suits stone, mortar, and wood. The idea is to build a pyramid of greater value than the dealer. There are thirty-six cards in a deck. Thirty regular cards, four wild, and two null. The wild cards can represent any card the holder desires. A null card is an automatic loosing card.

You bet after you get your first three cards.

There were now three older bears, Babs, and the dealer at the table. Ti requested he open a new deck of cards. Babs' first three cards were five of wood, six of wood, and six of stone she opened for two thousand credits. The two gentlebears next to her called. Mr. Brownstone folded in exasperation.

Babs' next two cards were a ten of stone and a ten of wood. She bet five thousand credits. The gentlebear next to her dropped his head and folded. The other one matched her bet.

The dealer dealt the last cards. Babs smiled. *So he wants to try and cheat does he fine.* "What are the table stakes?"

The dealer looked at her. "Twenty-five thousand credits a hand per bet."

Babs smiled. "Then, I will bet twenty-five thousand credits."

The older bear, that was still in, bet one thousand. He laid out his pyramid he had pair of seven's and a five of stone on the bottom and pair of three's and a two of stone on top. It was a good hand.

Babs laid down her cards, two ten's on the bottom two six's and her five on top but set her wild card off to the side.

The dealer assumed she played it as a ladder pyramid of three sets of pair. It was a good and safe play. However, not good enough he thought. He laid out a base eight pyramid with two nines and a four on top. He started to reach for the money.

Babs smiled. "I have yet to play my wild card. According to the rules I may set it aside till you lay down your hand. She placed it next to the tens this is now a ten making this a base ten pyramid. That beats your base eight."

Ti signaled the pit boss. He immediately came over, "My wife wishes to speak to you."

"Sir, I assume that these are supposed to be honest games of chance?" Babs said.

"Yes, my lady they are." The pit boss said.

"Your dealer has been manipulating the cards. He has been dealing from everywhere but the top of the deck. Haven't you darling? Oh he is good, but not so good another pro can't spot his tricks." Babs said so sweetly.

The pit boss looked at her. "I don't understand?" "It is quite simple; I use to be a dealer, and a good one at *Harrah's* on *Candaris Prime*. I was going to college there. Except, I never tried to cheat my customers, I never had to." The dealer started to reach across the table, when she grabbed his wrist. "You really don't want to start something. My husband takes after his father. After, I break your wrist. He might get real angry." She said, still smiling. She applied enough pressure to make him set down.

The pit boss signaled security, and had the dealer escorted out. "Mrs. Tornbow, do you wish to press charges?"

"No, I feel just terrible about interrupting these fine gentlebears entertainment. May I buy the table a couple of bottles of your best nectar? Then you can find us a new dealer." Babs asked as she pulled two large bills from her purse, "Will this be sufficient to also bring us some snacks?"

The pit boss almost gulped. "Yes my lady. I'll send a steward over immediately."

She had the older bears right where she wanted them. The conversation was lively. They talked about their families and their business. Ti just took it all in. The new dealer played it straight and kept the game friendly. The table took on a party atmosphere. After three cycles everyone but Babs had broken even. She was up seventy-five thousand credits. The party had cost fifty thousand. The casino was only down twenty-five thousand credits. They were happy because she tipped the help well as she left.

Ti smiled when they got back to the room. He scanned it again. It was still clean. "My love that was quite a show you put on."

Babs sighed. "I can't stand cheats. How much do you want to bet he is calling *Harrah's* to ask if I was a dealer?"

"He will be surprised to find out you are the owners nice." Ti said.

Babs shrugged, "Which I am. Can we lie down for a few cycles before dinner?"

Ti looked at the room, and its one large bed. "I..." but Babs had already gone into the bathroom and came out in a pair of pajamas.

After, she pulled back the covers and crawled in. She said "Well hurry up. I laid out your PJs."

Ti noticed she had hung everything up neatly. He hung up his suit and put on his bottoms. He walked back out and started to lie on the floor.

"Don't you dare," Babs said! "I trust you, now come lie down."

Ti looked at her. "Babs, what if I don't trust myself?"

Babs kissed him. "My Lord Maxumus, you may take what is yours. I would not stop you, because I love you. I would prefer if you wait till we wed and I give it to you with honor. For now I would just be a concubine."

"Babs, where do you get such ideas? That is not our way, Beary nor Octavious, has ever distinguished between members of the clan all share equally. You are a Regent; I am just a Knight Protector of the Clan. Angelina doesn't consider herself the ruler of the creatures of *Andreas Prime*, but their servant." Tiberius said

Babs snuggled into his chest. "Is this then the hold you Maxumus boars have on your females, that make us ache to be near you. Pompey said it was like a drug. Angelina told her it was a hunger. I need you to be strong for both of us Ti." She said as she fell asleep.

Great, six months of this and he couldn't even talk to his mom. Not that she would be any help. Maybe Beary, would but he doubted it. Not that he, had any experience, the great Scarecrow had always avoided these situations. The lone canus had been his style. Now he held the most beautiful female he had ever seen and he was scared to death. What would she say if she knew he didn't have any experience in the ways of love? Oh great new fears to think about. Tiberius, focus on the mission. With that thought he fell asleep.

Ti had woken up and quietly got dressed. He then woke Babs. "It is almost time for dinner. Babs..."

Babs looked at him, "What is it Ti?"

"Your honor is safe with me. Not because I don't desire you and not because I don't love you. I wouldn't know what…" Ti tried to say.

She kissed him, "I have never known a boar either Ti. It will be alright, I am an island girl. We are educated by our mothers from a young age. When we are wed I will give you my gift and teach you to give me yours."

Ti blushed but kissed her back.

She sighed. "You already know how to do that very well indeed. I think the black dress for dinner tonight."

Ti shook his head. "You are trying to drive me nuts."

The captain asked that they be seated at his table. Captain Thorn looked nervous. "Mr. Tornbow and Lady Tornbow please accept my apology for the incident in the casino this afternoon. The dealer will be punished."

Babs smiled a devastating smile. "Captain Thorn, please I understand the pressures some dealers feel. While I never cheated any customers, the temptation to manipulate the cards is always there. A good dealer can do it and never get caught. He just wasn't that good. His embarrassment of being caught will be punishment enough."

"I take it you were a dealer then?" the captain asked.

"Why yes captain. I worked at *Harrah's* on *Candaris Prime* to pay for college." Babs said "I went to school there at the *Institute for Geology and Mines.*"

"So you grew up there?" The captain asked as he drank some coffee.

Babs was enjoying this game. "No captain. My home is on *Bearilia Prime*, but I spent all my summers on *Candaris Prime* living with my uncle. He was the one that taught me to play cards."

"So, is your uncle a professional gambler?" Captain Thorn asked.

Babs laughed lightly. "Oh, no Captain, he says only idiots gamble. The smart ones, own the casinos. My Uncle is Maximilian Harrah."

The captain almost bit his spoon in two, "Your, Crusher Harrah's niece?"

Babs shook her head. "Uncle Max is a lamb. I don't know why people gave him such a horrible nick name."

Ti laughed to himself, sure Maximilian Svedberg, aka Maximilian Harrah, one of the greatest undercover cops ever. He had single handedly brought down the *Candarian Cartel*. Took over their legitimate enterprises and runs them as a shell company for the *Bearilian*

*Secret Service.* "He and my father are great friends." Ti added to the conversation.

Babs smiled and touched his paw. "That's the only reason we were able to go out."

On *Candaris Prime* in the office of Maximilian Harrah a meeting was taking place.

"Thaddeus and Angel, how good to see you. Please come in." Maximilian said.

Angelina walked over and kissed him. "Hi Max."

He turned to Octavious. "The room is secure we can talk. First my Highness, welcome."

"Max, not you too," Angelina said with a smile. "It is still just Angelina, or in this case Angel, on this trip."

Octavious smiled, as Angelina sat near a window overlooking the bay. "We have been friends along time Max." Octavious started out. "We've shared a lot of secrets."

Max looked at him. "Get to the point Octavious, your worrying me."

Angelina spoke next. "Beary and Babs found *Asador.* She joined your clan to his. He made her *Regent of Asador.* He gave your family the *Southern Palisades Island* also."

Max dropped his head. "So, the legend was true?"

Octavious started to talk, but Angelina shook her head. It was still her show. "Babs was prepared to sacrifice her life to protect the secrets they uncovered."

Max nodded. "It was our duty to protect their tombs. But you said Beary?"

Octavious smiled. "Beary, is the *Guardian of Vandar.* He is now the head of the *House of Maxumus.* I have inherited the *House of Caesar/ Maxumus* as First Knight apparent."

Max leaned back and smiled. "Ok, so do I kiss your ring or Babs to swear my fealty?"

Octavious laughed. "Technically hers as Beary's Regent."

Angelina looked at them. "You two old idiots still think this is a game! After all these years, after all the friends we've lost. Now we are sending our own children out to do the same jobs we swore we wouldn't let them do. Oh, we stopped the older cubs. But not Beary and Benjamin's twins couldn't wait to get in the game.

Beary and his family are heading into the unknown with a target on their backs. Along, with the entire crew of the *EAQ*. Plus we are sending Ti and Babs on a six month cruise with a big target painted on them, for what?"

Max nodded. "I know I never wanted this life for Babs. Yet I trained her. Do your children know about your past? The legendary Banshee of Death."

Angelina sighed. "Only seven creatures alive know that code name. Three are in this room and the two Heralds Deloris and Rebeca. We are retired remember."

Max nodded. "Except, when, Octavious drags you along."

Angelina shrugged. "You want to know what is real funny. On *Bearilia Prime* right now, I have two canus, a company of Marines, and my family detail all nervous because they're not here to protect little old me."

Max sighed, "The deadliest assassin that ever worked, for the Secret Service."

"Which brings us back to our present problem; Beary found and destroyed the *Devils Eye*. The creatures that used the seeking stones will want revenge. Shape shifters have already attacked the family." Angelina said.

Max hit a button. "Bring the casino to yellow alert scan all the guests and rooms, everything. We may have shape shifters. If you locate any use good judgment."

Octavious handed him a bracelet. "This is a gift. I have only enough for your key people."

"It's nice, what is it for?" Max asked.

"If you're a shape shifter it kills you." Octavious said.

Max got up and walked over to the window. "So you're telling me after all we went through with the Arcrilians and traitors in our own backyard. There is a new maybe more ominous threat."

Angelina nodded. "It could be worse Max. You could be responsible for the safety of an entire planet."

Max looked at her. "I am sorry Angelina; I should have realized your problems run deeper."

"No, Max it is not problems, it is responsibilities. I am responsible for the safety of my planet and its inhabitance. *Andreas Prime* is just now rebuilding. This threat affects all of the Federation and may have for some time. Think Max, Arcrilians never held territory after they stripped it, they left. We abandoned what twenty systems over four thousand years of war. What if another force doesn't want us to try and move back in?" Angelina asked.

Max considered her words. "Ok, then my Empress, how may an old scoundrel serve you."

Octavious looked at him. "Let your network know what is going on. Although, not through normal channels. We still don't know if all the traitors were accounted for. There are defense contractors and others that may have been involved. The Pompaius threat may still not be totally eradicated."

That night Captain Thorn was talking to the dealer in his cabin. "You idiot, if you weren't my wife's brother…I would throw you out an air lock."

"Look Hamilton…" the dealer started to say.

"That's Captain Thorn to you." Thorn said.

"Look captain, are you sure she is even who she says she is. What if she is a cop or something?" The dealer said. "Don't you think our friends would want to know?"

"Your right about one thing, they are expecting the old man. Not the kid and his new wife. The fact that she is the "Crushers" niece might bother them also. So I'll tell them. You stay in your cabin. At least till we leave *Candaris Prime* or I will feed you out an air lock." The captain said.

The dealer left and returned to his cabin. The captain locked his door and went to a small cabinet. He turned on a small micro burst transmitter. He composed a message which he sent.

Not too far away a small *BAF Scout Ship* picked up the signal. The computers quickly decompressed and decoded the message. The captain forwarded it to the regional intelligence center at the casino.

The duty officer looked at the message. He immediately took the message to Maximilian's office. He knocked on the door.

Angelina looked at him and nodded.

Max looked at the door, "Come!"

The duty officer looked at Octavious and Angelina nodded. "Sir, I though you would want to see this." He then left and closed the door.

Max read the message. "Someone sent a message informing someone that the senior Tornbows weren't on the *Dream of Night*. It was a sophisticated micro burst transmission. If the *BAF Bird's Ear* hadn't been in the area we wouldn't have picked it up."

Octavious looked at him. "Who sent it?"

"We can't tell, probable someone on the crew. Private cabin, that means officer. It was signed your friend on board." Max said.

Angelina thought. "Max, send a message to your niece. Tell her, that her father and mother-in-law are here. That they hope to see them during their lay over."

Max shook his head. "No Angelina. That would make you and Octavious an open target."

Angelina grinned. "That is precisely the idea. They send a team. We grab them and make them talk."

Octavious nodded. "The plan has its risks, but they are manageable. You have a good quick response team. We stay near the casino. Make them come to us, to our kill zone."

Max looked at them. "What if something goes wrong? After all Angelina…"

"I am quite capable of taking care of myself, Max. I do know what I am doing." Angelina said.

"Max, just play along Angel has made up her mind." Octavious said.

"Alright you two better check into your suite. I'll see you tonight." Max said.

Angelina got up and kissed him, "Max, send the message in the clear, nothing fancy. Nothing encoded. Ti will know what it means. Just that Thaddeus and Angel are here to see them."

Max nodded. "Ok Angel I understand. But please be careful."

Angelina grinned. "But Max, I am always careful."

# CHAPTER 2

# Candaris Prime

MAX DECIDED IT was time to do, what Angelina, had decided had to be done. He picked up the com unit; "Operator put me through to *the Dream in The Night*. Hello, yes, would you put me through to Mrs. Tornbow.

Allis, it is Uncle Maximilian, your father-in-law is here. He wants to meet with you and your husband here at the casino during your lay over."

Babs nodded. "Brinton and I will look forward to seeing him and you."

"Oh Angel is with him. She hopes you two can go shopping also." Max said.

Ti dropped his head Babs looked at him. "Tell Mom, I am sure Allis would love to. Well see you tomorrow Uncle."

Max nodded, "I love you both. We will see you soon."

The captain looked at the message. He had set it up so he could monitor all incoming communications. You never knew when you could find information that could be used for black mail. He would let his friends know that the old man Tornbow was on *Candaris Prime*. He would rather any problems happened on the planet rather than on his ship. He sent a message.

Babs looked at Ti. "Who is Angel? Your Mom..?"

"No, that's not one of her aliases. Angel is Angelina's alias, one of many." Ti said

Babs looked at Ti. "But the Empress…"

Ti shook his head. "There has always been a rumor about Angelina, mom, and Mrs. Maro. I have never been able to find out anything. I have asked mom. Her eyes get cold and hard then she laughs."

Babs thought. "My Uncle has a picture in his room. It had him and three others in flight suits. One was a Kodacian. There were three young females in the picture. He always laughed and said he was the only one that got away."

Ti sat down. "That picture was taken ten months before my mom and dad got married. Octavious had just asked Angelina to marry him. The Kodacian is Mr. Jim Maro. He works for the Senator. He lost his legs when his fighter was torn apart by a missile. They say he would have died but Angelina refused to let him go. She worked on him for twenty cycles straight. Despite losing his legs he and Mrs. Maro have six cubs."

"So you're saying that the other couples are your father and mother and Octavious and Angelina?" Babs asked.

"Yes, they were a lot younger then. I guess things are coming full circle." Ti said. "Babs, Angelina is setting herself up to be ambushed Octavious also. We are also bait, but you knew that." Ti said

"Why would she risk herself this way?" Babs asked.

"Someone attacked her family. She wants answers she plans to get them." Was all Ti could say. "We better get some sleep."

"But…" Babs tried to say.

"It is ok. I'll sleep with my back to the door. That way my body can shield both of us." Ti said.

Babs kissed him. "Ti you don't have to protect me. I am a big girl."

Ti looked at her. "Yes my love I do. Now let's get some rest. Tomorrow our troubles are going to start."

On a planet far away a sinister creature looked at the message. So the elder Tornbows and the young couple are both going to be on *Candaris Prime*. "Excellent have our agents grab both couples. The money, the jewels, plus the ransom we will receive for their return will help fund our crusade against Beary Maxumus."

The message was received on the *Orion Pirate Cruiser Devastator*. The captain read the message as did his first mate. The first mate slammed his fist into the table. "Captain you cannot be considering this?"

Captain Montage looked at his first mate. "Number 1, our friends are paying us well. We must not offend them. You forget they are powerful and have a long reach."

Number 1 shook his head, "Not as long as it used to be. They lost the looking stones. We and others have already lost crew members.

Why do you insist we take on this mission? There are ripe pickings in other sectors."

The captain looked at him. "We have already been paid. We are taking this job."

Number 1 looked at him. "If, you insist Captain, but know this, the crew is uneasy about your friendship with these devils."

"I note their concern. It is a paid contract and it was paid in advance. Number 1 I had no choice." The captain reasoned. A pirate captain had power till his crew decided they needed a better captain. Captain Montage was starting to feel vulnerable.

The next morning Ti and Babs got ready to visit *Candaris Prime*. They collected a few of their sample cases and an overnight bag. After all this was a three day lay over. This allowed the passengers to enjoy the pristine beaches. It also would break up the monotony of being trapped on a space ship for weeks at a time. Babs and Ti of course had a suite booked at Harrah's.

Ti smiled when she came out dressed in a simple sun dress. "You look beautiful."

Babs smiled, "I need to dress appropriately. This is what all the young ladies are wearing, along with a swim suit underneath. After all you must be ready for the beach."

Ti then noticed his father's ring around her neck. It was incased in what looked like a jewel. He walked over and touched it.

Babs kissed him. "It is a keepsake locket. I found in our case. It will protect the ring."

Ti kissed her again, "Marry me?"

Babs answered. "I already said yes Sir Knight."

"No Babs, I mean now, today or tomorrow before we leave *Candaris Prime*." Ti said.

"Ti… will you let a girl think about it. It is not like you to be this spontaneous." Babs said looking at him.

Ti sat down. "I have never wanted to be. Babs I love you so much it hurts. I have never allowed myself to feel this way. Then you came along and destroyed me. I know, I am asking you to give up a big ceremony for a small one. But we could have a second when this mess is over, if you wanted."

Babs sat on his lap. "Tiberius Maxumus, I don't care if I marry you in a shack or a cathedral. If it is just us or a thousand others present. If you want me I am yours. But since I am a Regent, Sir Knight you will be taking on a responsibility to my lands."

Ti laughed. "Yes my lady, but at least you won't have to change the monograms on the wall."

"Then it is settled. I always wanted to be married on *Candaris Prime* when I was a little cub." Babs said.

Angelina went to one of her bags and opened it. She took out a small communication unit. "Hello Helen, call Eliza and meet me on *Candaris Prime*. Bring your trumpets.

Rebecca Maro looked at her phone. "Alright Angel, we can be there in eighteen cycles, if we take *the Short Cut*."

Angelina thought. "Helen, it is dangerous."

"Not a problem Angel, I have driven it many times." Rebecca said.

Mrs. Maro hung up and called Deloris. "Eliza, grab your horn meet me at the tavern."

Deloris looked at the phone, "Understood."

Deloris looked at her office assistant. "Frank, I am not feeling well. I am taking a few days off. The Senator already knows."

Frank nodded. "Ok De, take care."

Deloris drove out to a secluded Airfield. Rebecca was waiting. They loaded their gear. "How is Jim," Deloris asked?

Rebecca smiled as she checked her instruments. "He is on *Antilis Zeta* for a conference. The *Antillean Council* wanted him to give a symposium on water management."

Deloris strapped herself in. "We're taking the *Short Cut*?"

"Yes, Banshee needs her Heralds a.s.a.p." Rebecca said.

"Does she know you been flying it twice a month to go to the Casino?" Deloris asked.

"No, does Octavious know you have been going with me to see Max?" Rebecca asked.

Deloris shook her head, "No."

"Oh come on De, Octavious and Angelina have been telling you for years that you needed to get on with your life. Ti would have wanted you to. You know that." Rebeca scolded, as she punched through the atmosphere.

"What will Tiberius think?" Deloris asked.

"He will be happy for you or that new partner of his might beat some sense into him." Rebecca said.

"Oh, did I tell you they are getting married. If they survive this mission, I might get grand cubs." Deloris said.

"So someone finally dented Junior's armor, about time." Rebecca said as she headed for a little known semi stable wormhole.

"No, this one didn't, dent it. She destroyed it. She took his breath away. You should see her. She is Max's niece." Deloris pointed out.

Rebecca laughed as they entered *the Short Cut*. This wormhole wasn't on any official navigational charts. It was considered too unstable especially for large ships. However, small two bear ships like the *Arrow* were perfect for it. It also helped to have an expert pilot at the controls and Rebecca Maro was one.

Though the *Dream in the Night* arrived two cycles before them at *Candaris Prime*, Deloris and Rebecca arrived at *Harrah's* almost thirty STU before Ti and Babs.

Rebecca and Deloris check in as Helen and Eliza Haines from *Darius V.* It was not uncommon in the *Darius system* for orphans to form families so no one question them saying they were sisters.

The two ladies were quietly led to Max's office. Deloris and Rebecca gave him a quick peck on the cheek. Angelina and Octavious came in. Octavious just sat down. "Ladies you made good time."

Deloris smiled. "Bec drove, how, are you, boss?"

Octavious sighed. "Concerned, you three tend to leave a mess when you get together like this. Angelina is in a bad mood."

Angelina scolded. "I am not. I just think it's time we had some answers. You know The Heralds and I are good at getting answers."

Max shook his head. "That was sixty years ago…"

Deloris shook her head, "Max, I work for Octavious. You should know better. Rebecca and I still do some minor jobs on the side."

Rebecca looked at Angelina. "So, what's the plan?"

"Simple, we have reason to believe someone is going to try and kidnap the Tornbows. That's us, Ti and Babs. You two are our back up. If they strike, I want some taken alive for questioning. Still, I want a message sent also." Angelina said.

"So if they have back up, we kill them. You take a few prisoners and one or two are allowed to escape." Rebecca said.

"Yes," Angelina said.

Deloris nodded. "It works for me."

The intercom flashed. Max answered it, "Yes?"

"Sir, Allis, and her husband are here." The receptionist said.

"Show them in," Max said.

Babs and Ti walked in. Ti's mouth almost dropped when he saw his mom.

Max smiled. "Brinton Tornbow may I introduce my floor show, The Haines Sisters, Helen, and Eliza."

Ti composed himself. "It is a pleasure to meet you."

After the door was secure Tiberius looked at his mom and Mrs. Maro, "What are you doing here?"

Rebecca shrugged. "We're your back up dear. After all The Scarecrow and Aphrodite deserves the best."

Ti looked at her, "Mrs. Maro..."

Octavious smirked. "It is ok Ti. She has a higher clearance than either of you. In fact I am about to read you two into information that only the people in this room know. You can never divulge it to anyone it is Ultra Top Secret."

Ti and Babs looked at each other, "Yes sir."

"Deloris and Rebecca's code names are the Heralds of Death." Octavious said.

Babs shook her head. "But they are just legends; they and the Banshee never really existed. No one could have pulled of the things they were credited with!"

Angelina replied, "My dear the missions really weren't that hard. There were three of us. We made a good team."

Ti looked at her, "You..."

"Don't look so shocked Ti. Who was it that taught you and Beary self-defense?" Deloris said.

Ti smiled. "Angelina. You taught me to shoot and Aunt Bec to fly."

Babs sat down, "My Empress, I am impressed..."

"Babs, it's just Angelina to family or for this mission Angel." Angelina said.

Angelina discussed her plan in detail. Babs was struck by its simplicity and deadliness. Angelina had a mean streak. She was tired of her family being targeted. It had become personal.

"Well since mom is here I have a request." Ti said.

Max looked at him. "What is that Sir Tiberius?"

"I want the Regent to make an honest boar out of me. I want her to marry me before we leave *Candaris Prime*." Ti said.

Max looked at Babs who smiled. "He is afraid I'll have my way with him."

Deloris, Rebecca, and Angelina broke out laughing. Octavious turned his head and smiled.

Max's mouth dropped open, "Allis!!!!"

Angelina grabbed her paw. "Come on Dear. We have some shopping to do. Ladies please follow discreetly."

Max looked at Tiberius, "You look a lot like your dad. I hope you are good to my girl."

Ti looked at him. "Sir, I am in love with her. I will protect her with my life."

Max shook his head. "You even talk like him. Son, Allis is as dangerous as those ladies that just left. Trust me, when I say that she can protect herself. Just love her and treat her like a lady."

Max then turned to Octavious. "I can get a preacher. It's the proper paper work I am worried about."

Octavious thought. "Not a problem. I can have the necessary forms and license here in ten STU. What is the law here?"

Max smiled. "Ten days."

Octavious called up Mr. Jenson. "Mr. Jenson I need a *Candaris Prime Marriage License* and forms signed and dated from ten days ago and placed in their system for verification…. I told them you could do it in ten STU…. Thank you."

Exactly ten STU later Max's printer printed out the necessary forms. Then the com unit rang. Octavious answered. "Yes, ok Mr. Jenson that shouldn't be a problem."

Max looked at him. "Well, what did he say?"

"All the necessary forms are there. A friend of his will bring the license over in two cycles. We are following proper procedures. Mr. Jensen called to ask why the paper work for Empress Angelina's cousin hadn't been processed. Since, it had been in their system for over two weeks. The Minister of Marriages found the forms on his personal computer. He apologized and said he would deliver them to your office personally." Octavious said.

Ti shook his head, "Are we risking our covers or yours?"

Octavious smiled. "No, Mr. Jenson made it clear that Angelina was on *Bearilia Prime*. You and Miss Svedberg are staying at a secluded beach house, which I hope someone tries to hit."

Ti raised an eye brow, "Why?"

Octavious replied, "Not your operation."

Number 1 led his team to Candaris Prime. He looked at Number 2 and 3. "You two will lead your teams. Number 3, you will back us up. Number 2 you will grab the females. My team will grab the boars. We will meet back at the shuttles, strike fast."

Babs and Angelina were walking down a street looking at windows. "Angel, we are being followed." Babs said.

Angelina smiled. "Yes, dear they will hit us soon. Let's turn down that alley to get away from the crowds. Our friends are nearby, don't worry."

"I am not my lady. I'll protect you." Babs said.

"My dear, I don't need protecting. They do." Angelina said as her eyes turned cold.

A beam reached out towards Angelina. She pushed Babs out of the way. Before it hit her, a blue dragon formed around her and turned the beam back striking the shooter. That's when five pirates charged. Before Babs could react all five were on the ground bleeding from several different parts of their bodies. Three more started to rush in but Babs dropped two. The third turned and ran; he made it another ten steps and fell.

Number 3 saw Number 2 go down. He started to charge in, with his twelve crew members. That was his last mistake. Two of the Pirates next to him toppled over. He was slow to respond when he saw a small hole appear in his chest. He didn't feel any pain as he fell to the pavement.

The other nine started to turn only to find their path blocked. Rebecca smiled as she opened fire at close range. Six pirates fell immediately. The other three turned down an alley, where Deloris met them. She pulled out two short swords and went to work. She wiped her blades off, joined Rebecca, and strolled off.

Number 2 couldn't move as Angelina picked him up by the front of his shirt. She looked in his eyes, "If this was set on kill you die. Oh, it was set on stun. You live for now. Your friends were not as lucky."

Across town at a small Café, Ti, and Octavious was having a cup of coffee. Ti took a sip. "On the left, I count five."

Octavious nodded. "I got seven more on the right."

Ti smiled. "You go left old boar. I'll go right."

"Remember, we let a few escape, I have a feeling Angel will forget that part." Octavious said.

The pirates rushed in. Number 1 held back. Octavious pulled out a staff. Three of the pirates fell. Two others fell back.

Ti dropped two with his paws. One pirate pulled knife and stabbed him. The knife folded like a piece of paper. Ti pulled a blade and stuck it through the Orion's throat. Number 1 blew a whistle and recalled the survivors.

One turned, stopped, and fired a phaser at the old boar. A blue dragon formed and blocked the beam. The beam shot back at the pirate. It struck him. He caught on fire and died.

Number 1 watched in horror. Five of his pirates were down. Two he knew were dead. He gathered his remaining five. "Run for the shuttles, hopefully the others have made it back."

Number 1 quickly moved towards the rendezvous point. He saw police and ambulances heading in the direction the other two teams had went. He climbed to a roof top. Tears flowed as he saw the carnage below. Number 2 was being loaded into an ambulance. He was the only one still alive. At least twenty-two crew members dead, six captured for what? These Maxmimus were not ordinary bears. They had strange ways and strange powers. No wonder the shape shifters feared them.

Number 1 returned to the shuttles. He looked at Number 4 who had stayed with the shuttles. Destroy the other two. They will not be needed. You are now Number 2.

Number 4 looked at him. "What about Number 2, and 3?"

"Number 2 has been captured. Number 3 and the rest are dead." Number 1 said. "It is time to leave."

Number 4 did as he was told. He then joined the five other survivors. One looked at him, "They are demons! I tell you a dragon came out of the old one and ate Number 16."

The other agreed.

Ti looked at Octavious. "What happened?"

Octavious shook his head. "I don't know. He fired at me. Then there was a blue flash and he caught on fire."

Security bears grabbed the survivors, and led them off. The head of the detail came over. "Sirs, your wives are safe. It appears they were caught in the middle of a fight between two groups of Orion Pirates. Twenty were killed in the fighting. Both groups might have been after your wives. We have one survivor but he can't seem to talk. All he mumbles is dragon."

Octavious sighed. "Thank you, officer. Could you give us a ride back to the casino?"

The security officer said, "Yes, Sir." Then he called a vehicle.

Max was waiting back at his office when they returned. Several shops had delivered packages that afternoon to his office.

When Babs came in she seemed shaken. "But, my lady, I failed you."

Angelina shook her head. "Nonsense, you preformed your duties perfectly. It was I who was clumsy."

Babs bowed her head. "No. You thought the shooter was trying to kill us. You pushed me out of the way to protect me. But what happened?"

Angelina shrugged. "He missed. I don't know how, but he did."

Max looked at them, "What happened?"

"Oh nothing, they were clumsy. I may have over reacted. I thought it was an assassination attempt. Instead it was a snatch and grab. I am afraid I didn't leave any standing, except the shooter. He may not be much help. His mind seems gone." Angelina said.

Babs shook her head. "She is amazing. I have never seen anything like it."

Max nodded. "Did they have back up?"

Rebecca and Deloris came in. Rebecca replied. "They did. They were pure amateurs. I shouldn't have wasted the ammunition on them. Deloris didn't on the three that escaped me."

Max shuddered and turned on the news. The pictures showed the aftermath of what they were calling a battle between rival pirate groups. There was only one survivor. It also told about an aborted attack on a visiting businessman and his son. These two were able to chase off the pirates. After one pirate's phaser exploded in his hands, burning him alive.

Rebecca looked at the screen. "One problem, phasers don't explode like that. If one had over loaded, it would have taken out a city block. It wouldn't have caught its shooter on fire."

Max nodded. "Your right so what happened?"

Angelina shrugged. "We will ask them when they get back. Now don't we have a wedding to plan?

Number 1 was fuming. So were the other survivors. He turned to them. "If you feel I failed you then take my life."

Number 7 looked at him. "No Number 1. You spoke out against this folly. It is the captain that has led us to ruin. Where is the profit? In six months forty of our mates have died for what? So we can be puppets to some unseen shape shifter. No we need a new captain!"

The others agreed.

Number 4 looked at Number 1. "All, hail Captain Santo."

Number 1 looked at them. "You realize, if you support me, this will be considered mutiny. If we lose then we will be killed."

"Captain Santo, if we follow Montage any longer none of us will live anyway. He will sacrifice us to the devils he serves." Number 9 said.

So these were his officers. Number 4 had no real ambition. He would be a safe Number 1. Plus he was smart. Number 7 would have moved up to Number 3 anyway so he would be Number 2. "Alright Number 4 you will be my Number 1. Number 7 my Number 2 and Number 9 My number 3. The rest of you will be rewarded. I promise." The other two smiled they were a long way down the food chain but they knew they were about to move up.

Number 1 watched as they approached the *Devastator*. His blood boiled. He knew what he would do.

Captain Montage was setting on his throne, as he liked to call it. "Number 1, what is this? Where are our prisoners? Where are our other shuttles? Did you fail me again?"

In response, Number 1 shot Montage through the head. Montage's body pitched back. Then fell out of his chair. Number 1 kicked his head as he went by. He turned to his new Number 1. "Throw this trash out an airlock." He then hit the ships intercom. "This is Captain Santo the *Devastator* is under new management. If you wish to serve me you may remain. If not stay in your berths, and you may leave the ship, when we return to *Orion* space."

He then composed a message. He had it placed in a buoy and launched it at *Candaris Prime*. "Number 1 set course for *Altair IV*. Take us away from *Bearilian* space. We shall not be returning."

Throughout the ship the crew cheered. Not one survivor would leave the ship.

Max and the others were talking. Ti and Octavious had returned, when an intelligence staff member came in. "Sir, turn to Channel 17. Our guest will want to see this."

On the screen was an *Orion Pirate Captain*, "This message is for Empress Angelina Maxumus of *Andreas Prime*. I am Captain Santo, of the *Orion Cruiser Devastator*. Our previous Captain, Montage, was working with shape shifter from the planet *Dark Doom*, in the *Caldron System*. His name is Dracdoran. I only ask that you use your influence, to help spare the lives of my comrades that were captured. We have left *Bearilian* space forever."

Angelina looked at the screen "Verify his information. See that the survivors receive proper care."

Max pulled up a space chart. "Bearilians have never been to the *Caldron System*. We only know about it because of the old charts we found on *Aldrin V. Dark Doom* is the seventh planet, a class M planet. It has an Oxygen and Nitrogen atmosphere according to their charts. The star is strange a *Black Dwarf.* Not a black hole. The light it emits is dark. The scientist theories it doesn't have the normal stellar materials for its fusion reaction, but some other rarer element."

Angelina looked at the chart. "So far away and they still are touching our lives. Yet we can't reach them where they live. Even with our fastest ships it would take one hundred years to get there."

Octavious replied. "Well if we can't go to them, then we will kill them, if they come to us."

Angelina nodded. "Let's see. I think we had some more pleasant business to attend to. If, I remember correctly someone wanted to get married. Babs, do you still wish to marry my cousin?"

Babs looked at her. "If, he wants me my lady, I am his."

Deloris laughed. "Babs, you got the fever bad. Octavious, go get my son ready. You're the closest thing he has to a father."

"Thank you De, it will be my honor. Max, why don't you come with me?" Octavious said.

Max nodded and followed them out to his private elevator. It took them to his private suite.

"Ti, there is something you should know. I have been seeing your mom." Max said.

Ti smiled, "I am glad Max. It has been a long time. I knew something was different lately about her. Dad died just before I was born. I think twenty-seven years is long enough to morn, don't you?"

"They had a lot of good years together Ti. He was so proud that he was going to be a father. He was my friend. I still morn him." Max said.

Ti touched his shoulder, "Thank you, Max. If, you can bring back the laughter in her eyes that I see in the pictures of when she was young. I will be indebted to you."

Max shook his head. "You are his son no doubt about it. Just put that laughter in my niece's eyes and will call it even."

Octavious shook his head. "You sound like two old boars trading mounts. Come on we need to get dressed."

# CHAPTER 3

# A Wedding

B ABS WAS LED to the elevator and taken up a floor to another suite. This one was for VIBs, Especially ones whose presents were not to be public knowledge.

Angelina looked at her. "Well we better make you beautiful for your wedding. Of course in your case that won't take much since you are already beautiful."

Deloris started to take off Babs' necklace, "Please don't... I promised Ti I wouldn't take this off."

Deloris looked closer. In the locket was Tiberius Sr.'s ring. "It is his dad's ring."

"Yes Lady Maxumus. I hope it is alright?" Babs questioned.

Deloris kissed her as a tear fell, "My son really loves you Babs. This is his most prized possession. It is the only thing of his Dad's he has."

Angelina looked at Rebecca. "If those two start blubbering shoot them, just kidding. Call the front desk; get the beauty shop to send a hair dresser and makeup artist up."

Rebecca smiled. "I am on it. I'll have them send up some food and drink."

Angelina nodded, "Now, let us turn on some music; take a look at the dress, and other necessities."

Babs thought. "Lady Angelina, it is our custom for the mother of the bride to tie the paws of the couple at the end of the ceremony. My parents can't be here. As Empress would you stand in for my mother giving your approval to our union? I don't want my family to lose face and I be considered a faithless daughter."

Angelina nodded. As Empress it was her right to bind Svedberg's in marriage. In fact it would bring honor to her mother that the Empress took her place. "I would be honored my dear."

Max called down to the front desk, "Have the small chapel set up for a wedding…No it is a private party. No publicity no announcements if any uninvited guests show up, I will personally fire the individuals responsible…Good take care of it."

Octavious sat down. "Well we have a few cycles. What do you two want to do?"

Ti dropped his head. "Talk, Octavious I am not sure what to do."

Octavious laughed. "I'll tell you the same thing I told Beary. There are some things in life you have to learn for yourself. Be gentle and relax."

Ti shook his head. "That is what you said about setting explosives."

Octavious replied. "What is your point? With Angelina it is about the same thing and the same result."

Max almost fell out of his chair. "If she heard you say that you might be in trouble."

"Max she is a doctor. You should have heard the lecture she gave Beany and Pompey before their wedding nights." Octavious said.

"Oh, anyway don't worry Ti; you are marrying an island female. Her mother has raised her to take care of her boar, when she gets married." Max said.

Ti shook his head. "You two aren't much help."

Octavious offered. "I could call Angelina down, I am sure she would be glad to answer your questions."

"Not that… Oh forget it. I need to get her a ring set!" Ti said.

Octavious pulled a box from his coat pocket. "This belonged to your Great Grandmother Juliann Maxumus. I thought maybe you would like to give them to Babs."

Ti opened the box inside was a gold band inscribed, Λοϖε Ηοπε Φαιτη (Love Hope Faith), the engagement ring had a red fire stone surrounded by blue diamonds. The band of the ring was engraved with two dragons that held the Red Fire Stone. "Octavious, I can't accept this it is a family heirloom."

"Tiberius you are family. She was your grandmother and we all want you to have it. If you think Babs will like it?" Octavious said.

Tiberius dropped his head, "Octavious thank you. I know she will love them. I don't know how to thank you and Angelina."

Octavious sighed, "I loved your dad. We grew up together. We were family, but we were also best friends. Ti, your Dad was a great bear he loved your mom. He was proud that he was going to have a cub. He would be so proud of the bear you have grown to be."

Ti sat down and lowered his head. "It is only because mom, you, Angelina, and Fred were always there for me. I especially wanted you to be proud of me."

Octavious walked over and touched his shoulder. "Ti you know Angelina and I couldn't love you anymore if you were one of our own. Especially since you are related by blood to both of us, you know you are Angelina's cousin."

Ti smiled. "Second mom's her first cousin. But ya I know Maxumus boars marrying Augustine females. What a scandal?"

Octavious laughed. "I was more afraid of Angelina than her father. I knew what she could do when she was mad."

Max sighed. "We had some good times. Sad thing is we can't talk about them."

Octavious nodded. "We can't even think about them. They didn't happen."

Ti nodded. "So that is how it was."

Octavious nodded. "The part that we played pales in comparison to the Banshee of Death and her Heralds. Angelina is the most loving and carrying female I know. The most carrying doctor I have ever seen. She also has a dark side. When it comes out it is scary. I am a combat trained soldier and still pretty good at the fast knife technique. I can complete it in ten to twelve SUBTU. Angelina can do it in eight SUBTU flat."

Ti looked at him, "Eight, that's impossible I can't get below twelve SUBTU."

Max smiled. "All three are deadly. Your mom could shoot the eyebrow off a mouse at a thousand yards. Rebecca can drive or fly anything plus she has no fear. They grew up together. Rebecca had been adopted by a member family of the Augustine Clan and was trained in their ways."

Ti stated. "Like the Artemus children."

Octavious nodded, "Similar to Maryam would be my guess, a companion protector."

Max looked at the time. "We better get dressed. We have about a cycle left before the wedding."

The hair dresser and makeup artist had finished and left. The ladies sat down for a moment to talk.

Babs looked at the three ladies. "May I ask a question?"

Angelina nodded. "Yes dear."

"You three have been together for a long time?" Babs asked.

"Yes Babs, Angelina, and I are cousins we grew up together. Rebecca was Angelina's companion. She was adopted by a member family of the Augustine Clan." Deloris said.

Angelina smiled. "We were more like three sisters, still are."

"So Maryam wasn't the first non Maxmimus companion?" Babs said.

Angelina laughed. "No dear, I hadn't thought about that, but your right. Rebecca was my protector we just never saw it that way, exactly."

Rebecca responded. "We were always a team. With Angelina in the lead, Deloris watching everyone's back and me getting us in and out of trouble and laying down massive fire power, of course."

Angelina added. "Don't forget running interference with father."

Rebecca and Deloris laughed at that.

"I don't understand?" Babs said.

Angelina explained. "My father thought it was a horrible scandal that an Augustus was marrying a Maxumus. That and my father detested Octavious. He could never tell me why. He says he doesn't know. He likes him fine now even voted for him."

"So, Ti is related to both you and Octavious." Babs said.

Angelina smiled. "Yes dear and we love him very much."

Rebecca laughed, "I am his godmother. So little lady, treat him right."

Babs nodded, "Yes Mrs. Maro, after what I saw today. I promise I'll be the best wife there ever was."

They all laughed.

Soon it was time to get dressed. Babs dress was a beautiful white dress. That due to her figure hadn't required any alterations to speak of. Plus, the lady in the shop wanted to please Angle Tornbow. She also knew Allis was Max's niece and no one wanted to upset the "Crusher".

Max led Octavious and Ti down to the chapel. A small nervous little priest was standing there. The priest looked at Octavious, Tiberius, and Max. "Senator Maxumus, I am Father Doran, I have been looking over the paper work, and while it meets the legal requirements it doesn't meet my ecclesiastic requirements."

Ti started to get angry. "Why you pompous…"

Octavious stopped him. "Father Doran, I am sure we can solve this give me a moment."

Octavious walked over to the house phone. "Angelina we have a problem can you join us for a moment."

Angelina smiled at the other ladies. "Octavious needs my help. I'll see you down stairs."

Angelina road the elevator down and walked into the Chapel. "Now what seems to be the problem?"

Octavious pointed to the young priest. "Father Doran doesn't feel we have met the ecclesiastic requirements to hold this marriage."

Father Doran looked at Angelina. "Your, position as Empress of *Andreas Prime* holds no sway with the church or my Cardinal!"

Angelina just smiled. "Who is your Cardinal?"

Father Doran leered. "Cardinal Shamus O'Malley is our Cardinal."

"Snuky, I'll just give him a call." Angelina walked over to a com unit. "Hi Joan is Snuky in? Thanks."

Cardinal O'Malley answered the Com. "Cardinal O'Malley here."

"Snuky its Angelina, how are you?" Angelina asked.

"Why Pumpkin, how are you? Or should I say your, Highness?" Cardinal O'Malley said.

"You can call me Pumpkin. You know Deloris's son Tiberius? He wants to get married. Father Doran doesn't feel you would approve." Angelina explained.

"What Ti found a young lady, who is she?" O'Malley asked.

"Max's niece," Angelina said.

"Little Babs Allis, I baptized her. Put that young… priest on Angelina and kiss both of them for me. If I wasn't two hundred KSMU away I would marry them myself." O'Malley said.

Angelina smiled at the young priest. "Father Doran, Cardinal O'Malley would like to talk to you."

"Father Doran, I have known both of these young people all their lives. I know that their faith is strong in the Creator and His Word. You will marry them. Or, I will send you to the mission field. Angelina and Deloris are dear friends of mine. I have known them since they were little and I was a young Priest working with Deloris' father, Senior Cardinal Paul Augustus. Do you understand?" Cardinal O'Malley asked.

Father Doran looked at Angelina and wilted. "Yes Cardinal O'Malley, I will see that it is a lovely ceremony."

Father Doran dropped his head. "Your Highness, how do you wish me to perform the Ceremony?"

Angelina put on her sweetest smile. "We just want a simple and Holly Ceremony."

"I will go prepare your Highness." Father Doran said.

Deloris came down, "Problem?"

Angelina replied. "No, Snuky says hi. He said to give both kids a kiss."

Deloris smiled and kissed Angelina. "Thanks, I might have just shot him."

"No this was more fun." Angelina said.

Octavious nudged Ti. "I told you the female is evil."

Ti smiled, "Ya and you love it."

"Every SUBSTU, she makes life worth living. I can never get enough of her...just being with her." Octavious said.

Deloris looked at Octavious. "He is giving you that look again."

Angelina sighed, "I know and I can't get enough of him. Never could especially when he gave me that look. It is a good thing he married me when he did or I would have did a very un-lady like thing I am afraid."

Deloris smiled, "Angelina, shame on you."

"You are one to talk." Angelina said with a smile.

"You know I have been seeing Max?" Deloris said.

Angelina nodded. "Of course you've been riding with Bec."

Deloris laughed. "Ya give's her, an excuse to play the slots."

Father Doran came in. "Sir Octavious if you, Sir Harrah, and Sir Tiberius would go to the front of the Chapel, we can begin. Who is giving the Bride away?"

Angelina smiled. "In accordance with her Clan's customs, I as Empress of *Andreas Prime* and my Handmaidens will be standing in for her mother and father. I will place my seal upon their union."

Father Doran looked at her, "You have this right?"

"Father Doran, In the *Pilgrim's Scroll* standard 16, paragraphs A- C; it states that the customs of a tribe or clan as long as it does not serve the dark one will not be questioned. Is that not so?" Angelina pointed out.

"Why of course my lady I a… we are ready to start whenever you want." Father Doran said.

Rebecca brought Babs down. She looked so lovely in her dress.

Angelina walked over. "Babs, you are so beautiful. Ti is a very lucky boar." With that she kissed her cheek as did Deloris and Rebecca. Then Angelina placed her vale over her face."

Ti watched as Babs was led down the aisle by Rebecca and his mom with Angelina escorting her. He felt like his knees were going to buckle and his breath was being sucked from his lungs. He had never seen anyone as beautiful as Babs. The universe seemed to stand still as she approached him.

Babs saw Ti sanding at the front of the chapel. She didn't understand this hunger she felt for him she only knew she wanted him, desired him. She felt she couldn't live another moment without being his wife. Her heart was beating so fast she thought it would burst from her chest.

Angelina squeezed her paw. "It all right Babs, we all feel that hunger. I still do."

Babs looked at her and smiled. "Thank you."

Father Doran gave an eloquent ceremony. He talked about the sanctity of marriage and the holiness of the union between a boar and a female. He final got to the point where he asked for the rings.

Octavious handed Ti the rings. Ti placed the ring on Babs' paw she looked at the brilliant red fire stone and the blue diamonds. Tears started streaming from her eyes as he placed the wedding band on with it.

Angelina handed her a ring and she placed it on Ti's paw. He realized it had been his Great Grandfathers. He looked at Angelina who just smiled.

Angelina stepped forward and tied their paws. "As Empress, I bind you for all times as Sire and Sirena."

Father Doran said. "You may kiss your bride."

Ti kissed Babs who kissed him back, she whispered, "You are now all mine and I am all yours my knight."

Father Doran solemnly said. "I give you Sire and Sirena Tiberius Maxumus."

Angelina walked over and thanked Father Doran. Then informed him that she and Octavious had never been here nor had the ladies. She gave him a generous donation for his church, but also made it clear that if he failed to keep her presence on *Candaris Prime* a secret she would see to it that Snuky sent him somewhere interesting. The young priest believed her.

Rebecca laughed. "I don't think we have to worry about the young priest."

Deloris shook her head. "No, Angelina got her point across."

Max said. "Ladies and gentlebears, please, if you will join me upstairs."

Once in Max's suite, he called his brother. Babs' father and mother appeared on the view screen.

Babs looked at her mother and father. "Mother and Father please forgive me, but Tiberius and I were married here on *Candaris Prime*. We are going to be on mission for six months and…"

Babs' mother looked at her. "But, I wasn't there to bind your paws, you will be dishonored…"

"Lady Svedberg, I would not allow my Son's Regent and my dear friends Niece to be dishonored. So, as is my right as Empress I took your place and bound their paws for you." Angelina said.

Lady Svedberg and Sire Svedberg both knelt before the view screen, "Our Empress, you have done us a great honor!"

Angelina replied sweetly. "No it is your daughter who honors us. She is brave and strong. You have done well and she has brought honor to the name Svedberg. As I know she, will the name Maxumus. Your lands await your families; we look forward to their return to *Andreas Prime*."

Tiberius spoke next, "Sire, I promise to love and to protect your daughter with my life."

Babs' mother looked strange. "Young boar it is my daughter's responsibility to see to your happiness."

Tiberius bowed, "Thank you Sirena, but just holding her paw takes my breath away. Besides is it not a boar's job to please his wife as well?"

Babs' mother looked at her, "Remember your training and treat this one well! Be happy my daughter."

"Thank you, Sir Tiberius for loving our daughter. May the Creator, bless you both." Sire Svedberg said.

The com link was broken. Max shook his head. "Babs they didn't say it so I will for them. Congratulations my love you look stunning. Ti thank you for your words, I know you are an honorable bear as your Dad was. May the Creator and His Word, bless you with many sons and daughters."

Octavious raised his glass. "Babs you were already a member of the clan but welcome to our family."

Babs looked at Angelina, Octavious, Deloris, Rebecca, and Max. "I don't know how to thank you all, especially you Uncle Max and you Angelina."

Max just smiled.

Angelina got up and picked up a glass of nectar, "Λοϖε, Ηοπε, Φαιτη, ανδ Γραχε φολλοω ψου αλωαψσ. (Love, hope, Faith and Grace follow you always)." Angelina gave the toast in the Ancient tongue.

Ti walked over and kissed Rebecca, Angelina, and then his Mom. "Thank you, Max and Octavious you know words can't express how I feel."

Octavious nodded as did Max.

Angelina handed Ti a key to a suite. "Two flights up, private suite no one will bother you. Have fun get some rest." She said with a twinkle in her eyes.

They quietly road the elevator to the suite, Ti opened the door. Babs looked at her husband. "May I go change for you?"

Ti said. "Sure, I'll get out of this monkey suit."

Ti slipped into a pair of slacks and a shirt. He turned around Babs was wearing an island sarong, loosely fitted around her body. He felt almost paralyzed as she came over to him and kissed him.

"Is this alright my husband?" Babs asked.

Ti looked at her. "You're wonderful."

"Come; let me make you more comfortable." Babs said.

Babs lead him into the bathroom. She had a warm bath drawn, "Come Husband."

The next morning Ti looked down at his sleeping wife. He had never known such passion. It seemed all the pampering and pleasure had been directed towards his happiness. Octavious words came back to him. "Just like handling explosives." He got up started, a bubble bath, came in and quietly carried Babs in to the bathroom. He kissed her awake. "It's your turn to be pampered my love."

Octavious hadn't lied about the results. Ti realized it was the same; Babs had been passionate last night because she had been told she had to be. This morning Ti's simple and gentle acts of love set off her true passion.

The com unit next to the bed went off at 11:00 Cycles. Babs quietly answered it. "Yes?"

"Hi Allis, we were wondering if you two would like to join us for lunch?" Max asked.

She felt a kiss on her neck. "Give us a half a cycle and we will be down Uncle."

"See you then Allis." Max said.

She smiled down at Ti, "Is that all right?"

Ti, kissed her, "Come on girl let's get dressed. We can't spend all day in bed."

Babs sat up with a pout, "But, I thought you liked being in bed?"

He kissed her and pulled her close "Girl, you are going to wear me out. I need food to keep up my strength."

Babs giggled. "Then we need to get you a good lunch. I want your strength up."

Ti put on a business suit, while Babs put on a nice afternoon dress. Both checked their weapons and smiled. Ti realized for them a phaser and a knife was no different than a ring and a watch for other bears. They locked the door and went down stairs.

# CHAPTER 4

# Off Again

TI AND BABS arrived in Max's suite. Lunch was being served buffet style. Angelina nudged the other two ladies. Max handed them a glass of nectar.

Babs smiled. "Thank you all, for the gift you gave us yesterday."

Angelina walked over and kissed both of them. "I am sorry we have to send you out on this mission."

Ti nodded. "I can't think of a better honeymoon. A long space cruise on a luxury liner and a visit to dangerous locations."

Babs giggled. "The only thing that could be better is if you throw in an attack by pirates."

Deloris laughed. "You sound like Angelina."

Babs smiled. "I hope to grow up just like her."

Max's com unit flashed. "Max, what... Ok I'll tell them. Let the other guests know. *The Dream of Night* is leaving early; it is leaving in three cycles."

Ti sighed. "Well, I guess that means we better get going."

Captain Thorn was not a happy bear. All his security people had been replaced. As was over half of his crew. His first officer had even been transferred. A new company bear had taken his place. His new security chief also had company bear written all over his face. It was also obvious that this one took good care of the bears under him. The one bear he wanted off the ship stayed his worthless brother- in- law. Who, had now been demoted to house cleaning. Only the casino staff had been unaffected by the transfers.

Captain Thorn looked at the company vice president, "I don't understand why my crew was broken up?"

Mr. M. Lakehurst dropped his head. "The new owners ordered all the ships to have their crews changed out. They noticed that your first officer had passed his *Ships Masters Exam* and want to offer him his own ship. It appears to be a short but possible lucrative run. I should tell you your new first officer is here to evaluate you also. If you pass you might be offered a new job as a district manager."

Captain Thorn looked at him. "New owners, this is the first I have heard of it?"

"Oh yes, bought out the entire line, they have even ordered new ships. This is your last trip on *The Dream in the Night*. They are grooming you for bigger things." the vice president said, *like a noose at Dragons Breath Prison if I am right about you,* he thought.

Captain Thorn was elated. He was also worried. He had seen the news reports from the surface. Something had gone wrong and the pirates had failed miserable. Then he got word his departure time had changed and his crew was being split. He had also known that for two years the family that owned the space line had been trying to sell it. So it might be alright.

The captain finally asked. "Who bought us out?

Mr. Lakehurst smiled, "It's called the *Gem Corporation*. It took some digging, but it only has seven shareholders five are family members. The Tornbows, the senior, and his son, their wives and Mr. Harrah, also two female entertainers the Haines Sisters they were quite an act sixty years ago. I guess they invested their money well."

Captain Thorn shook his head. "Just small timers brought in to give Tornbow and Harrah legitimacy. The kid said the old bear had got bored with the jewelry business and gave it to him. Now, we know why. One thing about it though everything those two touch turns to gold."

Lakehurst laughed, "Now you know why I didn't take the buyout. Take good care of Mr. Brinton and his wife they might be evaluating you also."

Soon orders were received, that stated that during their lay over at *Pandarus VI* the registration on the ship would be changed and a red fire stone with blue diamonds around it would be painted on with the word *Gem Lines* across it. The captain was to learn that each ship would have a different gem.

The Captain met Ti and Babs as they returned to the ship, "Mr. and Mrs. Tornbow, I hope you had an excellent time on *Candaris Prime*. By the way this is my new First Officer Mr. Julius Enfield."

The tall Kodacian bowed to Babs and extended his paw to Ti. "It is a pleasure to meet you Mr. Tornbow." The paw pass had been executed expertly. Ti felt the note being pressed into his paw.

"The pleasure is all, mine. Captain we wish to go to our cabin and get squared away." Ti said taking Babs' paw and pressing the note into it.

"Of course Mr. Tornbow," The captain said.

Babs looked at the note. "Bug on base of com unit. Accidently knock it over and find it. I will explain later. Enfield"

Babs rubbed her paws together and the note disappeared.

When they got to their suite Babs sat her bag by the com unit reached for it and accidently knocked it off. The listening device fell out. Ti immediately called ship's security and demanded they show up and explain what was going on.

The head of security and three other along with the first officer came in. They swept the room and found three other devices. They ripped them out and deactivated them.

The first officer and the security chief waited till their people stepped outside. "Regent, Sir Maxumus the room is now secure. Ti saw the device setting on the table and knew one devise was still active but was hearing another conversation. I am Lt. Commander Enfield Fleet Intelligence. This is Major Iqaluit of MSD 63. The tall Polarian just nodded."

Ti looked at him, "Red Paw?"

"No, but they are good people. I am of the Red Star Clan. We are from *Pratis VIII*. The Arcrilians never tried to land on our planet because it is too cold. But they did harass us until they left." The Major said.

"Mr. Enfield, why was the captain acting so strange?" Ti asked.

Enfield smiled. "A quirk of fate, you, and the Regent are the new owners. Justinian Maxumus bought the line from the owners four days ago. He licensed it under *Gem Lines* one of the shell companies Senator Maxumus uses as a cover."

The Senator worked his magic, made some calls; I ended up here along with sixty-three Marines."

Babs looked at him. "Then you both understand that Ti is in operational command."

The Major looked at Babs. "No my lady, I thought you were?"

"Gentlebears, first he is the senior partner. Second he is my husband. I am his second in command." Babs said.

Ti smiled. "Gentlebears, never argue with the lady."

Both smiled. "Do you want us to kill the last device?"

Ti thought. "No, just leave your toy. Tell the captain I am mad that our privacy was breached."

"That discussion is taking place as we speak. We have another two STUs before we need to go live." Enfield said.

"Good tell your people thank you. Keep a sharp look out." Ti said.

The light on the device turned yellow then red. Enfield nodded. "Alright sir, I will tell the captain." He and the major left.

Ti grabbed Babs by the paw. "Come on." He led her into the bathroom and turned on the shower.

She smiled and kissed him, and got undressed. "No point in wasting the water come on we can talk while we shower."

Ti leaned back into the warm water, when a thought hit him why not. He kissed Babs. "I think we deserve an up-grade in our accommodations."

She got an impish smile. "You want to really put the captain on his ear don't you?"

Ti nodded. "He has to be the link to the pirates and the shape shifters. He is the only one, other than a communications officer, who could pull it off. According to the Lt. Commander, Mr. Lakehurst suspects the captain."

She nibbled on his neck as she washed his back. "Alright, let's see if one of the bridge suites is open. I understand they have hot tubs in the bathrooms along with the bath tubs and showers. Also conference rooms, we may be able to sell some of our wears."

"They also have bigger beds." Ti said.

Babs pouted. "But, Sir Knight you don't need a bigger bed. I could make you happy in a hammock between two trees."

"Yes my lady," Ti said stroking her neck with his paw. "But could I please you there." Ti asked.

Babs' eyes sparkled, as she sighed and leaned into his chest. "Yes, my husband anywhere you please."

Ti lifted her chin and kissed her. "I think I'll go make that call."

She grabbed his paw. "Later."

Ti wrapped a robe around her and carried her to the bed. He placed her under the covers; she snuggled into the pillow and sighed. The female wore him out, but he loved it. He called the steward. "Yes, Mr. Bantelle the rumors are true. We do now own this ship…Thank you… Why no, I didn't know that such a suite existed. Off the bridge you say. Why yes, would you have it cleaned and have security go through it. Oh, you heard about that. Yes, I know a good steward keeps his ears open…About four cycles…Alright, see to it personally will you. Thank you."

Babs looked up, smiled, and patted the bed. "You look tired."

"Yes, I could use a nap." Ti said as he lay down.

The captain was really angry at his brother-in-law. "Why weren't you transferred off? I told you leave the Tornbows alone, especially now that they own this ship."

"But, I didn't put that bug on the com device. They didn't find the one I installed." The dealer said.

"I don't care they are moving to the owners suite. You stay away from it or my sister will be a widow. Do you understand?" The captain threatened.

"Yes captain, I understand but what about our friends?" The dealer asked.

"Our pirate contacts have left the area. I do not know who they would have me contact. Also, I do not want this ship attacked. The new security detail looks like they know their business." The captain said.

"Alright, I will stay out of their way also." The dealer said and left.

"Mr. Bantelle this suite is exquisite." Babs looked around the bedroom and the bath. Then she went into the parlor. "Are these the doors that lead to the conference room?"

"Yes my lady, they are. Also Regent Maxumus the lesser houses of the Red Daggers are here to assist you." Bantelle said.

Babs and Ti both swung around. Bantelle had his collar turned, and his Coat-of-Arms pushed up showing the *Seal of the House of Maxumus*.

Ti looked at him hard.

Bantelle smiled. "We of course will offer you our merchandise, at the family rate."

Ti shook his head. "We of course will accept."

Bantelle smiled. "I am sorry Sire, but I felt the code phrase inappropriate. There are four in my cell on the ship; they will be assigned as your maid, secretary, and purser. I will act as your steward."

"That will be fine Mr. Bantelle, but may I ask I did not fully recognize your Coat-of-Arms, who is the head of your family?" Ti asked.

"The Sage and his lady adopted us to protect the great bear, and the clan." Bantelle said with pride.

Ti nodded. "It will be an honor to have you with us, Son, of the First Knight and Lady Isadora."

Bantelle replied. "No Sire, it is we who live to serve the clan."

Ti responded. "So, do I, as a Knight Protector."

"Mr. Bantelle your staff may call me Allis. Mrs. Tornbow as my mother-in-law says is my father-in-laws mother." Babs said.

Mr. Bantelle took the hint, "As you wish Mrs....Allis.

Babs smiled. "Mr. Bantelle do you have a first name?"

"Yes Lady Allis it is Raphael. Father named me for one of the Creators Angels." Bantelle said. "I got to meet mother when we docked at *Andreas Prime*. If you, need anything just dial four and your staff will come. Oh, your maid is Teresa my daughter. Your purser is Andrew Re and your secretary is Annabelle Rosa, my brother and sister." Bantelle said.

Ti smiled, "Your wife?"

Bantelle smiled. "She moved to the *Palisade Islands* with our other seven cubs."

Babs nodded. "I understand there is a lot of work to be done there."

Bantelle smiled bowed and said. "If you need me just call."

Babs looked at Ti, "Now what?"

Ti thought. "We do what any other young rich business couple would do. We throw an exclusive party in one of the main ballrooms for the high rollers. Show off some of our better jewelry and try and make some money. We also find out who is still on the ship."

Babs paused then said. "I want to visit the bridge and tell the captain our plans."

Ti grinned. "Well alright let's do it."

Babs walked on the bridge. The Lt. Commander was on duty as the first officer. "Mr. Enfield it is nice to see you. So this is the bridge?"

Enfield looked at them. "Mr. and Mrs. Tornbow the bridge is off..."

Ti waved him off. "Nonsense, if the owners were not allowed on the bridge then why would their suite, be built with an access to it?"

Babs walked over to the engineering officer, a young female Pandarian. "Miss, do you enjoy your job?"

"Yes Mrs. Tornbow, I have learned much from our chief engineer. He is a good teacher." The Pandarian said.

"Call me Allis dear. What is your name?" Babs asked.

"I am Engineering Officer Third Class Fa Wang, Mrs." Fa said.

"And a very good student she is. Fa your shift is over. Do not forget to study for your exam over the new engines. The VMXDV are scheduled to be installed when we reach *Pandarus VI*. You must pass your written exam before we get there to be certified." The Chief Engineer said.

Fa Wang smiled at him. "Yes, Mr. Bancroft, I will take the test at 8:00 cycles tomorrow morning."

"Mrs. Allis do not worry. The *Vallen Institute* has promised it will only take two days to switch out the engines. We are scheduled for a four day layover. The increase in speed will cut two weeks off this trip and save two million credits in operational expenses." Mr. Bancroft pointed out.

"Very good Mr. Bancroft, I am Brinton Tornbow. Is there anything else you need?" Ti said.

"Since you asked, yes, new life boats the old ones are dangerous." Bancroft said.

"Then by all means order them and have the *Pandarus VI* shipyard have them available when we get there." Ti said.

Bancroft blinked. "But sir, they will expect payment on delivery. That will be twelve million credits for three new life boat shuttles?"

"Shouldn't this vessel have four or five?" Babs asked.

Bancroft nodded. "Yes Mrs. Tornbow, but the owners said the expense..."

"Mr. Bancroft, we run things differently. Order the *Mark 25* life boats not the *17s*. We want them armed and with shield generators. The small Mark 4 Gatling phasers won't hold off a pirate ship, but they will mess up a fighter." Babs said. "Also Mr. Bancroft, call me Allis."

"Lady Allis that will run you, twenty-five million credits. They will want a down payment and payment of the rest on our arrival." Bancroft said.

Babs smiled, wrote down a number. "Call this number. Tell them that Allis Tornbow authorized the payment of it in full for the cost of the life boats. Also, call Mr. Levant of *Levant Industries* and tell him that little Allis Harrah is now Mrs. Allis Tornbow. The owner of *The Gem Lines* and if he wants my business he will give me a good discount on *Mark 25s*. Go ahead make the call."

Mr. Bancroft made the call and did as he was told. He looked stunned. "My Lady, he says he won't sell you the *Mark 25*. They are obsolete, but he will sell you five *Mark 28s* on approval for twenty million, if you promise to consider upgrading the rest of your fleet at a later date."

Babs smiled. "Tell him to make it fifteen and he can send the upgrade contract to my uncle. We will start immediately."

Bancroft repeated her counter offer. "He says fifteen for the first five and twenty for each set thereafter."

Babs smiled. "Tell him if he uses the Vallen /Maxumus DMX4 Engines we have a deal."

Bancroft smiled. "He said to tell you he is using the VMDMX5C engines."

"Tell Mr. Levant it was a pleasure and give him the account number. He will take care of the rest. Oh, tell him when we will be at *Pandarus VI* and that I expect delivery." Babs said.

Bancroft gave him the information. "He said they will be there when we are. Thank you my lady."

Ti smiled. "*Levant Industries* as in George Levant your dad's sister's husband."

Babs smiled. "We might as well keep it in the family."

"Captain they just ordered the new life boats I was asking for. They got us the new Levant mark 28s!" Bancroft said excitedly as Captain Thorn came on the bridge.

Captain Thorn just stared at the Tornbows. "I have no authorization to make such a purchase."

Ti responded. "Captain Thorn my wife just authorized it. She made the purchase, it is done." Ti then sat in the Captain's Chair, "Now down to business. We want to throw a party, invite all the high rollers. You know who they are, especially, the ones with wives and girlfriends. I also want twenty of your prettiest female staffers to act as models to show off our jewelry. They will be compensated for their time."

Babs smiled. She could tell the captain was struggling to hold his temper. "We wish to use the Paradise Ballroom, say, 1800 cycles, tomorrow night. We will also use it as an introduction to the *Gem Lines*. Of course only the best nectars and finest food is to be served. You will see to it won't you captain?"

"Lady and Mr. Tornbow, I am the captain of this ship not a steward…" Captain Thorn started to say.

Ti stood up and walked over. "Captain Thorn, I own this ship. You work for me. I can make you rich or I can fire you and make the next captain rich. It is your choice."

Thorn slumped. "I will see to your wishes Mrs. Tornbow."

"Please call me Allis, captain." Babs said with a smile.

"Mr. Enfield you have the bridge." The captain said as he stormed off the bridge.

Mr. Enfield shook his head and walked over to Ti. "He didn't look very happy."

Ti laughed. "Good, but, I bet he will be pleasant by tomorrow and the party will be a big success."

The captain walked into his office. He was angry. *Why did he lose his temper, and why did he let that cub treat him like a lackey? Because the truth was he was a lackey. The Dream in the Night was not his; it belonged to the Tornbows and their friends. Oh, he had some power over the crew, but they could even under cut that. Brinton Tornbow said he could make him rich, or the new captain. Make him rich. The words sunk in. Or a new captain! A carrot and a club play nice and become rich. Disappoint my wife and be cast off like, old rubbish. Ok he would see to it that the party was perfect. He would also apologize, swallow his pride, and watch his temper. He had to remember the young Tornbow was his father's son!*

The captain called the head Activities Director, Miss La Rogue. "Maria, the Tornbows want to throw a big party in the Paradise Ballroom at 1800 cycles tomorrow. Fully catered, they want only the best food and finest nectars. Also they want twenty of our prettiest staff females to act as models to show off their jewelry line. They said they would compensate the ladies so ask for volunteers. Then pick the best. Also only, your best serving staff, and security but be discreet. They said to invite all the high rollers. They are going to introduce the name change of the line also that night."

"Alright, my captain, I will see to it. I will make sure it is the very best party ever. The ballroom will shine. It will be exquisite." Miss La Rogue said.

Ti and Babs were walking back towards their rooms when the two brothers stepped out of the shadows toward them. One had something in his paw.

Ti hit the first one driving him to the floor. Babs grabbed the other, pushed him against the wall, and twisted his arm behind him.

"Please Mrs. Tornbow don't hurt me. I didn't mean to scare you. We just wanted to show you these stones we mined from our mine." One of the brothers said.

The other brother cowered on the floor. "Please, please don't kill us. We didn't mean any harm. We have been trying to get up the courage to talk to you."

Ti and Babs stepped back; the one brother got up and stood shaking next to his brother.

Babs smiled. "Well, then come in and let's talk shall we."

"No, m my La…dy…We…don't want to intrude." The younger brother said.

Ti looked at them with half a smile and said. "I insist go in."

Babs led them into the room. "Have a seat please gentlebears, and let's talk, shall we."

The two brothers sat down on the couch and looked at Ti. Still not knowing whether to try and run or not.

Ti sat down. "I hope you will forgive us you see my wife and I were attacked on *Candaris Prime* by pirates. Needless to say we are a little jumpy when someone jumps out at us from the shadows."

"Mr. Tornbow and Mrs., We are so sorry, my brother Obadiah and I just wanted to show you our stones. We tried to sell a few on *Andreas Prime* and we did. Their jewelers just couldn't use very many of them. Then we heard you were going to be on board this ship so we bought tickets with the money we made. Oh, I am Zebadiah Worthnothing." Zebadiah said.

"Worthnothing that is, a strange name," Babs stated.

"Yes Mame, but that's the name the lady at the orphanage gave us. She said we were just two worth nothings. So that's the last name they gave us Worthnothing. They couldn't even sell us to the slavers. They said we were already just a sack of bones." Zebadiah said.

Babs smiled sweetly. "Well, call me Allis and this is my husband Brinton. Would you like some food or nectar?"

"Oh, Mrs. We can't…" Obadiah started to say.

Babs smiled her radiant smile, "Nonsense, we might have started off shaky, but we can get past that, you will be our guest for dinner. Perhaps a quite one here in our suite."

"If it is not a problem…" Zebadiah started to say.

"No problem at all, steak, potatoes, and greens, a dessert and nice nectar perhaps." Ti said.

Ti called in the meal order to Mr. Bantelle. He said he would see to it.

Babs then turned to the business at hand. "May I see your stones?"

"Yes Lady Allis." Obadiah handed a small sample to her. "We have some larger ones. But we thought these would make better jewelry."

Babs looked at the crystalline structure. "Brinton come here look at this."

Ti looked at the stone, took it over to a case. He put it into a devise and looked at the read out. "Do you cubs know what kind of crystal you have here?"

"No Sire, just that they are kind of pretty." Zebadiah said.

"Do you have your claim certified and registered with the Bearilian Government?" Ti asked.

"We filled out the papers. It's on a little moon in the *Tarsus System* called *Dryden*. We were prospecting there when the Arcrilians came. But we holed up real well and nobody found us. All the fighting was several hundred KSMU away from us." Obadiah said.

"Do you have a copy of your papers with you?" Ti asked.

"Yes Sire. I knew you would need to see them." Zebadiah pulled them out. They were just rudimentary forms.

"Gentlebears, these will not do. These will not give your claim adequate protection." Ti said.

"Sire, we couldn't afford no, fancy lawyer." Obadiah said.

"How many creatures know about this mine and its location?" Ti asked.

"Only twenty know it exists and two where it is at. We lost a small ruby mine on *Darius VIII* due to claim jumpers." Obadiah said.

"Good let's keep it that way, till we get you incorporated and your claim better established. I'll have my lawyers take care of it." Ti said.

"But why would you do that for us?" Zebadiah asked.

Babs smiled. "One, because it is the right thing to do, second we are both trained geologist and mineralogist. We know what these crystals are."

Ti smiled. "Besides you might become very good customers of our cruise line and our jewelry line. With all the money you're going to have."

"These are high grade Dylithiam Crystals. The military contact alone will be worth sixty billion credits if the mine is as pure as this sample." Babs said.

Zebadiah looked at Babs and Ti. "So, I guess you don't want to buy any?"

Babs looked at him. "Zebadiah what is wrong?"

"Lady Allis, we're broke. We don't have enough money to get home on. We can't pay you back for the lawyer and stuff." Zebadiah said.

Ti dropped his head. "Would you sell us a stake in your mine, say 10%?"

"Yes Sire, for a fifteen hundred credits?" Zebadiah said.

Babs laughed; she wrote out a draft for one point five million credits and handed it to Zebadiah. "I think this is more in line of what a 10% investment is worth. We will expect to receive dividends on our investment once the mine is profitable."

"Lady Allis this is too much! You can't, I mean, what if the mine fails or the vain runs out...." Obadiah said

Ti looked at them. "You two are hard rock miners right?"

"Yes Sire and good at it." Obadiah said.

"I'll send you some bears that are good at managing the business end of things. You hire the miners and run the mines. Two things to remember safety always comes first. No profit is worth a bear's life. Second, do it right the first time, treat everyone with respect, and share the profits. In relation to what someone does, and pay your bears a fair wage." Ti said

They talked late into the night. Ti called Mr. Jenson who set up *Worthnothing Mining Incorporated.* He also established a land and mineral rights claim deed on *Dryden* for the Worthnothings, of one hundred twenty thousand hectares around their mine. He also set up claims on a few other locations nearby.

It had been decided that the Worthnothings would get off at *Pandarus VI*. They would be met by a private transport. Mr. Amos Svedberg a mining engineer would travel to *Dryden* with them to inspect the mine. His report would make them all rich as would his management of the mine. The Worthnothings leaned on his management skills and returned to what they did best finding valuable minerals.

The next evening Babs and Ti looked over the young females that volunteered to act as models. Each was asked to wear a specific type of necklace or bracelet. The symbol of the *Gem Lines* was made prevalent as was show cases for the various stones and settings that were for sell. The guests were allowed in and seated.

Babs took center stage. "Ladies and gentlebears welcome to our little party. First I want to thank you all for being here tonight. We want to thank you all for being passengers on the *Dream in The Night*. The new flag ship of *The Gem Lines*."

The crowed, burst into applause.

Ti spoke next. "Ladies and gentlebears you see several beautiful young ladies walking around modeling some of our necklaces, bracelets, and earing set. All may be purchased from the models. In the next room we have a show case of some of our other pieces and some loose stones. Staff members will be happy to assist you, if you find something you like. Also, if you have a special request we would be happy to create a one of a kind piece or set for you. You can talk to me or my wife.

Please enjoy the food and the entertainment."

The guest mingled. Many of the wives led their husbands over to the models and into the other room. Slowly several of the models went into the other room and came out wearing a new set.

An older couple approached Babs. "Mrs. Tornbow, would you and your husband consider making us a ring, necklace, and broach set?"

Babs smiled. "If we have the stones and the necessary setting or can fabricate them on board we would love to. We have limited equipment on board. Or we could send your design to our factory."

The old boar spoke up. "No my lady, it is a simple design. Could we meet with you and your husband tomorrow to show it to you?"

"Yes Sire, about 10:00 cycles in our cabin. May I ask your names?" Babs asked.

"Coronado, Johnathan, and Silvia, we will see you then." Johnathan Coronado said. He then bowed and walked off.

Babs almost shivered, as she walked over to Ti. "What do you know about a Jonathan and Silvia Coronado?"

Ti looked at her. "Only that they are wanted in half the systems in the Federation, Why?"

"We have a meeting with them tomorrow morning." Babs said.

Ti shrugged. "It might not be them. It might be just a coincidence. That older couple might just have the same name, we'll check into it. For now let's just enjoy the party."

When the last of the guest left Miss La Rogue came over. "Madam was everything to your liking?"

Babs smiled a tired smile. "Yes Miss La Rogue, would you have your staff bring in their tally sheets starting with the models."

Miss La Rogue had them line up in order of the number of sets they sold. The first ten sold two each for twelve thousand credits each. Babs smiled, gave each a necklace, and two thousand credits. The young ladies beamed.

The next five had sold three sets each, and had made eighteen thousand credits apiece. These ladies were given three thousand credits and a necklace.

The next four had sold four sets for twenty-four thousand credits and were given four thousand credits and a necklace.

The last young lady looked embarrassed; La Rogue nudged her. "Go on Janet they are waiting."

The young Lady handed her slip to Babs. She had sold ten sets, worth sixty thousand credits.

Babs smiled. "You did very well my dear here is ten thousand credits and your necklace. Also, we are opening a jewelry boutique on the ship. How would you like to be the manager?"

"But, my lady, I don't know how?" Janet said.

"We have bears that will train you. Miss La Rogue seams very competent. I am sure she will help you pick a staff." Babs said.

"But of course, my lady, it would be my pleasure." Miss La Rogue said.

The other sells staff was paraded through. When it was over the evening had netted over one point two million credits in sells. They had paid out almost a hundred thousand in bonuses to the staff.

Ti called Miss La Rogue over. "You did a great job. My wife wants to give you a gift."

Babs handed her a box.

Miss La Rogue opened it. Inside was a beautiful necklace with a red fire stone surrounded by blue diamonds. It was similar to the necklaces the other ladies had received but bigger. It also had *Gem Lines* and *Dream in the Night* engraved on the gold ring holding the stones. "It is so beautiful."

Ti then handed her fifty thousand credits. "This is your bonus for tonight it was a smashing success. We moved a lot of merchandise and made a lot of customers happy. If you get tired of life aboard ships, we do own a few resorts also."

Miss La Rogue smiled. "I was born on a gypsy tramp freighter. I get uncomfortable confined to a planet. But thank you, maybe someday I take my test to become a ships command officer."

Ti smiled. "You let me know, and we will pay for the training."

Miss La Rogue looked at him. "You would do that?"

Babs replied. "Of course, we are always looking for good talent."

Miss La Rogue smiled. She had been thinking of quitting. Now there seemed to be a future here. "Thank you both, at least now I can dream and weigh my options."

Back in their suite Babs looked at Ti. "Well, I almost covered our investment in the mine."

"Not a problem I had the money anyway." Ti said. "I come from a wealthy clan remember."

"So you didn't marry me for my money?" Babs teased.

"No your wondrous body what else." He said kissing her.

"Me too, plus, now I won't have to change the monograms around the house." She teased as she touched his chest.

Ti laughed. "Marring you was supposed to make getting work done easier. You still distract me. We need to check on our friends."

Babs called up their secure data base. Sure enough there were Johnathan and Silvia Coronado pictures big as life. It was definitely them. "What now?"

Ti shrugged. "We arrest them quietly. Have the major hide them then turn them over at *Pandarus VI.*"

"It might risk blowing our cover?" Babs said.

"True, but they are thieves not assassins or traitors. So, we can't just eliminate them. Also, we can't just let them go." Ti said.

"You're right; I just am worried that's all." Babs said.

Ti took her in his arms. "Come on let's go to bed. You need your sleep."

Babs cooed. "Well bed anyway."

"Good morning Mr. Iqaluit... yes I was wondering if you could drop by." Ti asked. "Good, we will see you then." Ti hung up the com unit.

Babs looked at him. "Well?"

Ti smiled. "Well!"

Babs blushed. "Not the dress silly. When will he be here?"

Ti took her in his arms and kissed her, "In a few moments. You look amazing."

Babs smiled. "Thank you. But keep your mind on business these bears may be old, but they are dangerous."

Ti swatted her tail lightly. "Yes my love."

Just then Major Iqaluit arrived and knocked. Ti let him in.

"Sire Tornbow, my lady," He pulled out a small devise and scanned the room. "The room is clear. How may I serve you?"

Ti brought up the Coronado's picture. "This couple is on the ship they are wanted. We have an appointment with them. Then we are going to arrest them. You need to hold them quietly till you can hand them over to *Bearilian Security* on *Pandarus VI*. We want to try and protect our cover but we have to arrest them."

"Sir, I could..." Iqaluit started to say.

Babs shook her head. "They don't fall in your jurisdiction. They barely fall in ours."

Ti explained. "But once we cuff them, we can hand them over. That is legal."

The Major nodded. "Ok Sir, you are the boss." With that he left to make arraignments.

Mr. Bantelle, Annabelle Rosa, and Teresa Bantelle came in. Mr. Bantelle smiled. "My lady we are ready for your meeting the conference room is set up. Refreshments are also ready."

Teresa smiled. "With or without knock out drops, my lady."

Babs replied, "Without to start with, then we will see."

The Coronados arrived precisely at 10:00 cycles. Jonathan and Silvia smiled at the three staff bears.

Jonathan nodded. It was just as it should be the perfect trap. He and Silva would have been arrested before they knew what happened.

Had it not been, for the letters in his pocket. "See Silvia I told you, this couple was professional, they are even well mannered. They were going to feed us, give us drink, then probably drug us, and then quietly arrest us. Is that not so Sire and Sirena Maxumus?"

Ti smiled. "Not quite we were going to try and find out what you were up to first. I guess I should go ahead and point out that you are under arrest."

Silvia nodded. "Thank you, now that that unpleasantness is over, may we set down?"

Babs gestured for them to set. "Please, Lady Coronado, make yourself comfortable. Teresa, please serve our guests the good stuff."

Teresa put the bottle of sleeping potion away. "Yes, my lady."

Coronado looked at the three staff bears, "Team members?"

Ti shook his head, "Clan members, which, is better for you."

Coronado nodded as he sat down. "Well, first I better give you these two letters."

**Tiberius and Babs,**

Μερχψ ανδ Ρεδεμπτιον φορ τηεμ ισ ιν ψουρ παωσ
**(Mercy and redemption for them is in your paws.)**

**Octavious**

**To: Whom it may Concern**
**Subject: Pardon**
**From: President Coldbear Bearilian Federation**

**If Johnathan and Silvia Coronado, are successful in returning, the *Pandar Crown Necklaces* to *Pandarus VI* then**
**they will receive a full pardon.**

**David C Coldbear**
**President David C Coldbear**
**Bearilian Federation**

Ti showed the letters to Babs. "Both letters seem authentic."

Babs nodded. "So, what do you need from us?"

Silvia dropped her head. "We didn't get away clean. In all the years we have been at this we have never hurt any creature or been hurt."

"Mostly because the people we stole from were in on the theft." Jonathan said.

Ti looked at him. "I don't understand?"

"Insurance fraud, my friend, we steal the jewelry. Then return it quietly, for say 30% of what it was insured for to the owners, after they collect. We fence a perfect replica, but never the real thing." Johnathan said.

Babs shook her head. "So, what happened this time?"

"We got caught trying to fence a replica of the *Star of Vandar Necklace*. No one told us the real one had been found. We tried to do it on *Andreas Prime*. Our second mistake, our third mistake was the jeweler was a member of your clan." Silvia said.

Johnathan sighed. "We were given an option to help retrieve the *Pandar Crown Necklace* that was stolen by a Mr. Overa. Or go to jail. We thought it was our civic duty to help."

"Where do we come in?" Ti asked.

Silvia opened a velvet pouch. The necklace came out the chain and two halves of the pendant. "You see the problem. While we were escaping the necklace and Johnathan were hit. Empress Angelina fixed up Johnathan. She said you would have to repair the Pendant. Also, I am afraid the individuals we relieved this from are still following us."

Ti and Babs looked at the pendant.

Babs shook her head. "It can't be done. There is no way to solder it back together and not leave a trace."

Mr. Bantelle looked at the pendant. "The stones are floated into the pendant. Not set which means the metal was formed and cooled around them."

"So, what are you suggesting?" Ti asked.

Mr. Bantelle smiled. "Simple first we take very detailed scans of the necklace. Then we make a mold from it. We match the proof marks. Then we remove the stones. Gently melt down the platinum and gold mixture of the original and recast it."

Ti looked at him. "Even with using the original metal reheating it might change the molecular structure of the original."

"Annabelle Rosa, can manipulate the process enough, to see that, that is not a problem." Bantelle said.

Johnathan Coronado all of a sudden started looking pale. "My lady, may, I lay down…." He fell out of the chair.

Annabelle Rosa knelt down beside him. "He is breathing, but he is burning up." She unbuttoned his shirt the wound had started seeping again. "Did not the Empress give him some anti-biotic?"

Silvia nodded. "But we lost them when we boarded the *Dream- in-the Night* along with one of our bags."

Annabelle Rosa looked at Mr. Bantelle. "Raphael?"

Mr. Bantelle nodded. "I will call Andrew to help us. Once you heal him sister."

Annabelle Rosa looked at Ti, "But, what about Sire Maxumus?"

Mr. Bantelle shrugged. "Does not our young Prince know the truth?"

"Since the days of his youth, but…" Annabelle Rosa started to say.

Ti looked at her. "It was you. You were the one that found me that night. You saved me. I remember." Ti bowed, "My Lady Valorous."

Annabelle Rosa shook her head. "No Sire, I am only one of my father's three Roses. May I heal him?"

"Yes my lady." Ti said.

Annabelle Rosa opened her mouth and blew a fine flame around Johnathan Coronado. She then touched his wound. Her eyes changed to resemble that of a dragon's and she said. "Accept a dragon's blessing; be healed in body, mind, and soul."

Annabelle Rosa then turned to Silvia. "Be healed of mind and soul." She said as she touched her shoulder. Then she said. "Sleep to both of them."

Andrew Re arrived and helped carry both Coronados to a bed.

Babs looked at Annabelle Rosa. "That was amazing my lady."

Annabelle Rosa sat down. "Please Regent don't send me away."

Babs came over and kissed her, as did Ti. "You are family why would we send you away?"

Annabelle Rosa looked at them through her tears. "You want me, knowing what I am?"

Ti smiled. "You are the angel that saved me. When I was little and lost in the flood and the storm."

Annabelle Rosa looked at him. "But, you were so frightened of me. You were crying."

Ti shook his head. "I was crying because I was frightened by the storm. Angelina told me not to be afraid because special angels watched over us. I guess she meant you. I knew I had seen an Angel that night. I guess you're still watching over me."

Babs said. "Mr. Bantelle, will you prepare the mold and do whatever must be done."

Mr. Bantelle nodded. "Yes Regent."

Babs sat next to Annabelle Rosa. "Please, Lady Annabelle Rosa, tell me your story, if you can."

Ti coaxed her to tell. "I know Beary knows. I should have listened closer. You are the oldest of "The Seven." Am I right?"

"Yes Sire." Annabelle Rosa said.

Ti shook his head. "Lady Annabelle Rosa, I know you are a Knight of the Garter. To you I am just Ti a fellow Knight and one of lower rank."

"No, Sire Tiberius, father said we are to serve you. "The Seven" are servants to the *House of Maxumus,* the Empress, the young Prince, and his right arm. Beary asked that I be assigned to you and the Palisades. Father agreed. The others are going to, The Empress, Sire Gamey, and *The Home Island of Brigadoon*." Annabelle Rose said.

Babs asked. ""The Seven" I don't understand?"

"We are the true children of our father and mother. A Maxmimus doctor figured out a way to combine their DNA. The curse, had changed both, father, and mother a little. I was the first born more Maxmimus than dragon. Nota Rosa is the youngest she is more dragon than Maxmimus. Violet Rosa appears physically to be more Maxmimus, but she has even greater dragon abilities. We are fathers three Roses. The Four Rocks are Peter the Rock, Gabriel the Shield, Michael the Sword and Harold the Spear. They too share both Maxmimus and dragon traits. We were shunned by both dragons and Maxmimus. Sire Gamey's father called us an abomination. Only Sire Augustus treated us well. When father was hurt he ordered me placed on the transport with him. My siblings were all too young to fight. I should have stayed and fought by his side." Annabelle Rosa said.

"No," Ti said. "If you had I would be dead now. You might be also and perhaps Samuel. He always said his Rose saved him. He meant you."

Mr. Bantelle asked. "Andrew, are the Coronados alright?"

"Yes Raphael, I left Teresa with them. You and I can do what needs to be done. Then sister can do the rest." Andrew Re said. "Excuse me Regent, could you and Sire Ti move over to the couch, you also sister. We are going to remove the stones now. I need to set up a collection area so we don't lose any of the metal."

Raphael and Andrew carefully broke the necklace apart. They carefully placed the stones in the mold. They then gathered the metal and placed it in a crucible.

"Sister, we have all the metal shards in the crucible and the stones are placed in the mold at the proper depth and location." Andrew Re said.

Annabelle Rosa nodded. "It is my turn Regent."

She walked over and looked at the mold and crucible. She prayed over both. Then blew flames around the crucible slowly melting the metal, she then stared at the metal and moved her paws over it. Then she heated it some more. She then poured the metal into the mold. Again she studied the scan and moved her paws over the mold. She rose up. "I am finished."

Mr. Bantelle guided here over to the couch. "Rest now, sister."

"But, what about my duty…" Annabelle Rosa started to say.

Babs smiled covering her with a blanket. "Is to rest that is an order." With that she kissed her.

Annabelle Rosa let a tear fall. "Yes my Regent." She, reach out and took Babs paw. "I swear I will serve you and your children with all I am to the end of my life."

After two cycles, Ti removed the necklace. He compared it to the scan. It was perfect except for the proof marks. These Mr. Bantelle added with delicacy and skill.

Ti looked it over again he couldn't tell any difference. "It is perfect, as good as new."

Annabelle Rosa asked that they bring the necklace over. She looked deep into it. Yes, she had remembered to put it back, the signature, of the artist, who had made the necklace. "Yes, it is back to its original state."

"Thank you Annabelle Rose." Ti said.

She sighed. "It was nothing. It was too pretty to be marred that way anyway."

Babs looked at her. "Now rest, do you need anything to eat or drink."

"No my Regent," Annabelle Rose said.

"Ok enough of the Regent nonsense. While we are on this ship it is Allis. That is my middle name by the way. When we are home it is Babs, alright." Babs said.

"Mr. Bantelle smiled, "As, you wish."

Ti told them." I am supposed to be a stuffed shirt. Call me Mr. Tornbow outside the cabin. Once we're home I am Ti or Tiberius."

Annabelle Rosa smiled as she fell asleep. "You are just like him. You should be brothers instead of cousins…"

# CHAPTER 5

# Pandarus VI

THE CORONADOS SLOWLY woke up. Teresa smiled. "Good you are awake. Would you like some food?"

Johnathan Coronado shook his head. He felt different. "What happened to me?"

Teresa explained. "You were feverish, and your wound had become infected. Annabelle Rosa cured you and healed you. You are most fortunate that she was here."

Silvia looked at him. "She touched both of us."

"Yes, now I will bring in your food. While you are not technically under arrest, you are under our protection. Please, do not try and leave." Teresa said.

Johnathan looked at Silvia. "What now, Silvia?"

Silvia shook her head. "I don't know, I feel different and I am scared. You would have died if they had not helped you. Those two that were chasing us would not have given up."

Ti was listening. "That's why you're not making the delivery of the necklace. Babs and I are. Your part in this is done. I am going to make you an offer. I suggest you take it."

Johnathan looked at him. "What is your offer?"

"President Coldbear has offered you a pardon, but it was conditional. I will amend it to a probationary pardon. You will move to *Andreas Prime* and live on the *Southern Palisades Island*. You will work for Allis and me. You will report to a Mr. Jones he will assign you duties. Understand I will require you both to give a blood oath to one of the dragons of our house. If you break such an oath you die. Do you accept these conditions?" Ti said.

Jonathan looked at him. "What is in it for us?"

Ti told him. "You get protection, a nice place to live and an honest life."

"What is our alternative?" Silvia asked.

"Jail or I let you run. You can hope that Overa or his friends don't catch up with you." Ti said.

Silvia shook her head. The alternatives are both death sentences. "Johnathan, we have to take his offer. I can't live the way we were any more."

Johnathan searched his own feelings. "You are right Silvia. I can't either. You have a deal Sire Maxumus."

"Good, I will arrange transport for you. You will like your new home. It is a beautiful Island. Just stay away from the northern beaches. The fish in the trench grow very large, and are very carnivorous." Ti said.

Babs asked. "What skills do you have?"

Silvia shrugged. "Besides, opening safes and locks, we are good at designing jewelry."

"Alright, then we will set you up in a shop as artisans. You will pay twenty percent of your profits to the resort corporation. You will receive a percentage of the yearly profit of the resort." Babs said. "You are not family. So, your percentage as free artisans will be lower.

You will receive free housing."

Silvia smiled. "It might be a good life Johnathan."

"You mean an honest life." Johnathan said.

Ti nodded. "Would that be so bad? Plus we will protect you."

Silvia thought. "No, it would be good, we except Sire. I am tired of running."

Johnathan sighed. "Alright, Silvia, we are retired. We are going straight. My heart isn't in the game anymore."

Babs smiled. "Get some rest. We will make your travel arrangements."

Ti went into another room and summoned the Major. He and a Sergeant arrived shortly.

"Sir this is Sgt. Jo Fong he is from *Pandarus VI*. He can take the Coronados in for you." Major Iqaluit said.

"Change of plans Major." Ti said, showing him the letter from President Coldbear. "We are transporting them to *Andreas Prime*.

They returned the necklace to us. However, they are being chased by individuals working for a Mr. Overa."

"The Overa Crime Syndicate has been plaguing this section of space for years. The officials they can't buy, they kill. Stealing *The Crown necklace* was just another slap in the face of our ruling family." Sgt. Fong said.

Ti said. "Well we're going to return it. Would you like to help?"

Sgt. Fong came to attention. "Yes, Sir if I can."

Ti smiled. "Are there any other Pandarians in your unit?"

Major Iqaluit nodded. "I have two, Corporal Tongan, and Private Den Po."

Ti nodded. "Have them report to the Sergeant. Then have them, come here. They have just been temporarily assigned to the Secret Service."

"Sir," The major asked?

Ti explained. "Special Order 96, Major, you have to be a very Senior Agent to use it. I am a supervisor of section 85 Special Investigations. You will have a squad quietly deliver the Coronados to a Mr. Johnson. He is a Maxmimus; his partner is a female Kodacian. She will give the code word embrace. Your response is the moment."

The Major nodded, "Understood Sir."

"Major if you don't mind, I want to talk to the Sergeant alone." Ti said.

"As you wish, Sir," The major said and left.

"Sergeant Fong, you need to know that I may be putting you in harm's way." Ti said.

"Sir, I am a Marine." Fong said.

"Yes Sergeant I know. My Cousin was. He is now a naval officer. I think he is still a Marine at heart." Ti said.

"You mean the Ghost, Sir.' Fong said.

"Yes, but that is not the point. Your bears are going to be on your home world, not as Marines but as Secret Service Agents. You will have the ability to make arrests under certain conditions…" Ti was explaining.

"Bearilian Code 96A Section 15-27, Sir. Also Code 172, Section 52-107." The Sergeant stated, "I take the *Bar Exam* next month Sir."

Ti laughed. "Ok, then maybe you, know the law better than me. I have one rule; if they go for a weapon they are dead."

"I and my people can live with that Sir." Sergeant Fong said.

"Tell me what you know about Overa's organization on *Pandarus VI*." Ti said.

Sergeant Fong sat down. "Six years ago they started moving in. First it was mostly black mail, low level officials. You know the type Sir. Then they moved to extortion and murder. Police investigators families were attacked. My Brother and his family were killed in their own home. He was a sheriff in a small resort community. The Royal Family called in the Home Guard. That is when the *Crown Necklace* was stolen off the Princess' neck while she slept. No one knows how, her guards didn't hear a thing. No one should have known where she was sleeping."

Ti thought. "In the last month have the attacks increased or decreased."

"The threats have increased but not the attacks. In fact only two were attempted and they lacked the precision of previous attacks." Sergeant Fong said, "At least, that is what I have been told."

Ti whispered to himself. "They lost their eyes."

"I don't understand Sir." Sergeant Fong said.

"It is ok Sergeant it's just a theory. But, if I am right perhaps you and your friends can help get pay back for your people. I'll see you tomorrow." Ti said.

Babs came in. "The Coronados are in the spare bed room. I contacted Johnson he will meet the major at the spaceport. I told him we had all, the backup we needed."

"I think Overa and his cartel were using a seeing stone. Their operations changed and got less precise about the time Beary destroyed the *Devils Eye*." Ti said.

"That could explain why the Coronados are still alive." Babs said. "How do you want to play it?"

"I have three Pandarian Marines joining us under Special Order 96. The Sergeant lost a brother and his family to the cartel. We're going to return the necklace and shake the tree. See how many vipers we can get to fall out." Ti said.

Babs asked, "How old?"

Ti smiled, "Silvia's age, but sexy."

Babs shook her head. "No refined. I'll give you sexy tonight."

The next morning the *Dream in the Night* arrived at the space port at *Pandarus VI*. The major and a squad of security people escorted the Coronados off the ship. They met Mr. Johnson and his partner. Code phrases were exchanged and the Coronados were placed on board a four bear fast transport. They left for *Andreas Prime.*

Mr. Johnson reported. "Mr. and Mrs. Coronado you are safe now. We can out run and out fight most ships, except ships of the line."

His partner said. "*Hazzar's Passage* is coming up."

Johnathan Coronado's eyes got big. "You can't be serious! No one can fly through that."

"My Mother did it all the time. I can handle it with my eyes closed." Deloris Maro said.

Octavious and Angelina arrived back on *Bearilia Prime.* The Senator from *Pandarus VI's* house had been fire bombed. Luckily no one had been home. However the Senate was in an uproar. Octavious was called into a meeting to find out what he was going to do about it.

Captain Bandar had been dressed down by fleet. They were upset that Empress Maxumus had slipped off without him.

Also, the hospital was starting to wonder if it wasn't time for her to move her practice to *Andreas Prime.* They felt they were having more and more security issues. The Board of Directors had hinted strongly that she should consider opening a *Branch of the Institute* on *Andreas Prime.* They hinted she should think of setting up her practice there.

Angelina stormed into her office and slammed the door. "Bec, how would Jim feel about living on *Andreas Prime?* I could give him office space at the castle."

Mrs. Maro laughed. "So they asked you to start an *Institute* on *Andreas Prime?*"

Angelina's eyes flared. "Yes!"

"You didn't kill any of them. I am proud of you. Look Angelina my kids are moving there. De-De is working with Dave Johnson. She has already asked Johnathan Augustus for a small piece of land. The others have also." Mrs. Maro said.

Angelina said. "I'll give you some from the Caesar/Maxumus land."

Mrs. Maro replied. "That's fine Angelina. You know I love you and Octavious."

Angelina kissed her. "I am going home. I need to think."

Strong Heart stood up. "I already called Sire Jorgenson, my Lady. He is bringing the transport around."

"Dumb pet huh?" Angelina laughed.

He smiled a wolfish grin. "Mrs. Maro already knows my capabilities. I think I would like to hunt with her. She has the eyes of a hunter."

Angelina told him. "Don't repeat that to anyone. But you are right."

Strong Heart nodded. "He knew his Lady was one also, but he kept that to himself."

Captain Bandar was waiting for her. "Empress may we talk?"

"Yes, Captain what is it?" Angelina asked.

"Are you unhappy with us my Lady?" Captain Bandar asked.

"No Captain, Why," Angelina asked?

"Fleet has threatened to relieve us my lady." Captain Bandar said.

Angelina was mad now. "It is alright captain. I'll take care of it. Now, I need some exercise before I kill someone. My family detail won't spare with me. Ti and Beary aren't home do you think you have twelve Marines that would be willing?"

"My lady they are all trained Marines, some are combat veterans." Bandar said.

"That's Ok, captain have them wear protective gear. I won't hurt them." Angelina said.

Bandar brought the entire company down. Sgt. Fisher and Moon-Scare just sat down they told their Lieutenant that they knew her son and were not about to go up against her. Twelve volunteers were selected including 2nd Lieutenants each were given a pugilist stick.

Angelina smiled as she had Mr. Jorgenson tie a blind fold over her eyes. He then walked over next to Captain Bandar and threw her a stick which she caught.

Bandar looked at him. "What is she doing?"

Alexander Jorgenson smirked. "She is getting ready to beat your Marines. She is trying to make it fair."

Angelina motioned to them. "Come on Marines, I am one female and I am blind folded. Surly that is an easy enough target for you."

Two young marines charged in from different sides. Both went flying against the opposite wall.

Bandar looked at Alexander. "What happened? I didn't even see her move."

Alexander grinned. "Captain, your Marines are going to have to do better than that."

A 2nd Lieutenant organized a charge with five Marines. She side stepped or blocked each blow. She then dropped the Lieutenant with a blow to his midsection, followed by a blow to his head. She then sent two Privates sprawling in opposite directions. The other three retreated. The first two pulled the lieutenant off the floor he was out cold. They and the other two rejoined the eleven that were left.

They decided to attack in mass. In a matter of moments eleven Marines were laying around the work out mat. Six were unconscious and two had dislocated shoulders. The other three just refused to get up. They had bruises they didn't even want to think about.

Alexander yelled, "Stop! Angelina, you going to have to treat some wounded."

Angelina took off her blind fold. "Oh crap! I am sorry captain."

She walked over to one young private. He was holding his arm. She looked at it. "I am sorry son. It is not broken, but it is dislocated. I am going to put it back in. It is going to hurt, but then it will be better in a few days." She looked into his eyes grabbed his arm and snapped it back in place.

"Thank you, my lady." The young private said just before he passed out.

She made sure there were no concussions. Then had the twelve tended to by other staffers.

"I am sorry Captain Bandar." Angelina said.

"No my lady, that was the most amassing thing my Marines have ever seen. They said they would fight beside you anywhere any time." Bandar said.

"Thank you, captain and thank them. We will be leaving for home in about a week." Angelina said.

Later that night, General Zantoran was lying on a bunk, in his office at Marine Headquarters. He felt something cold press against his throat. He could tell his hands had been secured as was his mouth. A light was shining in his face. "General, your security detail stinks. This is supposed to be the most secure Marine base in the Federation, but I just killed you. Ok ladies turn on the lights." Angelina said.

General Zantoran looked at her. He cocked his head.

"Oh sorry, first General, don't yell or I will hurt you. I want to talk with you." Angelina said. She then removed the tape on his mouth. "Now General, before you say anything, this was a sanctioned security test. Your facility failed. You are dead. Most of your staff officers are dead. It was done by a three bear cell. If this was for real by morning this base would be burning."

"I don't understand?" General Zantoran said.

"It is simple General you made me mad. So, I wanted to prove a point. My ladies and I just infiltrated your base and killed you, most of your staff, and blew up your base. We would have walked out of here without any trouble. I have done this before General for real. That by the way is classified way above your pay grade. Leave Captain Bandar and his bears alone. They are doing a good job protecting my family. I don't need protecting." Angelina said as she cut his restraints.

"Empress Angelina, I don't understand?" General Zantoran said.

Deloris pulled off her hood. "There is a copy of my report to the Senate Committee on Base Security General. I can submit it or loss it, your chose."

"That's black mail." General Zantoran said.

"No, general that is giving you a chance to fix your problems before the next inspection team comes in." Mrs. Maro said with her mask still on.

"Alright Empress, and you were never here. I get it." Zantoran said.

"You're right General." With that they beamed out.

Zantoran hit his emergency button two guards flew in. "Check on the Xo."

All the staff officers were found gagged and tied to their beds with a target pined to them.

Zantoran called Admiral Starpaw, "Starpaw what do you know about Angelina Maxumus?"

Admiral Starpaw looked at a note from Octavious. "Zanny, don't make her mad. I don't know all the details but she use to work for Special Branch."

Zantoran looked at the com unit. "Are you sure it is used to?"

Starpaw shook his head; yes it was a secure line. "I am not sure of anything, just don't make her mad."

"You're telling me. Goodnight Admiral." Zantoran hung up.

He looked at the report on his desk. "Ok Marines, we have, work to do. I don't like waking up dead."

The three Marines had reported to Ti. Mr. Bantelle had helped change their appearance. Babs and Ti also looked different about ninety years older. Still fit and trim, but not two young agents either. They looked closer to middle age.

Babs looked at him. "Not bad, I think I'll keep you."

"You look good for an old lady too." Ti teased.

Annabelle Rosa came in. "I wish you would let us go with you."

Ti shook his head. "We are already risking too much exposure. Stay here and keep a look out for new arrivals. If I am right, the Overa Cartel will make a move on the Tornbows. The pirates are out of the picture at least one crew."

Annabelle Rosa nodded. She then kissed Babs and touched her face, "Προτεχτ." (Protect)

Babs looked into her eyes. "Thank you, Annabelle Rosa, for your blessing. Please do not put yourself in danger."

Ti kissed Annabelle Rosa. "Stay safe. We'll be back."

Sergeant Fong knelt before Annabelle Rosa. "My lady, I have seen you before, when I was young. I know you. I and my marines will protect them."

Annabelle Rosa touched him, "Βε βλεσσεδ." (Be blessed.)

Sergeant Fong kissed her Paw. The other two Marines kissed her paw, accepted a blessing, and followed Ti.

Ti, Babs, and their escort walked into the office of the *Minister of Antiquities*. The Minister seemed to be a nervous smaller Pandarian. There were four other bears in the room. None of which were Pandarians.

Fong signaled his bears to cover the four other individuals in the room. He then said, "Minister, I am Chen Fa of Special Branch. May I present Inspector Holms and Inspector Watson?"

The minister looked over his shoulder. "I was told that a Mr. and Mrs. Coronado…"

Ti cut him off. "They are a couple of small time criminals that we used as a diversion. We are returned the real necklace to you."

One of the other bears sneered. "That's impossible."

Babs responded. "Oh, perhaps you will be kind enough to explain how you know that?"

He looked at her. "No."

Babs shrugged. "We will see."

"May I have the necklace?" The minister asked.

"No, King Dang Chen asked to be here along with the Princess. We will wait for them along with their escorts." Ti said.

The four other bears started to head for the door. Two of the Marines blocked and closed the door.

Babs looked at them. "Gentlebears, please have a seat. I must insist."

One of them looked at her. "Female you can't tell us…"

Babs was on him in less than a fraction of a SubSTU. She had him thrown into a chair. She then put the heel of her shoe in his throat. "Play nice, I would hate to have to hurt you."

The other three started to move when they found Ti and one of the Pandarians standing in front of them. Ti told them. "Do as the lady says or I'll let her have you."

They looked at each other and set down. Babs handcuffed the first one to a chair. "Now behave yourself."

The Minister looked real scared now. "You can't come into…."

Ti explained. "Minister, I am an officer in Special Branch. I can take them outside, identify them, and if they are members of a known terrorist organization, say the Fusan movement or the Overa Cartel. I can just shoot them. No fuss no muss."

One of the bears looked at Ti. "But, I thought the Overa Cartel was just a criminal enterprise?"

"That was before they firebombed a Senator's house on *Bearilia Prime*. The Politicians and President Coldbear didn't think it was funny. So they were added to the list." Ti said, "In fact they are to be given special attention."

The four other bears just looked at each other.

Soon King Chen arrived with his guards and the Princess. "What is going on here?"

The nervous little *Minister of Antiquities* was about to come out of his fur. "Your Highness they say they have the necklace but they have failed to produce it. Then they attacked these bear that brought me information that the necklace was destroyed."

"Well," the King asked?

Ti waved off the statement. "It was cheap imitation your highness. It was made by a Johnathan Coronado. We used them as bait while we secured the real necklace and brought it to you. Mr. Coronado was severely wounded. He is not expected to live. The imitation necklace was badly damaged. But, as you can see this is the original." With that Ti placed it in his paw.

The king looked the necklace over checked the proof marks. "It appears to be the real thing. If the artist signature is not within, then we will know it is a fake."

He pulled out a scanner and showed it to Ti. Deep inside near a blue stone was the signature of Annabelle Rosa. The King smiled. "It is the real necklace. The gift of the Rose has returned."

Ti looked at Babs then at Fong who just smiled.

The bear handcuff to the chair glared. "That is impossible!"

Ti walked over. "You are under arrest for terrorism. You have a choice. Tell me what I want to know or die."

"I am not afraid of you. Even if you kill me the cartel will burn down your house, kill your wife, and your children. We see all and touch everyone." The bear boasted.

Ti leaned in. "Not any more. My cousin destroyed the *Devils eye*. Now will you talk?"

"Never," The bear spit at Ti.

Ti started to pull his knife, when Sergeant Fong stopped him. "My planet my people, Sire."

Ti nodded.

The Sergeant lifted him up. Then he cut his neck, clean through. The other three watched in horror.

Ti turned to the other three. "Well, what will it be?"

They all three looked at their cell leader's headless body. "We will talk."

The little Minister collapsed. "What have you done, they are holding my daughter!"

Ti looked at him. "Don't worry Minister. We will get her back. They will tell us where she is."

Ti grabbed one of the cartel members and dragged him into a closet. "I am going to only ask you one time. Where is she?"

"They are holding her in an old factory on the edge of town." The first one said.

He then grabbed the next, then the next. He then looked at all three "You all told me the same answer. If you lied I will give you over to the three Pandarians. If the girl dies, I give you to them. Do you understand?"

All three nodded.

"Good, Mr. Fa, take care of our guest till I get back. If I come back with the girl they live. If not then they are all yours."

Sergeant Fong nodded.

Ti looked at the King. "Sire, I need a plain delivery vehicle."

"Lieutenant, get this bear and his lady anything they want." King Chen ordered.

Soon Babs and Ti were rolling. She slipped into the back and put on a camouflage suit. "How do you want to play it?"

"You do the over watch and sniping. I go in and get the girl." Ti said.

"Why?" Babs asked.

"Simple even with the vest you could get killed. They might get lucky but unless they have a ships gun in there, they might hurt me but they won't kill me." Ti said.

"Don't get careless. I don't want to be a widow." Babs said.

Ti replied. "Ok, I'll do it right. Just keep them off me. Look in that case."

She opened up the case and looked at the rose wood fifty, caliber, rail gun rifle. "Sweet, I love the color."

Ti pulled into a hill overlooking the factory. Babs and Ti got out. They crawled over to the edge she looked through a hooded spotting scope.

Babs whistled. "There must be fifty guards down there."

Ti said. "That's why you're up here."

Ti scanned the building, "There are a lot of cells in there and a lot of bears in them."

Babs looked through the scanner. "Should we call for backup?"

"No, the noise might alert them. Then some hostages might get killed." Ti said. "Give me a few moments to get down to the gate. Then start taking out the guards. Start with the towers."

Babs kissed him. "Don't worry; I am as good a shot as you are. Just don't get hurt."

Ti nodded. "Stay alert, stay safe." With that he drove off.

He had put a spirits store logo on the side of the cargo transport. He also had placed several crates of spirits in the back. Plan A was to bluff his way into the building. Plan B was attached to the bottom of the clip board. The little gift from Andreios was only good for two shots. That was all he would need.

Ti quietly spoke into his com unit. "Aphrodite, wait and see how far I can bluff my way in."

Babs clicked her mike twice and moved her position. No one could hear or decode their transmissions. Still you didn't stay a live by taking unnecessary chances. Besides, she wanted a better shooting position. Overa's bears had snipers out also. They would be her first targets. She also knew they had all the likely spots for another sniper ranged in and marked.

She spotted her spot. It was just a shallow pot hole in the pavement of the parking lot next to where she was. The camouflage suit she wore made her invisible. She also carried a tarp that would blend into the terrain. She slowly moved over to the spot she selected. Poured some explosive crystals into the pot hole and covered it with the tarp. No one more than a few SMU away would have heard the pops. When they were done the hole was big enough for her to crawl into. She propped up the end of the tarp and started picking out her targets. She marked, each one of them, on her range card.

Ti pulled up to the gate. A big burly guard walked up. "What do you want?"

Ti gave him a friendly smile. "Hay dude my new boss just told me to drive this out here and give these crates to a Mr. Alex. He said to tell him to consider it interest, whatever that means."

The guard looked at Ti. "You work for old man Wu? You're not Pandarian?"

"Look I just spent six years on a tramp freighter. This was the first port we made where I could get off. None of his usual people would make the delivery. The law here says if you don't have a job you can't stay. I took the job. Do you want me to drop it here?" Ti said.

"No tough guy. I'll send you up to the Boss; he might have some more questions for you. He also might have a message for Wu." The guard said. "Drive up to dock five."

Ti did as he was told. "I am going in don't get in a hurry. You'll know when."

This time Babs didn't acknowledge. She just brought the rifle up and put a clip in and charged a round. She smiled he was going to play it loose. Part of her was mad. Yet she also knew that he knew he could do it. Partly because he was the Scarecrow and partly because he knew she was here.

Mr. Alex was waiting for Ti when he pulled up. Two bears jerked open his door and dragged him out. Mr. Alex threw a punch into Ti's midsection, only to grab his paw and wrist in pain.

"Mr. Alex that wasn't real smart. I am a Maxmimus you're not going to do much but annoy me doing things like that." Ti said.

One of his Henchbears pulled a gun and pointed it at Ti. Alex looked at him. "Put it away, for now. Let him go. Ok, why are you here?"

"Mr. Alex, I already told the guard. My new boss asked me to bring you these crates of spirits. He said to tell you they were an interest payment." Ti said.

"Why did Wu send you? You're not one of his usual bears." Mr. Alex asked.

Ti shook his head. "Come on Mr. Alex, I am been around. It's obvious he owes you money and couldn't pay it. So he sent you the spirits. High quality stuff too. In hopes that you would accept it and give him more time. His usual bears were afraid you would be upset. They refused to make the delivery. I needed the job. I figured you couldn't be worse than going back to the tramp freighter I was on."

Mr. Alex looked at him. "What was its name?"

Ti replied, "*The Flying Gull* out of *Darius IV* we were hauling organic fertilizer. The ship was a stink hole before, it was unbearable after. We were taking on a load of *Dan Po Cabbage* to take to a mining colony near *Zeta 8*. I had had enough after six years on that heap."

Mr. Alex ordered. "Why don't you come inside while we check out your story? If you were a crew member on the *Flying Gull* you might leave here alive."

"You four bring in the spirits." Mr. Alex ordered. "Put him in with Minister Hans' daughter she will be leaving soon also, one way or another just like this one."

Ti smiled, "Hi, little lady."

The young Pandarian girl cub looked at him. She held her paw to her mouth. "Shhh don't talk loud they are listening." She pointed to a guard.

Ti smiled took out a small device and placed it on the bars. "There Miss Han they cannot hear us. I am here to take you home."

She looked at him. "But, you are a prisoner also."

"No my Lady, they only think I am. Babs it is time. I have Miss Han. There are fifteen other cages they are filled with cubs and elderly." Ti said.

The guard could see Ti's mouth moving. But, all of a sudden he couldn't hear anything. He got up and walked over to the cage. "What is going on over here?"

Ti looked at him. "What I can't here you." He mouthed.

The Guard step next to the door. In a flash Ti reached through the bars and twisted his neck which snapped. He then grabbed the keys off the guard's belt and opened the door. He laid the dead guard on the floor in the cage and locked the door.

Babs had lined up on the first sniper in the far left Tower. She pulled the trigger. The fifty caliber round went through the side of the tower, hit the sniper, passed through him, and hit the guard behind him. Both slid down. She methodically moved to the next set of targets.

Ti looked at Miss Han. "Stay close we are going to secure this room. Then free the other prisoners."

Miss Han looked at him. "But how, there are so many of them?"

Ti explained. "I am a Knight my lady and we are not alone.

Ti, popped open a small capsule, he kneed the putty. Then he threw it at a guard that was setting in a chair near a window. The putty hit the chair. The guard heard it hit. He looked around and put his paw on top of it. Ti turned Miss Han away just as it went off. The guard's paw and the chair came apart. Parts of the chair buried themselves in his chest. The guard tried to scream but no sound came out as he died.

Babs had eliminated the other four towers. Now she decided to take out the guards on the roof. Four were lined up in almost a straight line she fired. Three went down clean. The fourth was only hit in the arm. The fact that it had been blown off didn't stop him from raising an alarm. Before, a second slug ended his life.

Mr. Alex came out of his chair. He looked out his window. He saw three of his bears fall in rapid succession.

Babs saw movement in a window and sent a round towards the wall below the window. One of Mr. Alex's bears grabbed him away from the window just as the wall exploded. He had thrown Alex clear but the round caught him in the side and blew him across the room. It almost tore him in half.

Five of his other bears were cowering behind desks and other furniture. "Let's get out of here. Kill the hostages now!" Mr. Alex screamed.

Ti had released the hostages. He moved them into an area where he felt they were undercover and protected. He asked an elderly couple to watch over, Miss Han. He then set up a barrier from where he could cover the door. He had taken the guards' weapons plus he had a few capsules of Andreios putty, his little blaster, and a few knives. He didn't see the thug that had sneaked in from a trap door from the outside.

The bear jumped him and stabbed him in the back. The blade just folded. Ti reached back and threw the thug over his shoulder. "You will have to do better than that." Ti twisted his arm till he dislocated the shoulder.

The thug stood up and tried to pull a gun. Ti put a knife through his throat severing his spine. Ti then pushed some crates over the trap door.

Babs was having trouble finding targets. Those still alive had taken to ground. She checked her ammunition. She had five clips left, thirty rounds, and two boxes. Ok, another ninety rounds. She slowly loaded another clip as she looked for a target. She saw movement. Someone was climbing a ladder on one of the towers. He had almost reached the top when she blew the rung and one of his feet off. She then put a round into the tower near where the upper part of the bear's body would be. It was thrown from the tower like a rag doll.

Mr. Alex gathered ten of his bears to him. No one knew what was going on. One told him that communications was down and he could tell that the towers had been wiped out. Also, the guards on the roof and the main gate were gone. He knew at least eighteen of his bears were dead out of fifty. He still had hostages. He would kill ten, throw their bodies out, and demand to negotiate. He would start with the Maxmimus and the Han girl. In the end he would kill all the hostages. Even the ones he might release. Just to prove a point.

He turned to five of his bears. "Go in and bring out the Maxmimus and the Han Girl. We will kill them first."

They burst into the holding room; Ti shot the first one in the head as he fell back. He shot two others before they got behind cover.

The two cartel members tried to return fire.

Ti had fashioned a sling shot and knead some more putty. He fired the sling shot just as one showed the side of his head. The putty hit him in the side of his head he tried to pull it off. He looked at his friend. That's when it exploded. His head just disintegrated.

The other cartel member had had enough. He ran for the door. He had almost reached it when he felt something hit him in the back of the head. He cleared the door, looked at Mr. Alex, just as his head exploded.

Mr. Alex lost his nerve. "Enough, torch the building. Let's get out of here!"

Ti heard what he screamed. "Aphrodite, they're going to set fire to the building. I am going to send the hostages out the trap door. Clear them a safe passage!"

Babs keyed her mike twice.

She fired two rounds at a post on the fence. The post disintegrated and the fence came apart. As it did a mine field exploded. Babs put a few rounds in front of the fence nothing happened. She then put three more beyond it. Again there were more explosions till the ground was churned all the way to the road.

Babs called. "They had it mined. I can't be sure I got them all."

"Ok, just keep the bad guys off. I'll do the rest." Ti moved the hostages into the tunnel.

"Don't; move until the building is in flames. Then move down to the end of the tunnel. When I tell you, head for where the fence is down stay on the ground that is churned up.

Mr. Alex got in his transport along with a driver and three guards. Only fifteen others had responded and got in the transports. They were going to charge the gate. Out of fifty-eight members of the cartel, eight were still gone. Fifteen were with him. The rest, thirty-five were probable dead.

Ti could start feeling the heat. "Ok, head for the end. Then wait till I get there."

The older Pandarians corralled the frightened cubs. Miss Han held Ti's paw.

"Scarecrow, I have movement. Three transports heading for the gate." Babs said.

"Try and stop them Aphrodite. I don't want them to reach the road." Ti said.

Babs clicked her mike twice and lined up on the first transport. The slug passed through the engine and into the passenger's compartment, smashing the leg of the bear in the right front seat. The hood flew off the transport. It careened out of control, smashed into a gas tank, and exploded.

She then lined up on the second car. This time the round hit the windshield in front of the driver. It disintegrated along with his head and the cartel member's behind him. The transport, speed up, then flipped sideways, rolling. It kept rolling through the fence on the other side and into the mine field. At which point it just came apart.

Mr. Alex didn't know what to do. His driver was weaving trying to throw the shooter's aim off. A slug slammed into the roof tearing out the back window. The next slug smashed into the side panel killing the bear next to him. Another slug hit the roof support and pealed part of the roof back. The bear in the front seat dropped down only to be killed when a slug passed through the wheel well.

Flames were starting coming out of the engine compartment. The engine coughed and died. The driver was trying to restart it when he slumped over. Mr. Alex pushed the body of one bear out and jumped out. He was followed by the remaining Cartel member. Alex looked stunned as he saw the bodies of his bears. That's when he saw Ti he screamed "You!"

Ti yelled, "Down!" He handed Miss Han to an adult Pandarian. Everyone dropped to the ground.

Mr. Alex and the other cartel member started running toward Ti. He was screaming. "I am going to kill you!"

The cartel member beside him pitched sideways, as a slug hit him and threw him off his feet.

Mr. Alex drew a gun.

Ti fired a blast from Andreios emergency phaser. It wasn't a well-aimed shot. Instead of hitting Mr. Alex, it hit his gun destroying it. Ti pocketed the phaser and drew his knife as did Mr. Alex.

Mr. Alex crashed into Ti. He was sure he had driven his knife deep into his stomach. He even tried twisting the knife.

Ti just smiled as he grabbed him by the neck. "That is not going to help." Ti put his knife away popped open a capsule. He kneads the putty and stuck it on Alex's forehead. "Goodbye Mr. Alex." He turned and walked away.

Mr. Alex stared at the bent knife in his hand. He then reached up and touched the sticky substance in his hair. "What?" That's when it went off.

Mr. Alex, the Overa Cartel's Terror of *Pandarus VI* and most of his organization lay dead. Ti looked at the carnage. "Ok Aphrodite, I am going to bring them out the main gate call for back up."

Babs made the call. Soon Ambulances and members of the Home Guard arrived along with Minister Han.

Ti walked over. "Minister Han, I am Scarecrow, I work for Inspector Holms. Here is your daughter."

The little Minister fell at his feet and kissed his paw. "How can I repay you?"

Ti told him. "Just give her a lot of love. She was very brave."

A Colonel came over. "The old ones say you refused to leave them behind thank you. Is there anything we can do for you?"

Ti looked at the mess he and Babs had left behind. "Could you, clean this mess up for us?"

The Colonel replied. "I would let them rot, but the buzzards might get sick. I will take care of it Scarecrow. Also, transport is waiting."

Ti walked up the hill. Sergeant Fong and his marines were with Babs. "We brought you both a change of clothes and a few bobbles. You have an appointment at a jewelry clearing house in three cycles. You can change in the back. We have a privacy screen."

Ti said, "Thank you Sergeant Fong."

On a hill half a KSMU away three bears stared in horror. One looked through a pair of binoculars. "It has to be his body. I can see his ring and his watch, but his head is just gone. Mr. Alex is dead. Everyone is dead."

"Ok, we better leave before we join them. We'll report to Mr. Overa. He is going to be upset. It looks like Mr. Alex torched the hostages. That will teach them. Let's go." The cell leader said. In the back of his mind he thought, but what if they survived.

Ti opened a com unit. "This is General Zen Tang." A voice said.

Ti spoke quietly. "Greetings General this is Scarecrow, I have a request."

The General replied. "Anything, that I can do for you my friend."

Ti explained. "Can you have your news agencies report that all the hostages were killed? It might be better for their safety."

General Tang responded. "I already did my friend. I also gave credit for the attack on the cartel to our Home Guard. I said that while the loss of the hostages was a tragedy. We as a free population could no longer live in fear and allow thugs to control our lives. It was a good speech. My forces raided four of their establishments. We have rounded up fifteen more cartel members and sympathizers. They have lost their grip of fear on us."

Ti sighed. "Thank you General Tang."

"No, thank you, Scarecrow and Aphrodite." General Tang severed the com link.

King Chen looked at the General. "Who are they?"

The General bowed. "They are friends, your Highness. More, than that I cannot say."

"Why can you not tell me?" The King demanded.

The General looked at him. "I gave my oath to a friend to take this secret to my grave your Highness. I will keep that oath."

The King nodded. "Such an oath cannot be broken not even by a King. Thank you General." *Such loyalty even to ones friends must be rewarded. I must ponder this.*

The Overa Cartel members that survived all made their way to exit points. Then they left *Pandarus VI*. Each vowed to return to seek revenge. None ever would.

Ti and Babs arrived at a small convention center. Miss La Rogue, Mr. Bantelle, and Annabelle Rosa were there.

Miss La Rogue ran over to them. "Monsieur and Madam Tornbow I am so glad they found you. Did you know that our Annabelle Rosa is a famous Artist? Anyway when word leaked that she was on board and that you had merchandise for sell, the calls came flooding in. Mr. Bantelle said you..."

Babs took her paw. "Did you bring the girls?"

La Rogue nodded. "Oui Madam Tornbow, they are getting dressed and are picking out their pieces."

"Good, now Maria, just relax and enjoy yourself you have done a wonderful job. Did the ship cater the food and drink?" Babs asked.

"Oui, only the hall and tables are rented. The security and everything else came from the ship." La Rogue said.

"Very good, make sure the staff is paid out of the event. Also, that the ship is paid for the event at the going rate. We should do very well tonight. Now, have fun." Babs smiled and kissed her cheek.

Babs and Ti walked into the room. She wore a stunning necklace made of yellow diamonds and green emeralds. The Pandarians bowed as she walked in.

One walked over. "Sire and Sirena Tornbow, I am Mr. Zing Fa. I am the head of the jeweler's guild. I want to thank you for setting up this gathering and bringing in the Rose. You also have many exquisite pieces and loose stones. Your prices also seem very reasonable."

"Thank you Mr. Fa. We hope you enjoy the evening." Babs said.

"Oh, yes my lady. By the way is your necklace for sell?" Mr. Zing Fa asked.

Babs responded, "Yes, Mr. Fa, but I am afraid it is the most expensive piece here tonight."

Two other jewelers came over. "My lady you must give us a chance to buy it also."

"Gentlebears please..." Babs started to say.

Ti stepped in. "Since more than one of you is interested in this piece. I will auction it off at the end of the evening. Does that seem fair?"

All three said, "Yes."

The twenty models were having a field day. They no sooner put on a set and walk out, than they found themselves running back to put on another.

Annabelle Rosa came over to Babs. "My lady may I make a few pieces for them. I will use the loose stones and get a good price."

Babs said, "If you want, my lady."

Mr. Bantelle assisted her in setting a small work area up. Several of the jewelers drew designs and purchased loose stones for her to use.

Annabelle Rosa spent time talking to each jeweler. Then she redrew the design to give them what they actually wanted. Then she took the stones some she rejected and replaced. Then she would make the necklace. She would heat strips of metal and form the base for the stones. Then she would pray over each piece and present it to the jeweler along with the bill.

Each jeweler would bow, go over to Mr. Bantelle, and pay the bill.

One, a Mr. Ta Zang came over with tears in his eyes. "Mr. and Mrs. Tornbow you have brought us the greatest gift. I will never be able to sell this piece. I shall give it to my daughter. Thank you, thank you." He said bowing as he headed for the door clutching his necklace. One of his assistance quickly bowed, gathered up fourteen other boxes, and followed him out the door.

After three cycles Ti decided it was time to start the auction. "Please ladies and gentlebears, I would like to draw your attention to my wife's beautiful neck or at least the necklace around it."

Everyone laughed as she twirled around.

"Ok, let's start the bidding at 1million *Bearilian* credits." Ti said.

Mr. Fa said, "One million."

Mr. Ta Sang bid, "One point five million."

Miss. Lu Way smiled. "One point seven five million credits."

Mr. Fa bid, "Two million."

Miss Lu Way smiled. "Let's not mess around Fa. Five million credits."

Fa dropped his head. "It is yours *Dragon Lady*."

Miss Lu Way sneered. "Thank you."

Babs said. "Miss Way this is called a *Dragon Heart Necklace* by the way. In our culture what he called you would be a complement. Many of our family members are actually dragons."

"You are most kind Mrs. Tornbow. However, in our culture it means that I am a shrew, a cold hearted business female, which I am. Do I pay you?" Miss Lu Way asked.

"No, pay Mr. Bantelle. Thank you for your business." Babs said.

The party lasted another cycle then broke up.

Fong came over. "The ship has been moved into dry dock. You have a suite at the *Imperial*."

Ti rubbed his shoulder. "What about the crew, the girls, and your security detail?"

"Sir, I am sure everyone will find some place..." Fong was saying.

"None sense call the Imperial. Tell them I want the top two floors. Tell them that if it inconveniences any other guests that I will pay for their rooms and tomorrows breakfast." Ti said.

"Mr. Fong, who did you say you were calling for?" The manager of the *Imperial* asked.

Fong replied. "Mr. Brinton Tornbow, owner of the *Gem Lines*."

The manager gulped. "Is he the son of old boar Tornbow?"

"Yes and he is as hard a bear as his old boar." Fong said.

"Tell him the *Imperial* is always glad to accommodate his needs. We will have the top two floors of suits cleaned and ready for your party's arrival. How many bears are we looking at?"

"Forty-four bears in all Sir. Just have the keys ready. I will take care of the room assignments." Fong said

Ti called everyone over. "Ladies and gentlebears, I know everyone is dead tired. I have rooms for everyone at the *Imperial*. Let's head over there. Get a good night's rest. Then tomorrow morning we will settle up. Mr. Fong and Miss La Rogue will see that everyone gets taken care of tonight. We will see each of you in the morning."

Ti and Babs got in the transport. The Pandarian private looked at him. "Sire how, how do you do it, you, and your Lady?"

Private, that is a…" Sergeant Fong was saying

Babs interrupted him. "It's ok Sergeant let him ask his question. We are professionals."

The Sergeant just nodded.

Ti explained. "Private, I was trained to be a warrior from the age of one. I am a Knight of my Clan. Killing is a horrible thing, but sometimes evil creatures don't give you any choice. When good creatures fail to stand up to Evil, then Evil wins. But remember Evil and evil Creatures tend to be cowards only preying on the weak and the old."

Babs added. "So for us it is about stopping evil. That for us is a commission from the Creator of the Universe and His Word. We are protectors. It is what we do. No matter the cost. As a Marine you should understand that."

The Private dropped his head. "Yes Mame, I understand now, thank you."

Sergeant Fong smiled, *Ok, these Maxmimus were different, but everything he had heard about them was true. Maybe that's why the bears that serve them are so loyal."*

At the hotel everyone was given a room assignment. They all slowly moved to their shared suites to crash.

Mr. Bantelle and his daughter took the suit next to Ti and Babs. Andrew Re bunked with them.

Ti and Babs asked Annabelle Rosa to share their suite. She didn't know what to say. Ti kissed her and pointed out that as a celebrity. She would be honoring them in the eyes of the Pandarians.

Octavious looked at Angelina. "Are you sure you want to do this?"

"No, I don't want this Octavious." Angelina said. "You can't spend all your time on *Andreas Prime* either. You would lose your seat."

Octavious shrugged, "That might not matter. I might have to give up my seat anyway."

Angelina looked at him. "Why? Not because of me!"

"No...Vice President Van Horn is very ill. He is going to have to resign. Coldbear asked if I would take his place. I told him I would have to talk to you about it. He gave me until the end of the weekend to decide." Octavious said.

Angelina looked at him. "What do you want to do?"

"I don't know. I would have more freedom and more responsibility. But I would also be seen as a lackey for Coldbear. David and I have been friends for a long time. He knows I am no one's yes bear." Octavious said.

"Who would take your place?" Angelina asked.

"Isaiah said he would like to try and run for the seat. He has Foreign Service experience. He also enjoys politics and the games involved. He also loves *Bearilia Prime* and has no intentions of going back to *Andreas Prime*. We could give him this house." Octavious said.

"What about Benjamin, Augustus, Maria, and Beany shouldn't they have a say?" Angelina asked.

Octavious shook his head. "You're their mother, the Empress, and you don't know what is, going on." he laughed.

Angelina's eyes flared and she hit him with a pillow. "What do you mean by that?"

Octavious explained. "Just that Benjamin has petitioned the council to start a University on *Andreas Prime*. Augustus sold his business here and has already started moving his family to *Andreas Prime*. Beany and her family are opening a law office in *Saint Elaina's*. She is moving into *Grace Castle* with Justinian, she pointed out he didn't need four hundred twenty rooms. Maria and Jim said that *Andreas Prime* needed more teachers. He passed his administrator exam. He will be a Principle at a new high school in *Angel Land*."

Angelina looked at him. "When did this all start?"

Octavious shrugged. "Alexa has been working on them for months. Isaiah complained. He said he didn't understand why she wanted everybody to follow her. Didn't she realize others might have other dreams? You know his usual speech."

Angelina sighed. "He was always compliant as a child. But, in some ways he is most like Alexa and Beary."

"Just more devious, that's why he will make a great politician." Octavious said.

Angelina leaned back. "Ok, so we move to *Andreas Prime*. You tell David you'll take the job. De and your staff go with you, and you're moving to *Andreas Prime*."

Octavious nodded. "Ok, that settles that. Now what can this Knight do for his Empress."

Angelina kissed him then smiled an impish smile. "Don't you mean to your Empress."

Octavious grinned *yes she still drove him crazy and he loved it.*

Ti looked at Babs sleeping she was so tired. She also slept so peaceful. He had trouble closing his eyes. He knew if he did the night terrors would start. Yet he had to sleep. The killings were proper they had deserved to die. But yet it bothered him. He slid in closer to his wife and forced himself to sleep. The terrors started. Mr. Alex's headless body was laughing at him. "I am going to kill your family, if I can't kill you. I'll kill her. You know you are not strong enough to protect her." Ti screamed at the headless body "I killed you." In his dream the body grew a horned snakes head. "No, you only removed a limb. See I have another head. I will kill her and everyone else dear to you." Ti started screaming.

Babs woke up and rolled over. She started kissing Ti and talking to him. "Ti what's wrong my love. It is ok, I am here."

Ti slowly woke up, tears streaming down his face. Babs kissed his face he looked at her, "I ... just had a bad dream."

Babs kissed him very passionately. "Then my husband we must exorcise those demons and I know the cure." She said as she leaned over him.

Ti woke up the next morning to singing coming from the other room. Two voices in perfect harmony were singing in an old almost forgotten language. He slipped on some clothes and walked out. Annabelle Rosa and Babs were fixing breakfast. He stood quietly listening to their song. When they finished he clapped. "That was amazing and beautiful."

Babs blushed. "It is a love song in the language of my race."

Annabelle Rosa explained. "The Charioteers were very passionate bears. Their songs are a little erotic. Not dirty, just suggestive visually. They are actually quite beautiful in the original language."

"I agree and when we get home you need to teach me the language. So I can help teach it to our cubs." Ti said.

Babs blushed even more.

Annabelle Rosa just laughed. "I think he meant so he could read the books and stories."

Ti looked confused.

Babs smiled and laughed. "I don't know perhaps if he taught our sons what he knows their wives would be pleased."

Annabelle Rosa laughed again. This time Ti blushed.

After breakfast Miss La Rogue and Mr. Bantelle came in. "Good morning sire." Mr. Bantelle said, "Lady Allis."

Babs smiled. "Morning did everyone sleep well and get breakfast."

"Yes Mrs. Tornbow." Miss La Rogue said.

"Maria, Brinton might be a little stiff but I am not. I am Allis or lady Allis if you prefer. Mrs. Tornbow as my Mother-in-law says is my father- in- Law's Mother. Now, how did we do last night?"

"After expenses, including the staffs' rooms for last night, the bonus you said to pay the girls and the salaries for the security guards. We cleared twenty million credits." Mr. Bantelle said.

"Did you and Maria take your cut? And did you give Annabelle Rosa, Andrew Re, and Teresa theirs." Babs asked.

"Allis, I have them here but they are…" Mr. Bantelle started to say.

Ti shook his head. "We share the risk. We share the reward Mr. Bantelle, everyone shares."

Bantelle nodded. "Yes, Sire Tornbow."

Maria looked at her envelope, "But Monsieur this is more than a year's pay!"

Ti replied. "Maria you earned it. We more than paid for this trip with this event. Just keep up the good work. Also, tell the girls thank you, enjoy the rooms, and the *Imperial* for the next three days. Along with the security staff here, the next three nights are to be charged to the *Gem Lines*. I'll go down and talk to the manager."

Maria was stunned. "But, Sire Tornbow the captain…"

"Maria, I own the ship. The rest of the crew, I know is staying at the port facility owned by the company. It will be fixed up in time.

But, your girls work for you and you now work strictly for me and Allis. As does Mr. Bantelle and his people. The security unit is here for our protection. I don't care how the captain feels about it." Ti said.

Maria bowed; she didn't know what to say. She knew she had just been promoted, but to what?

"Maria you like to travel. When we get back from this cruise we are going to make you regional director of marketing. Unfortunately, that will require you to get your deck officers certification. So you will have to go to school for about six months for the core classes. Then you can finish the others on line on the ship of your chose." Babs said.

Maria dropped on her knees and kissed Babs paws. "Mrs. Allis, I will make you and the Sire proud. I promise."

Babs replied. "Now go tell everyone to go have fun."

Ti went down to the manager's office. "Mr. Lee, I am Brinton Tornbow. I understand Mr. Bantelle settled my account."

"Yes, Sire Tornbow he did." Mr. Lee said.

"Good, I want to continue renting the top two floors for the remaining time *the Dream in the Night* is in space dock. You will charge it to the *Gem Lines*." Ti said.

"But, I have no authorization from Captain Thorn…" Mr. Lee started to say.

"Mr. Lee, I don't need Captain Thorn's authorization. He works for me. I own the *Gem lines*." Ti looked at him with cold eyes.

Mr. Lee wilted. "I am sorry Mr. Tornbow. It is just that, well ships crews are not usually treated so well."

"Mr. Lee, these ladies made me twenty million credits last night. If I treat them well they might do it again. The security bears are protecting my wife. If I treat them poorly they might decide to do their job poorly." Ti said.

Mr. Lee nodded. Brinton Tornbow might be as hard a boar as his father, but he was no fool either. "Well Mr. Tornbow, if your bears need anything my staff will be more than happy to see to their needs."

Ti smiled. "Make my bears happy and you will profit from it Mr. Lee I promise." He said as he left.

Mr. Lee understood the unspoken, don't and I will ruin you just as my father would.

The Pandarians finish securing their planet from the cartel's influence.

Ti and Babs visited the other crew members of *the Dream in the Night* and tried to improve their accommodations. They had food catered in and told the facilities cooks that they were fired. They also talked to the facility manager. He said that if they wished to replace him they could. However, that he had been fighting for years to improve the facilities. Ti believed him and gave him ten million credits. He told him to get started.

Soon the upgrades to *The Dream in the Night* were complete. She was moved to the *Embarkation Dock* at the spaceport. The passengers embarked and she headed out into space.

Captain Thorn looked at his navigator. "Miss Jacksen set course for *Helios IV,* warp 4."

# CHAPTER 6

# Changes

A NGELINA WALKED IN to the boardroom; the Directors of the *Medical Institute* were there. "Ladies and gentlebears, I have decided that the *Federation* needs a second teaching *Medical Institute*. I will be opening one on *Andreas Prime* and moving my practice there. I ask that Dr. Torrance be made Chief of Nero-Surgery here. He was always my best student."

"Lady Maxumus, we will be so sorry to see you leave. We are also glad that you will be starting another institute. With the *Federation* expanding *Andreas Prime* will be of great importance. Also, we concur with your recommendation of Dr. Torrance." Mr. Greenbrier said.

Angelina nodded, "Good day." She then left without another word.

Dr. Torrance was waiting for Angelina. "I wanted to go with you."

"No Tor, I need to leave someone here I trust. Besides, if you need me you can always call. The truth is your good enough, you won't." Angelina said.

"It won't be the same without you and Mrs. Maro." Dr. Torrance said.

Angelina just kissed him.

Rebecca handed her a coat. "Come on it is time. Take care, Dr. Torrance."

"You too Lady Maro," Dr. Torrance said as the two friends walked out the door.

Octavious looked at President Coldbear. "David, are you sure you want me. You know I am a pain in the tail."

President Coldbear smiled. "Octavious, Van Horn has to go under some risky treatment. The doctors only give him a 30% chance of surviving. He doesn't want to die in office. I will get Bob to appoint young Isaiah to finish your term. He owes me. I need you; I also want you to continue to run the Secret Service as Vice President. I will have Bill Henderson report directly to you. That way your little agreements with him can stay in effect."

"Ok David. I hope you know what you're doing." Octavious said.

"Octavious, if I wanted a lackey or a yes bear I would have asked Simon from *Darius V.* I don't. I want you because, I know you're honest, and so is Angelina." Coldbear said.

Ti, Babs, and Annabelle Rosa were watching the news; they were just taking a break from writing up, *After Action Reports*, when a news flash came on.

On the screen was Vice President Van Horn. He was standing before a joint meeting of the Bearilian Congress. Ti turned up the volume.

"My fellow Bearilians it has been my pleasure to serve my Federation since I was a young cub. Now, I stand before you a sick and dying boar. I do not fear death. I am ready to go to be with My Creator and His Word, if it be their will. However, I do not wish to die in servitude. So, as of this moment, I ask that you allow me that final promotion any servant of the general public may have, the simple right to become an ordinary citizen.

So, at this time, I tender my resignation as Vice President. I nominate a Senator, who by his leadership and honesty has proven his worthiness, Octavious Maxumus.

The uproar was immediate. The old bear just smiled. He held up his Paws. "Please, my friends, I ask only that you pray for me. Whether the doctors find a cure or the Creator takes me on the next great adventure. Pray that I find peace. Thank you." With that Van Horn left the podium, walked down the aisle to the doors of the chamber, and left.

Everyone stood in stunned silences.

Finally the Speaker of the House and the President of the Senate stood up. Mr. Freebear looked at the assembly. "It has been three hundred years since this body has had to replace a setting Vice President. One of our own has been nominated. A Senator we all know. Some like, some despise, but none question his integrity. I ask the House to vote." Of six hundred Congressbears: five hundred fifty voted yes. Fifty voted No. Mr. Freebear looked at Senator Coldspring. "The Bearilian House recommends Senator Maxumus be confirmed as the next Vice President of the Federation."

Senator Coldspring bowed. "Thank you Mr. Speaker. The Senate will now vote." Of two hundred Senators: one hundred ninety voted yes, nine voted no, and one abstained, Octavious.

Senator Coldspring called Octavious up. "Mr. Vice President."

Octavious looked at the gathered dignitaries and at the cameras. "My fellow Bearilians please join me in praying for Citizen Van Horn. Also, please pray for me that I may never betray your trust."

Ti looked at Babs. "What by the Moons of Bantine just happened?"

Widja smiled. "No my Angelina, that will not be a problem. I will ask the Council. I am sure they will agree. Having a major training hospital, along with the new university, they just approved, will not only help our local population, but all of the Races in the area. That includes the Antilleans and others."

"Thank you Widja. We will be home in about a week. I love you." Angelina said.

Ti called his mom's office. "Senator Maxumus office, Miss Jenson speaking, may I help you?"

Ti looked at the com unit. "Jenny, what are you doing at mom's desk?"

"It's not your mom's anymore. She has moved over to the Executive Office Building. When, she isn't going to be traveling. I am Isaiah's personal legislative assistant, and I do mean personal." Jenny laughed.

Ti smiled. "So, have you got him to set a date yet?"

Jenny beamed. "After ten years of dodging he finally decided it was time. We're going to get married here in two months by the lake. By the way congratulations, she must be a real catch to take you down."

Ti looked at Babs. "She is. Tell Isaiah congratulations. I'll call Mom on here personal phone. Take, care Jenny."

"You too Ti," Jenny said.

Ti called another number.

"Your Way Travel, may I help you?" The voice said.

"Yes, I would like book a trip on the *Gem Lines*. Can you send me a schedule for *the Dream in the Night*?" Ti said.

"Yes Sir." The voice said then hung up.

Deloris called him back on a secure line. "That was taking an unnecessary risk son."

"Mom, I knew a pro like you would know what to do. What is going on?" Ti asked.

"Simple, things have changed. You now work directly for Octavious as you always did. Now Bill Henderson and everybody else, does also. By the way, I have started building a cottage on the land you bought from Gamey. I figure you don't need the land anymore for a home. I do. So I am moving in." Deloris said.

"Mom that's fine, but we could give you a place...." Ti started saying.

"First, I am not an island girl. I like the mountains. Second, I need to be close to Octavious and Angelina. Besides, I can commute with Widja." Deloris laughed.

"Mom, I don't understand." Ti said.

"The Empress and the Vice President are moving all our operations to *Andreas Prime*. You will be met on *Helios IV*. Give Babs my love, goodbye." Deloris hung up.

Octavious looked at her. "Well?"

Deloris looked at him. "Octavious, it was kind of sudden and he found out by watching the news."

"Ok De, send a message to all our operatives. Let them know I am still in charge. They still work for you and me. By the way, figure a new title out for yourself. You're no longer a secretary." Octavious said.

Deloris told him. "President Coldbear took care of it. You're looking at your Chief of Staff. I even have a staff. I picked them. Most are Augustine. I hope you don't mind."

Octavious smiled. "Family is family, De."

# CHAPTER 7

# Helios IV

TI LOOKED AT Babs then Annabelle Rosa. "The more things change the more they stay the same. We still work for Octavious. We will get instructions on *Helios IV*."

Annabelle Rosa looked at Ti and Babs. "Perhaps it would be better if you stayed on board at *Helios IV*."

Babs could see the worry on Annabelle Rosa's face. "Why, Dear?"

"*Helios IV* was the home of the Mac-Ta Ra Cult. It might be better if you didn't go ashore." Annabelle Rosa said.

Ti looked at her. "The Helios government banned and destroyed the cult one hundred years ago. After they, caught them sacrificing cubs."

Annabelle Rosa shook her head. "Sometimes, if you cut the head off a snake it grows back. Ti they used seeing stones. Also and the jungles were and are thick in parts of *Helios IV*. The Government only controls the cities and the developed rural areas. Over half of the planet is still uncharted thick jungle. The Mac-Ta Cult thrives in this part of the planet unseen. They too will want revenge on any Maxmimus. Also, the Overa Cartel may be tracking the Tornbows."

Ti nodded. "That is exactly why we are out here, Annabelle Rosa. I and Babs are the bait. If the Mac-Ta Cult is going to strike, let them do it on *Helios IV*. Then we can decide how to deal with them. We need to find out who our enemy and their allies are."

Annabelle Rosa nodded. "I understand, but please, be careful. The Mac-Ta uses a dark magic. I am not as strong as a full fledge dragon."

Babs smiled. "It is ok Annabelle Rosa. We know what we are doing."

Two days later *the Dream in the Night* arrived at *Helios IV*. This planet was known for its unique pink sand beaches and warm mineral oceans. The resort city of *New Helarctos* was a strange mixture of modern and ancient architecture, with a small mixture of colonial thrown in.

*Helios IV* had been the home of two distinct cultures, The Mac-Po and the Mac-Ta. Both cultures built large temple complexes around the planet.

The Mac-Po with beautiful spiral spires, that raised to the sky in perfect symmetry, and bright colors. They wrote beautiful melodies and poetry. They lived mainly in the plains and along the coast.

The Mac-Ta lived in the thick jungle and the harsh mountains. Their temples had jagged spires and black facades. Their art, what was found of it, always depicted bears being devoured, and being sacrificed to an unseen entity called, Ta-Ra.

Ti, Babs, and Annabelle Rosa, along with Mr. Fong and his detail were shown into a beautifully decorated office building. A small Sunnarian met them. He bowed. "Lady Rosa, Mr. and Mrs. Tornbow, ah, it is a pleasure to meet you. I am Cultural Minister Muluzi Aziz. I am sorry Mr. Tornbow you…"

Ti smiled. "Please Minister Aziz; I have been getting that a lot this trip. Father has put me in charge of the business, along with my wife Lady Allis."

Babs bowed. "Minister Aziz, these paintings are breath taking. Who painted them?"

Minister Aziz smiled. They were his most prized possession. "They were done by a Colonial Missionary, one of the few that did not treat us like sub creatures, a Sir Homer Pierceville. But, they show those horrible temples."

Annabelle Rosa shook her head. "Minister, you of all creatures know better. They are Mac-Po temples. They were a gentle and cultured people who wrote beautiful music and poetry. Why would you a decedent of those very people say such a thing?"

Minister Aziz bowed deeply to Annabelle Rosa. "My pardon Lady Rosa most outsiders do not know the difference between the Mac-Po and the Mac-Ta."

Annabelle Rosa stamped her foot. "Then they should be taught."

Minister Aziz shook his head. "How my lady, very few can read the old language. Few know the history."

Annabelle Rosa shook her head. "This is totally unacceptable. Where are your scholars? Do you not understand the richness of your own heritage? If you do not shine the light of truth on the Mac-Po, then all you, can do is hide in the shadows from the Mac-Ta."

Minister Aziz shivered at that last statement. "What do you suggest then my lady. Who could we get to point us in the right direction?"

Annabelle Rosa looked at Ti and Babs. They nodded. "I can give you three days. Call in your best bears with some working knowledge of the language. I will teach them. Then I will contact a friend of mine a Professor Cambrian. He is actually a native of *Helios IV*, from Sandak. He has an intensive library on *Bearilia Prime*."

The Minister bowed again. "I will set it up my Lady Rosa. Please you must all be my guest at my home. It is on the beach. It's better than any hotel and more secure."

Ti nodded. "Thank you, Minister Aziz, for your hospitality. We will accept. I know you wish time alone with Lady Rosa. We will leave and tour your market area."

The Minister nodded. "Sire Tornbow, please be careful the tourist areas are the safest. Some of the neighborhoods closer to the edge of town have had an increase in crime, especially on wealthy foreign tourists lately."

Ti replied. "Minister, do not worry. I am not afraid of the Mac-Ta. I have nothing they would want."

Ti was wrong, he just didn't know it. He had everything they wanted.

Damien Overa was mad. He was also tired and scared. When news of what had happened on *Pandarus VI* had reached him, he had planned to take a force back and settle the score. He still hoped to. However, at the moment he just wanted to survive along with as many members of his cartel as he could.

He realized he had relied on the seeing stone too much. With it gone he had let his guard down. The Bearilian Government had named his organization a terrorist group. They had put it at the top of its list for extinction. Not only had several of his outlying organizations been hit, but an informant had given the Marines his main location. If it hadn't been for a dirty cop, at a local precinct, he would have been caught. As it was only he and twelve of his lieutenants and thirty members escaped the raid. Two hundred had been captured or killed.

He had tried to contact Montage. Only to find out he was dead, killed near *Candaris Prime*. His fortunes fell apart after Mr. Alex was killed on *Pandarus VI*. What was the connection? He had just been contacted to try and capture a Mr. and Mrs. Tornbow. They were on *the Dream in the Night* which was currently on *Helios IV*. It had been at *Candaris Prime* and *Pandarus VI*....No, it couldn't be just a coincidence. He didn't believe in those.

Damien Overa made a call.

In a deep hidden valley, in the jungle of *Helios IV*, stands a large black temple complex. Its, blade like jagged spires, jab at the sky. Tall black bears, similar to a sloth bear, move slowly from temple to temple in long flowing black robes trimmed in scarlet red. In the center of the temple complex is a statue of a beast, ripping the beating heart out of the sun. He is Ta-Ra the Destroyer. His golden horns seem to absorb instead of reflect the light.

A monk, wearing a black robes trimmed in gold, was setting looking out the window at the statue. His com unit went off. "Hello Damien, I knew you would be calling. I felt a trimmer."

Damien sighed. "Then you know that Montage is dead."

The monk shrugged at the view screen. "Yes, I knew. I also know you have suffered greatly."

"Our friends want us to capture a young Maxmimus couple, A Sire and Sirena Brinton Tornbow. So, they can be held for ransom. Can you do this without killing them?" Overa asked.

"Ta-Ra will want his blood. A Maxmimus has great strength." The monk said.

"Look Doom Ogre, drain him as much as you like. As long, as you deliver him to our friend alive the female also." Overa said.

"Yes, we can do that. He only said he wanted them alive. Not in pristine condition." Doom Ogre said.

"In one piece no hacking things off either." Overa warned.

Doom Ogre frowned. "How could he deny Ta-Ra his pleasure?"

"Perhaps after he is paid he will give them back to you." Overa observed.

"Yes, there is always that chance." Doom Ogre smiled.

The first afternoon was uneventful Ti and Babs made some purchases and sold some necklaces. They noticed the occasional shadow, but couldn't tell if it was friend or foe.

That evening Minister Aziz held a big party for the Rose and the Tornbows. Every dignitary from the government was there including the Bearilian Counsel General. He slipped a small disk to Ti as he shook his paw.

That night Annabelle Rosa came into see them. "Great evil is preparing to move against you. Please stay where I can protect you."

Ti told her. "Annabelle Rosa, we will be fine. You have a mission. Help these bears find the light. They already fear the darkness."

"Ti, do not underestimate their evil, or how dangerous they are. If they come for you they will use poisons and other dark magic." Annabelle Rosa said.

Ti pulled out a small pouch. "Ben Maritinus gave these to me and this tin of save. He said they stop most poisons. We'll be careful. Just take care of yourself and teach these people what you promised them. Besides Sgt. Fong and his detail are with us. I promise I won't head into the Jungle."

Annabelle Rosa kissed him. "You don't fear the storm anymore?"

"No, my lady, I am the storm." Ti said.

The next morning Annabelle Rosa prayed for them. Then she kissed them. She wanted to go with them. Ti said. "No, she had her own duty to these creatures."

Ti looked at the large armored limousine transport. "Fong, isn't this over kill?"

"Minister Aziz insisted Sir, especially when he found out you wanted to go out to the Mac-Po temple, near the Po-tan neighborhood." Sergeant Fong said.

When they arrived at the temple complex the market outside was bustling with families and children. TI and Babs bought a few books, other souvenirs, and a map of the temple, then went inside. After a cycle of looking at the frescos and statues, Sergeant Fong noticed that the crowd was thinning out.

"Mr. and Mrs. Tornbow we need to head back to the transport now!" Fong said.

Ti looked up and pulled a small weapon as did Babs. They started walking for the transport. Corporal Tongan sprinted to it and started it up. He was pulling it towards the entrance when the first wave struck.

Twenty black hooded robed bears advanced on Ti, Babs, Sergeant Fong, and Private Den Po.

Ti spun around. "Get Allis to the transport now!" He then fired, dropping two of the advancing Mac-Ta monks.

The black monks pulled long wicked looking swords and started to charge. Two jumped from a building and grabbed Babs. The Private stabbed one in the neck killing the monk. Only, to have his vest slashed open by another monk. This one Babs killed. Private Den Po dropped to his knees. "I am sorry my Lady." He said as he passed out.

Babs saw three more approaching and shot them through their heads. They each fell back. Then she felt something tear her sleeve. A small dart was sticking in her arm. She pulled it out killed two more. Then her world went black.

The first, wave of monks were dead. Ti looked around and saw Babs and the Private were also down. "Fong get the Corporal we have two down!"

Ti ran over. Both were unconscious the Private was bleeding from the wound to his chest. It wasn't deep, but it was long. Also the smell of poison was evident. Ti lathered some salve on the wound and bandaged it the best he could. He then forced three Arachnid Gallbladders into his mouth and made him swallow them. "Get him to the transport now before they regroup."

Corporal Tongan picked him up and carried him to the transport.

Sergeant Fong was kneeling next to Babs. "Sir, she is breathing, but she was poisoned."

Ti put salve on the hole made by the dart. Then forced three Gallbladders in her mouth and made her swallow them. "Sergeant, please get her to the transport. I will cover you."

"Sir, I will not leave you behind. We all go out together. They need medical attention now!" Sergeant Fong said.

As Sergeant Fong laid Babs in the transport, the next wave stated towards them out of the jungle. He jumped in, opened the sun roof, and pulled out a small multi barreled mini railed gun. "Here they come!" He opened fire.

Ti pulled some putty out of their capsules and kneed it together. He shot it at a tree at the edge of the jungle where the monks were advancing from. The putty hit then detonated. Shattering the trunk and sending wooden splinters into several of the attacking monks. The Sergeant was busy mowing down everything between the transport and ten SMUs into the jungle. "Get in Sir!"

Ti dove in. The Corporal hit the accelerator.

As they left Ti noticed about fifteen dead monks not far from where the transport had been parked.

The Corporal looked in the mirror. "I am sorry sir. I should have been faster."

Ti looked at him. "Were you hurt Corporal?"

"No sir, they came in dumb. I fragged them, but in the process of dogging a barrage of darts, I dropped the keys. It is my fault the lady got hurt." Corporal Tongan said.

"Nonsense, I knew there was a chance they would pull something like this. I lead us into it. I am the one that got Private Den Po hurt and Allis. Get us back to the Ministers."

The Sergeant dropped down. "We are not being followed. How are they?"

Ti looked at him. "Alive, the private would be dead if he hadn't been wearing his vest. As it is the poison might still kill him. Babs, I don't know. She seems to be suffering; it is like there is a battle going on inside of her."

Ti's eyes turned cold. "I am going to find these demons. I am going to find the hole they crawled out of, and I am going to burn them out. Then I am going to cut off their heads and burn their bodies."

Annabelle Rosa looked at Andrew Re and Raphael. "I tell you something bad has happened. Bring me my medical kit. I just know I am going to need it."

Andrew Re brought it in as the transport almost smashed through the gate. The transport screeched to a stop in front of the front door.

Annabelle Rosa ran for the front door. She saw Ti reach in and pull Babs limp body out of the transport. As he did the Sergeant and Corporal lifted out the Private.

She turned to the Minister. "Clear me space in the main parlor. Bring in two beds now!" she ordered."

The minister turned to two staff members who ran to the main parlor. They pulled two beds out of the wall.

Annabelle Rosa looked at Ti and the Sergeant. "Come!" Was all she said.

She started to go over to Babs. Ti stopped her. "Annabelle Rosa the Private first. He is hurt worse."

Annabelle Rosa looked at him, "But my lady?"

"Will have to wait," Ti said. "It is what she would want."

A tear fell from Annabelle Rosa eyes. She moved over to the Private. Her nose wrinkled as she removed the bandage. "Bovinus Salve, you also gave them each an Arachnid Gallbladder?"

Ti shook his head. "I gave them three."

"Three! Oh my…Ah, ok I can deal with that latter. It won't kill them it will just make them sick to their stomach. Also, it defiantly should have stopped the advance of any poison." Annabelle Rosa said shaking her head.

"Sergeant Fong and Corporal Tongan you should probable leave, unless you are hurt." Annabelle Rosa said.

Sergeant Fong shook his head. "No, my lady, he is one of my bears we will stay. You can trust us my lady."

Ti just nodded.

Annabelle Rosa looked at Raphael. "Prepare the special glass." She then looked deep into Private Den Po. She could see the poison. It looked like snakes were fighting very large spiders several places in the blood stream. A thin blue flame appeared around her paw, as she held it over the wound. Soon a greenish liquid started flowing out Den Po's wound. This she transferred to a large clear glass. She repeated the process several times, then searched some more. She found a small drop hiding and drew it out. The spiders seamed to go hunting along his blood stream. These images she left in his blood. With the last of the poison transferred to the glass. It started swirling and twisting soon a real snake seemed to start to form.

"No you don't." She said and engulfed the glass in an intense blue flame. The poison burned up and evaporated. She then placed a clean bandage over his wound.

Sergeant Fong looked at her. "You didn't close his wound?"

"No Sergeant Fong, I want the wound to seep. He is not losing much blood. I will heal the wound tomorrow after I am sure I got all the poison. The Salve on the bandage will has more time to work. He will live." Annabelle Rosa said.

Annabelle Rosa went over to Babs and touched her forehead. She seemed so cold. Then she dove into her mind. She found herself standing in darkness. She could hear the sound of a battle ragging and a cry or whimper. "I am coming, my love, do not fear." Then she lit a small light in the darkness. A blue flame appeared in Annabelle Rosa's Paw. She found Babs consciousness curled up in a ball crying. "It is ok my love. I am here. Touch my paw, see the light. See the spider is protecting you, do not fear him. He and I will destroy the snake. You must hold on to the light. That's right, hold on to the light. She then moved her other hand to the point over the darts entry point. She took a small scalpel and opened the wound. Then formed a blue flame around her other paw. "Come out!" She increased the light in Babs' mind and pulled with the other. Soon a dark shiny liquid came pouring out and into the glass. It immediately formed into a snake.

"How dare you interfere between me and my prey, Rose of the Maxumus Clan?" The Red Snake said.

"She is one of mine. You will not have her, nor shall your demonic followers." Annabelle Rosa said.

"I shall have you and her!" It said as it leapt toward her. Annabelle Rosa engulfed it in blue flame. It twisted and screamed, then burst into flames and disappeared.

Ti looked at her. "Is it dead?"

Annabelle Rosa shook her head. "No, I cannot kill it. It is hurt, it is gone, and it will not be back."

Babs slowly woke up. "Where...am I?"

Annabelle Rosa went to her. "You are with me my love. You are safe."

Babs shook her head. She saw Ti. "The Private..."

"He is hurt but alive. He will recover." Annabelle Rosa said.

Babs started shaking. "It was such a horrible dream. A large red snake said he was going to devour me. Then all of a sudden this very large spider appeared and attacked it driving it away from me. I was so scared then you came and saved me." Tears were streaming down Babs face.

"You must rest now. You are safe." Annabelle Rosa said.

Ti came over and kissed Babs. Then he walked out of the room.

Babs looked at Annabelle Rosa. "Stop him, please stop him!"

Annabelle Rosa ran from the room. Ti was heading for the outside door. "Where are you going?"

Ti's eyes were cold and empty as space. "You know where I am going. You know what I am going to do!"

"You can't go alone. Take...." She tried to say.

He walked over. "Annabelle Rosa, protect your lady. You, your family, and the Marines, with your lives, promise me."

"You know we will. But what of you?" she asked.

"I am no longer afraid of the storm. I became the storm. I am Scarecrow the Hunter. They will learn why others fear me. I will wipe them from this world." Ti said, kissed her, and headed out.

The Minister watched as Ti drove off. "Where is he going?"

Annabelle Rosa looked at the sky. "Minister Aziz, you might want to shutter your windows a bad storm is coming. One like you, have never seen before."

Sergeant Fong looked at her, "My lady?"

Annabelle Rosa looked at the Sergeant and the Corporal. "I am Annabelle Rosa Valorous Knight of the Garter, Knight of the Clan Maxumus will you serve me?"

Sergeant Fong and the Corporal saluted. "We will do it with our lives."

"Then you will help me, my brothers, and niece protect our lady at all cost." Annabelle Rosa said.

# CHAPTER 8

# The Jungle Storm

DOOM OGRE THOUGH he should be smiling. After all a blood red sun set over the statue of Ta-Ra was supposed to be a good omen. But, over one hundred of his followers were dead. Another fifty were wounded and their prey escaped. Was Ta-Ra mocking him because the seeing stone had gone blank while under his care? This he would have to ponder.

It had been a cycle since Ti had left the Minister home. He quietly boarded the ship and went to his cabin. As he was going in Major Iqaluit and Lt. Commander Enfield saw him.

They followed him in. "Sir, what are you doing?" They asked.

Ti turned and looked at them with cold dark eyes. "My job, take some of your bears and go over to Minister Aziz home. Bring my wife and the others back here. Find the rest of the crew, passengers, and get them on board. Protect the ship. Major you have one bear down. Along, with my wife, it was my fault. The Rose saved his life. Follow her orders; she will be in command till I get back. Leave on time, whether I am back or not."

"But Sir, how will you...." The Major started to ask.

"Major, this is what I do. I'll find a ride, if I need one." Ti said as he grabbed his gear and left.

Babs woke up. She heard voices in the other room. She tried to get up.

"Please my lady, stay where you are. Don't move around too much, you will get sick." Teresa said.

"But, I must talk to my husband." She sat up. That is when the nausea hit her. Babs threw up all over the floor.

Teresa came over and held her head. Then wiped her face with a cold rag and laid her back down. "He is not here my Lady and you must rest." Teresa walked over and grabbed a mop and bucket.

Private Den Po looked at her. "I am so sorry my lady."

"It is ok Private. This time it was not you. Just sleep and mend. I will change your bandage soon." Teresa said.

Major Iqaluit looked at Annabelle Rosa. "My Lady, I am sorry. I did not realize that you were The Rose."

"Major, why did you let him go into the jungle alone?" Annabelle Rosa asked.

"He forbade any of my marines to go with him. He said we were to protect you and the ship." The Major said. "I am to take orders from you. The ship is to leave on time."

"Alright major, we cannot move them for four more cycles. Secure the perimeter." Annabelle Rosa ordered.

She went in to talk to Babs.

"Allis," Annabelle Rosa said. "You have to know, I could not stop him. No one could, he is a Maxumus Knight. He knows what he must do. He must destroy them."

Babs looked at her. "I need to be with him."

"No, you need to get strong. The creature that was put into you was very powerful. If Ti had not given you the Anti-venom, he did it would have taken control of you. I could not have saved you. Unfortunately, he gave you a high dose and that has side effects. We are going to take you and the Private to the ship in about four cycles. Ti has ordered us to leave on schedule." Annabelle Rosa said.

"We can't leave him. I won't leave him!" Babs screamed.

Annabelle Rosa kissed her. "My lady you must do as he wishes. He will come back to you. He is not his father. He will live to see the greatness of his sons and daughters."

Ti worked his way through the jungle as the sun started to set. He had traveled twelve KSMU into the jungle. Tonight there would be a full moon in a couple of cycles. He had been heading north into the jungle. He climbed to the top of a ridge, sat down, and looked north.

According to the old native, the valley He was looking for was twenty KSMU northeast of the river. He could see below him the Rope Bridge below that spanned the rapids. He could also see the six black hooded monks guarding it on each side.

Ti sat and studied the bridge. It consisted of three large bradded ropes; two railings, one foot path, and hundreds of lacings that attached the three large ropes together. The large ropes were passed through metal rings on metal posts then anchored to concrete pilings. It also had built in sag. So a bear would have to climb up to the ends from the center. The Bridge was three hundred fifty SMU long.

Ti waited till it got dark. Then he moved down to the bridge. When he got down there three of the guards had entered a small shack to get warm. Three others were slowly walking the perimeter. One stepped into the jungle near were Ti was. Ti found him leaning against a tree preparing to light a pipe. Ti slipped his arms around the monk's face and shoved the pipe into the back of his throat. He then twisted and broke the monk's neck. One down eleven to go.

Ti heard voices. One of the monks had come out of the shack and wanted to know where the missing monk was. The other one said he didn't know. That he probably just went to go relieve himself.

The head monk cursed and called another monk out of the shack. They started heading into the jungle. They had gone about thirty SMU when they saw the first monk leaning behind a tree. They approached him. Ti rose up from behind them and sunk the blades of two of his knives into the back of their necks, severing their spinal cords. Both died instantly. Three down nine to go.

Ti knew he had to end things on this side quickly. Before, someone raised the alarm. The odds were now three to one on this side. He moved to the back of the shack. One of the monks was cooking. The rear window was open to allow fresh air in. Ti took out a small sharp blade and flicked it through the window. It struck the monk in the throat severing his wind pipe, passing through, and embedding in his spine. The monk knew he was dying he tried to scream. All he heard was a gurgling sound. He tried to move but his legs couldn't respond. He slowly sank to the floor. Four down eight to go. The last two guards were milling around the bridge. Ti could tell they were getting nervous.

He picked up a rock and threw it over their heads so it hit the water on the other side of the bridge. They turned their heads to see what made the splash. Ti was on them before they could react. His two short swords severed their heads. He ran onto the bridge with the agility of a tight rope walker. He ran down the first half of the bridge then dropped.

The moon was starting to rise. He quietly cut a couple of the laces and slid under the foot path rope. Using his feet and paws he slowly pulled his way across and up the underside of the bridge, till he was over the bank of the river. He then let himself down and climbed up.

He still had to eliminate these monks. He decided to take it slow and do it right.

He moved slowly around to the back of the hut and looked in. Four of the guards were setting eating at a table. The rear window was open to allow a breeze to blow through. Ti selected four thin blades; taking two in each paw he hurled them through the window. Each found its mark striking its intended victim in the neck or head. All four slumped over dead or dying.

Ti then moved around so he could see the Bridge. The two guards were looking across the river. He wasn't sure what they were looking at. Then he saw it a cat like creature dragging an arm in a torn monks robe. One of the monks started to turn and run for the shack. That is when one of Ti's knives caught him between the eyes and buried itself in his brain. He pitched backwards.

The last monk saw Ti and charged with his sword drawn. Ti calmly pulled a silenced pistol, shot him twice in the face, then twice in the chest. The last monk dropped backwards and into the brush. Ti quickly and quietly reloaded the clip and moved out along the trail leading to the northeast.

Annabelle Rosa and the others transferred Babs and Private Den Po to *the Dream in the Night*. Other guests had also been rounded up and brought back to the ship. The three bear unit, including the Private, was given a suite next to Babs. Captain Thorn was told they were executives of the shipping line and were not to be disturbed.

Babs was very agitated. She was crying. Finally Annabelle Rosa sat next to her and looked into her eyes. "Why are you crying? If it was him that was injured would you not be doing the same thing Ti is doing?"

Babs stopped crying, and wiped her eyes. "Yes, I would cut their hearts out. But…"

Annabelle Rosa smiled. "Have I not told you he is not his father? That you will both see the greatness of your children's children. Why do you doubt me?"

Babs looked at her. "I just love him so. I am his partner, I failed…"

"Nonsense, you are his strength. You are the reason he will return. I know the curse the wives of the Maxumus' suffer. But, it is your love that sustains them. That makes them who and what they are. Never forget that Regent. Just love him always." Annabelle Rosa said kissing her.

Angelina looked at Mrs. Maro. "You sure Jim is ok with this?"

Mrs. Maro replied. "Jim said he didn't know what took you so long. He actually has been talking to Octavious about letting him work out of *Andreas Prime*. Octavious said it would be ok. However, we needed to move into the castle for a while. I hope that's alright with you."

"Bec, you even have to ask. You know I couldn't love you any more if you were my sister." Angelina said.

"I know my Angelina. I just hope Widja don't mind." Mrs. Maro said.

"She thinks it is great. Remember you are family. Widja is big on family." Angelina said. "Well that's everything. The house is packed except what we are leaving for Isaiah and Jenny."

"Come on everyone is waiting. *The Valorous* needs to get back on patrol." Mrs. Maro said.

Angelina closed the door. A single tear fell from her eye as she headed into a new future.

Ti had made good time moving through the jungle. He was following the edge of the trail. He had gone fifteen KSMU. He saw a dull glow coming from a small valley about five KSMU ahead of his position. Ti moved deeper into the jungle. Ti started to head for the ridge overlooking the valley.

The sun was just starting to peek over the edge of the jungle to the east. Its rays were casting long shadows in the direction of the statue in the middle of the temple compound. Ti could make out the twisted features of the horned beast, which was the statue of Ta-Ra, the Destroyer. Ti could see about two hundred black robed monks with red trimmed hoods and sleeves. Then he saw him, a tall broad shouldered monk, with gold trim around his hood and sleeves.

Ti watched, as he had a young bear brought out before the statue. The young bear was in a torn blood soaked robe. Ti could see the wound on his leg was infected. The two monks that brought him out laid him on a table in front of the statue. The monk in the gold trimmed robe threw back his hood showing a disfigured head.

Ti recognized the face of one Doom Ogre, a wanted serial killer.

Ti watched as Doom Ogre took out a dagger and laid it slowly on the young monks infected leg. He could hear the screams where he laid hidden on the ridge. Then music and chanting started. Other monks came out beating on drums, swaying, and gyrating. Just as everything reached a fevered pitch, Doom Ogre raised his knife, and plunged it into the young monk's chest. He pulled out his beating heart, held it up to the statue, and threw it into a fire burning at the statues base. Then he rolled the rest of the body of the dead monk into the flames.

Ti's anger burned even deeper. He realized he or one of the Marines had wounded the monk that was just sacrificed. But, that was different than what he just witnessed. This was just cruel cold blooded torture and murder, of one of their own. If they were willing to do that to one of their own... Well, tonight they would find justice had arrived.

Ti blended back into the jungle foliage. To prepared for the night to come, a hunter's night.

Damien Overa, his closest lieutenants, and fifteen of his most trusted hoods were running again. This time the call from the local paid cop had been cut short. He had been caught making the call and had gone for his weapon. Well, at least he wouldn't have to pay him. However, he knew he was running out of places to run. So, he ran to the only place he thought he might be safe. He headed for *Helios IV* and his old friend Doom Ogre.

*The Dream in the Night* pulled away from *Helios IV* at warp 1. Captain Thorn was told that the engines needed to be recalibrated. He was also told that the Tornbows had caught a flue on *Helios IV*. They needed to stay quarantined in their suite for a few days.

Captain Thorn didn't like it. He knew something strange was going on. He was out of the loop and no one would talk to him. Also, the crew no longer feared him.

Doom Ogre had tried to appease Ta-Ra. That night the sun set was again blood red. He took it to be a bad omen this time. Especially, when a small white cloud blocked the sun's rays from the face of Ta-Ra, he went into his room to consider what he should do.

Ti slowly moved into the temple complex. There were only a few guards. Ti found the barracks area of the temple where the majority of the monks slept. It consisted of four stone buildings. With small slit windows and two massive balanced stone doors on each end. These Ti chained shut and then attached C4 to the outside support columns. Then, he placed it along the base of each building. He moved on. When he came to the statue he climbed up it lacing it with putty and C4. He then cut off one of the horns with a small torch. With all this done he walked behind one of the temple buildings. He set off the explosives.

The first explosions hit the barracks. The roofs caved in and caught on fire. The monks were trapped inside as the flames leapt higher.

The first explosions threw Doom Ogre out of his bed. He was looking out his window when Ti set off the explosives around the statue. The Ta-Ra statue broke into thousands of pieces. Some of the pieces smashed out Doom Ogre's window.

The broken glass and stone shards tore at Doom Ogre's cloths and skin. He was cut in hundreds of places, but none were very deep. His ears were bleeding from the concussion of the explosion.

Several other monks who had heard the first set of explosions had been caught near the statue when it exploded. Their broken bodies littered the ground.

Doom Ogre came out of his temple home flanked by four guards. He screamed for others to join him, but no one came. He called out for someone to answer his call. His only response was dead silence.

His four guards stared in horror at the destroyed statue of Ta-Ra and the bodies of the other monks. One of the guards thought he saw something. He started to say something when he was thrown ten SMU back with a hole in his chest.

Doom Ogre stared as a second guard's head exploded. It was hit by a fifty caliber round.

The two remaining guards tried to run only to be shot and killed.

Doom Ogre bared his chest. "Come on shoot me also coward! Ta-Ra will defend me!"

Ti laughed "Ta-Ra could not defend himself. I destroyed him. But, don't worry Doom Ogre. I want you to see my face. I want you to know the face of the Maxumus Knight that killed you." Ti stepped out into the light of the burning buildings.

"You," Doom Ogre screamed pulling a long curved sword and charged at Ti. "I will cut out your heart and eat it!"

Ti pulled out two short swords and also charged. As they meet, Doom Ogre swung at Ti's leg, only to watch Ti somersault over him.

As Ti was completing his turn over Doom Ogre's back, he swung his two swords cutting Doom's two Achilles tendons.

Doom ogre immediately, collapsed face first into the dirt. He dropped his sword. "I surrender." Doom Ogre screamed.

Ti picked him up and threw him up against a rock. "That might matter if I was here to arrest you, or if you were not a terrorist. I am not here as a cop. This is personal. You attacked my wife. For that you are going to die. Also, you are a mass murdering filthy terrorist. So, you're going to die."

Doom Ogre tried to pull a hidden dagger. Ti snapped his arm. Then he broke the other one for good measure.

"Oh, I took this from Ta-Ra." Ti said showing him the strange pointed golden horn. "I think I'll give it back to you."

Doom Ogre's eyes got big as TI raised the horn over his head. "No" he screamed as Ti drove the horn through his skull right between his eyes.

Doom Ogre the killer of children died with fear in his eyes.

Ti turned and walked into the main temple. He found some records and data crystals. He then planted some more explosives and headed into the jungle. There he set them off. Soon what was left of the temple complex was burning or had been turned into rubble.

That night about midnight a shuttle craft approached the valley. The pilot pointed out the flames.

Damien Overa pointed out a clearing four KSMU away to the southwest. "Land over there, it looks like they may be having one of their wild parties. We don't want to go in till it settles down."

Ti was exhausted he had only traveled three KSMU away from the temple complex. He built a hide and crawled in. He slept till morning. He thought he heard voices pass by. He looked out but saw no one. He gathered his gear and headed southwest. Two KSMU farther along the trail he saw a clearing with a poorly camouflaged long ranged shuttle setting in it. He quietly approached it. Ti found it shut down and empty.

Ti smiled, when he realized the owner was the Overa Cartel. Well he could go back and kill whoever they sent. Or he could just strand them and get back to his wife. Ti laughed as he fired up the engines and rotated off the ground. He headed into space.

Overa looked at the destruction of the temple complex. He then found the body of his childhood friend. His whole body shook. He could still see the fear in his friend eyes. That's when he heard his shuttle pass overhead and head into space. Damien Overa let out an oath, and then smiled. No he had survived again whoever had killed Doom and his monks had stolen his shuttle. Which means he didn't come back to kill him!

Overa turned to his Lieutenant. "I guess I was wrong. I was worried about someone stealing our loot, not the shuttle. The loot is safe and the shuttle is gone."

The Lieutenant looked around and shuttered. "Boss, let the so in so have the shuttle. I'll buy you another as long as he doesn't come back!"

"I think your right. Help me bury my friend. He was no good, but he was still my friend." Overa said.

Ti picked up a homing beacon for *The Dream in the Night*. He accelerated to warp 4. Much to his surprise the shuttle had a cloak. He engaged it. When it got in range he signaled Mr. Enfield, who had the engineer drop the *Dream in the Night* out of warp. Mr. Enfield dropped the shield near Ti's suite. Ti beamed on board. The Overa shuttle then went to Warp 4 and headed straight into the nearest sun.

Annabelle Rosa looked at Ti, the equipment, and bags he had beamed over. "Those we will take care of. First let me scan you."

Ti sat down. "Annabelle Rosa, thank you for taking care of Babs."

Annabelle Rosa touched him, scanned his heart and soul. "Be at peace my love." She said then kissed him. Then she slapped him.

Ti looked at her. "What was that for?"

"That my love was for putting my lady through so much worry and grief. If you ever intentionally hurt her Sir Knight, I will skin you alive." Annabelle Rosa said.

Ti kissed her. "My Rose, if I do then please use my own knife." Ti handed her one of his. "A gift my Lady."

"Go be with your wife you charlatan. She needs you." Annabelle Rosa said.

Ti walked into the bedroom. Babs was sleeping. He walked in and took another shower. After cleaning up, he came out, and crawled in next to Babs.

She snuggled into him. "Annabelle Rosa, I am having the strangest dream. I can almost feel Ti lying next to me."

Ti kissed her lips gently. "It is not a dream my love. I am right here."

Babs' eyes opened. Tears started flowing as she buried her head in his chest. "I failed you!"

"Never, do you love me Babs?" Ti asked.

"You know I do, with all I am." She said through her tears.

Ti kissed her again. "Don't you know? It is your love that sustains me. That gives me the strength to do the things I have to do. It was your love that gave me the courage to do what had to be done. Those devils will never hurt anyone ever again."

Babs melted her body into his. Holding on to him like she was afraid she would wake up and find him gone. The next morning she felt him next to her. She slipped out of bed and knelt next to it. She thanked the Creator and His Word for returning her husband. She then went in and took a shower. She put on a sarong and came back in. She had made a promise and she was going to keep it.

Ti woke up as she reached over and touched his face. "This morning you are mine. This is something very old and special our mothers teach us." Babs started singing a sweet melody.

Annabelle Rosa heard the melody coming from the room. Teresa had just brought in breakfast. "Niece they won't need that for a while. Just go take care of the private."

Teresa looked at Annabelle Rosa. "I don't understand?"

"Someday you will my love. They will not want to be bothered for many cycles." Ti I hope your heart is strong. Annabelle Rosa smiled.

Raphael came in two cycles later. "I have finished looking at the intelligence Ti brought back with him. I need to know what he wants to do with it."

Annabelle Rosa told him. "Make three copies. Send one to fleet intelligence, through the Special Services. One copy goes to the Empress and her bears. One is for our use."

Raphael Bantelle knew Annabelle Rosa was not going to let anyone bother the young couple. So he just smiled, nodded, then went and did as he was told.

Ti looked at his now sleeping wife. He just shook his head. He kissed the back of her neck and started to get up. That was when a paw stopped him. "Stay. They don't need you right now, but I do." Babs turned towards him and wrapped herself around him.

"Babs, I can't just spend the day in bed." Ti said.

"Yes, this day you can. I need you. I must have you against me. I almost went nuts. You left me behind. You went into harm's way without me. We are partners not just husband and wife. You're not a lone wolf anymore. I promised the Creator of the Universe, that if he brought you back to me, I would love you so hard you would never want to leave me again. Apparently I failed again!" Babs said with tears in her eyes.

Ti sat up shaking. "Don't you get it? They almost killed you! I didn't just kill them. I slaughtered them. I didn't spare a single one. I butchered them all. I burned two hundred of them alive when I dropped their barracks in on top of them. I torched the entire temple complex. I didn't leave one stone on top of another. I did that because they hurt you. I would do it again."

Ti had tears streaming down his face. Babs kissed him and then dropped her head. "I am so sorry Ti. It is just I couldn't live if something happened to you. I would rather die than live one moment without you. If you, would have been killed. I would have just died."

Ti shook his head. "No, you can't feel that way Bab's. I saw my mom suffer for years after my dad died. If it hadn't been for Octavious, Angelina, Jim, and Bec I don't think mom would have survived. You have to promise me that if anything ever happens to me you will live for the both of us."

Babs looked at him. He was shaking almost uncontrollable. She saw something she never seen before, fear. "All right, Ti I will try." She leaned into him.

Ti kissed her. "I love you Babs, more than life itself. I told you once it is your love that gives me the courage and strength to do what I must. We Maxumus Boars don't fall in love very easy. Because we hunger for the love our wives give us. It's like a drug we have to have."

Babs laughed till she cried. "So, the boars know our pain as well. Husband promise me you will never leave me behind again, unless you must. I know you felt you had to this time. But, you could have taken someone with you."

"No, Babs this was personal. I wanted Doom Ogre to know it was personal before he died." Ti said.

Babs looked at him. "So, it was him. He was the murder that escaped six years ago, after he killed those two cubs. You lost him when his transport exploded."

"Yes, I knew he had survived. We couldn't find him. Yesterday, I did. He will never hurt another cub or you again." Ti said.

"Husband, I saw fear in your eyes. That means I have failed to renew your strength. I think I will try again." She started singing to him again as she moved towards him and leaned him back.

The next morning Ti smiled at Babs. "I surrender. I will get your permission before I take off by myself. Then I will do it only if you are sick or with cub, ok. Now please Babs, we have work to do. Also, I am hungry."

Babs smiled, "Alright, but we need to shower first. Come on I'll wash your back."

Ti just shook his head and followed her in. They got dressed slowly and then came out.

Annabelle Rosa laughed. "I wish I could say you look rested, but you look happy Ti."

"Food please, I am starving." Ti said.

Babs just smiled. "He is such a baby."

As food was served, Ti asked. "Did we get anything useful?"

Raphael responded. "Yes, Rosa had me send copies on to Fleet and The Empress. This is a summery you can look at the raw data later."

Ti scanned the information. "No need, you found the needle in the hay stack for me. They are looking for something. *The Eye* was important, but the Shape Shifters are looking for something called the *Key of Epoch.* They believe it is it the *Aldrin System.* They wanted the *Devils Eye* to find it.

Apparently the ship they sent to search the *Aldrin System* got caught in a wormhole storm. It came out near *Andreas Prime.* Their engines were damaged and they crashed near *Pipet.* You know what happened next.

Without the *Devils Eye,* they gave their segregates viewing stones that were connected to it. As long as the *Devils Eye* existed they worked. However, none showed them where the *Key of Epoch* was.

Doom Ogre believed it was in the *Aldrin System. He* thought it was on one of the three temple planets.

Babs looked at Ti. "What is the *Key of Epoch?*"

Ti shrugged. "I don't know."

Annabelle Rose shook her head. "It is an ancient relic that opens the crossroads of time and space."

"What do you mean?" Babs asked.

"It is said to open a passage between time and space called the crossroads. The *Key of Epoch* allows a creature to travel anywhere and anytime in history. It is a dangerous artifact. The Evil One must never get a hold of it." Annabelle Rosa said.

# CHAPTER 9

# Wanderers & Arrivals

TI LOOKED AT Captain Thorn. "Captain, I am sure the chief engineer has everything under control. Surly you know new engines require recalibrating and restart after installation."

"Mr. Tornbow do you trust me as captain of this ship or not?" Captain Thorn asked.

Ti pondered the question. "Now, Captain Thorn that is, a good question. You are an average ship's captain. Not the worst and not the best. Your accounts have a few minor irregularities, but not enough that they couldn't be explained away. So, captain you are a thief, but not a greedy thief."

"I don't have to set here and listen to these insults!" Captain Thorn said.

Babs smiled at him as she laid open her badge in front of him. "Oh my dear Captain Thorn, I think you do. Unless, you want to spend the next say sixty years at Dragons Breath Prison."

Ti nodded. "At least, his brother-in-law is singing like a canary. Aiding pirates, in an attempted kidnaping of two federal agents, that is worth at least twenty-five years."

"You have no proof, that I have done anything wrong." Captain Thorn said. "Who is going to believe my worthless brother-in-law?"

Ti laid the transcript of the data crystals he had taken from Overa's shuttle and Doom Ogre Communications logs in front of the captain. "Your friends don't trust anyone. So, they keep everything to use as leverage and black mail. By the way Doom Ogre is dead."

Captain Thorn sank into the chair. He knew it was over. "What do you want?"

Ti looked at him with cold eyes. "I want you to tell me everything. How you got involved. Who your contacts are and how you got in contact with them."

Captain Thorn looked at him and licked his lips, "If I give you the information?"

Ti shrugged. "Then, I don't accidentally throw you out an airlock and you go to a nice agricultural prison planet. Captain Thorn, understand, I can kill you and no one will question it. You were working with two know terrorist groups, The Mac-Ta and The Overa Cartel. Not to mention Orion Pirates. Do to their involvement, I could kill you, and no one would care."

Captain Thorn was grabbing at straws. "So you owning the *Gem Lines* and this ship are shams."

Babs smiled, "Oh no Captain. I really am Maximilian Harrah's niece. And we really do own the *Gem Lines* and this ship. By the way you are fired."

Captain Thorn looked at them. "I'll cooperate. I will tell you everything I know."

"Good Mr. Thorn you just saved yourself a trip to Dragons Breath Prison, as long as you keep your promise." Ti said.

Babs called in Corporal Tongan. "Mr. Tongan, would you take Mr. Thorn to his new quarters."

The Pandarian Marine smiled, "Happily, my lady."

Ti walked on to the bridge and sat on the Captain's Chair. He hit the ship wide com button. "Ladies and gentlebears this Brinton Tornbow, I am sorry to inform you that our captain has taken very ill. We will be making an unscheduled stop at *Wanderer's Station* to let the captain off, so he may be transported to a medical ship. That is being sent to meet us. As you know the station is famous for its museums and shops. We will be there for twenty-four cycles before entering *Kalaallit's Passage.*

Please be advised Mr. Enfield your new captain is more than qualified to operate this ship." Ti then nodded to Enfield.

Babs looked at the chief engineer. "Mr. Bancroft may we speak with you?"

Bancroft nodded. "Yes my lady?"

"Mr. Bancroft you have your ships Masters Licenses do you not?" Babs asked.

"Yes Lady Allis, but I am just an engineer." Mr. Bancroft said.

Ti laid his personnel record down along with another. "Mr. Bancroft you failed to mention you were a Captain in the BAF."

Bancroft sat down. "Mr. Tornbow, I was relieved of my command. I ran my Destroyer Escort into an asteroid."

Ti shook his head. "You were cleared of any wrong doing. In fact they say your actions saved a hospital ship."

Bancroft shrugged. "Ten of my crew died including an Admiral's son. My career was finished. I had been an engineer and I liked it. So, I got out and ended up here."

Babs smiled. "We need a new first officer, now, and a new captain once we start home we want you to be that bear."

Bancroft looked at Babs and Ti. "But, Mr. Enfield...."

"Is strictly an evaluator and instructor for our company." Ti said. "Do you want the job?"

Mr. Bancroft thought. "Mr. Tornbow, I love this ship. I didn't like the way the old owners did things and to be honest I didn't care for some of the corners Captain Thorn tried to cut. If I am captain, I won't cut corners on safety, just to make a little more profit."

Babs told him. "If you did you would be fired. Mr. Bancroft, we want this to be the flag ship of the *Gem Lines*. It will be running a new route between *Bearilia Prime*, *Candaris Prime*, and *Andreas Prime*. We may add one other stop. But, it will feature beaches and resorts some owned by this cruise line."

Mr. Bancroft looked at Babs. "What about this route?"

Ti asked. "Is it profitable?"

Mr. Bancroft shook his head. "No not with this ship. Not even with the new engines. We are marginal for the *Kalaallit's Passage*."

Babs inquired. "What type of ship would be profitable?"

Mr. Bancroft thought. "That is simple, a *Seversons XXVI* Class. It carries two hundred passengers in luxury and five million KSWU of cargo. That is what you need for this run and it could do it in half the time. Also, it has Rollo Capability."

Ti nodded. "That's because if you own one it becomes part of the civilian ready reserves for the Fleet."

Mr. Bancroft nodded. "But they also pay 20% of the cost to build new ones."

Babs thought. "Then we will have to look into purchasing one for this route. If we get one you can decide if you want to be its captain or remain captain of *the Dream in the Night*."

Captain Nord looked at Angelina. "Empress Maxumus and Mr. Vice President it is an honor to serve you again."

Octavious smiled. "Captain Nord you can cut the crap. I know this is a real pain in your tail this time. But, thank you anyway."

Captain Nord replied. "Vice President Maxumus you and the Empress are always welcome on board this ship. We are now *Bearilia 2* while you are on board."

"Ok, Captain, take us home." Octavious said.

"Klein, you heard the Vice President. Let's take him and Empress Angelina home." Captain Nord said.

Widja was looking out her window. Gamey was standing near her. "What is it?" Gamey asked.

"It is silly. I am getting my wish. My Angelina is moving here permanently along with Mrs. Maro and Deloris Maxumus. Did you know that Rebeca Maro was an Augustine protector?" Widja asked.

Gamey nodded. "Yes, Grey Beard told me. She was adopted when she was three months old. Her maiden name was Hamilton. She was raised to serve Angelina, similar as to how Maryam serves Erin."

"It will be good then, to have her and Jim Maro, live in the Castle. What is his story?" Widja asked.

Gamey shrugged. "He flew with Octavious. He took a missile intended for Octavious's fighter, lost both legs as a result. He was married to Rebeca about a year. They say Angelina was acting as a surgeon on the hospital ship he was brought to. A senior doctor told her he was a goner, to let him die. She threatened to kill the doctor. Then she worked on him for twenty cycles. He died on the table twice, but she wouldn't let him go. She brought him back and saved his life.

The doctor tried to have Marine guards arrest her. She put three in the hospital before their captain arrived and told them to leave her alone. He told the other doctor that the ship's captain had relieved him."

Widja looked at him. "My Angelina put...."

Gamey laughed. "My love our Empress is one of the deadliest assassins that ever lived. Her cell included her two ladies. They are still a deadly trio.

Well, I better get back to work my Empress."

Widja smiled and kissed him. "I will see you at home tonight. Play nice with Mrs. Morrow."

"Shari, that Southern witch, I would be lost without her, but don't ever tell her that." Gamey said as he took off.

As he flew towards the Castle Maxumus he saw two lines of bears on war mounts on the road. He circled as one column peeled off and headed for the Maxumus Castle. The other headed for the Caesar/Maxumus Castle. He quickly dove for the Maxumus Castle and landed.

Mrs. Morrow came out. "Gamey, what in the world is that coming towards us?"

"Shari, I don't know but maybe you..." Gamey was trying to say.

Mrs. Morrow slid her dagger up and down in its sheath. "I like the view from here, my dear dragon."

The two riders at the head of the column jumped off their mounts and knelt. Then they took off their helmets. One was bright blond in color. He almost shined. The other was black as night and definitely, dragon in appearance. "Sir Gamey and Mrs. Morrow, I am Peter the Rock. This is my sister Nota Rosa. We are two of the "Seven". Father has sent us and our companies to serve you. If you will, accept us into your service, Sir Gamey."

Gamey looked at them. "Rise Sir Knight and Lady Rosa, no Maxumus kneels to anyone except the Creator and His Word, especially, not the children of, the First Knight and the Lady Isadora."

Peter looked at him. "But Sire..."

"Sire Peter, I have my father's memories. But, I am not my father. He was wrong, I ask your and the others forgiveness." Gamey said.

Nota Rosa touched him. "Be at peace Sir Knight. You, who are pure and honorable, we shall serve this house with are lives."

Widja smiled. "Welcome to the Caesar/Maxumus Castle."

"Empress Widja, we are Gabriel the Shield and Violet Rosa. We are here to serve the Empress and you." He started to kneel.

"None of that, no Maxumus kneels on *Andreas Prime,* except to the Creator and His Word. Besides, you are children of the First Knight and Lady Isadora." Widja said.

Violet Rosa looked at her. "Empress Widja, you are not offended by what we..."

Widja looked at the Violet colored Maxmimus with dragon eyes. "Children, who were born from the desire of two creatures in love to have children of their own, I am a mother. I would have done anything to have given Gamey a brood. Isadora loves Samuel as much as I love my husband. She gave him you seven, and then they have adopted many others. Is she not a good mother?"

Gabriel smiled. "Yes Empress, she is."

"Good then captains stable your mounts as their needs require. I know some are the children of Storm Cloud. See to your troops. You are Imperial Guards. Change into Empress Angelina's colors. However, maintain your banners to honor your house." Widja said.

On Brigadoon, Anna was in the communication center, when the call came in. "Emerald City, this is Transport 1567 requesting landing instructions."

Anna picked up the communication unit. "Transport 1567, this is Emerald City, please state your business."

"Emerald City, we are delivering two companies of Knights to serve Regent Fredrick Maxumus. Please inform him two of the "Seven" have been sent by their father to serve him along with their companies."

"Transport 1567 please land at these coordinates. You will be met by canus guides." Anna turned to Swift Paw. "It might be dangerous."

"If they are shape shifters, only for them, if they are family or friends it will be good will it not?" Swift Paw said.

"Yes, it will." Anna agreed.

With that Swift Paw was off with seven of his best hunters. He arrived at the landing field, as the pilot landed the large transport. He turned to one of his Lieutenants. "Stay hidden, if they are enemies you know what to do."

Swift Paw walked out into the open. Two Knights in Armor stepped out; one had red hair the other silver with a tail that resembled a dragon's.

The one with red hair looked at Swift Paw. "I am Michael the Sword, and this is Harold the Spear. We are sons of Samuel and Lady Isadora."

Swift Paw looked at them, when she appeared beside him. "Swift Paw do you know me?"

Swift Paw bowed, as did the two Knights. "My lady, I was told…"

"Yes I did, but I now am free to travel back and forth to protect my loves. These Knights are who they say they are. Samuel sent them at His and my request. Do you believe my words?" Star Firerena asked.

"Yes my lady, I trust your words." Swift Paw said.

Star Firerena looked at the two Knights. "These canus are Imperial Guards, treat them with respect, and trust them." With that she vanished.

Swift paw howled and his seven came out.

Michael smiled and called out his troops. Forty-eight knights assembled. "Sir Swift Paw, we are at your service."

Swift Paw responded. "I think it would be a pleasure to hunt with you." This was the start of a long friendship between the three of them.

At the stronghold Fredrick couldn't believe his eyes. The two head Knights started to kneel when Fred stopped them. "No Maxumus Knight kneels before anyone, but the Creator and His Word, especially not to another Knight of the Clan. You are two of Samuel's sons. Let me guess you are Michael the Sword his fiery Red head, and you are Harold the Spear the youngest of his sons. Where are the others, the three Roses, and your two brothers?"

"Sire Fredrick you are correct. Peter and Nota are with Sir Gamey with their companies. Gabriel and Violet were sent to the Empress with theirs. Annabelle Rosa is with Sire Tiberius. We hope you are not offended..." Michael started to say.

"First, it is Fred not Sire. I am Regent that is my job. Your job is to help me protect our home. We are family Michael and Harold. Your father is a dear friend. He was there for all of us when we were growing up. Maybe we didn't all listen to his stories as close as we should. But I did, when he talked about you. I also saw how Annabelle Rosa's eyes would light up. None of us understood how much she suffered. She never complained. You are two of the "Seven", children of the First Knight and the Lady Isadora; you are honored in the Clan Maxumus."

Michael and Harold both stood. "Fredrick Maxumus Regent to our Prince Beary Maxumus, we pledge our lives and that of our troop to you."

Fred dropped his head. "I give you ancestral land on the Island of *Brigadoon* to claim as your own. The land that is not marked is available. You may choose."

"Sire, is this mountain land taken, this land, with the deep valley, running to the west, near the end of the Island?" Michael asked.

"No." Fred said. "It isn't very good land."

"It is perfect for mounts and for sheep; our troops raise mounts and sheep, if we may have this land." Michael asked.

Fred smiled. "Then may that be the Realm of the House of Valorous. Now, I would like to introduce my staff...."

*The Dream in the Night* made its unscheduled stop at *Wanderers Station* much to the delight of the stations manager.

"Mr. and Mrs. Tornbow welcome to *Wanderers Station*. I am Mr. Yance Peabody the station manager. So you are old Thaddeus' son. How are the old reprobate and his charming wife Angel?" Mr. Peabody asked.

"Mom has made dad semi-retire. We are taking over most of the family businesses." Ti said. "I am Brinton and this is my wife Allis."

"Allis, no not little Allis Max's niece," Peabody said. "My how you have grown and what a beautiful young female you turned out to be."

"Thank you, Mr. Peabody; I wasn't sure you would remember me." Babs said.

"So what brings you to my station?" Mr. Peabody asked.

"The captain of *the Dream in the Night*, Captain Thorn has become ill. We need to return him to *Bearilia Prime*. We were told a ship with adequate facilities was returning and was here at the station." Ti said.

"Yes, the *BAF Banshee* is heading back in five cycles. They are going to retire the old girl and replace her with the *Banshee II*, a new Dreadnought Class. It will be the first of the class. It was going to have a different name but General Zantoran said the fleet needed a "Banshee". He said it was tradition. Strange for a Marine General.., Oh well listen to the ramblings of an old bear, I can make the arrangements." Mr. Peabody said.

Ti responded. "Actually, we already have bears taking care of that. I understand you have a huge library on the *Aldrin System?*"

Mr. Peabody's eyes got big. "Yes, the biggest, a large collection of relics, and logs from the *BAF Wanderer*. My great, great uncle was the Navigator, Percival Peabody. Would you like to see my personal collection?"

Babs smiled, "If, it wouldn't be any problem."

Mr. Peabody grinned. "For you, sweet Allis, I would do anything."

Ti just shook his head. The female was a sorcerous. She had to be, she could reduce even old boars to putty in her paws. "Thank you, Sire."

"It is nothing. I am just glad someone is interested in seeing it. No one seems to care about history anymore." Mr. Peabody said.

He unlocked a room. Ti was blown away by its size. Babs saw Ti's eyes.

"Mr. Peabody, have you ever heard of the Artist Annabelle Rosa?" Babs asked.

"Why yes, I am a fan of her work. I wish I could meet her someday." Mr. Peabody said.

"I am glad you said that, because she is interested in the history of the *BAF Wanderer*. She is on *the Dream in the Night*. May I call her and invite her, her brothers, and niece to see your archive?" Babs asked.

"Yes, please, by all means, then I would get to meet her!" Mr. Peabody said.

Babs called Annabelle Rosa and explained the situation. Annabelle Rosa asked if she could have a couple of loose stones. Babs said of course.

When she arrived, along with Raphael, Andrew Re, and Teresa, Annabelle Rosa gave Mr. Peabody a ring, with the insignia of the *BAF Wanderer* on it.

Mr. Peabody burst into tears. "Oh, thank you for your gift Lady Rosa. I am not worthy of such a wonderful gift." He then kissed her paw. "Allis please enjoy your selves. I must show it to my wife."

Annabelle Rosa stopped him. "Please, give your lady this. Tell her you did not forget this special day, as she thought. But had this commissioned for her."

Mr. Peabody stopped, turned, kissed Annabelle Rosa, turned pink, and ran to give his wife an anniversary present she would never forget.

Babs walked over and kissed her. "Thank you."

Annabelle Rosa shrugged. "We need him distracted. When she sees the necklace, he will be."

Mrs. Peabody was setting in her room. She had been crying. It was silly, fifty years of marriage. He was a good husband, just forgetful. He didn't mean to take her for granted.

Mr. Peabody walked in. "Grace, have you been crying?"

"It's nothing Yance, I am ok." Mrs. Peabody said.

"No Grace, it isn't. I did it again, but a beautiful and kind lady saved me this time. Here this is for you. It truly is happy anniversary, my Gracie." Mr. Peabody said.

Grace Peabody slowly opened the box. Inside was a brilliant yellow diamond surrounded by purple and blue sapphires. "I have never seen anything so wonderful in my life." She then saw the signature on the back of the gold band of the necklace and almost dropped it. "But we can't afford..."

Mr. Peabody placed his paw on her lips. "It was a gift from The Rose herself. I wish I could take...."

Grace Peabody kissed her husband like she hadn't in twenty five years. Yance Peabody was forgetful and a dreamer. But, he was honest and a good bear. She realized right then and there that was why she loved him and she was going to prove it.

Ti began reading:

Captains Personal Log. 15 Sorran 1880, of the Republic. It is hard to understand how these three cultures so similar in every way, still viewed their stars so differently. One as two demons fighting each other, another as two lovers embracing, while the third saw them as two twins struggling to hold on to each other, to stay alive.

Where did they go, the planets are viable? There is no sign of war or death do to disease or famine. It is as if the entire population of all three planets just got up and left on the same day and the same hour.

The more we find the less we know. There must be a key to this mystery. But this crossroads suspended in time and space is too valuable to be lost.

Ti read the last line again. Could it be that simple? Could everyone be looking for a key that never existed? Just a misinterpreted, line entry in an old Captain's Log Book, but that didn't make since either.

Babs shook her head. "None of this makes any since. Listen to this entry:

First Officers Log. 17 Sorran 1880, of the Republic. We are on the surface of the VII planet. I swear I have heard voices of Creatures speaking in a language I do not understand and the laughter of young ones. We found pictures of the inhabitance of these planets. They were a tall willowy race of humanoids. Not the Children of Adam or the Daughters of Eve but beautiful and statuses like Vulcans but not as stout looking. More like flowers.

Ti looked at her. "What did that mean?"

Babs shrugged. "I don't know, they were tall and had pointy ears. They were not the sons of Adam or the daughters of Eve. So, they did not come from *Earth* in the *Sole System*."

Ti shook his head. "Not stout like the Vulcans, but humanoids tall like them."

"Makes since two stars, *Vulcan* has two stars." Annabelle Rosa said.

Babs looked at her. "Have you ever been there?"

"Once, they are too stiff for my liking. They claim all they care about is logic. In truth they are just scared children afraid of their own emotions." Annabelle Rosa said.

"The cultural differences make since." Mr. Bantelle said. "The closest habitable planet probably still suffered from the effects of the push and pull between the two stars. The VI planet was in the ideal situation, still is. That is why the colony there thrives. The VII is a water planet. Babs, how would your people have viewed the effects of the gravity wells created by two stars, spinning around each other?"

Babs thought about it. "Probably similar to how they depicted it."

After several cycles Mr. Peabody returned. "My friends you all look exhausted. Did you find anything interesting?"

Ti smiled. "We found a lot of answers, and more questions. Mr. Peabody, you know my wife. You have since she was young. I ask that you trust us."

Mr. Peabody smiled. "I told you, I knew Thaddeus and Angel didn't, I. I have known them from the olden days. I know Helen and Elisa also. So just ask your question son." He said with a wink.

Ti shook his head, "The *Key of Epoch*."

Mr. Peabody shook his head. "Doesn't exists, I have looked for it for fifty years. The lines, the key to the mystery, the crossroads of time and space gave birth to the idea of a key that unlocked a mysterious door that the Ancients went through."

Babs looked at him. "Then why have Shape Shifters and others been looking for it since even before we got there."

"Allis, abandoned civilizations always leave some clue as to the why. It might take a while to find it, but it is always there. Well, it's not there in this case. We're not the first to look. That gives rise to legends. The Key is one of those." Mr. Peabody said.

"Prince Beary Maxumus destroyed the *Devils Eye*." Ti said.

"I have heard. A Sirius Captain Mac Dervish Scott said that the Shape Shifters and others have put a price on the young Princes head. They say it is twenty-five million gold bars. Scotty says there are some mercenary groups forming."

Annabelle Rosa smiled a dragon's smile. "It won't cover their funerals."

Mr. Peabody laughed. "Not if he takes after his mother."

Ti said. "You mean his father don't you."

"No son I didn't." Mr. Peabody smiled and handed him a box. "No one has ever figured out what this was or what it goes to. Bring it back to me when you come back. When you see your cousins give them a kiss for me. Your mom and godmother also, tell them the Raven says hi." With that Mr. Peabody smiled his mild mannered smile and waved goodbye.

Babs looked at Ti. "Did He say…?"

"Yes, I thought he was just a legend also." Ti said.

On *Helios IV* one of Overa's lieutenants came to him. "Boss, we got a shuttle we can leave. By the way you were right the Pandarian Militia is swarming all over the jungle near the temple complex. I took the scenic route getting here to avoid them."

Overa looked at his bears. "Load up, we're leaving this paradise."

Once in space his lieutenant looked at him. "Where to, boss?"

Overa thought. "*Break's Drift* we need a bigger ship we are leaving *Bearilian Space* for a while."

"I thought we were going after *the Dream in the Night*?" the Lieutenant asked.

Overa looked at him. "Do you want someone digging your grave? I don't. Death is riding on that ship. Wherever it goes, my friends die. I don't plan to join them."

Ti and Babs were back in their state room looking at the artifact. Ti couldn't decide if it was a piece  of a puzzle or a key of some kind. He did notice that it depicted the twin stars as just that, stars. Not demons or lovers or twins.

"What do you think Babs?" Ti finally asked.

"Well, if it is a key, it is a strange one; it looks more like a gold puzzle piece." Babs said.

"It is not *Aldrin* in origin then perhaps?" Annabelle Rosa said. "Perhaps, it is part of something else. Did not Maxumus put maps on Gold sheets?"

Ti looked at it. "Is it a corner piece of a map, with the *Aldrin Stars* in the corner?"

Raphael shrugged. "Well, then all we have to do is find the rest of the map. If you will excuse me, I am tired."

Ti looked at all of them. "Thank you, and good night."

That night Ti lay awake. His mind couldn't shut down. He walked over to his com unit and using a secure line called Alfa.

Mr. Blue answered. "Alfa command, may I help you."

"Blue, it is Scarecrow on secure bravo; do you still have a copy of that Shape Shifted Star Map Ghost recovered?" Ti asked.

Blue had been looking at it. "As a matter of fact, yes I do."

"Can you up link it to my unit?" Ti asked.

"Stand by… Ok, I scanned it in you should get it shortly." Blue said

"Thanks Blue, Scarecrow out." Ti turned off the com unit and printed out a copy of the map.

The star symbols were different. They didn't match. The shape shifters used "S" with lines through them to depict magnitude of the stars.

He found *Aldrin* on the map. It had two "S's" with two lines drawn through each and a swirling line around them.

Next he placed the puzzle piece on the shape shifter map and tried to line it up. It didn't, the scale was wrong.

He put the puzzle piece back in its box and went back to bed.

Babs nuzzled into him. "Husband, if you cannot sleep, I am here."

Ti kissed her. "Babs, I just had an idea it just didn't pan out. Get some sleep my love."

Babs sighed, "If you insist."

The next morning Ti came out. Star maps littered the room. Annabelle Rosa was stamping her foot. "No, it is not *Andorran* either!"

Ti smiled. "You couldn't sleep either."

Annabelle Rosa exhaled. "It is the dragon in me. I hate it when I can't solve a simple puzzle! I know it is a simple one.

I saw you eliminated the Shape Shifters. I eliminated just about everyone else."

Just then there was a knock on the door. Annabelle Rosa gathered her mess and answered the door. It was Maria La Rouge.

"Oh, la' la' did a storm hit this room?" Miss La Rouge asked.

"No Maria, a puzzle that has driven us crazy." Ti said.

"Monsieur Tornbow, perhaps I can help. I am great at puzzles." Maria said.

Ti looked at Annabelle Rosa who just shrugged. "We only have one piece." He showed it to Maria.

Maria looked puzzled. "You tease Maria, yes?"

"No Maria. I have been up half the night looking at maps trying to match those symbols." Annabelle Rosa said.

"These are not, map symbols; they are Signe panneau, a sign by road. They are used by gypsies. This one was a warning, the twin stars are for the *Aldrin System*. The three peaks are a mountain range with a very tall mountain facing the suns and two smaller mountains one separated by a small indentation and a valley. You see, whatever is in there is dangerous. This says stay out to other gypsies." Maria said.

"So," Ti said "we are looking for a mountain range."

Maria shook her head. "You do not understand this says stay out, danger. It is a very bad place a place gypsies do not go!"

"Maria that is why the bears you work for must." Babs said as she came out in her house coat.

Maria just sat down. "No, no, no, gypsies go everywhere. If gypsies say do no go, then it is very bad to go there."

Ti asked. "Maria if we showed you surface maps could you find…"

"No, please,' Maria looked almost frantic. "You must not go to this place. It is cursed, it is very dangerous. Why can't I make you understand?"

Maria was pacing now. "You are friends with Monsieur Peabody. He is a good friend of the gypsies. I know you are not who you say you are." Maria fell on her knees. "Even if you must kill me, it is ok, I understand. Please, listen to Maria. When you come on board Mr. Tornbow always looks like bear dying of thirst, even though he held a beautiful glass of water. Mrs. always looked like she was willing to be drunk, as she still does. But, now Mr. Tornbow looks like a man who will never thirst again. He changed after we left *Candaris Prime*. Mrs. had family on *Candaris Prime*, yes?"

Babs sat down. "Yes Maria. Max Harrah is my uncle and yes we were married there."

Maria nodded. "You are Allis, but also not. But, you are not a Brinton. The name is not as strong as you are."

Ti shook his head. "Maria, I don't know what we are going to do with you. Ok, since you work for us, I guess you are going to have to really work for us. I am Tiberius Maxumus. By the way we do own the *Gem Lines*."

Maria nodded. "I already knew your true name Sire Maxumus. I had contacted friends."

Annabelle Rosa shook her head. "The oldest intelligence system, there is in the universe, the gypsies."

"Lady Rosa, we gypsies know where you go miracles and trouble follows, usually for evil creatures. So, I sent inquires." Maria said.

"You must also know that danger awaits you in the *Aldrin System*. Great Evil is coming. They seek a Beary Maxumus, but they will try and take anyone of your clan." Maria said.

"Would you or your people sell us out?" Ti asked.

"Normally information is a commodity for sell. However, the Rose is part of your family, we gypsies know this. We would protect her with our lives. As such we will protect any member of the Clan Maxumus with our lives or die to protect their secrets." Maria said.

Ti shook his head. "Maria, I would prefer if you lived to protect it."

Maria smiled. "I would prefer that also, Sire."

Babs replied. "Then it is official. You just joined the team. I hope you understand what you have let yourself in for."

Maria looked at the small sign, "Mon!"

Mr. Bancroft looked at Mr. Enfield. "You sure you don't want to do this?"

"No, this is going to be your ship. You take the seat might as well get your feet wet." Enfield said.

"Miss Jacksen, if you please take us in, half impulse power. Watch for the forming wormhole." Bancroft said.

"Yes, Captain Bancroft." Miss Jacksen said.

# CHAPTER 10

# The Aldrin System

THE PASSAGE THROUGH *Kalaallit's Passage* was quick and uneventful. The wormhole deposited them near *Aldrin IX*, a large gas giant.

"*Aldrin Control* to ship that just came through *Kalaallit's Passage*, please identify."

Mr. Enfield smiled. "Well, Captain Bancroft you better respond."

Bancroft looked at him. "*Aldrin Control*, this is the *Gem Line* luxury transport *Dream in the Night*. We are in route to *Aldrin VI* for a layover. This is Captain Bancroft requesting instructions."

"*Dream in the Night*, what happened to Captain Thorn? *Aldrin Control* out."

"*Aldrin Control*, Captain Thorn had a medical emergency and was transferred to the *BAF Banshee* at *Wanderers Station*. I was the engineering officer and was hired by the owners to take over as captain." Bancroft responded.

"Ok, Bancroft we found you. You have your ships Masters License. Sorry, but we have a lot of fakes come through here. Proceed to *Aldrin VI* space station for docking. *Aldrin Control* out."

Ti walked on to the bridge. "Mr. Bancroft how long is our stay over here at *Aldrin VI*, before we head back through *Kalaallit's Passage*."

Mr. Bancroft looked at him. "Sir, we normally put in for two weeks periodic maintenance. This is the final stop for all our current passengers. Only you and Lady Allis are scheduled on the return trip. Of course, we have over four hundred passengers for the return trip. We are scheduled to leave in three weeks."

"Alright Mr. Bancroft, if the accommodations are substandard for the crew here, as they were on *Pandarus VI,* put them up in the Ambassador. Rent out the top four floors if necessary." Ti said.

"But, Mr. Tornbow, I know the facilities here are bad but the cost..." Mr. Bancroft started to say.

Ti told him. "Tell Mr. Bollinger, I said he was to give us the family rate. Also, don't worry; Miss La Rouge is planning a party, or two. We will cover the cost. Mr. Bancroft, evaluate the companies holdings here, if they are salvageable have the manager fix them up. Or, fire him and find someone that can. If not sell the property and we will rent better accommodations."

"Yes Sir," Mr. Bancroft said.

Ti nodded and walked off the bridge.

Mr. Bancroft looked at Mr. Enfield. "I have never known bears like him and his wife."

Mr. Enfield nodded. "You never want to be on their bad side. But, if they like you and trust you they show that also. Don't disappoint them."

Mr. Bancroft nodded. "No I won't. It is scary to be given that much trust, but I'll prove I deserve it."

Maria was setting. She was scared, she was also happy. These bears had been good to her she would help them. She would fight the evil that had taken her parents. She was a gypsy. She could not join any clan. But, she could give here loyalty in the gypsy way.

She walked over to Ti, who had just got back. She pulled out a small knife, sliced her palm, and handed it to Ti. He carefully cut his and she placed her palm in his. "I as a gypsy cannot ask to join your clan. I cannot be untrue to my own kind. But, I give you this, my blood oath to serve you till I die, and beyond if possible."

Ti responded. "To my kind only the family bond is stronger than a blood oath. So, know this Maria La Rouge you will be honored by the clan Maxumus and sheltered in our halls. This, I Tiberius Maxumus Jr. Knight Protector of the Clan, so swear."

Babs came over, slit her paw, and grabbed Maria's. "I Babs Allis Svedberg Maxumus, Regent of the Palisades, also accept your oath in the name of our Prince Beary Maximus, if it be your will."

Maria bowed. "Yes, I give him my oath also."

Annabelle Rosa came over. "Maria it is our custom for a dragon to seal such an oath. It has consequences. But, if you wish, I have the ability to finish this ceremony."

Maria nodded. "I know Lady Rosa that if one breaks such an oath they die. It is the same for a gypsy. It is our law also. I will finish the ceremony."

Annabelle Rosa came over, her eyes changed to that of a dragon. She blew a fine flame around Maria. Accept my blessing Maria."

Maria smiled. The scar on her paw had disappeared. She also felt a peace she had not felt in years. She kissed Annabelle Rosa. "Thank you, Lady Rosa."

Annabelle Rosa healed Babs paw. Then she looked at Ti's. His had already closed. "You and Beary should be brothers; you are more like him than his own brothers."

Ti shrugged. "The gene is rare even among the Maxumus clan. Even rarer in the Augustine, somehow Mom and Angelina, Dad and Octavious each managed to have a child with it. Even then, Beary's is more pronounced than mine. Dad and Octavious had the gene also."

Maria looked at him. "I do not understand. What gene?"

Ti smiled, picked up a knife, and stabbed his arm. The knife folded like paper. "I normally do that little trick a little more dramatic. But it makes Allis angry."

Maria just stared. "It did not hurt you?"

"No Maria, a knife cannot hurt him. He is impervious to blades." Babs said.

At the *Ambassador* Ti and Babs was taken to their rooms. Mr. Bollinger smiled as he personally showed them in. "Raphael asked that he, Andrew and Teresa along with Lady Annabelle Rosa be put in an adjoining suite. Also a Miss Maria La Rouge is in the suite across the hall. Who is she?"

Ti replied. "A new member of the team, she is connected to another intelligence organization, Joe."

Joe Bollinger raised an eyebrow. "Are you sure you can trust her?"

Annabelle Rosa nodded. "I give my word that he can."

Bollinger bowed. "I understand my lady. Well, what can I do?"

Ti sighed. "Stay undercover. You're a target also. Remember, the red dagger serves us best when they stay hidden."

Bollinger nodded. "Yes sire, enjoy your stay. Our staff is here to serve your needs."

Maria came in and sat down. "Lady Allis, do I set up a party or do, we... I know someone on *Aldrin VII* that might give you some answers. But, going there may be dangerous."

Ti asked. "Maria, we have put you in a bad situation haven't we?"

"No, Sire Tornbow, I have my own selfish reasons for wanting in. I am seeking revenge on the devils that killed my parents. Your enemies are mine. The Shape Shifters killed my parents. So, you see, I am not being noble. I am just being a gypsy." Maria said.

Ti nodded. "Ok Maria, first thing first we put the girls to work. Raise some working capital, pay the bills. Throw a big party. Mr. Bollinger will assist, I am sure.

"Oui since he is family. I know it is a secret, but I saw how he looked at you and the others." Maria said. "I will set it up for tomorrow afternoon. On *Aldrin VI* most business closes in the afternoon and opens at night. The Afternoon is for play, love, and parties."

"Maria you might prove to be very useful or a real pain in the tail." Ti said with a smile.

"Oui, but you and Mrs. are not busy this afternoon no parties. So you go play or perhaps she has better ideas." Maria said smiling at Babs.

Babs smiled back. "Perhaps both, Oui."

Ti just shook his head. "Don't we have work to do?"

Maria laughed waved and headed out the door.

Babs grabbed his paw. "Come on, we should go shopping for some local items and hit some of the local shops."

Annabelle Rosa frowned. "Not by your selves. There are real dangers here. At least take Sgt Fong and the Corporal with you."

Ti looked at her. "Alright, but you stay here and stay safe. You are also a target for them because they know you are a true threat."

Annabelle Rosa smiled a dragon smile. "It would be a mistake for them to come for me."

"Still, we all need to play it safer. We all go home." Babs said.

Babs saw a small shop on a corner. She asked the Corporal to stop.

Corporal Tongan got out and looked around. "It looks clear sir."

"Thank you Mr. Tongan." Ti said, as he got out he also scanned the area. He then helped Babs out."

"Shall we Brinton, it looks like a lovely little shop." Babs said.

As they walked through the door a small bell rang. A small little girl cub came out. "Hello, may I help you?"

Babs smiled. "Are you the proprietor?"

"No silly, the shop belongs to my grandfather. He is in the back...," She looked around; "I can show you what you are looking for. It is over here." She led Ti and Babs over to a shelf by the door. "Please, you must leave. Some bad creatures are holding my grandfather. They will hurt him and you if you don't leave."

Babs took her paw. "Come, you can show me the shop you mean." Babs took her and put her in the car. The Sergeant and Corporal took defensive positions.

Ti had stayed inside. He moved towards the blind side of the shop.

One of the thieves stepped out to try and figure out what was going on. He wasn't happy the girl cub was gone. "Get the old bear to open the safe. Then kill him the girl is gone."

That is when Ti hit him. The blow to the back of his neck knocked him out. Ti cuffed him and took his weapon.

Babs had moved around to the back door. There was a look out in a getaway vehicle. He was looking the wrong way. That is when Babs hit him in the side of his head, with the butt of a knife. She gaged and cuffed his paws behind his back.

The old bear was still refusing to open the safe. The third criminal raised his weapon; hit the old boar across the face, driving him to the floor. "Open it or I'll kill you right now!"

Ti stepped into the door. "Drop your weapon."

The third criminal turned and fired. His energy bolt went wide and hit the door frame. Ti fired twice; his first bolt hit the criminal in the chest. The second hit him in the head above the right eye. He was dead before his body hit the floor.

Babs came through the back door.

Ti yelled. "Clear, Babs call the police."

Babs nodded and went out front.

Ti looked at the old boar. "Are you alright Sire?"

The old bear looked at him with penetrating eyes, "My granddaughter?"

Ti nodded. "She is a very brave cub. She warned us and tried to get us out of the shop to protect us. We gave her to our security people and decided to take care of the situation."

The old bear looked at him, "Marine?"

"No Sir, Special Forces *Hazard's Rangers*." Ti said.

The old bear smiled. "Not many Army units left son. But you picked a good one. So why did you leave?"

"My dad said it was no place for a married boar. He wanted me to take over the family business. I still do reserve time. I am Brinton Tornbow." Ti said holding out his paw.

"Old boar Tornbow's son, I met him once and his lovely wife Angel. She bought a necklace from me." The old boar said.

"The pink crystal heart" Ti asked?

"Why yes." The old boar said. "I am Ben Weizmier"

Sergeant Fong brought the little girl cub back in. She ran to her grandfather. "She wouldn't stay outside any longer."

Ti nodded. "It's ok Fong, can you help Mr. Weizmier into the other room. Tend to his wounds till the police and the ambulance arrives."

"Yes Sir Tornbow." Fong said and helped the old boar into the other room and into a chair.

Babs brought in a first aid kit and helped clean the wound. She put a bandage on the gash on the side of his face. "It's going to require stiches."

"You are very beautiful Mrs. Tornbow. I can see leaving the service for you." Mr. Weizmier said.

"Well, only partly, he is still a reservist, as am I." Babs said.

"Oh, what branch?" Mr. Weizmier asked.

"Fleet intelligence, I am a mineralogist and geologist by trade. Fleet feels that has its uses in the intelligence area." Babs said.

"So, old boar Tornbow had a marriage made in heaven for his business." Mr. Weizmier said.

"Brinton is a fine geologist in his own right and gemologist." Babs said very proud like.

Weizmier smiled. "You have done well for yourself young Brinton, almost, as good as your father or as good maybe."

Ti bowed. "Thank you, Sire."

The criminal on the floor started to come around. Sergeant Fong picked him up and threw him in the backroom. He landed next to his dead partner and screamed. Fong tapped him and he passed out. "He was too noisy, I put him to sleep."

A half a cycle later, the police and an ambulance arrived. A burly police Sergeant stomped into the shop. "What is going on here?"

Ti stood up. "Attempted robbery and attempted murder. One suspect is dead. One is detained in the getaway vehicle and one is detained in the other room."

"Just how do you know what was going on? Maybe Weizmier faked the whole thing and you killed an innocent bear?" The police sergeant said.

Ti was getting mad. "I tell you what sergeant, you grab the other two. I'll go down to the precinct with you and give you a full statement."

"Maybe, I should just cuff you while I am at it?" The police sergeant said with a sneer, "Since you like his kind."

Babs looked at the old boar. "What is his problem?"

"We are followers of the Creator of the Universe, just as he is. But we follow an old way, on the old *Scrolls of Creation*." Weizmier said.

"So you are Followers of the First Ones." Babs said.

"Some call us that. It is not what we call ourselves." Mr. Weizmier said.

"A good friend of mine told me, we are all Children of the Creator. How we serve him is how he chooses. As long as we recognize that we are his children and that he is the Creator of the Universe." Babs said.

Mr. Weizmier bowed, "Thank you."

"Maybe I should run you in also." The police sergeant said.

Ti walked up to him and looked him in the eyes. "Mr. Fong, load the prisoners into the squad car. Mr. Tongan, protect your lady and Mr. Weizmier see he gets proper care. Sergeant, I have had enough of you. We are leaving. We will see if you even have a job after today."

The police sergeant was fuming. "I will have you thrown into a hole; no one will ever find you. You will rot before you get out!"

Ti looked at him. "Pull over now."

The sergeant did and looked at him, "Now what you going to beg?"

Ti hit him, tossed him over his lap, cuffed him, and slid into the driver's seat. Then he headed for the precinct. "Sergeant, you are under arrest for dereliction of duty and any other charges I can come up with."

The police sergeant looked at him. "Who do you think you are? You can't…"

Ti opened his badge. "Oh, yes I can and you made me mad."

The police sergeant had turned white. He didn't know what to do. "But, he was just an old Firster. No one cares about them. They don't worship right. They have strange ways."

Ti looked at him. "I am a Maxmimus. I have family members who are dragons and dogons. One of my priests is a dragon. A more devote follower of the Creator and His Word you will not find. But, in your universe there would be no place for him would there?"

The police sergeant looked at Ti in horror. "Then it is true, your race has dragons in your families! You truly are an abomination!"

Ti hit him again. This time he knocked him out.

Ti arrived at the Precinct. "Those two are under arrest for attempted murder and robbery. The police sergeant is under arrest for threatening a federal officer, dereliction of duty, and violation of code 12A of the Bearilian legal code."

A Police Lieutenant came over. "By what authority..."

Ti showed his badge. The lieutenant got white. "I am sorry Sire. Do as he says, now."

"Lieutenant, you have a problem. In fifteen days you're going to have a lot of help to fix it. Two squads of Special Investigators are going to descend on your precinct and on the others. If, they find the kind of corruption I think they're going to find, heads are going to roll." Ti said.

The Lieutenant bowed. "Praise the Creator. I have been begging for such an investigation. Inspector it is bad here. Half my police officers are on the take, including the Sergeant you busted. The corruption is wide spread. The Overa Cartel started it, but sold out to another Cartel."

"Lieutenant, drive me back to my hotel will you. By the way, I am undercover. My employer, Mr. Tornbow doesn't know I work for the Secret Service." Ti said.

Sergeant Fong saw Ti bringing in the Police Lieutenant; he turned to Bollinger. "Quick, give me a spare room key, something away from everyone else."

"Not a problem this room isn't on the room chart, it is special." Bollinger said.

"Mr. Holmes, Mr. Tornbow is furious that you left the lady's side this afternoon." Fong said.

"It is ok Fong; tell him I'll be up in a little while. I need to talk to the Lieutenant." Ti said.

"Ok sir, here is the key to your room. I'll tell him you have been detained." Fong said.

Ti looked at the key and nodded. "Come on lieutenant."

Once in the room, Ti sat the Lieutenant down and handed him a bracelet. "Put this on Lieutenant."

The Lieutenant put it on. "What is this?"

Ti told him. "Simple, if you had been a shape shifter you would be dead right now. Keep it on it is the only way my people will begin to trust you."

The Police Lieutenant nodded, "Ok now what?"

"Simple, you tell me everything you know." Ti said.

After half a cycle Ti stopped the recorder. "You are sure it is this bad."

"Yes Sir, bears I have known for years changed... I couldn't explain it. Crime went up and this hatred and intolerance for bears with slightly different beliefs. We are not talking Mac-Ta worshipers here. But, Firster and Baptizers have had their houses of worship burnt. In one case it was another Baptizer church that set fire to the other Baptizer church. None of it makes since." The Police Lieutenant said.

"Alright, I'll make the call." Ti opened a case and turned on a com device. Bill Henderson appeared. "Sir, Inspector Holmes reporting..." Ti laid out the situation.

"Holms your unit can't handle an invasion, give me a moment." Henderson was back in a moment. "Ok Holms, the *BAF Carnise Drift* with its Marine Expeditionary force, will arrive in twelve cycles. General Puller is in charge. Tell him what you know and clear out, boss's orders."

"Understood Bill thanks, I'll hide the Police Lieutenant till he gets here." Ti tuned off the com.

"Sorry Lieutenant, you're under protective custody. Do you have family?" Ti asked.

"No Inspector Holms, not good enough life expectancy if you don't play their game." The Police Lieutenant said.

Ti made a call. Three Marines showed up and escorted the lieutenant blind folded to another safe room.

Ti briefed the others.

Maria thought. "Could we not give these bracelets as party favors?"

Ti considered it. "We don't have enough Maria. Besides, the General gets here after the party tomorrow night."

Babs pondered her suggestion. But, if we get a hit on a scan maybe we could sneak a bracelet in. If it was a big enough target. "Maria, don't totally shelve your idea, let me sleep on it."

"Oui Allis." Maria said.

Annabelle Rosa shook her head. "But, we still need to clear out."

"Yes, so we go visit Maria's friends on VII and let the General do his thing." Ti said.

The next afternoon Maria's girls were dressed in their finest cloths and finest jewels that were left in the collection. Annabelle Rosa had created several special pieces from the loose stones and had them properly displayed.

As each guest came in they were quietly scanned. Four Shape Shifters were found to be among the attendees. One was a high minister; the others were local political officials.

Babs smiled; Maria's plan was do able. No one would understand what happened. The shock that it would cause, when it was revealed that these officials had been replaced by Shape Shifters, would be enough to give the General cover. The bracelets had been disguised as watches. They would be presented to them just before they left.

Ti greeted their guests. "Ladies, gentlebears, and other guests welcome. Please enjoy the food and refreshments. If you see any jewelry you like the models will be happy to assist you."

After three cycles, the merchandise and the crowd started to thin out as the party came to a close. The watches had been given out as planned. Over twenty were given including the four designed to kill shape shifters.

Everyone put on their watches and left.

Maria went to figure the receipts and to pay the staff.

High Minister Bronchi had just arrived home with his wife. He had seen the targets. He would have to let their leader know. The other three had also seen them, but they all reported to him. All of a sudden he felt a pain in his chest. Then he saw his leg change shape everyone was staring at him. At the last instance he wondered if this was how the real Bronchi felt when he died. Then his world went black.

One of his attendants looked at the misshapen form lying on the floor. Then he called the local military barracks. The call was diverted to General Puller.

"You say your boss was a Shape Shifter? No, you believe he was replaced by one and it just died of an apparent heart attack. Who was your boss? High Minister Bronchi! That means the entire government of the planet might be compromised! Yes, by all means you did right. Thank you, we will deal with it." General Puller said. Three other calls came in.

"Ok Marines, that's our cue launch. Take over every police barracks and governmental offices. If you find Shape Shifters kill them." General Puller said.

"Fong tell everyone to stay in their rooms, for the next seventy-two cycles. Captain Bancroft, you must keep the crew in the *Ambassador*. Mr. Bollinger will take care of you. Things are going to get real ugly for seventy-two cycles." Ti said

"Sir Tornbow, where are you going?" Bancroft asked.

"I, Mr. Fong and a few select others have an appointment elsewhere. We have to leave now or we won't get to leave. I have been given a very narrow window." Ti said.

Bancroft looked at him. "Sir, who are you really?"

Ti smiled, "The owner of the *Gem Lines* along with my wife, my cousin and his wife, and a few other investors. The rest, I'll explain on the way home. For now trust me."

Bancroft looked at him, "Yes sir."

Fong pulled a transport up to the front, Ti jumped in. Fong hit the accelerator, "Where to Sir?"

"Out of the city to the east about five KSMU, there is supposed to be a dagger waiting for us." Ti said.

Fong looked at him. "Sir, I don't know how to fly one."

Babs, Ti, and Annabelle Rosa all said. "It is ok Sergeant I do." at the same time.

Corporal Tongan smiled. "Well, I guess we have a pilot. Private Den Po how are you feeling?"

"I am good Corporal; Miss Teresa took good care of me. I am ready for duty." Private Den Po said.

A Marine Lieutenant and his squad were waiting when they arrived. "You Scarecrow?"

"Yes Lieutenant Walsh, I am." Ti said.

"The Ensign isn't real happy about you taking his ship. Try not to scratch it. General Puller said if you do you'll buy him a new one." Lieutenant Walsh said.

"Tell the old pirate that if I ding it, I'll buy him two to replace it." Ti said. Walsh saluted. "He said you would say that. Good hunting sir."

"You too Marine," Ti said as his small group loaded up.

After they got airborne Babs looked at Ti. "You know the General?"

Ti nodded, "For about five years, he was a Colonel then working intelligence. Had just one of those things happen, you know wrong place wrong time. Anyway, I went in and got him out. He is a real professional."

Babs looked at Ti, coming from him that was high praise. He also wasn't saying any more. She nodded. "Maria you better come up and tell us what we need to know."

Maria nodded, the Shape Shifters will be real mad now their quiet foot hold will be broken. "There is an island on the equator. It is shaped like a crescent moon. The main Gypsy Camp is on the island. We will have to meet with La Noire. He is the King of the Gypsies on *Aldrin VII.*"

Babs looked at Maria. "You seem worried."

"Oui, he will not be pleased that I brought you to see him." Maria said.

Ti said. "If he doesn't want to help us it is alright."

Maria said. "He will help. He has no choice. He owes me. He will help whether he likes it or not."

# CHAPTER 11

# Aldrin VII Home of the Gypsies

A S THEY APPROACHED the island, Ti noticed a black craft as it fired on the island. It also started to spray a chemical over the island.

Babs' blood started to boil. "Weapons are up. Tracking target, I have good tone, Fox 1- 3 away."

The missiles tracked into the black craft. The first one exploded against its shield. The next two punched through. The craft exploded and crashed into the ocean.

Two more black fighters appeared and fired at the dagger. Its shields flared.

Babs fired three more missiles at one fighter, as Ti opened up with the Gatling phaser. Both black fighters exploded.

A fourth rose from near the surface and streaked for the atmosphere. Babs lined it up and launch three missiles after it.

The Black fighter had almost reached the cold of space when it exploded.

Annabelle Rosa turned to Raphael. "Get my medical kit ready. There is bound to be wounded. Also we need to determine what they were spraying."

Ti nodded. "I am working on it. It seems to be a virus, no its Plague, *Hedrick's.*"

Annabelle Rose nodded. "I can treat it. I have enough antibiotics to start. Then we will have to produce medicine. Luckily these islands have natural antibiotics available. Let me see the scan. This is a modified plague; it is designed to attack the very young and the very old."

"They are the ones that gather the fire wood." Maria said.

Annabelle Rosa fixed two injectors and gave everyone a shot. She carefully gave Ti his behind his ear.

"Ouch, that hurt!" Ti said.

Annabelle Rosa replied. "It worked and I got the medicine where I needed it. Don't be a baby."

Ti landed near the village. The destruction was minimal. A water tower had been hit, along with what appeared to be a defensive position."

Maria stepped out. "Is anyone here, it is La Renard."

La Noire stepped out. "So, Maria La Rouge you have returned. Who is this you have brought with you, uninvited?"

Annabelle Rose looked at him. "I am The Rose your populaces have been infected with the *Hendricks's Plague*. If I am going to help them, I must start now."

La Noire looked at her. "How do I know...?"

Annabelle Rosa got in his face. Her eyes changed to those of a dragon. "Do you wish to challenge me gypsy?"

La Noire dropped to his knee. "No Lady Rose, please help my families. The cubs and old are very sick."

"Then get out of my way. Teresa, Raphael, Andrew Re, and Mr. Po you are with me." Annabelle Rosa said.

Maria shook her head, "I thought you would have gotten smarter after all these years. Father taught you better than this."

La Noire looked at her. "He also told you not to bring strays home!"

Maria slapped him. "This is Sire and Sirena Tiberius Maxumus. He is a Knight of the Maxumus Clan. His wife is Regent to Prince Beary Maxumus. I have given them my blood oath."

La Noire looked at her. "You brought them here, knowing that those devils have been attacking us."

"No because no one told me. I didn't know till they destroyed the four craft that were attacking our people. Where were your defenses?" Maria demanded.

"Gone a traitor sold us out. He is dead. Lobo found him and eliminated him." La Noire said.

"Lobo, is he alright?" Maria asked.

"Yes, he is well and we scanned him. The traitor was not one of the devils. He just was greedy. His name has been erased." La Noire said.

Ti looked around, "Your tribe?"

La Noire shrugged. "We have always had underground bunkers to live in. For us life has always been hard. Whether living in tramp freighters traveling from system to system or trying to have a home. No one wanted these islands. My father started moving gypsies here fifty years ago. Since no one wanted us, it seemed like a good match.

The other colonies have not been attacked yet, only ours. I am not sure the Shape Shifters know about the others."

Ti shook his head. "No there is something on this island they want and you're setting on it, whether you know it or not. The question is what it is."

Maria looked at her brother. "My pledge to him is also binding on you. You know this don't you."

Lo Noire looked at her. "Maria, you go too far. I am King…"

"Only as long as I say you are brother. Do not forget, I am the head of this tribe and this family. Or do you wish to challenge my authority!" Maria asked.

"He, will not La Renard, he knows he cannot take you. I might try for the fun of it. But you would spank me." Lobo said.

Maria smiled. "This is Philipp my youngest brother. He is Lobo our hunter."

Ti smiled. "Call me Ti."

Philipp looked at him and Babs. "Two hunters, very dangerous, I think it would be more fun to be killed by her, she at least would make your last moment a pleasure."

Babs grinned. "Some creatures have thought so."

"Brother, do not be an idiot they are our friends. The Rose is helping our cubs and old ones. She is family to this one. Also, Maria will just end up making you help them." Philipp pointed out.

"Come it is safer inside." La Noire said.

Fong and Tongan came over. "Camouflage and landing shield is up and running on APU."

Ti nodded. "Stay loose and try and help Annabelle Rosa."

As they walked in Annabelle Rosa walked up. "I have exhausted my antibiotic supply. I have treated everyone. The young ones are responding already, but some of the elderly are very sick. I strengthened a couple, but they are still very week. I need to produce more medicine."

Maria looked at her. "Lady Rosa you need to rest. Please tell us what you need. We will send gatherers to find the items you need."

Annabelle Rosa nodded. "Thank you, tell them to hurry. I need to have more medicine produced in twelve cycles."

La Noire called ten of his bears over. He told them what was needed. Then gave them the list and told them to take armed teams out and bring back the items.

One spoke up. "Don't, worry; Lady Rosa gave us an inoculation to protect us."

La Noire nodded. "Come this way, Lady and Sire Maxumus."

He led them down a tunnel, then down a stair case, then into another tunnel. "We found the inhabitants of these islands had built these underground shelters deep into the bed rock of the islands. Mainly, because the storms are so devastating, also the tsunamis that strikes periodically."

Maria nodded. "Father said that is why the Bearilian Colonist abandoned *Aldrin VII*. They hadn't figured out how the ancients had lived here.

They built simple structures topside. Their cities were underground except the temple city on this island, fifteen KSMU from here. It is on high ground. This was a large village with a center of learning."

Noire opened a massive set of doors. "This was their library. This is what the Shape Shifters want. What we must not allow them to have or anyone. It is our Treasure." Noire looked down. "Except you Sire Maxumus, our tribe is bound to you by our law."

Ti pulled out a sack of loose gems and threw them to La Noire. "Then this is a gift to show my appreciation."

La Noire looked at the first yellow diamond; it was at least five carrots. It was worth twenty-five thousand credits at least. The sack was full of gems of similar value. "Thank you Sire, your gift will bring my sister honor." Not to mention myself he didn't say.

Babs gave him a cold look. "As Maria will tell you those that share the risk share the reward. La Noire, understand if Maria's trust, was betrayed in any way. I would take it very personal. She is my friend; you are her brother if her trust in you was betrayed. Well, this Universe wouldn't be large enough for you to hide in." Babs then smiled. "Shall we see what we can find?"

La Noire felt a shiver go up his spine. So, this is what it is like to look death directly in the eyes. "My lady, I love my sister I could never..."

Babs nodded. "Call me Allis; I just wanted you know your sister is very dear to us. I would hurt anyone that hurt her."

"Yes Lady Allis." La Noire said bowing.

Maria looked at him. "What is wrong?"

"Nothing Maria, you have made a friend. That one said that if anyone betrayed your trust or hurt you. She would hunt them down and kill them. I believe her." La Noire said with a smile.

Maria sighed. "Their kind, do not lie. That one is fearless, so is her husband. They will not betray our trust brother."

La Noire showed her the sack of gems. "I know they even know our ways and honor them."

The library was extensive. The language was giving the translator fits. Till, Ti realized that he was reading it from the wrong direction. These documents were written right to left instead of left to right.

"These documents are older than others that have been found on the other planets." Ti said.

La Noire nodded. "Yes, that is what I thought also. I think this was the original language. We have found other libraries that mirror the documents on the other two planets. But, this library is unique.

Tell me Sire Maxumus, did you look up at the stars?"

Ti shook his head. "No, I didn't think to look."

"The Afternoon storms will be coming soon, but come look." La Noire took them up a small tunnel opened a small portal. They walked out on to a stone balcony. "Look, what do you see?"

Ti and Babs both looked up at the suns. "Only one, they look like one sun from here!"

La Noire smiled. "Exactly, they are so close together that from this orbit they appear to be one star. So how did the ancients know there were two?"

La Noire looked at the Eastern sky. "A storm is coming; I hope the gatherers are back."

Just then the head gatherer reported, that everyone was back, showered off, and that the tunnels were sealed, for the coming storm. La Noire led them back in and sealed the portal. "Is your Dagger tied down?"

Ti called Fong. Fong answered. "Yes Sir, one of the gypsies actually had me move it to a shelter in the rocks. It was a hanger of some type a long time ago."

Ti looked at La Noire, "A hanger?"

La Noire smiled. "Yes, ship docks, even a submersible pen. They mined the ocean bottom. They had space flight at the height of their civilization. These documents that you were looking at are at least sixty thousand years old. Their civilization disappeared ten thousand to fifteen thousand years ago, from what we can tell."

Ti looked at him. "So what happened, and how did the early inhabitants know there were two stars?"

La Noire shrugged. "I have spent fifteen years studying every document. I know that they achieved space flight and space travel at two different times. Space flight was accomplished with ships around thirty thousand years ago. Then they developed another system twenty thousand years ago, that was said to be faster. None of the documents say what it was."

"So the *Key of Epoch* is based on more than just a misinterpreted log entry." Ti said.

La Noire shook his head. "Yes and no, there is no *Key*. Not in a physical since. What there is; is a mystery, a hole in the history of the *Aldrin* people, spanning five thousand to ten thousand years. Plus, a combine population of three planets, close to two hundred seventy billion, intelligent beings that just up and disappeared. No record of what happened. They just were gone."

"So, since then everyone has tried to discover the secret and find the *Key*." Ti said.

"Exactly, The Shape Shifters want this library because they think the answer is here. But, it isn't. It is thirty thousand years to old. However, the music and poetry is so beautiful. Their culture was so rich. I am planning to publish it." La Noire said.

Maria laughed. "It is a scandal. He is King of the Gypsies, and he has a PHD in Ancient Literature, Poetry, and Languages."

Babs replied. "If you didn't have two life times of work here, I would have a job for you."

La Noire nodded. "If we don't stop the Shape Shifters it won't matter."

Ti told him. "So, we stop them. On *Aldrin VI* I am sure they are having a very bad day."

General Puller's Marines were all wearing bracelets. One shape shifter ambushed a Marine, killed him, and took his bracelet. He believed it was an Identification badge. He took five steps, when the bracelet activated killing him. The Marine's buddies found him and the dead Shape Shifter. They placed his bracelet back on him, marked his body for pick up, along with the misshapen body of the Shape Shifter. Then they moved on in threes.

By the end of the first day the fighting in some precincts had been fierce. Officials, who had sided with the Cartel and the Shape Shifters, and the Shape Shifters themselves, had tried to organize some type of resistance. Over two hundred Shape Shifters were dead along with fifty corrupt police officers, which tried to shoot it out with the Marines. Twenty-five Marines had been killed another sixty wounded.

The Hospital ship *Mercy* along with its escorts and the *Dreadnought Relentless* arrived and took up station near *Aldrin VI*.

Admiral Hazard was a small Red Pandarian. Though small in stature he was known for his brilliant intellect. "Mr. Percy, have the *Mercy* move to a stationary orbit away from the nearest wormhole exit points. Set guard ships on each one. If a hostile comes through, tell the captains to shoot first and ask questions later. Tell all inbound traffic that *Aldrin System* is a quarantine zone, till further notice. Send beacons through each known wormhole"

The *Sirius Freighter Airedale* was preparing to enter *Kalaallit's Passage*, when the beacon came through. Captain Mac Dervish Scott, a small pipe smoking Scottish terrier, read the message that was transmitted. "By a cat's whiskers what is going on now? Mr. AJ call *Wanderers' Station* tell them *Kalaallit's Passage* is closed and take us back."

"Yes Captain, the company won't be happy." Mr. AJ said.

"True but they would be even unhappier, if we were blown apart." Mac Dervish Scott responded.

A distress signal was received aboard the Shape Shifter *Battleship Doomsday*. Admiral DevMorda read the message. Their clandestine colony on *Aldrin VI*, which had been so important to their plans to destroy the Bearilians, had been discovered. Four of the replacers he had sent in had died mysteriously revealing their true selves. Bearilian Marines had landed and declared Marshall Law over the territory. They and their supporters were being decimated.

Admiral DevMorda fumed. His plans were falling apart. "Prepare the fleet. We are attacking the *Aldrin System* immediately. Launch from

Alfa, Bravo, Tango, and Zeta wormholes. They will not expect a four pronged attack we will catch them sleeping."

"Destroyer detachment 2A and 2B cover Sector 3"

"*BAF Fire Sword* you and *Hammer Claw* cover Sector 4

"*Purple Dragon Wing*, use your Valkyrie III to help cover Sector 4."

"*Red Dragon Wing*, fly cover over *Mercy*."

"*BAF Death Sword* and *Mace Claw* cover Sector 2."

"*The Relentless* and the *BAF White Sword* will cover Sector 1"

"Destroyer Squadron 3, wheel to where you are needed."

"Destroyer Detachment 2D stay in reserve in case we are attacked from more than four points."

Admiral Hazard sat back. He had given his orders. He knew that they could use standard wormholes, but he didn't expect that. These were almost uncharted and led to empty space between systems. Or, perhaps to where long dead systems had been in one or two cases.

Ti could hear the storm raging outside. Annabelle Rose came in and sat down. She looked at all the scrolls. "The answer is not here. These scrolls are too old. But oh, what wonders they must hold."

La Noire nodded. "Yes my lady the music, the poetry, and the novels. Also over there are some books on medicines."

Annabelle Rosa responded. "So this is your treasure?"

"Yes my lady. I want to bring their beauty back to life." La Noire said.

"Then you shall." Annabelle Rosa said. Then she walked over to Ti. "Evil, is coming. I feel it."

"Yes Annabelle Rosa and *Bearilian Fleet Ships* are waiting to meet it head on." Ti said.

# CHAPTER 12

# The Battle for the Aldrin system

DEVMORDA WAS SURE of his plan. No one had reported anything other than the usual Bearilian Cruiser and five destroyers that were usually assigned to the *Aldrin System*. The last cruiser reported wasn't even a front line cruiser, but an old tired warship ready for the scrap yard. Well, he would send it there.

He had his new battleship *Doomsday* and six cruisers and thirteen destroyers. He would send one cruiser with four destroyers through three of the wormholes. Then attack with three cruisers and a destroyer with his battleship through the fourth. The small Bearilian fleet would be so over whelmed it wouldn't know what to do.

DevMorda smiled. "Give the command to begin **Operation Overload**."

The command was received. The various Shape Shifter Commanders gave their orders. The first through were four destroyers.

Attacking through a wormhole can have an advantage, if you have total surprise. You can get in close to your target and close with the enemy. However, it has two major disadvantages. For one STU shields and weapons are off line. If your enemy is caught unaware, that time lag is not a problem. But, if your enemy is waiting for you near your entry point you die.

One other point about wormhole mechanics, once you start through you can't reverse course.

Admiral Hazard watched as four wormholes started to form, just where he expected. "Give the command to open fire as soon as the enemy ships start through."

"Yes Sir, To Fleet, open fire as the enemy ships appear, *Relentless* out."

The Shape Shifter destroyers started to emerge. As they did they were smashed by rail gun and phaser fire. Without shields and weapons, it was like being put through a meat grinder. The first four destroyers died quickly. They were pushed through by the tidal force of the wormholes.

Believing, his first wave was already wreaking havoc on the Bearilian Fleet, DevMorda ordered four of his cruisers through.

The bridge of the Shape Shifter Cruiser is just back of the forward weapons area. As the Captain of the *Cruiser Death Song* came through he gazed right at the *BAF Relentless* and her massive rail guns. He ordered shields and weapons brought on line.

His weapons officer just shook his crystalline head. "Forty-five SubSTU to go, we are dead."

Six massive rail gun shells from the *Relentless* smashed into the area around the *Death Song's* bridge. Then three more from the *White Sword* smashed into the front weapons area. One skimmed the outer skin of the cruiser and smashed through the bridge killing everyone.

The captain was dead. The first officer, in axillary control, was trying to do something. The wormhole just kept forcing them out. He tried to send a message, but communications was down. More rail gun shells ripped into the *Death Song* soon it just came apart.

The other three suffered a similar fate. The Valkyrie III's dive in on one of the cruisers and hammered it. The *Fire Sword* smashed it with rail gun fire.

The destroyers used their photon torpedoes on the other two. These weapons are normally not the first chose of destroyer captains, because they have limited effectiveness and accuracy. But, in this situation they are a perfect weapon. Eight photon torpedoes exploded against the hull of each cruiser, their warheads expanding and burning deep into the cruisers internal structures. This they followed with eighty missiles each. The one hundred sixty Mark 4's missiles burned deep into the now battered cruisers. Hitting their engineering sections causing core containment fields to fail, the cruisers disintegrated.

Admiral Hazard was beginning to wonder how big a fleet he was facing. He had the *Red Dragon Wing* and the *Purple Dragon Wing* switch places. Then ordered the *Purple Dragons* rearmed. He waited for the next wave to come through.

Admiral DevMorda had received a garbled message. However, it had stopped. He decided he needed to find out what was going on. "Take us in order the remaining cruisers to stand by."

Admiral Hazard smiled. "Jack, I think something big is going to start coming through. Hit it with all forward batteries and a full load of missiles, as it breaches the leading edge of the wormhole."

The Shape Shifter *Battleship Doomsday* was a big ship. Its battle bridge was built slightly aft of front third of the ship. This area was filled with massive energy weapons and launch bays. Over one hundred twenty fighters were prepared to launch once they cleared the wormhole.

As the leading edge of the *Doomsday* cleared the edge of the wormhole, six massive rail gun shells, followed by ten smaller caliber shells, two hundred fifty Mark 4 Death Hawk missiles streaked for it from the *Relentless*. These were followed by three rail gun shells and one hundred twenty Mark 4 missiles from the *White Sword*.

On the *Doomsday,* the forward weapons were smashed by the rail gun shells that gouged deep into her armored hull then exploded. The first one hundred Mark 4 missiles tore at the outer hull of the ship as the rest burrowed through to the launch bays. The Shape Shifter pilots died in their fighters, unable to launch and unable to escape the burning and exploding fighters. One missile hit a weapons bunker for the fighters setting off their own weapons stores, which added to the fires and internal explosions. The *Doomsday* was burning.

Admiral DevMorda was thrown out of his chair. His aids helped him back into it. He was staring at the *BAF Relentless,* as it fired another salvo. "Give me weapons, shield, something!"

"Thirty more SubSTU Admiral." Was all, the weapons officer, could say. As the large rail gun shells hit the area around the battle bridge.

DevMorda marveled at how big the shell looked as he watched it smash into the front of his bridge and as it burst through. The shell hit his command chair as it exploded, ripping the bridge apart.

Ten decks bellow, the ship's captain was trying to save his ship. When word that the battle bridge was gone reached him, he said. "Order the rest of the fleet to retire. Save what they can. I doubt that we will survive."

The *Doomsday* had finally exited the wormhole. Its warp engines were gone. Its fighters destroyed, along with its main weapons area.

Most of his secondary weapons were destroyed. But, he now had weak shields and a few phasers. He opened fire.

The shields on the *BAF Relentless* flared. Admiral Hazard smiled. "So, it can still fight. Let's finish this."

*The Relentless* turned sideways and fired all her port rail guns at the *Doomsday*, along with three hundred Mark 4 missiles. Sixteen large caliber and twenty smaller caliber rail gun shells streaked at the wounded ship.

The weakened shields manage to deflect three of the large rail gun shells and fifty of the missiles. The rest burned through. The thirteen large rail gun shells tore mercilessly through the *Doomsday* exploding deep inside its structure. The smaller rail gun shells and missiles destroyed the few remaining weapons. Five Mark 4s burned through to the engineering section smashing the plasma containment field. The containment field failed and a blue haze enveloped the center of the *Doomsday*. Then crashed in on itself. The explosion ripped the battleship in half. Soon, the rest of the ship just came apart.

The Commander of The *Shape Shifter Cruiser Death Tone* sent a recall message to the remaining nine destroyers. He left one destroyer briefly at each wormhole, in hopes that a ship would come through. However, only one escape pod with the dead body of a shape Shifter came through.

They failed to notice the small tracker probe that followed in its wake. After one STU the probe's cloak activated. It pulled away from the escape pod. It headed for the destroyer sentinel. Soon it attached its self to the Shape Shifter Destroyer and prepared to transmit data back to the fleet.

Back in the *Aldrin System* several of the Bearilian Captains wanted to pursue the remains of the Shape Shifter fleet. Admiral Hazard shook his head. "Have you not learned anything? Don't you think that they have ships waiting for you to make the same mistake? We will send a probe through and see what intelligence we can glean."

The first micro burst show the destroyer setting in ambush. Admiral Hazard smiled. "You see Jack, they understand what happened. We will not make the same mistake. Hopefully it will be recalled soon and lead us to their base."

Lt. Commander Jack Perry nodded. "But, it won't be us that get to go after them. Our orders are to secure the *Aldrin System* and let others know we mean it."

Hazard looked at his staff. "No, but I think we sent a message today. We will gather up this junk and use it for something."

Commander Diaballein pulled the *Death Tone* into its slip at the star base. It was near a rogue planet suspended in space near a quasar. The remnants of what had been a large star before it went Supper Nova and exploded destroying the solar system that had revolved around it, except one small dead rock of a planet. Here they had built their advance base. Now, only the *Death Tone* and the *Curse Mark* sat in their berths along with five of their destroyers. Four others were on their way back. Still, the *Doomsday* and four cruisers and four destroyers would never return. Eleven thousand Shape Shifters lost on the nine ships. The hidden colony accounted for another two hundred.

Commander Diaballein was the senior commander. He would have to make the report. "Communications Officer, come to my cabin please."

The Communications Officer came in. Commander Diaballein changed in to the red crystalline creature with horns that the Fuehrer demanded Shape Shifters turn themselves into when they talked to him. He claimed this was their true form. A form so frightful, that other creatures were supposed to run from them in fear. Perhaps it was true, but no one seemed to be running from them today.

He walked over to the metal circle and knelt. An image of Fuehrer Dracdoran appeared before him. It spoke. "Who are you, where is Admiral DevMorda?"

"I am Commander Diaballein, of the *Death Tone*, my Fuehrer. Admiral DevMorda and the *Doomsday* are no more."

Dracdoran's cold red eyes grew even colder. "Tell me, what happened to him, Commander, exactly."

"My Fuehrer, we received a distress signal from our colony on *Aldrin VI*. Some of our replacers died suddenly, disclosing their true selves. Bearilian Marines moved in declaring Marshall Law. The Admiral decided to move in to save our colony. We were expecting a small disorganized Bearilian detachment. He launched a surprise attack through what we thought were four unmarked wormholes. A full Bearilian Battle Fleet was waiting. They destroyed our ships as they came through, including the *Doomsday*. Its Captain warned the rest of our ships off saving two cruisers and nine destroyers. We lost The *Doomsday*, four cruisers, and four destroyers. Also, the colony was decimated. Eleven thousand two hundred Shape Shifters died today my Fuehrer."

Dracdoran's eyes grew even colder as he looked at the Cruiser Commander. He wanted to kill him for bringing him this news. But he had not sent an underling to do it. Instead he did it himself, knowing that death was a possibility. "Commander Diaballein, bring your flotilla home. Leave a few destroyers to protect the base."

"Yes my Fuehrer." Commander Diaballein said. The com unit went blank.

"Inform Section 3 they will be staying to defend this base. The rest of the fleet is to return home immediately, Fuehrer's orders." Commander Diaballein said.

Soon the two cruisers and five destroyers headed for deep space.

The tracking probe watched them go and detached itself from one of the remaining destroyers. It went a short distance away and started micro burst transmitting its information.

Six days later the *BAF Bugle,* a listening outpost picked up its signal and forwarded the information to fleet headquarters.

Fleet Intelligence marked its location. A battle plan was being drawn up to deal with the threat.

But, for now, they just wanted to get a strike force closer. *Strike Force Delta* built around the new *Dreadnought Van Horn* was sent to the *Tiramisus System*. It was little more than a small mining colony, orbiting around the small Star *Tiramisus*. The two planets in this system had harsh environments but were rich in minerals. The system also had six good wormholes that led to other parts of the galaxy. One would take the task force within a day of the enemy base.

# CHAPTER 13

# The Search for Clues

TI'S COMMUNICATION UNIT goes off, "You Scarecrow?" Admiral Hazard asked.

"Yes Sir, I am Scarecrow." Ti said.

"I am Admiral Hazard, General Puller told me to inform you that *Aldrin VI* is secure. Also, son I stopped a Shape Shifter Fleet, which was attacking the system. Now son will you tell me why a Marine General, in command of a Marine Expeditionary Force, and an Admiral in charge of a Battle Group is reporting to a much younger bear? Who do you work for son and who are you?" Admiral Hazard asked.

"Admiral, who I am, really doesn't matter. I know you are famous for hating call signs. However, I also know that you will recognize the one I am going to give you. I work for Golden Dragon 1." Ti said.

Admiral Hazard dropped his head. "Ok Scarecrow, that is good enough for me. Stay safe son, Puller, and I will take care of the rest."

"Thank you Admiral, We have a mystery on our paws." Ti said.

"OK Scarecrow, stay loose, if you need us we are here. Hazard out." Hazard smiled.

Lt. Commander Perry looked at the Admiral. "Do you know this Scarecrow, Sir?"

The Admiral felt of the pilot wings on his uniform. "No Jack, but I bet I could pick him out in a room." The Admiral pressed a button and a bottle appeared with two glasses.

"Sir, that is against Fleet Regulations..." Lt. Commander Perry started to say.

"Quite right Jack, except I am an Admiral and this is my Battle Bridge. This is for only nonessential crew members, which truthfully you and I are." He poured two small drinks. "A toast, to old friends, some who were lost, but they will never be forgotten." Hazard said as he drank his drink and smashed the glass, and put his bottle away.

"Ok bears, let us, get back to work, and see what intelligence we can find among the wreckage." Hazard said.

Lt. Commander Perry looked at his Admiral. He didn't understand him. He did know that the bears on this battle bridge would follow him to the *Moons of Bantine*, and never question it.

Ti looked at Babs. The storm was raging outside. "They have secured *Aldrin VI* and the rest of the system. The Shape Shifters tried to send in a fleet to take the system, it was decimated."

Babs looked at him. "That is just going to cause more problems Ti, in the long run. You know that, as well as I do."

Ti shrugged. "We killed a bunch and secured this system. They were taking it from us slowly. We didn't even know it."

Babs nodded. "Come to bed husband. We will figure it out tomorrow."

Ti lay down next to his wife. His mind was still reeling, what was he missing? Everything apparently, none of it made any since. His mind went back to the little gold sign. It had to be the missing piece to the puzzle.

Babs rolled over and kissed him. "Tiberius, you cannot solve this puzzle without sleep. Come and hold me and sleep please."

Ti kissed her back. "Your right, it can wait till morning."

The next morning Ti woke to find Babs already up and gone. He got dressed and went looking for her. He found her, Maria, and Annabelle Rosa setting around a table talking. Maria was nodding. "Oui, it is our best move from here we go to the temple. Then we head on to the other two. I will ask Noire about the sign post. He will know. I still do not think it is wise to ignore its warning."

Ti walked over and said. "Maria, if you don't want to go, you don't have to."

Maria smiled. "As they say in for a pinch, in for a full measure, besides you do not know our signs. I do."

Babs nodded. "It is her territory. The storm is still ragging up top. There are tunnels that lead to the temple complex. I think we should take them."

Ti nodded. "How are your patients Annabelle Rosa?"

Annabelle Rosa shrugged. "All but one older couple is doing fine. I need better medicine for those two."

Ti nodded. "Send someone for it. Sgt. Fong can go, but you need a pilot."

Andrew Re spoke up. "I and Raphael are qualified in daggers and jump ships. We will take him. Sister, just write down what you need and have Ti sign it."

"Which hospital ship is in orbit around *Aldrin VI*?" Annabelle Rosa asked.

Ti thought, "They said it was the *Mercy*."

"Good, Doctor Gullstrand is in charge of the *Mercy*. He owes me. I will call him. Andrew, take off now please. The medicine I want will be waiting for you when you get there." Annabelle Rosa said.

"Ti, my Lady, I will collect the other two and get started." Andrew Re bowed slightly.

Maria smiled. "That one is very formal even when he is informal. He is also very handsome. Is he married?"

Annabelle Rosa stifled a laugh. "No, Andrew Re is still single."

"Hmm good, if we survive this, I may wish to talk to you Lady Rosa." Maria said.

La Noire walked in. "I understand you wish to take the tunnels to the temple city?"

Babs nodded. "Maria said it was possible, yes. We need to start finding answers."

Ti looked at Maria who shrugged. "We also have this clue. Maria is reluctant about it because of what it means. Still, we need to pursue it."

Ti showed La Noire the small metal piece.

"Where did you get this?" La Noire asked.

"*Wanderer's station*, The Station Master had it." Ti answered.

"He must have purchased it from the thief, which took it from where it was placed. It is too bad Lobo killed him." La Noire said.

"Could it be on this planet?" Ti asked.

La Noire shook his head. "Look you saw that from here you only see the twins as one star, yes?"

Ti nodded. "So, wherever, this was, you can see both stars in this position."

"Yes, probable at dawn. At higher latitude, but not near a temple there is no symbol for a temple." La Noire said

"Which planet would you guess?" Ti asked.

La Noire shook his head. "Maria, told you what this means did she not? It says danger! Do not go here."

Ti nodded. "Yes she did. We still have to go. We will find it La Noire somehow. We might survive with your help."

La Noire looked at Maria. "You are going with them?"

She cocked her head. "Yes, I gave them my word and my bond."

La Noire sat down. "I am a gypsy. What you ask ..."

Babs asked. "What is your greatest wish La Noire?"

La Noire thought. "I wish to publish my treasure, to share its beauty, and make money from it, of course."

"Done, *Gem Publishing* just signed a contract with you. I'll have my lawyer draw up the papers. We get ten percent of the profits after expenses." Babs said. "We can set up an office here and one on *Andreas Prime*. We will distribute your books through our resorts and cruise line." Babs said.

"You mean you actually do own the *Gem Line* cruise line?" La Noire asked.

"Yes, and I am connected to *Harrah's* on *Candaris Prime*. I own two hotels on *Andreas Prime*." Babs said.

"We are connected to a few more also. We also have other enterprises." Ti said.

"So, now you go into publishing to help me." La Noire said skeptically.

"No, you believe that these stories are worth saving. Also, that the music, poetry, and stories have value. If you are right, then you will make us richer, while you and your people also become wealthy from your resource.

If you are wrong, we still help save these stories for their historical value." Babs points out.

La Noire smiled. "You must have gypsy blood."

Babs shrugged. "I don't, know but I married a pirate."

Ti shook his head. "We were seafaring collectors of valuable goods."

"Ok, we will leave for the temple city this afternoon. We will want to be in the temple at high noon tomorrow." La Noire said as he walked away.

Babs called Mr. Jordan. She told him what she needed. He told her he would take care of it.

That afternoon they headed deep into the tunnels. Then turned northwest in the direction of the temple city. Every so often tunnels branched off and headed toward the surface.

Ti spotted a door that had large bars on it. "What was in there?"

"Weapons storage, would you like to see?" La Noire asked.

"Yes, I would." Ti said.

Inside were some strange weapons. Some were blades others were strange energy weapons. They seemed to be very light weight. The energy packs still showed that they had power. Ti raised an eye brow.

La Noire explained, "We figured how to recharge and refurbish these weapons. We expected the Shape Shifters to attack. I guess they are not coming now."

Ti shook his head. "Don't lower your guard just yet. We won a battle, but, maybe not the war."

They closed the doors and started out again. Maria smiled at Babs. "He is a good one, your boar."

Babs winked. "Thank you Maria. Will we get there tonight?"

Maria nodded. "Yes, but we will not enter the actual city, till morning. So, that we do not disturb the city. It is haunted at night. We will not go in. You will hear the noise for yourself Lady Allis."

After several more cycles of traveling they arrived at the outskirts of the temple city. La Noire dropped his pack. "We spend the night in this house tonight and enter the city in the morning."

Ti looked at him. "Why not proceed and stay closer to the temple?"

La Noire shook his head. "No you will disturb the spirits of this place. We will go no further tonight."

Babs took Ti's paw. "I am weary, we need to rest."

"All right, if you need to rest. It has been a long day." Ti said.

Maria smiled and nodded at Babs. "I will fix supper for us. You two should rest, you also brother."

La Noire nodded. "Ok Maria." He sat at a window and stared out at the tunnel leading to the city gate.

After they had eaten, they started to settle in. That is when the first sounds were heard. They weren't distinct. It sounded like distant music or laughter. The sound of children at play, but a long ways off carried on the wind. The problem was there was no wind.

Ti started to get up when Babs stopped him. "Leave it be, just rest. We will figure it out in the morning. This is not a time to go charging in."

"But, what if..." Ti tried to say.

Babs kissed him. "Your mind will play tricks on you. I think I know what it is. But, you need to just stay here for now. Trust your partner and wife for once Sire Maxumus."

Maria looked at her. "You know what is making this sound?"

Babs thought. "Perhaps, have you lost bears in the temple city at night?"

La Noire looked at her. "Yes, three young boar cubs recently."

Babs nodded, "I don't want to get your hopes up, but if it hasn't been more that forty days they may still be alive. Perhaps not, but at first light we should go look for them somewhere high and dark above ground."

La Noire thought. "There are two towers still standing near the pyramid. They are both almost as tall as the pyramid."

Babs nodded. "I hope you brought some weapons with you."

La Noire nodded. "Oui, energy weapon for each of us, but why?"

Babs leaned back. "I will explain in the morning, by then I will be sure."

La Noire looked at Maria who shrugged and said, "Trust her."

The next morning, Babs got up, made coffee, and breakfast for everyone. "Eat up everyone. Then we head straight for the towers you told me about. Hopefully we will find the young cubs still alive."

Ti looked at her, "Ok Babs, what are, we looking for?"

"A Siren Spider, they produce music and other sounds to lure their pray in. Then they put them a state of suspended animation for about forty days. Then they inject them with enzymes to dissolve them. Prior to eating them." Babs said.

Maria looked at her, "How big are these spiders?"

"They can grow as big as four to five SMU in length and two to three in width." Babs said.

La Noire whistled. "They are big!"

Babs nodded, "But they are not overly poisonous. Their venom produces sleep paralysis, which is easy to reverse. They are hard to kill, shoot for their eyes and legs. Their under bellies and top parts are armored in most cases. They are usually territorial, so there should only be one or two around."

"Wouldn't it, had been better to hunt them at night?" Ti asked.

"No, they only sing at night. That is their main weapon. The closer you get the more hypnotic it is. You forget what you're doing and they sting you. Also, they will usually attack from above, but they will attack from below." Babs said. "Their stinger is in their abdomen. That is their only offensive capability, except their song. As far as I know, they never sing in the day time."

"Alright, then follow me to the surface. We will head for the towers." La Noire said.

They followed a tunnel to the surface. The storm has blown a few trees over, but other than that no other damage was visible. In fact the storm seemed to almost clean the city. The polished white marble facades of the temple complex still glistened in the early morning sun light.

It took them almost a full cycle to reach the first tower. Its walls were almost twenty-four SUBSMUs thick. Inside they found a stone spiral stair case that led towards the top of the tower.

Babs pulled a phaser and started up the stair case. She was followed by the other three. Ti went up watching backwards. About half way up they came to a landing with rooms off to one side. In this room they could see the shapes of four cocoons.

Babs entered the room carefully and sliced open one of the cocoons. A red crystalline face stared back with dead eyes. She opened the other three all were in the process of some type of transformation. "I take it these aren't anyone you know?"

La Noire shook his head, "No, Shape Shifters?"

Ti looked at them. "I think so. How long have they been here?"

Babs noticed a green fluid dripping from them. "Sixty days, it has been feeding on them. That means your cubs are still probably alive."

They moved on up the tower till they reached the top. They didn't find anything else. But, the top of the tower intrigued Ti, it appeared translucent.

La Noire told him. "The towers were some sort of auxiliary observatory. If you stand in the middle of the floor and look in the direction of the stars, you will see what I mean"

Ti did. That's when he saw it. What the creatures of *Aldrin VII* depicted as a whirlpool. "I see it, the vortex caused by the solar winds from the two stars colliding it looks like a whirlpool."

La Noire nodded. "Yes, and you can only see it from *Aldrin VII*."

Babs looked at them. "Gentlebears, we need to find the cubs. They are not in this tower. So, they are probable in the other. If they are, then so is the Siren."

They quickly moved toward the next tower. When they reached this one the door seemed to be barred. It was not locked. It was more like something had pushed something against it.

Babs nodded. "It is in there, and it knows we are coming, so be careful."

Ti said. "I'll hit it high. Noire you hit it low. Babs and Marie follow us in."

Babs whispered. "Wait, just crack the door, and throw in a flash bang. Then push open the door. Our main objective is to reach the cubs."

Ti pushed the door open a crack and tossed in a flash bang. It went off with a load bang and a blinding flash. There was a high pitched scream from inside and the sound of scurrying feet against the stone.

Babs pushed through the door, and took the stairs two at a time, heading toward the top of the tower. Ti followed her up. Noire and Marie were close behind.

"Babs, don't be so reckless." Ti said.

"It's ok; it went down to escape the light from the flash bang. I think I found them!" Babs yelled.

Babs quickly cut into the silk covering the first cub. She found that he was still breathing. She pulled him out and gently laid him on the floor. Then move to the next. Soon, she had all three cubs lying next to one another.

"It is a good thing we got to them when we did. Call back to your camp, have Andrew Re fly over here, and take them back to Annabelle Rosa." Babs ordered.

La Noire nodded. "Their parents will forever be in your debt."

"What of the Siren Spiders?" Ti asked.

Marie noticed the paintings on the wall as did Babs. "No we should not hunt them. They are the guardians of the temple. We are intruders. We may find a way to communicate. For now we should leave the tower and go to the main temple, once the cubs are safe."

Ti looked at them. "You're sure about this?"

Babs nodded. "Diplomacy first, you can always blow something up, if it doesn't work."

Ti shrugged. "Yes, but if you blow it up first, you don't have to mess with the problems of diplomacy."

They carried the cubs out into the sun light and called for the medevac. Soon, Annabelle Rosa and Andrew Re arrived. They woke the cubs up and tended to them. Then they took them back to the gypsy camp.

La Noire led them to the temple. He positioned Ti and Babs in the center of the chamber and told them to look up. As they did, they noticed the suns start to separate into two distinct stars. The solar flares seemed to reach out to each other like arms trying to embrace. They also could see the tidal forces that looked like a whirlpool, which seemed to form slightly behind the two stars.

Ti smiled. "Ok, so the temple shows the two stars reaching out towards one another. Also, what looks like a whirlpool trying to pull them in? So, that is how they depicted it."

"Yes, but it is the crystals, in the dome of the temple, that allow you to see the stars separately. This is a stationary observatory. It only allows you to view the stars for one cycle." La Noire pointed out.

"But that was enough for their purposes." Babs pointed out. "They may have had other observatories for star gazing. From the pictures on the wall this was more. It was more important. It was almost a religion."

Marie nodded. "At, least at first perhaps, still you had three planets with similar races, with, three different interpretations, of the relationship between their stars."

Babs nodded. "Three different environments, three different effects, and three different interpretations of the same relationship, it makes perfect since."

"Until they gain space flight and start interacting." Ti pointed out.

La Noire shook his head. "But, there is no indication they changed their beliefs, from one planet to the other. Nor, that it caused strife between the planets. In fact the writings seem to suggest that they accepted the interpretation of the other planets, as being real for their reality, but not theirs."

Babs pondered that statement. "They believed what they saw with their eyes and their hearts. Each temple presented a different view, a different reality."

La Noire nodded. "Yes, as does the environments of the three planets."

"So representatives visited each temple and decided all three interpretations were correct?" Ti asked.

Marie nodded.

Soon the stars moved and were no longer in line with the top of the temple. It was time to leave. Babs and Maria convinced Ti to leave the spiders alone. After all, they killed the Shape Shifters. La Noire would make the temple off limits, except during the day light hours. Food would be offered periodically to the spiders. Maria noted that the Ancients would feed them deer carcasses. It was decided the gypsies would try the same thing, to establish a truce, if not an understanding.

Ti, Babs, and Marie found a corner of La Noire's library to discuss their next move.

"It is obvious what we are looking for is not here. The Shape Shifters thought that the clue was here." Ti pointed out.

"Oui, but as you have seen it is not in this library or in the temple." Maria said. "What else is there?"

Babs sat up, "Your father's, ledgers, and writings! You said that he surveyed *Aldrin V* and *VII* before deciding to settle your people here. He was the one that would have placed the markers."

The light bulb went off in Maria mind. "But, the papers are not here. What few survived I have on the ship. There were not very many, most were destroyed when the Shape Shifters killed him and my mother."

Ti looked at her. "None of his charts or maps, anything survived? He had to make backups."

"Yes, but when they attacked he was in the process of moving his belongings and office here. Everything was in the open. The first strike destroyed his files. The second destroyed his back up computers. When they came for him, he destroyed the rest and they killed him." Maria said as tears swelled in her eyes.

Ti got up and paced the floor. "Ok then we will go to *Aldrin V.* We know it's not here and it is safe to assume it is not on VI."

# CHAPTER 14

# Aldrin V

TI AND BABS gathered their team. It was time to leave *Aldrin VII*. It was obvious what they were looking for was not on this planet.

The parents of the three cubs that Babs and Ti had helped rescue brought them gifts. They told them that they would pray for their safety. Annabelle Rosa was also given gifts by the families of the sick. Several gypsies asked for a blessing from The Rose. Which Annabelle Rosa gladly gave them and admonished them to follow the Creator and His Word faithfully. Which the gypsies said, they had always done, after their own fashion.

La Noire also talked to Lobo. He told him to stay near the camp since he was going with La Renard and the others. That Lobo would be in charge till he returned. Philippe had just smiled and nodded.

Soon the Dagger was packed and the group headed out for *Aldrin V*.

Ti made a call back to *Aldrin VI* and checked on the crew of *The Dream in the Night*. He was told that everyone was safe and well taken care of.

He was also informed that the Marines had finished securing *Aldrin VI* and that all Shape Shifter had been eliminated. None had been willing to surrender and had chosen death to capture.

Ti turned to his small band. "Well, *Aldrin VI* is secure. I wish I was sure about *VII*?"

La Noire told him. "You do not have to worry. We have developed our own bracelet like devices, long ago, to detect and kill Shape Shifter. Did you not notice the amulets all the gypsies wore? If you are found without it you can be killed. If one puts one on it affects them the same as your bracelets do."

Babs smiled. "You were ahead of us."

Maria shrugged. "We have fought them longer, and the Bearilian High Council had other concerns."

Ti shook his head. "The Arcrilians, but what if this is all connected."

Annabelle Rosa spoke up. "Perhaps it is Ti. However, for now keep that thought to yourself. We need to stay focused on our current task, which is unlocking the mystery of the *Key*. Or at least what happened to the creatures of this system."

Babs shrugged. "We might just be the latest in a long line chasing that wild goose."

"Oui, but we might not be alone on *Aldrin V*. We should be careful. The Shape Shifters had a presence on *VI*. They tried to force my people off the Temple Island on *VII*. No one lives on *V*. The last colonist left twenty years ago." Maria pointed out. "And they were gypsies."

Ti nodded, "Andrew Re, cloak the ship."

"I am doing so now." Andrew Re said.

On *Aldrin V* at the temple complex in the central desert region just north of the equator a Shape Shifter Major was staring out over the sand dunes. Major Bandura was not happy. He knew that the colony on *Aldrin VI* had been destroyed, as had the fleet. He figured it wouldn't be long before the Bearilians decided to check out *Aldrin V*. He had wanted to evacuate, but the scientist in charge Dr. Van Doom had refused. He said that the Bearilians were slow minded creatures and wouldn't bother with this planet. Since they knew it was abandoned. The Major had his doubts about the good Doctor's assessment of the situation.

The major turned to one of his Captains. "Extend our security zone and double the guards."

The Captain dropped his head. "I cannot major. I do not have the personnel."

"What?" The major exclaimed!

"Dr. Van Doom pulled another twenty of our troop to add to the excavators and to help with the dig. I am having trouble maintaining our current security zone." The Captain explained.

"Bloody… Captain, I want those troopers pulled off the dig now. Put them back on security. I want the security zone increased. Tell the good Doctor, I do not care if he objects. I believe we are at risk. Do it Captain, now." Major Bandura ordered.

The Captain did as he was ordered. As expected the good doctor was not happy.

Dr. Van Doom changed himself into an almost clear crystalline state and went to find the Major. He was mad. How dare this Major Bandura countermand his orders? Well he would see about that!

He found the Major overlooking the sand dunes. "How dare you take those troopers from duties I gave them?"

The Major turned on the scientist he had had enough. His job was to protect this pampered snob. Not put up with his stupidity. "My good Doctor let's get one thing straight. My troopers' job is to protect you and your people. Not to act as your slaves. I and only I give them orders."

Van Doom was taken back. "How dare you talk to me like that? Do you know who I am?"

"Yes Doctor, but do you realize that we are on a hostile planet behind enemy lines with no hope of support?" The Major paused to let his words sink in. "Our fleet was destroyed, our colony on *VI* discovered and destroyed. We are alone behind enemy lines. I have twelve fighters and fifteen small transport drop ships to evacuate your people and my troopers off this Rock. There is a Bearilian Battle Fleet out there. You are supposed to be a great mind. You do the math."

Doctor Van Doom paused. "But, we are safe here they will…"

The Major shook his head. "Wake up Doctor. They are coming it is only a matter of time. You have been digging in this sand box for ten months. What have you found?"

Van Doom blinked. "We have found several interesting…"

The Major shook his head. "*The Key*, Doctor what about the *Key of Epoch?*"

Van Doom lowered his head. "No, nothing, but the answer must be here. We just haven't found the right chamber!"

"No Doctor, it isn't here. I don't think it even exists. Everyone is looking for a myth. These creatures just left. Why who knows? Maybe they found a better place to live. Somewhere, they didn't have to explain their different beliefs, to anyone." The Major said.

"The Fuehrer would not be happy with your assessment." Doctor Van Doom said with a sneer.

"Nor your lack of progress my good Doctor. Do not forget you promised results. I expressed my doubts about this venture based on the intelligence we had gathered." The Major pointed out. "Doctor, you should get back to work." With that the Major strolled off.

Dr. Van Doom slowly walked back to the dig site. He was even madder, but he was also scared. No one had ever talked to him the way the Major had. Did the Major know something he didn't? Was the situation really that desperate? Or perhaps the major had received a communication from the Fuehrer expressing his displeasure with the slowness of the digs results? All of a sudden the good Doctor was scared. Every option he saw lead to his death.

The Major walked back to his command bunker. If the Bearilians came he would have to resist. However, surrender would be an option, if he could get them to spare the lives of his troops. He had no illusions about their chances. His one hundred twenty troopers, sixty scientist, and workers were no match for a division of Bearilian Marines. Plus, his troopers were too spread out. He had given the order that none of his troopers could take bear form, and all had to stay in uniform. They were soldiers not assassins or spies. One of his Lieutenants questioned the order. The major explained to him that if a trooper was wounded and did not try and deceive the Bearilians they might treat his wounds and treat them honorable. However, if they practiced deceit they would be killed without mercy.

Andrew Re had passed over the temple and saw the activity below. He pointed it out to Ti.

La Noire looked at Ti. "What will we do?"

Ti looked at Babs who just smiled. "Our job."

Maria shook her head. "But, there is but a few of us and many of them. Also, we do not wish to damage the temple."

Annabelle Rosa nodded. "True, but who is to say what damage they have caused. At the least the fighters and jump ships must be destroyed."

Sgt. Fong spoke up. "We could use the missiles for that. Launch them in stealth mode. They wouldn't know where they came from. Then call in a Marine Strike Group."

Tiberius agreed. "Ok, but we keep them busy till it gets here. Just harassment, but enough to cause them concern."

Babs nodded, "We need to hit them from more than one side."

"OK, Fong you stay with Andrew Re. Target the fighters and jump ships. Don't waist all our missiles. Just use what you have to too get the job done. Then call in the cavalry. We'll keep them busy." Ti said

"Yes, Sir, Corporal you're with Sir Tiberius. Private you're with Lady Maxumus." Sgt. Fong ordered.

Ti nodded.

Annabelle Rose looked at Ti. "Teresa and I will go with our lady. You take Raphael and Maria.

La Noire looked at Ti. "Where do you want me?"

Ti thought. "Protect the ship if you don't mind."

La Noire nodded.

Ti called up a 3D map of the temple and the enemy positions. "If we can set up near these two dunes, we will have a good field of fire on their positions."

Babs nodded. "My team can approach from this ravine. It should take fifteen STUs"

Ti nodded. "We can circle around and go up this ravine. We will use long range sniper weapons. Stay hidden and move to your positions quietly.

Once we're in position we will notify Andrew Re and he will start the fire works."

Babs nodded. "Ok bears we rattle them, pin them, and wait for reinforcements."

Everyone nodded.

The two groups took off, while Andrew Re and Sgt. Fong set up the firing solution. La Noire climbed up the side of a dune and dug in. From here he could watch the approaches to the ship and provide cover to the two ravines, if need be.

Back in his command post Major Bandura was worried. He just didn't have enough troops to cover this sight properly. He thought about putting up a Combat Air Patrol, but what good would that do? He should withdraw his troops and the scientist. The suns would set in eight cycles. He would be facing a wormhole. Hopefully, away from a Bearilian Destroyer, even then the jump ships were small and fast. If they ran into trouble the fighters could buy them enough time to escape. After all that was their job.

He called in his captains. "We are going to evacuate as soon as the suns set. We will head for the nearest wormhole and head away from Bearilian Space."

One young Captain spoke up. "What of our mission? Dr. Van Doom said we were close to finding the *Key*."

"Captain Turlock, the good Doctor lied. We are behind enemy lines, surrounded by a Bearilian Battle Fleet and a Marine Expeditionary Force. Our Fleet was destroyed; our Colony on *Aldrin VI* discovered and wiped out. It will not be long before the come here. There is no *Key*. The good Doctor has been searching for ten months and found nothing. Our luck and time is running out." Major Bandura said, "Also, *Special Order Five* is still in effect. No trooper is to violate that order under any circumstance."

"But, Major our ability..." Another captain started to say.

"Has been neutralized by the Bearilians and will only lead to the unnecessary killing of the civilians and wounded. Remember, you are soldiers. You are to remain in uniform and a shape that is not Bearilian." The Major stressed. "If you fail to follow these orders, they have the right to kill you, if you are captured. If you follow them they will obey the Rules of War."

Another captain looked at him. "Why should they, we haven't."

"Because they have honor." the Major said.

Captain Turlock's anger flared. "What you two said could be taken as treason against the Fuehrer."

Major Bandura sighed. "If we survive, then you can report us."

Just then the first missiles arrived and the fighters started exploding. Major Bandura spun around. Too late, he thought. He had waited too long. "Get the scientist into the shelters. Take up fighting positions."

Captain Turlock, the young political officer, was the first to run out of the bunker. He was yelling at troopers to follow him. He had changed, into bright red crystalline shaped features, which resembled his hero the Fuehrer. All of a sudden he was thrown fifteen SMU back towards the bunker opening. Half of his head was missing. The other officers had left the bunker by slit trenches and saw him die.

An older captain shook his head. The young idiot thought he was invincible, now he is dead. He dropped down lower, as a slug dug in above his head. How many more would die and would he be one?

The Major put up a periscope to try and get a feel for what was happening. He could see the last of his fighters explode and his jump ships start to explode. A couple of pilots had tried to get airborne. Only to have their crafts hit as they took off. Then the periscope took a direct hit and was destroyed. He exited the command bunker along with his communications NCO, just moments before the roof was destroyed by two missiles. They crawled along the bottom of the trench.

Ti and Babs and their teams were a little frustrated. The fighters and jump ships were all destroyed. Only seven Shape Shifters had shown themselves well enough to be eliminated. Ti was sure one had been an officer.

Andrew Re called over the com net. "Marines will be in bound in three cycles. They want to know if we can hold out that long."

Ti thought. "Shouldn't be a problem, they don't seem to want to play."

Dr. Van Doom crawled over to the Major. "You have got to do something!"

Major Bandura looked at him. "Just what do you suggest Doctor Van Doom? Our fighters and jump ships are destroyed. My troopers are pinned down. What do you want me to do?"

Dr. Van Doom looked at him, "Charge them, and drive them off!"

The Major shook his head. "We do not know where the enemy is. They have struck us with missiles once, and probably could do it again. If I grouped my troops for a blind charge they would be slaughtered. Is that what you want Doctor?"

Dr. Van Doom's eyes got wide. "No, I want to escape!"

Major Bandura laughed. "We are not going to escape my good Doctor, but we might survive."

"No, I cannot be captured. I must escape!" Van Doom screamed.

The Major dropped his head. "This trench runs to the edge of that dune, then to a ravine, and the desert beyond. You have no hope of survival, but you may try if you wish. Here is a small pack with food, water, and a weapon. Good luck Doctor."

Van Doom looked at him. "You must give me an escort!"

Major Bandura dropped his head. "No, if you must escape your only chance is on your own. I don't believe you will make it, but if you stay low and move quietly you may. We will try and draw their attention. Goodbye Doctor."

Van Doom cursed him and headed down the trench.

The Sergeant looked at the Major. "What now sir?"

"Have Alfa Company open fire on the dunes in front of them. Even if the enemy is not there, it might pull their view away from the good Doctor." The Major said.

Alfa Company opened up. In response Babs and her group opened fire on them from behind. Three troopers were killed before they dug deeper into the ground. But, Dr. Van Doom had made the ravine he started running full out. That was his mistake.

Ti saw the movement and started following the curves of the ravine. He saw a spot where he had a clear shot down a length of it and waited.

Doctor Van Doom was running full out. He heard the shooting behind him. That pushed him even faster down the ravine. He hit a straight section and ran right down the middle. That's when it happened. Something hit him. He felt his body being picked up and thrown to the ground. He slowly picked himself back up and started to try and run again. His legs felt so heavy. Why was he so tired? He thought as the second slug arrived.

Major Bandura watched as Dr. Van Doom was thrown sideways a second time. This time he knew he would not be getting back up. "The idiot might have made it if he would have taken it slow and stayed in the shadows."

A slug burned in, smashing into his field glass and ripping them from his hands. He looked at the Sergeant. "Durban, it is enough. Let us see if Bearilians are honorable, open a channel."

"To Bearilian Commander, this is Major Bandura of the Forty First Escort Division, Sorlovian Imperial Construction Guard. I wish to discuss terms of surrendered."

General Puller turned to his communication officer. "Answer them and call the Scarecrow. This is the Command Center of the Bearilian Marine Expeditionary Force. Your troops will lie down their arms, remain in uniform, and stay in a non Bearilian form. Or they will be shot. These terms are not negotiable. Your troops that comply will be treated in accordance with *Galactic Treaties on the Treatment of POWs*. I will make no other concessions."

"Please inform your General, I have wounded and civilian scientists." Major Bandura said.

General Puller came on the line. "Major if your troopers and scientist behave I will personally guarantee that your wounded will receive proper medical care. However, if there is any treachery, I will wipe you out."

"I understand General. Please call your forces off. I will meet with their Commander." Major Bandura responded.

"I'll set it up Major, Puller out." Puller turned to the Com officer, "Get those Marines moving now, and give me Scarecrow."

Ti looked at his communication unit. "This is Scarecrow."

"Scarecrow ceases fire. They are surrendering. But they are expecting a military unit." Puller said.

Ti smiled. "Not a problem General. All my bears are in desert camouflage. Aphrodite and I carry military rank. She is a Naval Reserve Lieutenant, and I am a Ranger Captain."

General Puller smiled an Army Ranger. "Not too many of you around."

"No sir, the few and the proud, anywhere and anytime when death is on the line." Ti said

"Ok Captain, help is on the way. Their commander is Major Bandura stay loose, Puller out." Puller smiled. "Erase the last part of that transmission."

"Babs and Andrew Re stand down. Issue everyone rank emblems. We are taking prisoners." Ti said.

Soon a white flag could be seen. The Major and one Captain and a Senior Sergeant walked out, into the open.

Ti looked at the Corporal. "Feel like going for a walk?"

Corporal Tongan looked at him. "You really a Ranger."

Ti smiled. "Reservist now, but yes and I hold the rank of Captain."

The Corporal smiled and saluted. "This Marine would be honored Sir."

Ti and the Corporal walked out. The Major came to attention as Ti saluted him. "Major I am…"

"Maxumus, Tiberius Jr. Knight of the Maxumus Clan, Second Cousin to Beary Maxumus the *Destroyer of the Eye*. Yes, I know you Captain. I am Major Bandura. I have twenty wounded troopers and six civilians in need of medical care. I also have thirty dead. I have seventy combat capable troopers' forty-three civilians that are unhurt. Also, I have one dead civilian, the chief Scientist Doctor Van Doom." Major Bandura reported.

Ti looked at him. "How?"

The Major shrugged. "Our dear Fuehrer has made your family our public enemy number one, especially your cousin. Your family has affected his control over the Sorlovian Empire. That is why he sent us here to roast in this desert. To have us look for a nonexistent *key*."

"Ok Major, I have a small medical team. Have your troopers drop their weapons, all of them. Bring out their water, food, and any medical supplies. If you have medics, have them report to my medical bears. Put your wounded in the shade of that dune. The civilians over there and have your officers take command of their troopers. Major no funny business, I will have missiles rain down on top of them and us if necessary." Tiberius said

"I understand Captain Maxumus. Captain Nordura, give the orders, do as he said. Bring out the wounded." Major Bandura said.

His troopers pilled all their weapons neatly and went and sat were they were told. Two young lieutenants were brought out on stretchers. One was clutching a picture of his family.

Ti saw that and called Annabelle Rosa. "Get down here fast. There are many wounded."

Annabelle Rosa looked at the young Lieutenant. "You are hurt bad. I will try and save you. Will you let me?"

"I have a family. If I live the Fuehrer will kill them. If I die they will starve." He gasped.

Annabelle Rosa looked in his eyes, touched his head, and prayed for him. His pulse strengthened.

The young Lieutenant grabbed her arm. "You are a follower of the Word and the Creator?" He whispered hoarsely.

"Yes, I am The Rose." Annabelle Rosa said.

"Pray for my family Annabelle Rosa, Rose of the Stars." He pleaded.

Her eyes changed and she focused more energy into his body. Soon, his wounds started healing. "You are still hurt. But you will live. Behave and I will come and talk to you about your family."

The Lieutenant held her paw. "I am Kalona Atta."

Teresa and Annabelle Rosa moved from wounded soldier to wounded soldier. The Shape Shifter medics aided them. Soon they got to the civilians. Again two were just workers. The medics were gentle with them. All of a sudden one Medic grabbed a scientist and wrenched his hand clear of the blanket. He pulled a syringe from the scientist's hand.

The Medic showed it to Annabelle Rosa. "Poison meant to kill you."

Annabelle Rosa's eyes change. They changed to that of a dragon. She looked at him. He screamed and withered in pain. "He is faking and he tried to commit murder. Take him out to the Captain."

The Medics did as told. Ti searched him. He found that he was gestapo agent.

Major Bandura walked over. "Captain Maxumus please give me a weapon."

The Major turned to the Gestapo Agent. "You tried to kill their doctor."

The Agent spit at him. "She is the enemy…"

The Major shot him. "Thank you Captain, here is your weapon."

Ti nodded.

The Corporal walked over and quietly lowered his weapon. "You trusted him, why?"

Ti shrugged. "He wants out. His troopers want out. Look at them. They are disciplined solders. They are not afraid to die. He knows they out number us. He also knows that Marines are coming. He wants his people to survive. He doesn't blame us for those we killed. That is just the nature of the job. But that one risked the ones we are trying to save. That was intolerable to him."

Soon several Marine jump ships started landing. A Marine Lt. Colonel jumped out. "You Army?"

Ti Saluted. "Captain Maxumus, Rangers 14th Special Detachment."

The Lt. Colonel raised an eyebrow. "Special Forces, ok son what do we have?"

The Major walked over. Ti introduced him as the Major saluted. "Sir this is Major Bandura, he has proven honorable. His troopers are professional and are behaving properly."

Major Bandura dropped his head. "Thank you Captain Maxumus, but Lt. Colonel Jefferson there was an incident. Unknown to me a Gestapo Agent was among the Civilian Scientists. He tried to kill the Lady Doctor. One of my Medics stopped him and the Captain allowed me to execute the scum. But, it did violate my promise to your General…"

"Major, he was not one of your troopers. He was a spy. Who, you had no control over. You did us a favor. You have acted honorably. Your troopers will be treated properly. We will have to incarcerate you however." Lt. Colonel Jefferson said.

"We understand Sir, but may I make a request. Please send a signal that we were all killed. If not our families will be. What I have done will be considered treason. But my troopers did not deserve to die here,"

The Major said, "at least not for our dear Fuehrer. Also could you please incarcerate us some where it is green. Not this infernal sand color."

Several cycles later, after all the Shape Shifters had been transferred to a POW transport and hospital ship, except Major Bandura and Captain Nordura, who were quietly setting in a tent, Ti approached Lt. Colonel Jefferson.

"Sir, I, my wife, and Doctor Rosa would like to talk to the Major and the Captain before you take them away." Ti said.

"The General thought you might Scarecrow. He also said you're getting a little clumsy. The Admiral figured out who you were." Jefferson said.

"He flew with my Uncle and my dad. He was Golden Dragon 5. That is why he refuses to use call signs." Ti said.

Jefferson whistled. "That must have been some squadron."

Ti dropped his head. "Fifty percent KIA, another ten percent wounded in Action, and the survivors have gone on to make names for, themselves."

Jefferson dropped his head. "That high, I didn't realize it had been that bad."

Ti nodded. "Seventy-two combat engagements. Not counting special assignments."

"Ok, but make it quick. I need to get them off this rock also." Lt. Col. Jefferson said.

Ti, Babs, and Doctor Rosa walked into the tent. Major Bandura and Captain Nordura stood up and bowed. "Lady Rosa, thank you for treating our wounded. Some would not have survived without your care. I know it was not pleasant for you to treat our kind." Captain Nordura said.

Annabelle Rosa looked at the Fish symbol on a chain around his neck. "You are a follower of The Creator of the Universe and His Word, Captain are you not?"

The Captain dropped his head and touched the necklace his wife gave him. "My wife's faith is stronger than my own. I know that evil exists as does the evil one. I have seen his manifestations often enough. But yes my Lady, I believe. Though, to profess such faith is considered treason to our Fuehrer."

Annabelle Rosa then turned to the Major. "What about you Major Bandura?"

The Major dropped his head and laughed. "Lady Rosa, you already know that answer don't you."

"Yes Father Bandura I do. It must have been painful for you." Annabelle Rosa said.

"I died a little with each soldier I lost. That is the nature of war. A war our Fuehrer forced on you and us. I wanted to evacuate before you got here, but the lead scientist refused. He is dead. I told them the *Key* does not exist. I have been here before, during a time of peace. Sixty years ago I met a gypsy who had explored this planet grain of sand by grain of sand. If it had been here he would have found it. I found out ten years ago our dear Fuehrer led a raiding party back here and killed that good bear, for what? They found nothing. Now this, more creatures have died for a myth that does not exist. It is madness." The Major said.

Maria and La Noire were listening. "You knew our father?"

The Major shrugged. "We were both very young. I was with my father and he was maybe thirteen years. He was an explorer even then and he knew the desert better than anyone."

Ti took it all in, but it was Babs that asked the next question. "Your families what will happen to them?"

The Major and the Captain both looked down. "If the Fuehrer and his followers find out what happened here, they will be killed. In fact our entire settlement will be destroyed."

"Where are your families located?" Ti asked.

The Major looked at him. "Our unit is from the *Agricultural Penal Colony of Agora* on the Planet *Havenia* in the *Haverdine System*. We use to be a free colony providing agricultural goods. But then Dracdoran took over and declared himself Fuehrer. He moved his capital from *Balderas* in the *Medusa System* to *Dark Doom* in the *Caldron System*. They are followers of a Dark Way. As you know we are all capable of changing our shape. But this hideous crystalline shape is not our true shape. At least we don't think it is. But the Fuehrer and the followers of Waerloga the Yenaldlooshi require us to use this shape."

Annabelle Rosa looked at him. "Who is this Waerloga the Yenaldlooshi?"

"He is the deity that the Fuehrer and his followers follow. He is the creator of the seeing stones and the *Devil's Eye*. His name means oath breaker the one who walks on all fours the first Shape Shifter. It is said that he changed himself into an animal to get close to the Dark one to steal his eye, and make the seeing stones. The Dark one caught up with him after he had made the seeing stones and after seeing the evil that could be done rewarded him instead of destroying him. But he also made him a slave to his evil ways." The Major said.

"So those that live on Dark Doom are followers of Waerloga?" Babs asked.

"Yes, and those that lived on *Viper* in the *Medusa System,* also, but the three habitable planets in the *Caldron System* are the main stronghold of the Yenaldlooshians. The strange star gives them unusual powers." Captain Nordura said.

"Don't forget his allies. There are many evil group that follow similar deities and Dracdoran has made allies with many of them. They are all gunning for your family." Major Bandura pointed out.

Ti thought. "Ok Major, you help us and we will see what we can do to help your families. I can't make any promises. I know The Bearilian Government will not want to take any chances. However, I know someone who might want to try and help your families get out, again no promises."

Major Bandura nodded. "Thank you if it is possible. If not, I understand. We will cooperate and tell your people all we can."

Ti nodded. "Lt. Col. Jefferson, they are all yours. They were very helpful."

Annabelle Rosa looked at the Lt. Col. "Treat them well."

Jefferson bowed. "Yes Doctor Rosa."

The major stopped. "I remember something my friend told me so many years ago. Why does everyone look for things of science and space travel, in a place of worship and culture?"

Ti stopped and looked at him. "What?"

Major Bandura smiled. "Come on Sire Maxumus you of all bears should understand. A House of Worship is not a space port or a research facility. Come on Lt. Col. I should check on my troopers."

# CHAPTER 15

# Answers Hidden in the Sand

A FTER THE MAJOR and the Captain left, Annabelle Rosa sat on the edge of a sand dune and started laughing. "The Major knew they were looking in the wrong place!"

Ti looked at her. "What, I don't understand? I mean, I see his point…"

Annabelle Rosa shook her head. "No Ti, he knew they were looking in the wrong place. He let them. He didn't want them to find the proper place to look. He gave you a clue. We are looking for a city, an old spaceport."

Maria looked at her. "A lost city?"

La Noire nodded. "Shotoba, it has to be. Dad mentioned it, but never said were it was."

Ti looked at the golden piece. "This is the clue, were the mountains line up with the two stars at dawn."

They took out a map and looked for a mountain range that matched the piece. Ti threw the map down in frustration. "Nothing on the map matches."

Maria smiled. "It wouldn't. I told you it says do not enter. You would have to be seeing the mountains from the direction it shows at dawn, when the stars are at that angle."

Annabelle Rosa looked at it. "The Stars, raising from the southeast in front of the mountains, so the mountains are facing the rising suns in the northwest. If the angle is about right, I would say above the fortieth parallel but below the fiftieth."

La Noire nodded. "Yes, that seems about right."

Ti looked at his Team, "Any suggestions?"

The three Marines looked at each other. "Well since we are here, could we at least look at what they found? Maybe we could tour the complex?"

Annabelle Rosa looked at the setting stars. "Not tonight, tomorrow we should. Also, we should get in the jump ship and go to sleep. Night is falling and this is the desert."

Ti nodded. "We will set up a sensor watch. No one leaves the jump ship. Babs and I will take the first watch."

Sergeant Fong nodded. "Corporal Tongan and I will take the second watch."

Raphael responded. "Andrew Re and I will take the third watch. That way Private Den Po, Teresa, Annabelle Rosa, Maria, and La Noire can get rested."

Ti nodded. "Good idea, they can team up tomorrow night. That way everyone gets at least a couple of full nights of sleep."

Everyone grabbed a quick meal and went to sleep. Except Ti and Babs, they watched the sensors, as the desert came to life. Large scorpion like creatures tunneled their way out from under the sand. They started their hunt for food. As did other animals that hide from the day time heat created by the two suns. Here and there creatures struggled to see who would eat who, in the never ending cycle of survival, which such a harsh climate requires.

Babs watched as one scorpion pulled its prize back underground. "The people that lived and worked at this temple complex would have lived under ground also. Only the temple complex would have been above ground. Just like on the islands. They would have had to, to protect them from the desert heat and sand storms."

Ti thought about that. "Yes, but, not in the mountains and the hills, there they would have done it different. Wouldn't they?"

Babs shrugged. "We are missing something. I just don't know what. Everyone, I think has missed the same thing."

Ti shrugged. "I don't know what it is. I think your right, pieces don't fit right."

Babs sighed. "It is so lonely here at night. Almost depressing, I remember briefly thinking it was beautiful earlier in the day. At night it is cold and stark, even with a full moon."

Ti looked at the moon. "That's right *Aldrin V* had a small moon. *Vardus* was what the ancients had called it. Little more than a lifeless asteroid caught in the planets gravitational pull."

Babs sighed. "Still, it is a companion, for a lonely and sad planet. I wish we could go home."

Ti looked at her. "Babs are you alright?"

She shrugged, "Tired, that's all. Frustrated also, I know I am missing something simple."

"It is ok. We are not alone in that department. But, we will figure it out." Ti said.

"Or not, I guess it doesn't matter, if the *Key* truly, does not exist." Babs said.

"It is our turn, sir, and Lady Allis. It is time, for you to get some rest." Sgt. Fong said.

"Ok Sergeant, just some big critters running around eating each other. Stay loose and in the jump ship." Ti said.

The Sergeant and Corporal saw a large centipede appear on the scanner and disappear again into the sand. "Yes Sir."

The rest of the night, pasted quickly. At dawn everyone was up and moving. Breakfast was served. A plan was laid out. Raphael, Andrew Re, and the Marines would make up one team. They would explore the dig sight and search the area where the scientist had kept the artifacts they found. The rest would search the temple itself.

In the temple Ti gazed at the picture on the floor. That is when he noticed it. The two figures, one was wearing the skin of a large bear with blood dripping from its fangs. The other the skin of a large white, what? Bovines, no that wasn't correct either, but similar. They were locked in a death struggle.

"What if the symbols have nothing to do with the stars?" Ti said out loud.

Everyone looked at him. "What?"

Ti turned to them. "Why do we assume these symbols relate to the two stars?"

La Noire looked at him. "Because...it says... *Aldrin the Destroyer.*"

Babs cocked her head. "But, does it? Or has everyone just accepted that translation."

Maria thought. "How did they translate these symbols?"

Ti smiled. "From an old map, it was labeled the *Aldrin System* and below that name were these symbols."

"What about the word destroyer?" Teresa asked.

"That is easy, in their literature these symbols were first related to the person dressed as a blood drinking bear. A symbolism, I find a little revolting, a vampire bear. He was called Blood Bear the Yenaldlooshi, the Destroyer of Souls, and then just the Destroyer." La Noire said. Looking at the picture on the floor for the first time in light of the stories he remembered reading.

"If that is Blood Bear...then the other one has to be Shaman White Buffalo, the Pure of Heart, and this depicts their battle." La Noire said.

Maria looked at him. "If that is the case, then the symbols at the temples have nothing to do..."

Ti smiled, "With the stars at all."

Annabelle Rose shook her head. "The Major and Captain Nordura already knew that."

"But, if they did why..." Teresa started to ask.

Ti looked at them. "They were Shape Shifters. These planets originally belonged to them. He knew it. Let's go. I need to talk to him."

Two cycles later Ti, Babs, and Annabelle Rosa were on the *BAF Sledgehammer*, a POW containment and hospital ship. The others had opted to stay on *Aldrin V* and search some more.

Major Bandura and Captain Nordura were brought into a conference room. Ti sent the guards away.

Annabelle Rosa smiled. "I checked on your wounded. All are healing well and should recover completely. Are you being treated well?"

"Thank you Doctor Rosa. Yes, we are being treated better than I would have expected. Considering, we invaded your territory." The Major said.

Ti shook his head. "That is not totally the truth is it Major?"

Major Bandura dropped his head. "It is a matter of perspective Sire Maxumus. If you abandoned a house with no intention of ever moving back in and someone else did. Then improved it according to your own laws who would own it?"

"If they truly abandoned it...then it would be considered salvage. After, an appropriate amount of time had passed." Ti said.

"Six thousand five hundred forty-two years seven months three days to be exact, our peoples left these worlds. Those of us with the curse separated ourselves from those without the curse.

But, that doesn't tell the whole story either. The original people of these worlds, the Old Ones were collectors. They brought humanoids from all over the galaxy in the hopes of saving their race. Including eighteen members of the Blood River Clan, unfortunately all were Yenaldlooshi, witches that feed off of greed and other negative energies. Originally they had to use animal skins to aid in the transformation. They would put on the skin of an animal and become that animal. The radiation from different stars changed our people growing part of the brain that allowed for the transformation.

Anyway, the Yenaldlooshi took over the ship carrying them. They killed the crew and captured another ship. Nine took it and went to the *Caldron System* and became even more powerful. The other nine lead by Blood Bear continued on to the *Aldrin System*." Major Bandura explained.

"So, are you related to one of them?" Babs asked.

"No, I am descended from the Shaman of the White River Clan. They came and asked to save them from the evil they unleashed on themselves. Nine young Medicine Men Warriors stepped forward. I only know the name of three, White Buffalo, Wild Elk, and Bronze Moose. I am descended from Bronze Moose, and Captain Nordura from Wild Elk." Major Bandura said.

"I see, so they came to hunt the Yenaldlooshi?" Ti said.

"No, they came here to kill them and to return the harmony to these creatures that the Yenaldlooshi had destroyed. They killed the nine here. Six of the Shamen were killed. Only White Buffalo, Wild Elk, and Bronze Moose survived the battle. White Buffalo killed Blood Bear in the last great battle." Major Bandura explained. "The final battle took place on *Aldrin V*."

"The Pictures on *Aldrin VI*, what do they celebrate?" Babs asked.

"The wedding between White Buffalo and the one he called his Spring Flower in their language Lady Atta." Captain Nordura said.

"The Lieutenant's last name is Atta." Annabelle Rosa said.

Major Bandura nodded. "He is descended from Lady Atta and White Buffalo. The Third temple celebrates the birth of their twins one a shape shifter, one not.

The other nine were and are led by Waerloga. Well, the six that survived. Two perished on a strange planet when their spacecraft got caught in a wormhole storm and crashed landed with the *Devils Eye*.

That is where your Clan first enters the picture. They had been sent here to locate the *Gate of Ages* and what they believed was the *Key of Epoch.*"

The Ancient Ones understood wormholes. They also understood they were at a nexus of several here. They also learned to make artificial ones connecting gateways from one planet to the next, even one galaxy to the next. After centuries of harmony problems started to occur, the old ways were slipping away. Fewer young people were interested in becoming Shaman and some were more interested in using their abilities to change shape for evil purposes. So, it was decided those without the gift would leave by ship and gate. Some went to the other side of the galaxy, some to another galaxy. Our people also departed, some to a distant galaxy. Others went across the *Milky Way.* Our Clan went to *Haverdine.* We were responsible for destroying the *Gate of Ages* and the other gates on these planets."

"Time travel where did the Yenaldlooshi get the idea that it was possible?" Ti asked

"I don't know, it never was, perhaps they misunderstood the name of the *Gate of Ages* to mean gate of time. It didn't, it was the main gate, one that could connect to all the gates." Captain Nordura said.

"Ok, I understand which planet…" Ti started to ask.

Major Bandura smiled. "You already know. Why do you think the final battle was there? Blood Bear was trying to escape to reach *Caldron,* even though there wasn't a gate there."

Ti looked at him, "Where was the city?"

"We don't know really. The last time I was there I was a child. I remember the mountains, one tall, one short, and one slightly taller. The valley it was in was through the saddle between the short and medium mountain." Bandura said.

Babs nodded. "It is a small piece of a clue, but no real help."

Ti smiled, "Thank you Major Bandura and Captain Nordura."

"Sire Maxumus if you find the lost City. Destroy anything that can help the Evil One. Do not let them find any clues to the Old Ones secrets." Major Bandura said.

"I give you my word." Ti said.

"Sire Maxumus you do know *Andreas Prime* was not your original home world?" Bandura said.

Ti looked at him. "What are you talking about?"

"Your people migrated there with your canus. The dragons know the truth. You come from a system near the *Dubhe System*. Your clans left, I do not know why." Major Bandura said.

Two cycles on *The Sledgehammer* and four cycles of flying, Ti had answers and more questions. Some Annabelle Rosa said didn't matter. Yet he felt he had wasted six cycles. He understood more of the history. Now he knew that a loss of what they called harmony had caused them to abandon their worlds. It had made since to them perhaps a way to prevent war? The Major had purposely seen to it that they had been digging in the wrong place and had told Ti where to look to the best of his ability. Why? Ti shook his head.

Babs came over and sat next to him with some tea. "It is an old battle husband good vs. evil. Our kind has prided ourselves in being involved in that fight for a long time. Apparently your family has been involved in this story even longer."

"Only, since the *Battle on Pipet*, where we apparently killed two of the main Yenaldlooshi, or whatever they were. Demons, Shape Shifter, or witches whatever, they were or are a threat. Yet, I do not believe the Major is or the Captain." Ti said. "Hopefully the others have more."

Maria and La Noire were waiting for them. "It's good you are back. We could fill a museum with the artifacts they uncovered. But, we believe your suspicions were correct."

"Only partly..." Ti went on to explain everything they had learned. "That pretty well sums it up."

Maria shook her head. "Such a structure would require immense energy. I have heard of other races that use such gate travel, but it only works over short distances. Not galaxy to galaxy, that is impossible."

Raphael was listening and smiled. "Ti, what do you see around you?"

"Sand and lots of it, so what is your point?" Ti asked.

Raphael shook his head. "And you're a gemologist. Look at the sand."

Ti and Babs scooped some up. "You have got to be kidding me."

"No, I tested it, thirty percent Dylithiam crystalline based sand. I am willing to bet there are some huge mines on this planet somewhere. You could build a power plant to supply the energy you need." Raphael said.

Babs thought. "What if the core is made of Dylithiam? You could tap into it as a power source. This sand in depleted. But, we know there is at least one active volcano on this planet."

Ti smiled. "Ok, now we find what we came here for."

"But, how do we do that?" Maria asked.

"I launched two orbital probes before we landed. I had them looking for structures. Now, I'll have them look for old Dylithiam mines or geothermal fields. Even if they haven't been in use for almost seven thousand years, they should still give off an energy reading." Ti said.

Soon areas in the mountains both north and south of the desert started showing up. The mines were the first things they spotted. Then the faint signal of geothermal plants, long abandoned started to show up. All but one, that seemed to still be operational, though at a low setting. It was northwest of their location almost seven hundred fifty KSMU away.

They took off and headed in the direction of the signal. Once they arrived in the area Ti soon discovered he couldn't fly into the narrow canyon. Night was falling so they landed in an open valley southwest of the canyon and set up camp.

Here there was green grass, flowing water, and cool breezes. Ti was still concerned about wild life. Maria had convinced him that they were safe here unlike in the desert.

Ti and Babs walked into the meadow and looked up at the mountains. The suns were setting behind them and stars were becoming visible in the east. As the last beams of light were fading in the west, Ti saw something out of place, straight lines. One universal fact nature never makes straight lines. He marked their location.

Babs looked at him. "What did you see?"

Ti smiled. "Straight lines, up towards the saddle. I think they are some type of walls."

Babs nodded. "Well, we can check it out tomorrow. How do you want to set up the teams?"

Ti thought. "We leave the Marines, Andrew Re, and Teresa here. You, I, Annabelle Rosa, and Raphael go in. Of course Maria and La Noire go. Their dad was part of this story."

Babs nodded. "Ok, we leave a security team and head into the valley tomorrow morning. What about tonight?"

Ti shrugged. "I still think it is safer staying in the Dagger. Yet the view is magnificent."

Babs looked at the sky. "Your right, but we set a watch, and stay in the Dagger. Maybe cloak also, why give way our location?"

Ti kissed her. "That is why you're the brains of the outfit." They walked back. "Ok, everyone inside and button up and cloak." Ti said.

The night, pasted quickly. The next morning the team moved out into the early morning light. Ti looked back up at where he thought he had seen the straight lines. In the morning light it now looked like the side of the mountain had a rock face. Still he wasn't sure. Well, they were heading that way this morning.

Ti walked back over to where the others were finishing their breakfast. "Ok, once you're done get your gear and we will head out. Andrew Re, why don't you move the dagger to a more defensible position, you are exposed here."

Andrew Re nodded. "Why not let me take you closer to the saddle. I would rather have that cliff behind me. That way any one attacking will have to come down the valley."

La Noire smiled. "It will save us several KSMU of walking."

Maria shook her head. "You are lazy even for a gypsy."

"Ok, let's load up. We need to get this show on the road." Ti said.

As they flew towards the saddle they started noticing the straight lines in the cliff again. As they got closer they realized it wasn't one solid cliff face but a series of stone walls fourteen SMU high. Build above one another.

"It was a layered defensive position protecting the pass." Babs commented.

Ti looked at the structures. "Yes, but they are old, older than the temple complex."

La Noire turned on one of the optical scanners. "There is some writing on the third wall on the left. It is a very old script, maybe eighty thousand years. It is very old."

"So, these fortifications have been here a long time. They predate the Shape Shifters involvement with the creatures that lived here." Ti pointed out.

Raphael nodded. "I have been wondering about that. The Major called them collectors. Why? What did he mean by that and that they were trying to save their race?"

La Noire shrugged. "I told you, there were holes in the historic record. Most were short, only a few decades some longer. These may have been times of war or famine. I do know. They had colonies in other systems. I know some systems broke away. That is in some of the younger literature, found in the libraries on *VI*."

"This fort and your library predates that period. So, at least part of this valley has nothing to do with what we are looking for." Ti said

Annabelle Rosa shook her head. "Why would you assume that? Have we not learned that everything is connected? We should proceed with caution and take everything in."

Andrew Re cloaked the dagger and looked at Teresa. "You monitor the scanners and communications. I think the Marines and I will explore these fortifications."

Private Po looked at Teresa. "Sir, should she be left alone? I mean is it safe…"

Andrew Re laughed. "Private, she has unique gifts that you do not understand. However, you are correct, it is better for there to be two of you here to watch the ship and guard it. Sergeant, is that alright with you?"

Fong said. "You're in charge Sire Re. I think you, the Corporal, and I can search this fortification."

Andrew Re checked the scanners. "They have reached the top of the saddle. I guess we better get started also. Stay vigilant Teresa."

"Always Uncle, you be careful also." Teresa said.

Ti and his group crossed the saddle between the two mountains. Off to either side were small waterfalls falling down to a pool below. From the pool a small river flowed down into the valley.

Raphael pointed to a well-worn trail that still led along the edge of the canyon wall. They started down it. After traveling a few KSMU they started noticing stone buildings built into the side of the canyon wall.

La Noire shook his head. "How did they build these structures and why did they build them like this?"

Babs looked at this city like structure built into the canyon wall. "It is well hidden from above. If an attacker got past the fort, it would have been difficult for an attacking force to attack down this path. Then to try and attack those structures would have also been difficult. Only a narrow path leads up to the base. All the entrances are on the second level, which can be reached by ladders."

Annabelle Rosa just walked on by. "They are only ancient structures of the First Ones. There are only ghosts in those structures. Not what we are looking for. We should keep moving."

Maria slowly followed as did Ti. Babs and La Noire took one more look and slowly moved down the trail.

Raphael brought up the rear, but took one more look. His eyes changed slightly. Yes, there was movement, but he wasn't sure what it was.

At noon Annabelle Rosa called a stop. "We are at a good spot to stop, eat, and rest. We have a source of clean water and shade. Also, we can get off the trail and not be near any structures."

Ti looked at her. "Fine, but what are you not telling me Annabelle Rosa?"

Raphael spoke for her. "We are being watched and followed. I don't know by what."

Annabelle Rosa nodded. "It is keeping its distance, moving from structure to structure as we pass them. Or, should I say, they, I don't know if it is one creature or more than one. They are tracking us as we move down the canyon. It may even be just an animal. Raphael?"

"I don't know. That is the problem. I know it is there, but it is not giving off a normal heat signature." Raphael said.

Babs looked puzzled. "I don't understand?"

"There is a reason father adopted his children. We were born different, as misfits. Father, strengthened what he called, our gifts. Among other things, I can see in all light spectrums. Whatever is following us does not show up well in the inferred spectrum, but does in the ultraviolet." Raphael said.

Teresa was monitoring the scanners. She picked up two shuttles entering the atmosphere heading for the canyon's rim. They were civilian shuttles not military. "Den Po we have company coming. Please inform my uncle. I will let Tiberius know."

Private Den Po looked at her. "Yes Teresa." He turned to do it. "Sir Re this is Po, we have visitors coming. They may be hostile."

Andrew Re spoke into his com unit. "Private stay close to Teresa, she will protect you."

"Sir, I am a Marine…" Po started to say.

"He meant no offence Den." Teresa said, "But he is correct. You need to trust me and let me protect you." She said in a soothing voice, "I am Teresa of the Light; no harm will come to you, and this I swear."

Den Po looked at her she seemed to almost shimmer. "Yes My lady."

"Sire Tiberius, we have two shuttles landing on the rim of the canyon. One near our location, one closer to you, each has fifteen black hooded individuals in them. All have red trim but one, he has a silver trimmed robe. I am up linking the images to you." Teresa said.

Ti and Annabelle Rosa looked at the images.

"I thought you killed them all." Annabelle Rosa said.

"The ones that were at the temple, I did, all of them." Ti said.

They looked at the one in the silver trimmed robe, the satellite pulled in on him as he threw back his hood. Ti looked at him.

Annabelle Rose looked at him." Do you know him?"

Ti looked at the image again. "Only by reputation, that is Demon Ogre, The older brother of Doom Ogre. He was supposed to be dead."

"Alright, we need to move! We also need to separate. I need to take Babs with me and Raphael. The Red Snake will be back. We need to prepare. You need to take Maria, La Noire, and eliminate this Demon Ogre and his followers." Annabelle Rosa ordered.

Ti looked at her. "How did they find us?"

Raphael looked at him. "Simple he followed *the Dream in the Night*. Then they had Shadow Demons look for us. They found us. Remember we are dealing with Mac-Ta devils. Show them no mercy."

Maria looked at Annabelle Rosa. "What about Andrew Re, and Teresa?"

Annabelle Rosa told her. "Do not fear for them Maria. They will kill the devils heading their way. Do as Ti, tells you. He will protect you. He is a hunter."

Ti kissed Babs. "Do as Annabelle Rose tells you. She will protect you.

Babs looked at him and smiled. "I am not helpless. This time, I get pay back."

Ti started to head out when Annabelle Rosa grabbed him. "The Red Snake will be coming for her. I can protect her thanks to the gift of the Red Paw in her blood. However, you must find the three Mac-Ta priests, strengthening and controlling the demon snake and kill them. They will have Red Snake tattoos on them."

Ti looked at her and kissed her. "Stay safe my Angel."

She watched as he, Maria, and La Noire disappeared into the jungle. "You also, my Prince, come we need to find a defensible position and prepare for them to come for us."

As they moved through the jungle Raphael moved up next to Babs. "My lady you should know that Andrew, my wife, and I were the only survivors of a freighter that was caught in a strange cosmic ray storm. All the adults on board died, but we three babies survived. Our DNA was changed. Andrew Re secretes a metallic substance from his pores that encases his body when he becomes frightened. I along with changes to my eyes can produce energy from my body similar to lightning. My wife is just amazing; even I cannot describe her gift. We were found by slavers and sold to a freak show. That is where father and Annabelle Rosa found us and rescued us. Father blessed us and taught us to use our gifts properly. Teresa received a mixture of her mother's and my gifts."

Babs smiled at him. "Raphael, I live with Dragons and talking Canus. Why would your gifts bother me?"

"Thank you my Lady." Raphael said as he dropped back.

Annabelle Rose saw a lone tower on the opposite side of the canyon. "There, we will set up there. Raphael search and destroy."

"Yes Sister." Raphael said as he accelerated toward the tower. He quickly climbed the wall and flew through a window. He scanned the inside and saw movement. Two shadows moved toward him. "No you don't."

Lighting danced from his skin, then struck out at the two shadow demons, which were illuminated in bright blue light. They screamed and twisted. Raphael increased the intensity of the lightning till they shriveled up.

On top of the canyon two Mac-Ta priests screamed in pain as their tattoos caught fire and started to burn. Another Mac-Ta came over and killed them.

# CHAPTER 16

# Battle in the Valley of the Shadow

DEMON OGRE LOOKED at the two dead priests. "This is what happens when you fail Fa-Ra. We must revenge Ta-Ra. His great mother demands we hunt these unbelievers down and feed them to her. Gray Tor, take your team and find their ship. Kill any you find. I will release Cobrais the Red Snake Demon, so that he can hunt his prey."

Annabelle Rosa helped Babs into the tower. Babs seamed fidgety. "It is alright my love. I know it is here. Look into my eyes." A blue flame appeared on the tip of her paw as she touched Babs' forehead "Awaken, you are needed."

An image of a large green spider appeared. On its back was the symbol of the Red Paw. "How may I and my children serve you, dragon?"

Annabelle Rose thought. "The Red Snake is coming for our lady?"

"I and my children will guard her from within, but you wish more?" The image asked.

"Yes," Annabelle Rose said. "It will be coming in a physical form."

"You are a dragon, you know what to do." The image said.

"Yes, but not without your permission, your child may not survive." Annabelle Rosa said.

The image laughed. "We are antibodies; we exist to protect our host. I give you two of my children. They know their duty and will live and die doing it. Fear not for them."

Annabelle Rose drew out a single drop of blood and placed it on the back of two spiders Raphael had found. They grew and turned green with the mark of the red paw on their back.

They turned to Annabelle Rose. "We Hunt." They left out the window.

Babs looked at Annabelle Rosa. "What just happened?"

"Dragon Wraiths, in the form of the spiders in your blood stream. It is an old battle technique that dragons used to fight dangerous enemies." Annabelle Rose said. "They will hunt the Red Snake Demon and hopefully kill it. If not, they should at least give Ti time to find and eliminate the priests."

Gray Tor split his team. He led nine of his warriors towards the old fort. He sent five others to find the dagger. He wished that Demon hadn't killed both of the shadow warriors. They had lost their eyes. Yet, he knew he could release the green snakes.

He had the two Green Snake priests release their demon snakes tattoos. The tattoos slithered off their bodies and joined to form a large green snake. Gray Tor turned to it. "Find your prey."

Private Den Po winched in pain. Teresa walked over and touched his forehead, "Awaken."

Inside his body the image of the green spider emerged from a cocoon. "Use my children, if you can."

Teresa took two small spiders and dropped a small drop of the private's blood on them. They grew into large green spiders and looked at her. "We go."

Den Po looked at her. "What just happened?"

"I created Dragon Wraths, from the anti-bodies in your blood. They will hunt the Green Demon Snake that is hunting you. They were created by the arachnid gallbladders that Ti gave you." Teresa said.

"But, you're not a dragon?" Den Po gasped.

"No, but I have been trained in dragon medicine and can use some of the techniques. Den, I am a child of two that were chosen by Samuel. I inherited some of their gifts and grandfather strengthened my gifts. We are different, but we are still bears. We serve the Creator and His Word. Remember also my grandmother is a dragon and though she does not look it, Annabelle Rosa is also one." Teresa said. "Now, let's see if we can target a few of these devils."

Den Po thought, *why would, I fear her now, she took care of me when I was sick.* "Yes Teresa, I want some payback."

"Ok then, we, have six missiles we can use. Let's put one each on the shuttles and then we will try and pick other targets." Teresa said.

"This group has split; these five are moving toward us. Something is with them, but they are spread out. The other nine are closer together and are moving on the Sgt. and your uncle. There is another group of about thirteen moving through the jungle. Something is with them also. They are moving toward your aunt. Tiberius is moving towards them, but is at a safe distance." Den Po reported.

"Put two on the nine and two on the thirteen. Cloaked, then we will leave the dagger, and find a better place to fight." Teresa ordered.

Den Po targeted the shuttles, the two groups, and launched the missiles. Then grabbed his pack, his weapons, and followed Teresa out.

The missiles quickly launched and headed down range. Teresa locked down the dagger, recloaked it, turned, and then took off across the valley. Den Po followed quickly behind.

The missiles streaked toward their targets. The first to tip over were the two targeted at the nine approaching Andrew Re.

Grey Tor thought he heard something, but he couldn't see anything. Then all of the sudden the jungle around him exploded he was thrown to the ground by the concussion. The second explosion rolled over him, as did a ball of fire. He laid there for several STU. Then he slowly got up.

"Come to me!" Grey Tor called out.

Slowly five of his followers crawled out from under the broken trees. He slowly started looking for the other four. He found the first one with a large tree lying across his back. Gray Tor reached down and checked his pulse, there was none. He moved on. One of his other followers found the next missing member. His head was missing. The last two were found in the center of a crater. Their bodies were charred.

Grey Tor looked at the survivors. "Let's go."

A few moments later the missiles struck the shuttles destroying them. Demon Ogre looked surprised when he heard the explosions. That is when the next two missiles arrived.

The last two missiles tipped over; near the front of the group Demon was leading. One of the Red Snake priests was torn in half by the explosion. The Red Demon Snake withered in pain, but recovered. Five other monks were killed in the explosions.

Demon Ogre picked himself up off the ground and pulled a wooden splinter from his arm. He looked around six of his group were dead. They were struck down from the sky by an unseen attacker. Was Fa-Ra angry at him? Why had she not protected him? Was she angry at him because his brother had failed to protect Ta-Ra? "Cobras hunt your pray?"

The Red Demon Snake hissed at him. "Do you believe you can order me around Ogre?" Cobras hissed.

Demon Ogre looked into the eyes of the Red Snake. "No great Cobras, it is just that in my grief, because we had failed to secure your prey, and something seems to stand in our way, that I miss spoke."

The Red Demon Snake hissed. "It is the dragon. I will eat her soul also!"

Ti, Maria, and La Noire heard the explosions. They moved to get around the monks moving towards where the others were.

Maria looked at Ti. "What was that?"

Ti smiled. "Teresa is trying to cut down the odds and stranding our friends. She took out their shuttles and hit them; at least that is my guess."

La Noire shook his head. "She is so young."

Ti smiled, "She is a Knight of the Maxumus Clan. Do not forget she was trained to fight from the time she was old enough to walk. Also, she is part of the First Knights Family. She is worth twenty normal bears. Let's keep moving"

The five that escaped the missile attack broke into the valley. They saw Den Po and Teresa reach the edge of the trees, on the far side of the valley.

The Green Demon Snake started slithering quickly across the valley after them.

Teresa stopped. "This is where we stop. Den, I want you to lie down and use this sniper rifle. When I tell you to, kill the Monks with their robes open. There will be two of them. They will have green marks on their body, but do not open your eyes till I tell you. Or you will be temporarily blinded."

Den Po looked at her. "Yes my lady."

Teresa sighed. "Den, we are friends it is just Teresa." With that she stepped out into the valley two swords drawn.

The monks saw her as did the snake. They picked up their pace, started yelling, and cursing.

Teresa just smiled. "I am Teresa of the Light, come, dance, and die vermin." She flashed the swords out to her sides. All of a sudden she pulsed with a blinding white light. The light wave crashed across the valley.

The five monks were blinded by the searing white light. The Green Snake withered in pain but recovered and started back towards her. That's when the Dragon Spider Wraths appeared out of the ground.

"Now Den, take out the monks!" Teresa yelled.

Den opened his eyes and lined up on the first monk with the green snake tattoo. He fired the small rail gun. The slug covered the distance across the valley in less than two SubSTU. It hit the monk in the chest picking him up and throwing him like a rag doll.

The Green Snake was distracted for a moment by the death of the monk. This gave one of the Spiders an opening. He sank his fangs deep into the snake's neck, just behind his head. It pumped several units of anti-bodies into the Demon Snake, which immediately started attacking its internal systems.

The Demon Snake threw off the Spider and struck out with its poisonous fangs. Though the poison had no effect on the spider, the long fangs pierced its hard shell and delivered a fatal blow.

The spider reached out with one of its front legs and stabbed it into the Green Snake as it died.

Den located the second monk. He was running in circles screaming. Den lined up and sent another round down range. He caught the monk in a turn. The slug caught him just below the jaw and destroyed his head.

The Green Demon Snake screamed and hissed. It was burning, its priests were dead. It couldn't retreat and the other spider was circling it. The Demon Snake lunged at the remaining spider and missed. It jumped on its back and sank its fangs deep into the snake's head. It then started winding a web around the snake and itself. Sealing both inside an egg sack made of flammable silk.

Den fired again. A third monk dropped.

Teresa ordered. "Den, the last two are mine."

Den nodded. "Yes my …Teresa."

Teresa ran across the valley. One of the monks heard her coming. He swung his weapon in the direction of the sound. She slid under it and cut him in half with her sword and continued on. The last monk was chanting as Teresa approached.

Teresa saw shadows gathering around him. "Monk, I am here. Do you wish me to wait to kill you till you finish calling your demon? So I can kill him also."

The Monk stared with burned out eyes, "I am Gadard the wicked. The Green Snake…"

"Is dead, destroyed by Dragon Wraths." Teresa said.

"The other five monks..?" Gadard asked.

"Also dead, you are the last." Teresa said.

Gadard stood up and bared his chest. A large dark shadow started moving. A black shadow dragon started to form. Its red eyes started to glow.

Teresa held up her paw toward it. "I am Teresa of the Light, Grand Daughter of Isadora Valorous. By what right do you hold a dragon spirit?"

Gadard laughed. "He lost his name to me and his heart. Kill her Bradius."

The Black dragon started to fly toward Teresa. She held up her paw. A flash of energy hit the Black Dragon and bound it. "I told you, I am Teresa of the Light, dragon. I free you; he has no power to hold you. Let your spirit be free."

The Black Dragon twisted in the air. The monk withered in pain as a round object pulled out from under the skin in his upper arm.

Gadard screamed. "No, it is impossible! No one can break my hold on him, no one?"

Teresa hit Gadard, with another beam of energy from her paw knocking him off his feet. Teresa picked up the stone heart, "Bradius the banned one, whose name was erased. I feel your sorrow and pain. I forgive you in the name of the Clan Maxumus. Which is my right, be at peace lost soul."

The Black Dragon bowed and vanished.

Gadard was crawling on the ground. Cursing and screaming for Fa-Ra.

Teresa found him. "She cannot help you Gadard the Wicked. She is only a stone statue far away. You are now going to pay for your crimes." He rolled over and screamed, as she stabbed him through the heart.

As she walked toward the egg sack, she felt the presence of the second spider. "Teresa of the Light, burn, the egg sack quickly. Fully destroy this demon for good. I am near the end."

Teresa held up a paw and muttered one word "ϑυστιχε" (Justice). With that a fine blue light pulse engulfed the egg sack. It instantly burst into flames and disintegrated. Within a moment only ashes remained.

Den Po came out. "Teresa, now what do we do?"

Teresa smiled. "We return to the dagger. I begin the preparations to ask for forgiveness from Gamey the Brave."

"But why, I don't understand?" Den Po asked.

Teresa dropped her head. "I forgave the spirit of a dragon whose name was erased and recovered his stone heart. I am now responsible to see that is allowed to be buried properly. It was the heart of a traitor."

Grey Tor had seen the aura of the blinding white flash. It had struck the valley. He wondered what it was, but there was no time to worry about it. His prey was before him. There were three in the fort below him. The odds were still in his favor. Still, he knew that they had lost the element of surprise. "Spread out, find them, and kill them."

The monks did as they were told. They move toward the first door way. They drew their weapons and started to enter. The first two through the door had gone from the bright light of the suns into the darkened interior of the fort's last wall. Their eyes were slow in adjusting to the lighting conditions. They never would. One thought he heard a metallic sound bounce off the wall next to him. He started to scream. It was too late. Both monks were shredded by the explosion.

Sergeant Fong smiled to himself. Two down, how many were left? He wondered.

Grey Tor watched as his other three monks fell back from the wall. He also backed away. Just then two more were picked up and thrown to the ground by an unseen hand.

Corporal Tongan slid back behind the wall. It had been an easy shot. They had been standing close together. The builders' of this fort had designed it to be defended by just a small force, from concealed positions. He was glad he wasn't trying to take it.

Gray Tor and the remaining monk fell back into the trees. He didn't know what to do. That was when Andrew Re appeared out of nowhere.

He grabbed the other monk, just broke his neck, and dropped him.

Grey Tor stared at the metallic creature standing in front of him. "What are you?"

Andrew Re laughed. "I am a protector of the Maxumus Clan, prepare to die."

Grey Tor charged with his wicked curved sword. He slashed down at Andrew Re, who just blocked the blade with his left paw. The blade snapped when it came in contact with his metallic shell. He then hit Gray Tor with his right paw.

Grey Tor felt his jaw snap and shatter. He flew through the air and landed on his back. He thought why? Why hadn't Fa-Ra helped them?

Andrew Re looked at him and shook his head. "No stone statue can help you now." He flared out his paw slowly. A metal pole formed. "This is made from my sweet glands, now Justice."

Grey Tor screamed in horror as Andrew Re pinned him to the ground. He felt no pain as this strange creator broke off the pole from its own body. So, this is death, he thought as the darkness enveloped him.

Andrew Re walked back towards the fort. He started to shed his shell. Sergeant Fong came out. Andrew smiled. "Here its titanium, it should be worth something. No point wasting it."

Fong smiled. "You secrete metals?"

"Yes, whenever there is danger or my body detects an attack." Andrew explained.

"Nice trick." Corporal Tongan said.

"It is actually bothersome, but it does have some advantages." He produced a small gold nugget in his paw and gave it to the Corporal. "I am never without resources."

"Like, I said a real nice trick!" Tongan said pocketing the nugget.

Ti, Maria, and La Noire reached the top of a hill and crawled behind some boulders near the edge. Down below them they saw eight monks and the Red Snake slithering beneath them.

Ti turned to his companions. "Try, and take out the Monks with the red tattoos they belong to the Demon Snake."

Maria looked at him. "I only see two. Where is the third?"

"Maybe he is already dead. A couple of them look injured and there is not as many as there was." La Noire said.

"Alright you two take out the Snake Monks. I'll try and kill their leader. Ti said.

All three fired at the same time. The Red Snake Monk La Noire was aiming at was on the outside. The slug caught him under his left arm and tossed him sideways. Another monk stepped into the slug meant for the second Red Snake Monk and was killed. The Red Demon Snake rose up in pain at the death of the first monk. Ti's slug burned into its flared hood.

In response The Snake sprayed the hill with venom. The rocks they were hiding behind started to disintegrate.

Ti yelled. "Go get out of here!"

All three scrambled down the back side of the hill and down a ravine for close to a hundred SMU. They then took to ground.

Ti looked at them. "Is everyone alright?"

"Yes, but I missed. Another one stepped in front of my target." Maria spat angrily.

"It is ok, mine hit the snake, and almost got us, melted." Ti pointed out.

"Mine is dead for what it is worth." La Noire grinned.

Cobras, was angry now he hissed. "Find them, kill them. What are you waiting for?"

"You two see if you can track them. The rest of you spread out." Demon Ogre ordered.

The two monks cautiously climbed the hill. When they reached the top they found nothing. They came back down and reported, "There is nothing up there, no tracks to follow. The venom erased everything."

Demon Ogre nodded. "Cobras, we will continue on towards our prey. We will find them together."

Cobras calmed down. "Yes, you are right hurry this way."

Ti climbed the next hill he could see the Red Snake moving in their direction. Below them he saw two large Green Spiders digging in either side of the trail.

Maria pointed toward them. "What are those two?"

Ti replied, "Dragon Wraths, I have heard of them but never seen one used before. Only the most powerful and ancient dragons were powerful enough to create them. They are a weapon designed to kill a foe without getting close to it. A guided missile of sorts, you could say."

La Noire looked at Ti. "But, we don't..."

Ti shook his head. "No La Noire, we do, and she is more powerful than even she understands."

Maria nodded. "Brother did you not understand? The Rose is a dragon at least part dragon."

"She is one of the "Seven" the children of Sire Samuel Valorous and Lady Isadora Valorous. Her father is the Sage of *Harvenger's Glenn*. The First Knight of the Maxumus clan." Ti explained.

"I still don't understand." La Noire said.

Ti shook his head. "It is a long story. Let's just say Annabelle Rosa is older than she looks and leave it at that."

"They are coming in range. What do you want us to do?" Maria asked.

Ti thought. "Wait for the Wraths to attack. Then hit them."

Maria and La Noire nodded and spread out. La Noire was still thinking about what Ti had said. He thought the Rose was in her sixties. Still, young for a bear of course. But, Ti had said she was older than she looked and she did have those weird eyes. Oh well, he would ask later.

Demon Ogre was now worried. He was down to only five monks, and only one could serve as a refuge for the snake. This was not good he should withdraw, but his shuttles were destroyed. The only thing left to do was continue and kill the prey he had come for.

The Red Demon Snake broke into a clearing. Cobras, was about half way across when the Spider Dragon Wraths attacked. The two Green Spiders came out of the ground on either side of the Snake driving their fangs deep into his side and pumping their poison into him.

Cobras thrashed throwing them off. He knew he was hurt. He was also angry. He turned and smashed his body down on one of the spiders. It turned over as he came down on it and sank its fangs into him pumping its venom into him as it died. Cobras, was a strong demon, but these anti-bodies were made from his demonic poisons. So, they attacked his internal systems. He was experiencing intense pain. That is when it occurred; his third and last monk pitched back and was thrown to the ground.

On a hill not too far away Maria lowered her rifle. "Well, I didn't miss that time."

Ti said. "Ok, let's fall back."

Back in the valley below Cobras hissed and screamed as his third monk died. He then sprayed poison in every direction. Some fell on one of the other monks. His cloths caught on fire as did his exposed skin and fur. He screamed in pain then died. Cobras winched when he realized it had no effect on the last spider that was now circling him.

The Green Spider looked at him and spoke. "Let us end this. It is time for you to return to the fires that spawned you forever."

Ogre pulled his last three monks away from the battle. Cobras and the Spider started maneuvering around each other. He could tell the Snake was at his end and would lose this encounter. He just didn't understand how it was possible. Cobras was a strong demon. Yet, here he was about to be destroyed on this strange planet.

The four monks quickly moved through the trees. Demon Ogre was in the Center. He heard what he thought was a single pop. All of a sudden his three remaining monks were thrown from their feet. Two were missing part of their face. The third had a hole in his chest and a large pool of blood was spreading out around him.

That is when Demon Ogre felt himself being picked up and thrown to the ground.

Ti started to smile until he saw Demon Ogre stand back up. Then he heard Ogre scream. "You will have to do better than that!"

Ti lined up and fired again. This time he saw Ogre's head snap back again. Ogre was thrown to the ground. Again he stood back up and laughed.

Annabelle Rosa was watching from the tower. She spoke into her com unit. "Ti, fall back to my location. You cannot kill him. This is a job for a dragon."

Ti signaled the other two to follow him. They moved back to the tower.

Demon Ogre sat on the ground and untied his robe. Well, it was time. He knew Cobras was dead, so was everyone else. How long had it been since he and the beast had fused together? It had been a benefit to both. It had made him invincible and it had allowed the beast a hiding place. Come my friend, it is your turn to take over our body and transform us into your form.

All of a sudden Demon Ogre was thrown down on his front paws as two large wings protruded from his back. A long tail sprouted out of him as his feet and front paws changed into that of a large cat. Then his head changed into that of a large hawk. He screeched.

Annabelle Rose looked out. "So it is her. Very well, it ends here."

Ti looked at her. "What is it?"

"Behold Cyllene the Griffin, Cyllene the wicked Queen of Evil. She is mine. Stay here this is a dragon's fight not yours!" Annabelle Rosa said.

Annabelle Rosa jumped from the window and sailed down to the ground below. She ran into the woods. As she approached the clearing she heard another high pitch screech.

Annabelle Rosa let out a dragon's roar that pierced the forest around her.

Cyllene snapped her beak in response to the sound of a dragon's roar. "You have called me forth to face a dragon? Are you a fool? That is the only creature in the Universe that can kill us!"

Annabelle Rosa broke out into the edge of the clearing. She called her name, "Cyllene, I have come for you. Shall we dance and end this once and for all?"

Cyllene's head snapped towards the sound, her bird eyes widened. "It is you the hidden dragon!"

"No Cyllene, I am not hidden. I am Annabelle Rosa Valorous Knight of the Garter of the Maxumus Clan. Daughter of Isadora and Samuel Valorous, First of the Seven Children of Harvenger's Glen, the first Rose of my father, and a Dragon of the Clan Maxumus. Fear me." Annabelle Rosa said.

Cyllene snapped her beak. "I remember you! You are the Rose! You tried to kill me before. It was you that forced me into hiding all these years! Why must you torment me? Leave me alone or...or I will be forced to destroy you!"

Annabelle Rosa just smiled a dragon's smile. "Come on, are you a Griffin or a pigeon. Demon Ogre whose body you share is braver than you. Come let's dance one last time."

Armored scales stared to form on Annabelle Rosa's body as she became slowly more dragon in appearance. "I said come and dance Cyllene. I will meet you on the ground or in the air your choice!"

Cyllene looked at her and took to the air. She screeched a fireball out in Annabelle Rosa's direction only to find that Annabelle Rosa was no longer there.

That is when Cyllene felt a stream of flame hit her left wing and sweep down her left side. Her wing folded and she tumbled and crashed head first into the ground. As she stood she screeched in pain. "How did you get above me?"

Annabelle Rosa landed and drew her sword. "I knew how you would attack. Now I am going to kill you."

Cyllene had fought many battles in her long life. She had won all but one. That one had left her scared, had forced her into hiding, and merging with a half dead follower of Fa-Ra. Now that same dragon stood before her. Cyllene could tell that her left wing was not only burnt, but also broken. She could no longer fly. A bird on the ground was at a disadvantage, but half her body was that of a lion. She charged at Annabelle Rosa. Her front claws ripping at her clothes and scales. Cyllene could feel her razor sharp claws connect. She smiled as she passed her pray. Then it happened all of a sudden, her strength left her. She heard Demon Ogre scream in pain deep inside of her. She crumbled on the ground.

Annabelle Rosa walked over. "Both of your lives end here Cyllene; Demon Ogre has already died within you."

Cyllene looked up at the Rose. Her vision was blurring. "But, I know I got you!"

Annabelle Rose half smiled. "Yes Cyllene, you have wounded me. Few ever have. Remember, I am a dragon. Now die Griffin." With that Annabelle Rosa twirled her sword and removed Cyllene's head.

She walked over and sat on a stump.

Ti and Raphael ran over. Ti saw the blood running down her side. "My Annabelle…"

Annabelle Rose smiled a tired smile. "It is alright my Prince. It looks worse than it is. Give me two of your arachnid gallbladders."

Ti did. She swallowed them as Raphael inspected her wounds.

Raphael looked at his sister. "You are going to have to shed your scales so I can treat you."

Slowly the armored scales retreated beneath her skin. The gash in her side looked bad, but Raphael just cleaned it out and examined it. "It is not too deep your scales prevented her claws from cutting beneath your layer of bone plating. It is good that you are both dragon and Maxmimus. The two armors work well together. I will close the wound. It will hurt."

Annabelle Rosa nodded and took Ti's paw. Raphael formed a small ball of blue lightning in his right paw. He placed it over the leading edge of her wound and followed it along its length about ten SubSMU. The skin sizzled as it sealed together. Raphael then bandaged her side. "Teresa can fix it up better when we get back. This will do for now sister."

Annabelle Rosa let out a small breath of flame and let go of Ti's paw, then kissed him. "My young Prince this time you came to save me. Come we still have work to do."

She walked over to Cyllene's decapitated body. Then she covered it in dragon's fire. Raphael assisted with lightning fire. Soon all that was left of her and Demon Ogre was ashes.

"Now for the snake, come on." Annabelle Rosa said as she slowly walked towards the clearing.

In the clearing was a large red and green egg sack made of spiders silk. A voice called out from inside it. "Please my lady burn the sack. I am near my end. The snake is near death finish it!"

Annabelle Rosa breathed in a deep breath. Her side hurt as she released her flame. The egg sack almost exploded from the intensity of the dragon's fire. Then it, Cobras, and the spider were gone.

Annabelle Rosa slumped to the ground. "My lady is safe from that curse once and for all."

Ti looked at her. "My sweet lady, are you going to be alright?"

"I am alright my sweet Prince. We should call the others and get going." Annabelle Rosa said.

Ti shook his head. "No, we return to the tower and call Teresa."

Two cycles later Teresa came out of the room where Annabelle Rosa was resting. "I am glad you called for me. Father did a good job and she took a poison anti-dote. But, she fought a Griffin, an old and treacherous one. If it had been any of you that fought her, you would have died. Even you father. I had to reopen the wound and put in a drain to pull out infection. Maria and Allis are with her now." Teresa said.

Ti looked at her. "Will she be alright?"

"Yes, but she will require at least a week to recover. I want to keep her sleeping at least for twenty-four cycles. She will not be happy but I am now in charge." Teresa stated mater a factually.

"Well, in the morning I'll continue down the valley by myself. The rest of you can..." Ti started to say.

"No, did I not say I was in charge my Prince. I am the only Medic left. I cannot leave my Aunt and I will not have any lone wolf antics out of any members of this team. The Marines and I will stay with my Aunt along with Lady Allis. You will take uncle, father, and Maria with you. La Noire can choose." Teresa said

"I will stay here." La Noire said.

Ti looked at Teresa. "What about the dagger?"

"I secured it. You know no one can find it with it cloaked. My prince you know that I am right." Teresa said.

Babs laughed. "What you didn't argue with her?"

Ti shook his head. "No, I have known too many female doctors that use that tone of voice, when they want to make a point. Besides, she is probably right. You would probably back her. However, I thought you would insist on going."

Babs nodded. "I would have, but, Annabelle Rosa and I have the same blood type. Teresa convinced me she might need me here to make a serum for her.

I made up a room for us up stairs. Come on let's get some rest."

Ti followed her up the stairs, she quietly undressed him. The next morning Ti looked down at his sleeping wife. He smiled. He was a lucky bear, probably the luckiest in the universe. Of course he knew that was how Beary, Octavious, and even Artemus said they felt. Yet, here on this rock orbiting around these twin stars, he knew he was.

Babs reached up and touched his face. "Ti, what are you thinking?"

"Just how lucky I am to have you love me, Babs Allis." Ti said.

She reached up and kissed him as a single tear fell from her eye. "No my love it is I who is lucky to have you."

Maria was standing at the door and smiled, then knocked, "I am sorry but it is time for us to go."

Ti smiled and kissed his wife. "Duty calls, I'll be right there Maria."

# CHAPTER 17

# The Temple of the Crossroads

TI LOOKED AT his little band. Raphael, Andrew Re, and Maria all three smiled at him. He waved at Teresa and Babs. Sgt. Fong walked over.

"Sir we will guard them with our lives, I promise, especially, the Rose and Lady Allis." Sgt. Fong said.

Ti nodded. "Listen to Teresa Sgt. She may be young but…"

"Don't worry Sir; we know what Lady Teresa can do. She is smart and totally ruthless." Fong said.

Raphael smiled. "She takes after her mother."

Ti replied. "Still, be careful. If necessary evacuate the Rose and the others and come back for us."

"Yes Sir, I understand whatever the Rose needs." Fong said.

With that they headed down the path. Ti looked back and waved.

Babs smiled and waved back.

"It is ok my lady, you are safe with me. They will protect him." Teresa said.

"Teresa I am a warrior also. I have killed many times. Some of my kills were up closes and personal. I am not afraid. Also, Ti is a hunter. He is a Knight Protector of the House of Maxumus as am I. You are also, but we all serve the Clan and each other." Babs said kissing her.

Teresa grabbed her paw and kissed it. "But, Regent, Grandfather said we were…"

Babs held her paw. "Remember Teresa, no Knight of the Maximus Clan kneels before anyone, but the Creator of the Universe and His Word. I work for Beary. He is now head of the Family. He works for his mother for she is the Empress. She works for all the creatures of *Andreas Prime*. It is a big circle."

Teresa smiled. "You love Tiberius. What is love like?"

"Has not your mother told you?" Babs asked.

Teresa shrugged. "She has told me to be careful of my powers and not to let my passion get out of control."

Babs smiled. "Well, I can see where that could be a problem. However, passion is very important, but so is tenderness. It is hard to explain. I was raised by our ways, the ways of the islands. Where it is a wife's job to please her husband and give him cubs. Ti has shown me there is more to it. That is even harder to explain. I am in love with a Maxumus boar. Angelina calls it a hunger. Pompey says it's a need like air. It is an addiction like a drug. I hurt when he is not with me. I need his touch. It is not always like that. Ti was my first; however I have dated other boars. I never felt or fell for them the way I did him."

Teresa nodded. "But, how did you know he was the one?"

"You will laugh. I saw his face in a dream years ago. I figured he was just that, a dream. Then there he was." Babs said.

Teresa smiled. "So you dreamed of him. Is he everything you hoped for?"

Babs shrugged. "Ti is no dream. He is reckless with his own safety and stubborn to a fault. He allows his emotions to override his common sense, just like he did on *Helios IV*. He is also the most tender and loving boar in the Universe. Our mothers instruct us at a young age, on the duties of a wife to her husband. They never mention a husband's duty to his wife. Ti taught me that they exist also. His simple acts of love allowed my passion to soar to even greater heights. In the end we both benefited from what he taught me."

"I still don't understand?" Teresa asked.

"Love is tricky. It is like so many things in life, it is about balance. A husband and a wife are not slaves to one another. They are missing pieces of a puzzle. When the pieces fit you get the right picture, one of balance. A picture where hope, love, and faith are the foundation and corner pieces, of the picture you build. It does not mean there are not storms or strife in the picture, there always are. When you get married you become one with your partner.

For Ti it has been hard to share all of his deepest fears. Most revolve around the loss of his father. Then, I went and got careless. When you get married you have to learn to share all of who you are. That can be real hard." Babs pointed out.

La Noire was listening. He smiled, and then walked into another room. He wasn't sure why he hadn't gone with the others. He knew the danger was over. He just felt the sign post was meant for him. So, he had stayed behind.

Ti and the others had covered several KSMU. Then the trail turned towards a sheer cliff about a quarter of a KSMU away. They slowed down and started to survey the area.

Raphael shook his head. "That is where the trail leads. There is nothing but, game trails leading away from it."

Ti thought about it. "Well, we might as well see where it is taking us."

Andrew Re nodded and led off. Ti followed. Maria and Raphael brought up the rear.

Maria was watching Andrew Re. "Raphael does Andrew have anyone waiting for him?"

Raphael looked at her. "What do you mean?"

"Annabelle Rosa told me he has no mate." Maria said.

"That is true he is unmarried and unattached, why?" Raphael asked.

Maria smiled. "I like Andrew. I am interested…"

"Maria, we are not normal…" Raphael tried to explain.

"Raphael, I know about your gifts remember. Plus, I am a gypsy remember. Do you think such a thing would bother me? Do you think he could go for me?" Maria asked.

"I don't know Maria? I cannot speak for my brother. However, he could do a lot worse." Raphael said with a smile.

It wasn't long before they had covered the short distance to the cliff. The trail followed its base for another one hundred fifty SMU. Then it seemed to turn into it. What they found was what appeared to be a vine covered cave entrance. They soon realized it was an artificial tunnel. It had been bored through the mountain. At one time an Iron Gate or door had covered the entrance. Time and tectonic activity had displaced the doors. They had fallen to the floor of the entrance.

The tunnel was only eight SMU wide and twelve SMU high. The floor, sides, and ceiling each seemed to be made of interlocked stone slabs. Each was fitted so tightly that even the slimmest blade wouldn't fit between them. They continued to move slowly down the tunnel. After twenty STU they began to see a glint of light toward the other end of the tunnel.

Ti slowed them down a little more as they got closer to the end. He started looking for traps or triggers but found none. When they final broke out of the tunnel, they were standing on a ledge overlooking a valley. Hundreds of small waterfalls rushed down the sides of the mountains surrounding this bowl shaped valley. In the middle was a small lake and in the middle of the lake was a large pyramid shaped temple with circler arches all around it. Some were broken others still seemed intact.

Ti looked at the stairs, which were cut into the side of the cliff. They led down to a trial, which led to a stone bridge. It led to the island in the center of the lake. He signaled the others to follow.

Maria reached out for Andrew's paw. "Is it not breath taking?"

Andrew looked at her. "Lady Maria I… yes, it is a wondrous sight, but we should stay vigilant."

"Oui Andrew, you are correct. It could be dangerous here. I almost forgot the sign by the road. You will protect me Andrew, Yes?" Maria asked in a sweet voice.

Andrew looked into her eyes. "Of course Maria, I will protect you…"

"Will you two wait till we get back to the ship? We have, work to do." Raphael scolded. He then laughed as he moved passed them to join Ti.

Ti stopped at the bridge. There seemed to be a force field in front of the bridge.

The others joined him. Andrew Re reached out and touched the force field. He was pushed back with the same force he had applied.

"It is a simple barrier field, but a variable strength one. The harder you try to force it, the harder it will repulse you." Andrew Re reported.

Ti nodded. "Ok, so we are probable not going to overpower it. So, there has to be a door bell."

Maria looked at him. "Why do you say that?"

"Because your father was here and my guess is he got inside. He figured out a secret. All we need to do is figure it out." Ti said.

He saw a small slot in a pillar near the bridge. "Maria where do you hide something you don't want people to find. That you know they will look for and will tear everything apart to find?"

Maria looked at him. "I am not sure?"

Ti grinned. "You hide it in plain sight, with the words danger written all over it. Give me the sign."

Ti took it and put it in the slot and turned it, a holographic image appeared.

"Welcome travelers, you may select one from your party to cross to the temple, to see if you are worthy to proceed to your destination. If your purpose is pure, then all may proceed." The Hologram stated.

Ti told them. "Wait here, I'll be back."

The others nodded.

Ti spoke to the Hologram. "I am the leader. I represent my party."

"Then you and you alone may cross and be judged." The Hologram stated.

Ti slowly walked through the force field. In a blink of an eye he found himself standing inside the temple. Had the bridge just been an illusion he wondered.

Ti looked around. He was standing on a platform. A beam scanned him. Another Hologram appeared. It was humanoid in appearance wearing a white robe. "Welcome Prince of the Maxumus Clan. To *The Crossroads*, are you here to fulfill your destiny?"

Ti looked at the Hologram. "I am just Tiberius Maxumus, a Knight of the Clan. Not my Prince."

The Hologram scanned him again. "But, you are the son of an Augustin and a Maxumus?"

"My mother and her cousin the Empress fathers were twins. They married cousins. Beary is my third cousin and my Prince. He is the one that destroyed the *Devil's Eye*." Tiberius explained.

The Hologram shimmered. "You are still a Prince of the Clan. You are a direct decedent of Justinian and Augustus and Caesar Maxumus, the sons of Paul Maxumus. So, you may be the Prince we have waited for."

"I do not understand?" Ti said. "What do you mean waited for?"

"Long ago, when the last of our race left these planets, we sent an emissary to your people. We ask that they wait a specific amount of time then come and destroy the *Crossroads Gate*, and seal its secrets away forever. That time period has come. If it is not done soon then evil could gain control of the gates and spread. Your people destroyed *The Eye*. They now must have the *Gate of Ages*. You did come to destroy it?" The Hologram asked.

Ti dropped his head. "I did not know of the promise made by my ancestors. Still, I was drawn here to protect this site from evil."

"So, Providence guided your steps here anyway. Plant explosives at these locations and you will destroy *The Gate* forever. The other gates do not matter, just the *Gate of Ages*." The Hologram explained.

Ti nodded. "How do I know this is what is right?"

Just then she appeared. "Do you know me, my Tiberius?"

Tiberius bowed to the Red Dragon Spirit. "Empress Star Firerena, I recognize you my Lady."

She smiled and kissed him. A small mark of a dragon appeared on his forehead. "You are so much like my Augustin. You think only of serving your brother Beary. Yes, I know he is your cousin, but your spirits are brothers. Know that this recording tells the truth, my child."

Ti bowed his head slightly. "Yes, my lady."

"Do not fear Tiberius; your father is proud of the boar you have become." She said as she faded away.

Ti started to work. He set the explosives, he carried in his pack, and at the locations the hologram had instructed him. When he was done he returned to the platform. "I am done."

"One more thing Prince Tiberius, open this panel. Take what it contains to your home, and keep it safe." The Hologram pleaded and illuminated a recessed panel in the wall.

Ti opened it, took out a long crystalline and metallic object. Ti looked at it. He returned to the platform. "What is this?" He asked.

The Hologram blinked. "Set off your explosives. I will return you to the bridge. If you were successful you will be able to cross to the island, if not I will return you here."

Ti set off the remote. As he was being sent back to the bridge, he heard. "Guard *the Key of Epoch* well, Prince of the Maxumus Clan."

In a flash he was back at the bridge. His three companions were waiting for him. He turned and started walking across the bridge. The others followed. They searched the entire complex. They did not find the chamber that Ti had been in or the *Gate of Ages*. Ti knew that he had been in the temple complex. That he was sure of. Still, somehow the chamber he had been in was now gone or at least unreachable.

After four cycles they had search the island. They had recorded many of the paintings and even gathered a couple of scrolls. Then they headed back across the bridge. Ti put the sign back in the slot and turned it. The force field didn't come back on. He then understood. When he blew up *The Gate* this portal had also been deactivated. Ti smiled, he had kept his Clan's promise. "Ok bears, it is getting dark and I want to sleep in my wife's arms tonight. Let's go." Ti said with a smile.

After five more cycles they made it back to the tower. A light was shining in the top windows.

As they approached, they heard Corporal Tongan call out a challenge. "Halt, Advance and be recognized."

Ti and the other slowly stepped forward. "Is everything alright Corporal?"

"Yes Sir, just getting back to being a Marine. Lady Allis had you coming in almost a half a cycle ago. She has a sniper over watch with an inferred scope up top. The Rose refused to leave till you got back. She is healing, but we should get her to a hospital ship, Sir." Corporal Tongan said.

"Thanks Corporal." Ti looked at Andrew Re who nodded.

"I think I'll stay with you awhile Tong, if that's alright?" Andrew Re said.

The Corporal smiled. Yeah, I would play it the same way. "I told Teresa that Ti would be suspicious of a sentry out here. However, she wanted some eyes down the trail. I was getting claustrophobic in that tower."

Andrew Re smiled. "I figured that. I wanted to talk. I didn't want to go back in there either, right now."

Tongan looked at him. "Why?"

"Maria has been acting strange… Asking if I would protect her, stuff like that. She is a very competent female. She doesn't need a boar's protection." Andrew Re pointed out.

Tongan laughed. "My dear Andrew, it is not about needing. She was flirting with you. She has a desire for you."

Andrew Re dropped his head. "I am not normal, you know that."

Tongan shook his head. "Andrew, first she is a gypsy. To her it would not mater. Second, you from what I can tell belong to the Clan Maxumus, and are related to the Rose, as her brother. Is that correct?"

Andrew nodded.

"My people were blessed by her and her father years ago. I do not believe that you are held in any lesser importance by your Clan, than any other member. I know Sire Tiberius would die for you, because you are part of his, family." Tongan said.

Andrew Re looked at him. He started to say something when Ti came back.

"Andrew, come on. I need you to come with me. I need another pilot to help me fly this canyon. Corporal, go help Babs." Ti said

"Yes Sir, I will join Lady Allis." Tongan said with a smile.

Ti took off down the trail, with Andrew following to catch up. "What is wrong my Prince?" Andrew asked as he caught up to Ti.

"Andrew let's drop the prince stuff. I am just Ti or Tiberius, a Knight like yourself. Beary is the Prince of the Clan, and he would tell you that it's just Beary. We are family. That truth is you are Samuel's son. That makes you more of a true prince than I or Beary, adopted or not. Or don't you know your father's full true name?"

As they pounded down the trail, Andrew looked at him. "I don't understand?"

"Samuel, the Sage Priest of Harvenger's Glen, Samuel Valorous, First Knight, of the Maxumus Clan, and Samuel Valorous Caesar the IV Emperor of *Andreas Prime*, He dropped the last when my Great, Great many times over uncle Caesar Maxumus took up the name Caesar as his last name. He and Isadora joined the Maxumus clan under the name Valorous. So Andrew you are every bit as much of a prince as I am. We can both trace our linage back to the same grandparents. Empress Constance father was Samuel's twin brother." Ti explained.

Andrew Re shook his head. "Father is correct you have strange ideas. Just like your cousin. We serve the main House; I serve you and our lady the Regent, Ti. That makes you our Prince."

Ti just shook his head. "Thank you Andrew. Now let's get that shuttle and get my Angel to a hospital ship."

They ran without stopping. After several cycles they reached the spot, on the top of the ridge near the fortifications, where Teresa had moved the Red Dagger.

Ti looked at Andrew Re. "We are going to have to thread the needle, where the canyon walls open up, about fifteen KSMU down the canyon. Then try and land on that small field east of the tower."

Andrew Re nodded. "Alright, let's do this."

They rotated the Dagger off the ground and headed for the canyon roof. It didn't take long till they reached a point they could enter the canyon. The floor of the canyon was plenty wide enough to land the Dagger. However, the ledge of the canyon curved up and out over the canyon wall. Ti was worried that if they clipped the overhang they might cause a catastrophic cave in of the canyon roof and a landslide.

"Andrew, this is going to be a touchy ballet. We are going in vertical but I am going to need you to watch the horizontal thrusters. Keep us away from the sides of the overhang." Ti said.

Andrew nodded. "No problem, just take us in slow and steady."

Ti slowly started lowering them down. Andrew carefully adjusted there horizontal stabilizers to push them slightly to the left. Then again back to the right. After several STU they cleared the roof and let out a collective sigh of relief.

"Ti, do me a favor, bring Raphael the next time you want to do something that crazy. I didn't think it would be that hard or that nerve racking." Andrew said as he peeled some metal off his paws and pocketed it.

Ti nodded. "After we get out of here, let's try not to get into a situation like this again." They flew along the canyon and landed in the clearing near the tower.

The others came out carrying out Annabelle Rosa on a stretcher. Soon everyone loaded up. Ti had Babs take over the other pilot seat.

"It was a little rough coming in and it might be a little rough going out. Can you handle the horizontal thrusters?" Ti asked.

Babs told him. "Gun it. I'll keep you away from the sides. Just thread the needle, and let's get her to the *Mercy*."

Ti flew towards the opening. He started to slow.

"Just shoot through. I'll keep you away from the sides. Don't slow down just go for it." Babs ordered.

Ti nodded. Andrew Re turned almost white as Ti gunned the engines. Babs' paws flew over the controls like she was playing a piano. Before Ti could blink, they were out of the canyon and heading out of the atmosphere.

"Sergeant Fong contact the *Mercy*. "Tell them we have a medical emergency. Use the call sign Hazard's 7." Ti ordered.

Fong smiled. "If you're going to use that call sign Captain, you better change into an Army uniform, the Lieutenant a Naval one."

Babs told him. "Not a problem. By the way I am Ultra 26, if they ask."

"If they ask, tell them we are from Joint Command 26." Ti added.

Fong's eye brows went up. "Wont Special Forces Command, get upset with us posing as a 26 unit."

Ti shook his head. "No Sergeant, I command a 26 Unit. It is part of my cover. As I said, I am a reservist in Hazard's Rangers."

Babs smiled. "I am part of the same 26 Unit now."

"So we were incorporated into the unit." Sgt. Fong smiled.

Ti nodded. "Yes, when you signed the paper work."

"Alright, *BAF Mercy* this is Hazard 7 declaring a medical emergency." Fong reported.

"This is *Mercy* standby. Hazard 7 that is an Army call sign, please explain?"

"*Mercy* this is Ultra 26 we are a JC26 Unit, do you understand? We have a wounded member and have declared a medical Emergency. Do we need to call General Puller?" Babs asked.

There was static then, "Ultra 26, Hazard 7 sorry for the inconvenience. We have some incompetent communication watch officers. We are ready for you, Surgeon 42 out." Dr. Gullstrand looked at the communications officer, "You really are worthless right now. Go get some rest."

A cycle later the Red Dagger landed. Dr. Gullstrand was waiting as Ti got off. "How many wounded do you have Captain Maxumus?"

"Only one my Medical..." Ti started to explain as Gullstrand pushed past him.

"Annabelle, where is she?" Dr. Gullstrand yelled.

Teresa looked at him. "She is here doctor. She is stable."

He looked at her. "Raphael, Andrew help Teresa get her to exam room one alpha now!" With that Dr. Gullstrand flew past Ti and grabbed his arm. "What happened to her?"

Ti looked at him "I..."

Gullstrand took a breath. "Tiberius, you will tell me everything or you will need the protection of that plating beneath your skin. I will try and beat it out of you. I know Annabelle Rosa is a dragon. So, cut the diversion."

Ti looked at him, even for a Maxmimus Dr. Gullstrand was large. He seemed to grow a little. "She fought a Griffin. She killed it, but it cut her with its front claws. The wounds were not deep but the claws had poison on them. She took two Arachnid Gallbladders to counter act the poison."

Doctor Gullstrand turned almost scarlet. "That little idiot! She knows better. Had she taken any before that?"

Babs spoke up. "Earlier yes, about twenty cycles before she took one. In fact she gave everyone one, but me and the private."

Ti looked at the doctor. "I don't understand?"

Gullstrand took a deep breath. "She is allergic to an enzyme in the gallbladder. She probable took an antihistamine with the first, to prevent a reaction. She forgot when she took the other two. So, she is having a bad allergic reaction not to one, but three gallbladders. She probably had gone dragon. That means her metabolism slowed. Even though her appearance reverts back in an instance, her metabolism doesn't. I need to start treating her. My Rosa is just lucky Teresa was with her. Even if, she didn't know what the problem was, she kept Annabelle stable. I have to go."

Four cycles later Annabelle Rosa woke up in a hospital bed with an IV in her arm. She started to reach for it when a voice stopped her.

"Touch that and I swear I will paddle your tail." Gullstrand said as he sat up next to her and kissed her. "You scared me."

"Vegus!" Annabelle Rosa exclaimed. "You shouldn't..."

"Why not," He said with a smile. "Can't a boar kiss his wife, if he wants too?"

Annabelle Rosa touched his face, "But father..."

Dr Gullstrand smiled. "Samuel is a hard boar when it comes to his Rosa. However, Isadora explained to him that he of all creatures should not be so stiff necked. He did make one demand. I must leave the service and move to the *Palisades* with you. The young Regent might need me anyway."

Annabelle Rosa kissed him. "I am sorry; I got careless with the Arachnid Gallbladders."

Dr. Gullstrand kissed her again and said. "I will punish you later. You are a better doctor than that."

Ti had walk in and looked at him. "Do you always kiss your wounded doctor and then talk about punishing them?"

Annabelle Rosa smiled then laughed. "Ti please, it is a joke between lovers."

"What?" Ti said.

Babs shook her head. "Forgive him Annabelle. He is a little slow at times. Ti, Dr. Gullstrand is Annabelle Rosa's husband."

Ti looked at her. "How long have you known she was married?"

Babs smiled. "Since she and I started singing together."

Dr. Gullstrand stood and bowed. "Regent Maxumus, I Doctor Vegus Gullstrand Valorous, offer you my services."

"Thank you doctor, I accept in the name of our Prince Beary Maxumus. Since you are already of the clan no other act is needed." Babs said.

"Regent you should know before Samuel adopted me. I was a slave to the Pompaius Clan. They…" Dr. Gullstrand started to explain when Annabelle Rosa touched his paw.

"Ti, Babs he is a good bear and a great doctor. The friction, which exists between him and father, is my fault. I fell in love with him and seduced him. His other secrets we can explain later. May I be alone with him for now?" Annabelle Rosa asked.

Ti smiled, and kissed her cheek. "For you, my Angel I would do anything."

# CHAPTER 18

# Homeward Bound

T I CALLED ENFIELD. "How is the crew of the *Dream in the Night* doing?"

"Everyone is ready to head home. Any idea when we can board the ship?" Enfield asked.

"Tell Captain Bancroft to prepare the ship for departure in two days. We are done here. Have him send a shuttle to the *Mercy* to pick up an additional passenger and the Rose. I'll, be back in thirty-six cycles." Ti told him.

"Alright Sir, I'll let everyone know." Enfield said.

"Fong you and your Marines stay with the Rose and protect her. I don't think Dr. Gullstrand would allow anything to happen to her but, I would feel better." Ti said.

"Sergeant Fong saluted. "We will see she gets back to the ship alright, Captain."

Ti nodded.

Babs looked at him, as they walked back to the dagger with La Noire, Maria and the others. "Do you ever wish you had stayed in uniform, instead of following the coarse you did?"

Ti shook his head. "No, I like being the Scarecrow. I like the freedom it gives me to do my job. If I was in uniform, I would have to play by rules that we don't. How, about you Babs, do you miss fleet intelligence?"

"No, I hated my job there. Photo interpretation is tedious and boring. I was good at it. I like field work. I am even better at that, as you know." Babs said.

Ti looked at everyone. "Ok, let's get La Noire home. Then get back to *Aldrin VI*."

La Noire looked at Maria. "You are going to return with them aren't you?"

"Yes, I can serve our people better serving them. Besides, they have offered me my dreams. As they have you. Your own publishing company, it will mean jobs for our people." Maria pointed out.

"True, but I will just be a partner in their enterprise." La Noire said.

"They are good, honest, and you will be also. For I, will have little brother watch you." Maria pointed out. "My bond to them is also binding on you as well."

"Yes, my Empress Maria, even a King of Gypsies must bow to the Supreme Empress of all Gypsies." La Noire said with a laugh.

Maria smiled, yet among her kind that was who she was. La Renard, *The Fox*, Supreme Empress of all Gypsies. "Just stay safe my brother. I think I will sleep now."

La Noire nodded and leaned back. He would keep his word after all he was honorable, for a gypsy. Besides, La Renard would kill him or have Lobo do it if he didn't. He smiled as he went to sleep.

"I am glad father is going to let Vegus join us." Andrew Re said.

Raphael looked at him. "I bet that was a fight. I don't know mother very well, but she must have insisted."

Ti looked at them. "Isadora is Samuel's conscious. He always said she tempered his steel and forced him to look at both sides of an argument."

Raphael looked at Ti and Babs. "Vegus is only a few years younger than Annabelle Rosa. You won't remember him Ti. Beary met him once when he was four. That was probable the last time father and he talked. Of course they fought. Samuel had sent Annabelle Rosa somewhere. Vegus had come home on leave and wanted to see his wife. Samuel exploded that they had married behind his back and had disgraced themselves and the family. Vegus said that he had told him of their intent. Samuel countered that he had never agreed to such a union. What could he expect from a Pompaius dog? Vegus stormed out.

Annabelle Rosa was furious with father and threatened to leave and never return. She did leave. Vegus sent her home, and made her apologize to father. He told her that what they had done was not wrong, because they were in love. Still, they should have did it better."

Babs was almost in tears. "It must be hard for them."

Raphael shrugged. "Is love ever easy? You learn to take the good with the bad. I can understand both sides. Though Samuel was pleased, when I and Solara got married, but then it suited his purpose."

Andrew nodded as he looked at Maria. "She says she likes me but what will father say?"

Ti shrugged. "What do you feel Andrew?"

"Confused, she is very attractive, but I am not a normal bear. I am a monster to most of the worlds we have visited. It is true Sgt. Fong and the other Pandarian Marines seemed to except us as we are but..." Andrew's voice trailed off.

Babs got up and touched his face. "Andrew, do I or Ti treat you like a monster?"

"No my lady, you have only been kind to us, both of you." Andrew Re said.

Babs smiled. "Andrew you are family. We are heading home. At home I am Babs or Allis. If you want you can call me Babs Allis, which is my name. Regent is my job, my responsibility to the clan. Do you understand? You, Raphael, Teresa, his wife, other children, Annabelle Rosa, and Vegus are family to me and Ti. As are Alpha and Bravo teams."

Shari Morrow and Gamey were looking over the plans Mrs. Bantelle presented them.

Mrs. Morrow spoke up. "It is a good idea. Beary said he wanted to make the northern island a resort for family only. This would allow it to still be profitable."

"Thank you Mrs. Morrow. May I ask a question? Do I work for you or are we equals." Solara Bantelle asked.

Gamey responded. "I am the Head Protector of the Clan and brother to the Prince. Mrs. Morrow is the Head of all Household Staffs."

"That said Solara, if I may call you that, by the way I am Shari, I have my paws full with the main castle. You are responsible for this island and will support Mrs. Svedberg on the other island." Mrs. Morrow explained.

Solara beamed. "Thank you Mrs. Morrow, I mean Shari. I will not disappoint you."

"Come on Solara, the big overgrown lizard has other work to do. Let us girls go talk in the garden." Shari said with a smile and a wink at Gamey.

Blue walked over. "You really would be lost without her wouldn't you?"

"Yes, but don't tell that Southern Witch that. How are things here?" Gamey asked.

Blue smiled. "Good, I want to stay on so does my team. So does Jones' Bravo. Some of Mrs. Morrow's people are ready to leave, but they are not needed any more."

Gamey looked at him. "Blue losing both, you, Jones, and your teams could put me in a jam."

"Not really Boss. Look, if we are stationed out here and you could get us two daggers, we could be back over the castle in no time, with two or three hunt Parties. Besides, I know Samuel sent you two companies of Knights. You don't need us. Babs does, even with the people she has coming. You need us here also, so does Beary." Blue pointed out.

Gamey thought about it. "I'll discuss it with Beary. You are probably right."

Out in the garden Solara and Shari were talking.

"Solara that is a beautiful name, does it have special meaning?" Shari asked.

Solara dropped her head. "Father said if you asked, I was to explain and show you. I, my husband, and Andrew Re, his brother were the only survivors of a cosmic storm that struck a freighter we were on. We were all three new born cubs. The ship was discovered by slavers as it drifted. They soon discovered our abilities and sold us to a traveling freak show. That is where Samuel and Annabelle Rosa found us. The manager had named me Solara the living Star. May I show you, the young Prince knows? Please put these on."

Mrs. Marrow put on the glasses and watched as Solara started to glow, then ignite into flame. She slowly rose off the ground as she pulsed. Then she slowly lowered herself down and dimmed.

"That was wonderful, so beautiful." Mrs. Morrow said.

Solara looked at her. "You were not frightened?"

Mrs. Morrow walked over and kissed her. "Solara my dear I work with a dragon, I have a talking canus bodyguard and a dogon to deal with on a daily basis. Plus, I have been a fleet officer's wife for a long time. Also, I was Beary's Nurse. I knew about you dear, Samuel told him he could tell no one but me, because Beary could not break his promise to me, or I to him.

You have grown into a remarkable female, as has your oldest daughter. She is what sixteen and already a trained Physician's Assistant and medic."

"Yes Shari, she is very good at it also. We hope to send her to Medical School." Solara said.

"I'll tell Angelina. She is opening a teaching hospital here. Teresa will make a good candidate." Shari said.

"But we can't bother the Empress!" Solara exclaimed.

Shari laughed. "Oh Solara you have a lot to learn, Angelina would be upset if you didn't. You are family, you are a Maxumus. You are not a servant, we each have are jobs and responsibilities to the clan and each other. Gamey and I are not our jobs. Don't tell that overgrown Lizard but I love him like a son. I am proud of him. He is good at what he does and he has a good heart."

After fifteen cycles they dropped out of orbit and landed on La Noire Island. Philippe was waiting.

"Did you succeed?" he asked.

Ti nodded. "The *Gate of Ages* is no more."

Philippe smiled. "Then our father did not die in vain. Those evil ones will never find it or learn its secrets. This is good, yes La Renard."

"Yes Lobo, but stay vigilant and protect our people. Help your brother." Maria said.

Ti then pulled out a nap sack full of old manuscripts and gave to La Noire. "Translate these for me before you publish them and only if Angelina says it's ok." He then handed him a signet ring, with a blue diamond in the center and red fire stones out lining a thunderbird around it. "This is a token of our bond of trust between you and me."

La Noire looked at the ring. It was an ancient gypsy symbol. Ti knew its meaning. If La Noire accepted it, he would be bound to the Maxumus by his own oath, not just La Renard's. This ring would also give him status among the other Kings, not that being La Renard's brother didn't. He bowed and accepted the ring.

Maria kissed her brothers. Ti and Babs said goodbye and joined Raphael, Andrew Re, and Teresa on the dagger and headed for the *Dream in the Night.*

Maria smiled. "It will be good to get home to the ship. I have laundry to do."

Everyone laughed.

Maria walked up to the pilot's seat. "Ti, you knew the meaning of that symbol on the ring, yes?"

Ti nodded. "It was a symbol given by a pirate to a group of gypsies a long time ago. A promise of shelter, in times of storms and persecution, it also bound that group of gypsy to the pirates family."

Maria looked at him. "I do not understand?"

Ti smiled. "Maria, there is a lot I don't understand. However, I know the Maxumus seal and I know that the *Thunderbird* was one of the ships of our founder. His ring was a blue diamond with a *Thunderbird* outlined with red fire stones. I found his ring with a note from your father. It asked that if it was found by a Maxumus that it be given to his oldest son.

Your tribe and mine have been connected for a long time. So Maria, know this, you and all your gypsies will find refuge in our halls. This I swear, not only for myself but also for my Prince Beary Maxumus." With that he handed her a ring with the same symbol. "I talked to the Empress she said to have this one made for you Maria. Why didn't you tell me who you are?"

Babs was watching and smiled at Maria's reaction when she saw Angelina's crest inside the Thunderbird.

Maria's mouth opened then she smiled. "Ti I have pledged myself to you, Babs Allis, and Beary Maxumus."

"Yes Maria, but we are now reaffirming our pledge to you and your tribes. If you present this ring to any member of our clan you will find shelter or aid." Ti said.

Maria kissed Ti then Babs and walked back to the passenger's compartment. She kissed Teresa on the cheek, then Raphael. When she came to Andrew she drew his face to hers and gave him a very passionate kiss. She then peeled the light film of gold off his lips. "I may keep this, yes, as a souvenir of our first kiss."

Andrew Re just nodded, as she smiled and walked with her hips swinging back to her seat.

Raphael smiled. "That one is trouble."

Teresa just chuckled and went forward.

Eight cycles latter they landed on *Aldrin VI*. They returned the dagger to a very relieved pilot, who found that even his weapon stores had been replenished. "It is all yours Lieutenant. Now if you could get us a transport into town." Ti asked.

"Yes sir, not a problem, one is waiting for you behind the trees over there." The Lieutenant pointed to the left.

Ti walked over. The others followed. An armored limousine was waiting. Sergeant Fong waved. "Annabelle Rosa and Dr. Gullstrand are on board. The Private is with them along with the rest of my squad. The Corporal and I thought we would come after you all."

"Thanks Fong, we need to stop at *The Ambassador* and talk with Mr. Bollinger." Ti said.

"Alright Sir, but I could drop the others off at the ship on the way." Fong said absent mindedly.

Babs nodded. "Good idea, but I will go with Briton." Everyone got the hint.

Fong bowed, "Yes lady Tornbow, I mean Allis."

After a cycle Maria, Andrew Re, Raphael, and Teresa got out of the limo and went on board the *Dream in the Night*. Sgt. Fong drove Ti and Babs to *The Ambassador*.

Mr. Bollinger escorted them into his office. The Sergeant and Corporal waited outside. He hit a button securing the room. "I am glad you are back safe."

Ti nodded. "Annabelle Rosa was hurt, but she is alright. Luckily, Vegus was the Doctor in Charge on the *Mercy*."

"Luck had nothing to do with it. Your cousins saw to it." Bollinger told them. "I am sorry I failed you so badly. I should have known how bad…"

Ti held up his paw. "How many are in your cell on *Aldrin VI,* or even in this system."

"Only six, most work here. One owns a coffee shop across the street." Bollinger said.

Ti nodded. "I reread your reports. You reported everything that was happening. All the clues were there. No one was looking for a clandestine invasion of this system. Yet, the information was all there. You did your job but, I do want to send you some help. If I can, I want to send you two canus pups. They can smell Shape Shifters and they are silent killers. Yet, they are gentle and intelligent. They have been part of our clan forever."

Bollinger thought about his family. It would be added protection. The Marines would stay for a while. Still, sooner or later they would withdraw leaving a small garrison behind. He had seen it happen before.

No one on *Bearilia Prime* understood how important this system was. "Thank you Ti, any help you can get us would be appreciated."

Ti nodded. "Maria is, La Renard, *The Fox*, her brother La Noire is the King of the Gypsies on *Aldrin VII*. We and they are bonded to each other. Julius the Scared gave one of their founders, his ring. If you need their help call on them, if they need yours, give it. That is Her Highnesses orders."

Mr. Bollinger nodded "I understand Ti. Now about your bill, I am sorry but it is quite large." He handed it to Ti who handed it to Babs.

She went over it. "Mr. Bollinger you did promise us the family rate."

He looked at the bill reduced it, 20% and handed it back.

Babs nodded and wrote out the check.

Mr. Bollinger smiled. "Captain Bancroft mentioned that you wanted to sell the crew facilities at the spaceport. He had fired the management team which is a good thing; most were Shape Shifters and are now dead. Unfortunately, they fought it out at your facilities which damaged their value. Also, they had dropped the insurance."

Babs replied. "Luckily Uncle Justinian insured all corporate property against loss due to war or acts of nature or fire etc., when he bought the cruise line.

Mr. Bollinger, you will act as our agent. Turn in the claim to the insurance. See that they settle the claim. Then sell the property."

Mr. Bollinger hesitated. "I have a buyer for the property. The insurance will settle for three point six million credits. About twice what the actual structure was worth, but since the Marines razed it. The buyer I have in mind is not a wealthy bear. But, he could offer about one point five million for the property. The *Gem Lines* would realize five point one million credits for that property. Also, the new owner would promise a better facility for the cruise line crew and guests."

Babs laughed. "Mr. Bollinger it is yours. Just reinvest your one point five million and half the insurance settlement. If it becomes profitable, we get 10% is that fair. Also, we get a 30% discount for our crews."

Mr. Bollinger looked at Ti.

Ti shrugged. "I am a gundog; she is the business bear along with Lady Pompey. Beary and I stay out of it."

Mr. Bollinger bowed. "Lady Maxumus, it will be as you say. I now know why our Princes do so well. They marry brilliant females."

Ti and Babs said their goodbyes and headed back to the *Dream in the Night*.

Maria was waiting for them. "We depart in three cycles. Everything is good to go. The Captain knew you would be tired. He asked if I could talk with you since he is tied up with custom inspections etc."

Ti stretched. "Thank you Maria, for everything."

"Ti you need to tell Captain Bancroft the truth. He is a good bear he needs to know who he really works for." Maria said.

"I know Maria. Just as soon as we go through the wormhole and head for home." Ti said looking at the empty jewelry cases. "I guess we sold out. I won't have much extra work for the ladies."

Maria looked at him. "Ti, you hired me to be marketing director, oui."

Babs smiled. "Oui, Maria he did."

Maria said, "Then you should have known I would insure that I would have plenty of high quality merchandise to sell, and plenty of parties to throw on the way home. I do not plan to be a poor gypsy. If I must, I will seduce Andrew Re. He produces very high quality metal from his sweat glands. This," she showed them a necklace made from the kiss, "came from a kiss. Can you imagine what would happen if I really came onto him."

Babs laughed. "Maria you are evil."

Maria smiled an impish smile, "Of course, I am gypsy."

Captain Bancroft looked at his bridge crew and smiled. "Second Engineer Fa, are my engines ready to take us out?"

Fa replied. "Yes Captain, we are ready."

"Mr. Zing, take us out head for *Kalaallit's Passage.*" Captain Bancroft ordered.

Mr. Zing responded. "Yes Captain."

Enfield just sat back and watched. Bancroft was good. His bears respected him. The fleet messed up. They should have never let this one go.

Ti slipped on to the bridge and found an empty chair. He watched as they headed into the wormhole. Soon they were heading for *Wonderer's Station* to give back the sign post.

"Captain Bancroft, can I see you in my cabin." Ti asked.

"Alright, Mr. Tornbow, Mr. Enfield you have the Bridge." Bancroft said.

Captain Bancroft came in Babs, Annabelle Rosa, Vegus, and the others including Maria was there. Raphael secured the door.

Bancroft looked at him. "Mr. Tornbow what is this about?"

Ti smiled. "Captain Bancroft, have a seat please." Ti and Babs produced their badges. "I am Inspector Tiberius Maxumus of the Bearilian Secret Service. This is my partner and wife Inspector Babs Allis Maxumus. Mr. and Miss Bantelle, Andrew Re, and Annabelle Rosa are part of our team. Maria joined our team for this investigation because of her connections on *Aldrin VII*."

Bancroft looked at them. "I don't understand, then you..."

Babs smiled a radiant smile. "Oh no Captain, we do own this Cruise line along with my husband's cousin's Wife and a few other investors. *Gem Lines* is owned by the Maxumus clan and Max Harrah my uncle."

Bancroft looked at her, "Crusher Harrah is really your uncle?"

"Yes Captain he is. A dearer bear you would never meet." Babs said.

"But...old boar Tornbow?" Bancroft asked.

"Captain, if I read you into that you would have to take a blood oath that if you broke would kill you." Ti said. "Let's just say they are very senior field operatives."

"I take it if I divulge anything you tell me I will go to jail." Captain Bancroft said.

Babs sighed. "Captain Bancroft we don't threaten our friends. Really nothing has changed. You still work for us."

The Captain looked at them and dropped his head, "But you are connected to a criminal enterprise. I mean Crusher..."

Ti started laughing. "I am sorry Captain Bancroft, maybe we are going to need you to take that oath after all."

Bancroft looked at him, "Alright Sir, I have a feeling it would lead up to it sooner or later."

Ti handed him a knife and had him slice his paw. Ti sliced his. Captain Bancroft took his paw. "I give you my oath to guard your secrets with my life."

Ti smiled. "I Tiberius Maxumus, Knight Protector of the Clan, accept your oath."

Annabelle Rosa came over. "Captain, it is our custom for a dragon to seal an oath. I am a dragon of the Clan Maxumus. If I seal your oath it has consciences. If you break your oath you will die."

Captain Bancroft looked at her. "I don't understand."

Annabelle Rosa's eyes changed and she surrounded him with a fine flame. "Accept a dragon's blessing."

Captain Bancroft felt at peace, but he was also confused.

Vegus looked at his wife. "Ti, she is still a little weak. I am taking her back to our suit."

"Alright, doctor, take care of my Angel." Ti said.

Vegus nodded.

Bancroft looked at Ti. "Ok, please explain."

"Captain all except Maria are members of my Family. Even Maria is connected to my clan by an ancient treaty. Max Harrah is an agent of the Bearilian Government. The casino is one of our intelligence centers. Babs is really his niece." Ti said.

Bancroft shook his head. "Enfield, who is he?"

Ti smiled, "Lt. Commander from Fleet Intelligence. Your security team is MSD 63."

"The elder Tornbows," Bancroft asked?

"They love this ship, when they travel under their aliases. They are Vice President Maxumus and Empress Maxumus." Ti said.

Bancroft whistled. "Ok, I understand. What about the promises you made the crew."

Babs asked. "Captain, do you still wish to work for us? We do really own this ship along with the *Gem Lines,* a couple of resorts, and an ocean going cruise line on *Andreas Prime.* Plus, I own a small interest in *Harrah's* and just bought a small interest in *The Ambassador* on *Aldrin VI.*"

Captain Bancroft thought. "Thank you, Mr. Enfield said if you trusted someone you proved it. I guess he was correct. I am your bear."

Ti smiled. "Good, I'll still be Brinton Tornbow till we arrive at *Andreas Prime.*"

Bancroft nodded. "We have a full ship for the return trip. Most of the passengers are getting off at *Pandarus VI* and *Candaris Prime.*"

At *Wonderer's Station* they returned the sign post and thanked Mr. Peabody. Ti also gave him an artifact from the *Wonderer* that was found on *Aldrin V* by the Shape Shifters. It was a small plaque with the names of the crew on it. Mr. Peabody was thrilled.

A day later they headed out for *Pandarus VI. Helios IV* was not on the return trip. The Government had quarantined the planet to search for more members of the Mac-Ta.

The return trip was quite. Maria had thrown four parties by the time they reached *Pandarus VI.* She had also depleted over half of her goods and had made a healthy profit. Her girls were almost embarrassed by how much they were making at the shows. One told Maria she had made more in the shows, than on the cruises she had worked for the last three years.

Annabelle Rosa had stayed in her suite with Vegus for most of the trip. Ti was worried till Babs explained that he shouldn't be.

Maria continued to pursue Andrew Re who didn't know what to do. But they started spending more and more time together talking and walking around the ship.

Babs interviewed the different crew members. She asked them about their jobs, their likes, and dislikes.

She also checked out the casino operations. Here anything that was not up to her standard was changed. She was a stickler on every detail.

Ti filled all his reports back to headquarters and to Octavious. Then he started formulating his plan. He would present it to Angelina, to help the Major's men's families. He knew the Bearilian Government wouldn't care, but he felt he owed Major Bandura.

When they reached *Candaris Prime*, Babs and Ti went to talk to Max at the casino.

Max smiled as they came in. "It is good to see you both." He walked over and kissed Babs. "How is my girl?"

"I am good Uncle Max and happy." Babs smiled.

Max turned and hugged Ti with a crushing bear hug. "You did good son. Your dad would have been so proud of you."

Ti smiled. "Thanks Max, here is a copy of my final report. Also, here is something for your eyes only. I know Angelina will want your input."

Max sat down and read the quick summery. "There is no way Bearilian High Command will agree to this."

Ti nodded. "I know, but I owe Major Bandura. He knew they were digging in the wrong place and was willing to sacrifice his troops to protect *The Gates'* secrets. If we can help them, we must."

"By the Moons of Bantine, Ti, what do you want!?" Max asked.

Ti shrugged. "Everything you can get on the planet *Haverdine*, its population, and garrison, especially the penal colonies on the planet. These are the names of the men in the unit and their family's names. They are the creatures we want to help escape."

"Alright, Ti, I know Angelina. This is just the kind of stunt she would love. I'll get the information you need to make it work." Max said.

"Thanks Uncle Max. It is still just uncle isn't it?" Ti asked.

Max smiled. "I am willing Ti, but she isn't yet. I know Tiberius wouldn't mind. He was my best friend. I loved him too. But, she just can't let go. I know she loves me. But...It's ok it is enough for now, just to share her, with his ghost."

Ti put his paw on Max's shoulder. "No Max, it isn't. Dad would be mad at both of you, you for allowing her to put you off and her for not living her life to the fullest. But, thank you for not getting impatient with her."

"Allis you did well when you married this one." Max said giving them both a hug, "You better get going. You're leaving in a few cycles."

Babs nodded. "We will see you soon. Come to the *Palisades* for a visit. Our beaches on the southern island are better than these."

Max smiled. "Maybe next month."

Ti nodded. Then he and Babs left.

Three cycles latter The *Dream in the Night* left for *Andreas Prime*. The trip back had not been the leisurely cruise the out bound trip had been. The *Dream in the Night* was going into space dock at *Andreas Prime* for overhaul. The crew was getting three months paid vacation at a new resort on the *Southern Palisades Island* which just happened to be owned by the *Gem Lines* Company or vice versa. During which Captain Bancroft would get a look at *Traveler's Dream,* a new Rollo Cargo Transport. It was designed to carry five million KSWU of cargo, two hundred fifty passengers in luxury. It was also, able to make the trip to the *Aldrin System* in seven weeks from *Candaris Prime*, eight weeks from *Bearilia Prime* and seven point five from *Andreas Prime*. He smiled, he would keep the *Dream in the Night*, but it was nice to be given the option.

# CHAPTER 19

# Home Coming

T HE *DREAM IN the Night* arrived early in the morning over St Elaina's. The passengers were disembarked at the new orbital space terminal and shuttled to the surface, after they and their luggage had been screened.

The crew was busy preparing the ship for space dock. The engineers were shutting down, securing the warp engines, and signing ships systems over to the space dock crew.

Captain Bancroft was going over the books, since he took over the ship had made a nice profit. In fact thanks to the new owners they had paid for the new upgrades to the engines and life boats. They still made a small profit of thirty thousand credits. Not a great performance, but they were in the positive side of the column. Of course the new upgrades would wipe that out in a heartbeat.

He picked up the books and carried them in to Babs.

"Lady Maxumus..." Bancroft started to say.

"Captain, I told you, Lady Maxumus is my Mother in-Law, not me. I am Babs or Allis your choice."

"Yes lady Allis, I have the books. We made thirty thousand credits after all expenses." Captain Bancroft said.

"Really, we did that well? Good did you get your bonus?" Babs asked.

"Yes My Lady, but it was too generous. If you had cut the bonus to the crew the profit would have been greater." Captain Bancroft pointed out.

"Captain we made money on a trip we expected to lose money on. My husband and I actually made close to ten million credits on this trip clear from the jewelry we sold. That is after we gave the ship its cut, which helped your bottom line. We also bought interest in a Dylithiam Crystal mine. According to our experts our 10% ownership is going to be worth one hundred million credits. It was a profitable trip, Captain."

"But the upgrades you have ordered..." Captain Bancroft started to say.

"Are being done by my own space dock, well that's not totally true I only own 15% of the space dock." Babs said.

"Captain, Ti's cousin Justinian owns the port facilities at *Saint Elaina's*. Pompey Maxumus, his other cousin's wife owns *The Maxumus Vineyards* and nectar bottling plant. Along with a large sheep herd and land in the southern continent. She is also my partner in the ocean cruise line and the resorts as well as the *Gem Lines*. Her husband was the designer of the Vallen/Maxumus warp engine series, as well as the Maxumus APU's and other systems. He also owns part of the *Vallen Institute*, though that is not common knowledge." Babs concluded.

Captain Bancroft shook his head. "Do you people own everything here?"

"No, The clan system in the Northern Continent divided power between six major Clans, the Caesars, Pompaius, Augustin, Maxumus, Delinian and Charioteers. The Caesars were the ruling clan. The Delinian Clan controlled the southern ocean and its islands. The Maxumus, the islands in the Northern Delinian Ocean, and a strip of land from *Saint Elaina's* to the northern plain. The Charioteers controlled the mountains to the east of that strip, to the Ocean. The Pompaius controlled the land to the south in the plains. The Caesar clan had the land west of the Maxumus Strip. The Augustine had a small strip to the east. The clans of the southern continent were nomads and pledged allegiance to no one. Just like the Frigorific Dragons of the north. The Caesar and Pompaius clans are no more. In fact out of one hundred forty clans only forty still exist. The Maxumus and Augustine are two of the largest and they are connected by marriage."

Bancroft looked at Babs. "What about the Charioteers?"

Babs shrugged. "We are few. Our families were decimated, but not wiped out by the first incursion. But, low birth rates have doomed some of our families to extinction. Some of us have joined larger clans including my family."

"What about dragons, Annabelle Rosa said she is one?" Bancroft said.

Babs smiled. "Oh Captain, that is a long story. Let's just say that dragons are part of who we are. They are members of our family. The rest you can read about in our library at the resort."

"Yes Lady Allis, we will be disembarking soon for *Saint Elaina's.*" Captain Bancroft said.

Babs nodded and waved.

Soon the crew had shuttled down and was being transported to the *Southern Palisades Resort.* Maria was with Ti, Babs, and the rest of the team. When they arrived in *Saint Elaina's* Mr. Jorgenson was waiting for them.

"Welcome home. Ti, you, and your team have been requested to go out to the house with me.

Also, Empress La Renard, Her Majesty was wondering if you would join them." Jorgenson handed her an engraved invitation with a Scarlet Rose.

"It would be my honor Sire." Maria said, "May Sire Re, accompany me?"

Jorgenson bowed. "If it pleases you, your Highness."

"Oui, it does." Maria said.

Teresa stopped and dropped to a knee. "Sire Jorgenson, I cannot go."

Jorgenson picked her up. "Lady Knight no Knight of the Garter ever kneels to another Knight of the Clan. How may I serve you, in your distress?"

"I must, I am compelled to see Sire Gamey immediately." Teresa said with tears in her eyes.

Jorgenson replied. "That is not a problem. It is on the way. I'll call ahead and make sure he clears his schedule for you."

They drove toward the Maxumus Castle. Maria was struck by the beauty of the hills. Then she saw the Castle Maxumus. Jorgenson drove up to the Gate. Teresa begged everyone to stay in the transport as she walked through the gate, with her bag rapped in her arms.

Mrs. Morrow met her. "You must be Teresa Bantelle child. I will take you to Sir Gamey's office."

"Thank you Lady Morrow. You are as kind as grandmother said you were." Teresa said.

Gamey was setting in his office when Teresa walked in. She saw the Symbol of Vandar on his shoulders. She bowed, dropped to both knees, and wept before him.

Gamey leaped up. "Child, what is it?"

"Sir Knight, I have come to ask you to right a wrong. To give back to one that which was taken from him and give him peace." Teresa said.

"Teresa, do not grovel before me. Please stand up and have a seat. Tell me what is on your heart." Gamey begged.

But she refused. "I am *Teresa of the Light*, arbitrator for the lost. I have recovered your brother's heart, and set his enslaved spirit free. But, Bradius did not ascend. He retreated into his heart. He had been made a slave to a Mac-Ta devil. I killed the swine and forgave him." As she said all this she started to glow with a golden light."

Gamey looked at her. His father's anger, weld up inside of him. Bradius the egg killer, how dare she! But Gamey forced the memories aside. "Please Teresa set up and tell me what you know."

Teresa looked at him. She could see the conflict in him, but saw that he controlled it. "Your brother suffered from an illness that caused uncontrollable seizures. He had one and fell into a nest containing two eggs. One was destroyed. Your father did not believe he could father a sickly child. He refused to listen. He had your brother charged as an egg breaker and banished."

Gamey nodded, as his father's memories screamed that she was a liar. Finally Gamey whispered. "Enough, I have my father's memories. But, I am not my father. Give me his Heart Teresa of the Light."

Gamey took his brothers heart. A single tear fell and touched it, "Bradius," he said in a whisper that echoed, "You are home. You are forgiven. I give you back your name. I will place you in our chapel and write your name in the family book. This I swear as Knight of Vandar."

The dragon heart pulsed, a black dragon spirit materialized, and bowed. "Thank you brother, I can now join our ancestors, be blessed."

Teresa looked at Gamey, "I am sorry…"

Gamey smiled and kissed her.

As he did she glowed and touched him. "Accept my blessing Sir Gamey"

Gamey sat down and watched as she walked out of the door. Mrs. Morrow came in.

"Gamey, are you alright?" Mrs. Morrow asked.

He started crying. She came and held him. "It is ok my son you can tell me when you're ready." Mrs. Morrow said absent mindedly.

Gamey wrapped his arms and wings around her and held her. "I don't have my mother's memories, I can't even remember her. But, I know she must have been like you. She must have been Shari or I would have turned out hard like him."

Mrs. Morrow whispered. "I love you too you overgrown lizard, don't you ever forget it."

Teresa came back out and got in the transport.

"Is everything alright?" Ti asked

"Teresa smiled. "Sir Gamey is wonderful, probably the greatest dragon of our time."

Ti shrugged. "I doubt he would agree."

"But, don't you see that just proves it!" Teresa said.

After another cycle of driving they came to the Caesar/ Maxumus Castle. Maria stared as two large dragons in red uniforms and a canus wearing a red jacket came forward and bowed. "Empress La Renard, I am Strong Heart, Empress Angelina's personal bodyguard." He smiled at Mr. Jorgenson. "If you would come with me I will show you into the garden."

Maria bowed. "May Andrew Re, come with me?"

Strong Heart smiled. "Of course he is a Knight of the Clan and a son of the First Knight."

Jorgenson smiled as Strong Heart led Maria and Andrew Re off. "That pup is taking over my job."

Ti asked. "Do you mind?"

Mr. Jorgenson shook his head. "No, it frees me up to secure this place, Jermain also. Thanks to them we are getting more done. Plus, Angelina lets them go places we never were allowed to go."

Babs smiled. "They suit her, not that you don't."

Jorgenson felt of his chest. "No, we have too much of a history together, and I owe her way too much."

Ti said. "She tells it a little different."

"Come on she wants to talk to all of you later." Jorgenson said showing them in.

Mrs. Maro saw Ti, came over, and kissed him, then Babs. "Come on you two, I'll show you where to freshen up."

The others were shown their rooms.

Maria was shown into a beautiful rose garden. Widja came over and greeted her. "Empress La Renard, I am Widja Caesar/Maxumus,

Empress of all Dragons and Handmaiden to Empress Angelina Maxumus."

Maria nodded. "Your Highness it is a pleasure."

Widja smiled. "Andrew Re Valorous welcome home, Sir Knight.

Andrew Re, saluted, "My Empress Widja."

"Come Empress Angelina awaits." Widja said.

Angelina was setting in a simple sundress at a table among the roses. The table was set for midmorning tea. Maria smiled this one was following protocol treating her as she would any visiting dignitary, even though she didn't have too. This was who Angelina Maxumus was. Angelina stood up and walked over.

"Empress La Renard, I am Angelina Maxumus, welcome to my home. Please come set. I hope you don't mind meeting in my rose garden. I hate the throne room and refuse to use it." Angelina said with a devastating smile.

*Could this charming female actually be the famed Banshee of Death? Her people believed so though there was no proof to back it up.* "Thank you Empress Maxumus."

Angelina smiled. "Please, this is my home, just call me Angelina."

*Again a voice like Angels singing* Maria thought, "Then please just call me Maria, your Highness, I mean Angelina, I am after all just a simple gypsy."

Widja laughed a dragon's laugh. "Can we now drop the excrement?"

"Widja, such language in front of a guest," Angelina laughed.

"Better than what you said to the Tholian Ambassador last week." Widja retorted with a laugh.

"Yes, but it was anatomically accurate." Angelina pointed out.

At this point Maria lost it and laughed also.

Andrew Re just turned away to look at the roses.

Angelina smiled. "Maria, I wanted to honor you. To give your visit the dignity you deserve. However, I and unfortunately, Widja hate the pomp and circumstance. I hate it as a politician's wife. I hate it even more as Empress."

"Oui my Angelina, but you have already showed me more hospitality than a gypsy ever receives." Maria pointed out.

Later that afternoon Angelina met with Raphael and Teresa in her office.

"Teresa, I see that you are already a trained and gifted Physician's Assistant and Trauma Medic. You are also trained in dragon medicine and can do some of the procedures." Angelina said.

"Yes your Highness, I can." Teresa said.

"Teresa you are family it is just Angelina. We are opening a teaching hospital next month. Would you like to train to become a doctor? Both, Doctors Valorous say you are good enough?" Angelina commented

"Yes, Angelina that is my dream." Teresa said.

"Good. You will all rest here tonight. Then go to see Samuel and Isadora, and then head to the *Palisades*. Then Teresa you will return here in one month and live here with me." Angelina said.

"But…" Raphael started to say

Angelina just smiled that smile.

"Thank you my Lady." Raphael said.

The next day Ti drove everyone out to *Harvenger's Glen*. Maria was setting particularly close to Andrew Re.

Raphael smiled. "Miss La Rouge, what are your intentions towards my brother?"

Maria smiled. "Quit shameful I assure you. I plan to have my gypsy ways with him and make him mine."

Everyone could hear small pieces of metal breaking off of Andrews paws as he tried to keep it from building up.

Raphael smiled, "Very well."

Ti pointed out the old fortress to everyone.

Maria smiled and took Andrew Re's paw.

He looked down at it in his. It seemed to fit nicely. "Maria," he whispered, "do you really want to be with me? Knowing, I am a monster?"

Maria looked into his eyes, and whispered back, "Oui, I love you Andrew, all of who you are." Then she kissed him sweetly.

Annabelle Rosa took Vegus Paw. She was nervous.

Vegus looked at her. "It will be alright."

Samuel and Isadora were standing outside. Storm Cloud was standing next to Isaac.

Storm Cloud smiled. "This will be interesting your oldest sister is coming home."

Isadora looked at Samuel. "Be on your best behavior old boar. I am warning you."

"But, he is going to be with her." Samuel said.

"They are married; it is as it should be. They are in love." Isadora countered.

"But, it wasn't a proper ceremony!" Samuel said and knew he had fallen into her trap.

Isadora countered. "Well my dear husband, you are a priest after all. Fix it!"

Annabelle Rosa looked at the others. "Please, let Vegus and I go first please." Everyone nodded as they got out.

Vegus took his wife's paw as they walked towards their father. Vegus stood tall as he greeted them. "Hello Father, Mother, and greetings Great Storm Cloud."

Storm Cloud whined greetings. "Vegus Gullstrand and Annabelle Rosa may you always find happiness."

Samuel shot him a look. Storm Cloud just smiled a War Mounts gin that said so what.

Isadora smiled. "Welcome home my children. It is so good for my old eyes to see my dear children." She then kissed Vegus and then Annabelle Rosa. "You look beautiful my dear, but you have been ill."

Vegus nodded. "She fought and killed the Griffin Cyllene. Unfortunately she was poisoned by the griffin's claws. She took three Arachnid Gallbladders as a precaution. She then had an allergic reaction to an enzyme in the gallbladders. She is a better doctor than that. She should have known better. But, when it comes to herself my Annabelle is a little careless."

Samuel exploded. "Your Annabelle, by what right do you call her yours!"

Vegus looked at him. "She is my wife remember!"

"You were not married properly!" Samuel retorted.

"Why, he was a minister a follower of the Creator and His Word. You always said that there was no difference in the faiths." Vegus retorted

Annabelle Rosa was getting upset. Red scales were starting to form as both husband and father were getting angrier.

Finally Isadora had had enough. "Quiet both of you idiots! I will not have you two fools upsetting my daughter. Vegus, Samuel loves you he is not upset that you are married to Annabelle Rosa. Only, that you did not have him perform the ceremony. He is a priest after all. So you and Annabelle Rosa will reaffirm your vows tonight at our chapel."

Annabelle Rosa fell at her father's knees. "You would do that for us father?" She said with tears in her eyes.

Samuel looked into her eyes and picked her up. "For you, my Rose anything, if it will make you happy. You really do love him?"

Annabelle Rosa kissed her father. "With all my heart and soul."

Samuel looked at Vegus. "It will be as your mother commands, and there will be peace between us my son."

Raphael smiled. "I am not sure what all was said, but mother settled it. I guess it is our turn Teresa."

Ti nodded.

Raphael and Teresa got out and walked up. They kissed Samuel and Isadora.

Isadora asked. "Where are Solara and the other children?"

"Mother, they are already in the *Palisades* working with Alpha team." Raphael said.

"Then we will have to come and visit some time." Isadora said.

Samuel shook his head. "Teresa, I am told you did well on your assignment, and are being rewarded by the Empress."

"Yes Grandfather, she is sending me to medical school, and is having me live with her. But, I am afraid; I might have hurt Sire Gamey's feelings." Teresa said.

Isadora retorted. "Nonsense my child. He told me you corrected a wrong and restored his families honor. He loves you for it. He also said to tell you that his brother sleeps in the Chapel of his ancestors.

Teresa do not judge Gamey's father too harshly. He was a great dragon, probably one of the greatest. It is just that he had a strict interpretation of Dragon Law and Custom. He did not allow for any leeway in its interpretation, right was right, wrong was wrong."

"Is that why Sir Gamey is so conflicted?" Teresa asked.

Isadora smiled, "No." but that is my secret, my gift to him, and why he will become greater than his father ever was. "Please join the others inside."

Andrew Re got out and turned to Maria, "Come La Renard let me introduce my Lady to my adopted parents."

Maria just looked at him, "Oui."

Andrew Re walked up holding her Paw. "Father, Mother this is Empress La Renard Maria La Rouge."

Isadora smiled. "So you are *The Fox*. It is my pleasure to meet the Empress of all Gypsies. I also see you have a modified ring of Julies the Scared with our ladies seal. Welcome to our home Lady La Rouge."

Maria nodded. "Please Lady Isadora, call me Maria. After all I am just a gypsy that has been treated kindly by your clan."

Samuel shook his head. "More importantly my young female, what is your intention toward my son?"

"Samuel, do not be so rude!" Isadora scolded.

Maria smiled and held her head high, "No my lady, it is fine. I shall tell him. Great lord, I am gypsy. I plan to seduce him, carry him away, and make him mine."

Isadora broke out laughing, especially after she saw Samuel's face. She wrapped her wing around Maria. "I like you girl. Come, I will talk to Andrew Re if he agrees we will see if we can come to an agreement."

Samuel was left looking stunned as Ti and Babs walked up. "Did you hear what that female said?"

Babs smirked. "Yes, I thought her honesty was refreshing didn't you?"

Samuel looked at her blank faced.

Ti sighed. "Come on Samuel let's go inside."

Storm Cloud was rolling on the ground laughing. "Go on cub, my children will watch your flock, be with your family."

Five young stallions and six mares formed a circle around the sheep.

Samuel looked at Isadora. "You want to adopt her, don't you?"

Isadora smiled. "She offered me ten thousand credits for Andrew's Paw in marriage."

"What did you say?" Samuel asked.

Isadora shrugged. "Andrew Re likes her very much. I told her I wanted more, ten thousand and five grandchildren. She offered to start right away. I told her she should wait till after the wedding."

"Don't you care what I think?" Samuel asked.

"When it comes to most things my husband I will always defer to your wisdom. But not when it comes to the hearts of our children." She touched him tenderly. "You are the love of my life, but you have always had trouble understanding others feelings." Isadora said.

Samuel kissed her. "Alright Isadora, I won't fight it. I guess I could do two weddings tonight."

Isadora asked. "Good, when was the last time you, did a gypsy wedding?"

Samuel shook his head, "One hundred twenty years ago."

"Good it should still be fresh in your memory." Isadora said.

Isadora went and found Ti and Babs. "Babs you look wonderful my dear. I was wondering could I ask you to help Annabelle and Maria prepare for their weddings. It appears we will be having a double header."

Babs bowed, "Yes my Lady."

Isadora stopped. "Princess Maxumus, while I appreciate you honoring me, it is just Isadora."

"But my Lady, I am just a daughter of the islands, a Regent at best." Babs said.

Isadora touched her face. "No my dear, you are a Princess of the Maxumus Clan. Please, I need to talk to Tiberius alone."

Babs nodded still perplexed, "Alright Isadora." She then turned and walked into the old fortress.

Ti looked at Isadora. "Isadora, I am not a Prince, Beary is the Prince. Technically his brothers and sisters would be also. I am just a Knight."

Isadora shook her head. "No Tiberius you are wrong. Beary wanted to tell you but time ran out. Your Grandfather and Beary's were twins. Your Father and Beary's married cousins. Their fathers' mother was Maria Caesar Augustus, the last true Empress of *Andreas Prime*. You are your father's only child that makes you a prince."

Ti shook his head. "My only purpose is to serve the clan, Angelina, Octavious, and Beary."

"Yes, but you are the hidden prince. You are just below Beary and above his siblings. You also have the gift like him. He has entrusted you with *Asador* and *Ashland* for a reason. They are yours to guard, yours and the Lady Maxumus. He wanted you to know that he loves and trusts you Ti." Isadora said.

Ti sat down. "It is *The Eye* isn't it? He expects trouble. He wanted me to know that if something happened to him, I was to care for Pricilla and Erin."

Isadora smiled. "And the rest of the clan. Do not worry though he is being protected."

Ti shook his head. "Beary isn't the kind to be protected. He is more like Storm Cloud, he will charge into danger."

That evening two weddings were held. The first was very solemn, a very dragon wedding with a sermon. Annabelle Rosa cried with joy. She didn't understand why she was so emotional, but she was so happy.

Isadora just smiled.

The next wedding was a little wild. Samuel conducted the service with abandon; it was fun, and beautiful.

At the end Isadora and Samuel looked at Maria. "You have joined Andrew Re. Will you allow us to adopt you into our family?"

Maria looked at them. "Lady Isadora will it allow me to still…"

"Yes dear you will still be gypsy, but maybe a little more." Isadora said.

Maria kissed her. "Oui"

Isadora and Samuel took her paws. "Accept our blessing." Maria was surrounded by a bright light that glowed around her then faded.

Maria bowed then kissed them. Then she flew into Andrew's arms. "Come let me teach you what it is like to love a gypsy."

Samuel shook his head. "What have I done."

Isadora nuzzled him. "Given one of our children a great gift."

The next morning goodbyes were said. Andrew Re and Maria curled up next to each other and fell asleep. So, did Annabelle Rosa and Vegus. Raphael and Teresa smiled at them. Babs and Ti got in the front seat and started driving to *Saint Elaina's*.

Six cycles later they boarded an amphibian and took off for the islands. The pilot introduced himself. "Sir Maxumus, I am Conrad Jones. I'll be you and the Regents new pilot. I can fly just about anything Sire."

Ti looked at him. "You related to Bravo's Commander?"

"Yes Sire, I am his kid brother, I just got out of the Marines. Not by choice." He taped his left leg. It sounded metallic, "Pirate missile, I survived. My gunner in my dagger didn't. He was a good kid." Conrad said.

Ti nodded. "We have been there Conrad. It is never easy is it?"

"No sir, but it is part of the job. We killed sixty of them and lost five of ours. One dagger completely destroyed and three damaged.

We have an eight cycle flight. We need to out run another storm that is probably going to hit the northern island. Most miss the southern by twenty KSMU.

Eight cycles later Babs looked out and saw *Asador* below. She also saw the storm closing in from the south.

"I think we should land on the plateau and park in the upper hanger." Babs suggested.

Conrad looked at the storm. "I think you are right Regent."

"Alpha Command, this is Alpha 1 requesting priority landing at sight two."

"Alpha 1 come in fast, hanger is up and waiting. That storm is going to hit soon."

Conrad banked in, landed, and drove right into the hanger. The doors slammed shut just as the winds started picking up.

"That was close my lady, good call." Conrad said.

Soon everyone disembarked. Conrad led them down the tunnel. Soon three canus approached and bowed.

"Welcome home Regent. I am Gray Back, Sergeant of the Guard, part of Wolf Banes hunt party. This tunnel will take you into the stronghold. The path is clear Conrad can show you." Gray Back said.

Babs smiled. "Thank you Gray Back."

When they got to the door leading into the stronghold Gray Mane and White Mane were waiting. They saw her ring and howled for joy. "My lady you are now Lady Maxumus!"

Babs smiled. "Yes, Ti married me when we got to *Candaris Prime*."

Grey Mane replied. "Then Lord Ti, you as a Maxumus Prince, are Lord of the Stronghold. We pledge ourselves to you, our Prince Beary, and Empress."

Ti looked at him. "Grey Mane, I am just Tiberius or Ti nothing more."

Grey Mane laughed. "You are so much like him. How is it you are not liter mates? Both Star Firerena and Isadora have told us different Ti. But, Beary refuses to go by prince. So, we will follow your wishes also. Yet, our pledge still stands. We serve the clan as we have always served our clan."

Ti nodded, "Gray Mane. This is Dr. Vegus Gullstrand Valorous and Annabelle Rosa Valorous.

This is Raphael and Teresa Bantelle Valorous, and his brother Andrew Re Valorous and his new wife Maria La Rouge La Renard Valorous."

Gray Mane looked at Dr Vegus and talked to Ti and Babs. "The doctor smells like a canus, but she does not smell like a fox."

Doctor Vegus broke out laughing. "I am not a threat to your pack Great Gray Mane, but you are correct I am part canus part Maxmimus an experiment gone wrong. I was saved by Samuel and Lady Isadora."

Gray Mane nodded. "Then you are a brother to our pack doctor, and will be honored by our pack. Dogons were once from our pack also. The swine Pompaius stole one of our packs pup's years ago. He is probably part of you."

Maria looked out of one of the storm windows as the storm raged outside. She looked at her sleeping husband and smiled. She would let him sleep, he needed his rest. After all she had a debt to pay and she needed him to help her pay it. But, he was worth it.

Annabelle Rose felt funny. She felt queasy to her stomach. It couldn't be. "Vegus, could you come here."

Babs woke up. She felt strange. She walked into the bathroom and threw up. She called Ti, who came in, held her, and called for Dr. Vegus.

Dr. Vegus looked at Annabelle Rosa, "But how?"

Annabelle Rosa smiled. "You're a doctor. Vegus do you really need me to tell you."

That is when Ti called. "Doctor Vegus, Annabelle come quick Babs is very sick."

Dr. Vegus and Annabelle come out of the room. "Well, I want to call in an expert as soon as the storm is over."

Ti looked worried. "If it's that serious, I can fly her to the main land. I can handle this storm."

Dr. Vegus looked at him and laughed. "Ti with the infirmary I have here Annabelle and I could do major surgery with no problem. I have already prescribed and given her the vitamins she needs. I just want Alexa to come out and check her and Annabelle Rosa out."

"Why do you need to call Alexa?" Ti asked.

Vegus looked at him. "Ti, I am a trauma surgeon. I really want an expert in cub birth to check over my wife and yours."

Ti looked at him, "But how?"

Annabelle Rosa shook her head. Why did intelligent boars become idiots over a simple thing? "Go talk to your wife."

Ti came in to the room. Babs looked at him. She didn't know whether to laugh or cry.

Ti buried his head into her chest. "So, we are going to have a cub?"

Babs looked at him. "Are you angry with me?"

Ti looked at her and kissed her. "How could I be angry, when you are giving me such a great gift? I love you Babs Allis don't you know that?"

Babs wrapped her arms around him. "I love you Tiberius, so very much."

Yes, Beary was right this was living. Ti thought.

# EPILOGUE

CAPTAIN BANCROFT COULDN'T believe this resort. The beaches were pristine. The rooms were comfortable. Everything was so relaxing. The only area off limits was the northern beaches and an area they called the trench.

He asked a Mr. Jones why. Mr. Jones told him that since he was head of security. He would take him out to the cliffs and show him the reason. While out there they saw a large sea bird flying over the water. That was when a large shark leaped from the water and snatched it from the air. Mr. Jones pointed out that is why the northern beaches and the trench were off limits. Bancroft decided that was a good reason.

The rest of the crew was just having a good time.

Mrs. Svedberg ran the resort like a general. The service staff seemed happy, despite the fact that she seemed demanding to work for.

He also was confused by the large canus that seemed to have free run of the island. Till he was told they were part of the security detail. Yet, he liked what he saw. These Maxumus were good at what they did. Bancroft decided he was a lucky bear. At the very least his life would probably never be boring. He was going to be right.

CPSIA information can be obtained
at www.ICGtesting.com
Printed in the USA
LVOW10s1620210217
524951LV00002B/295/P